THE
DIRTY
SOUTH

Center Point
Large Print

Also by John Connolly and available from Center Point Large Print:

The Woman in The Woods

This Large Print Book carries the Seal of Approval of N.A.V.H.

THE DIRTY SOUTH

JOHN CONNOLLY

CENTER POINT LARGE PRINT
THORNDIKE, MAINE

For Carolyn Mays

THE
DIRTY
SOUTH

1

Vengeance and retribution require a long time; it is the rule.
—Charles Dickens, *A Tale of Two Cities*

NOW

CHAPTER
I

The tide rolled in, erasing the first of the footprints in the sand, like the memory of a presence gradually being excised from the history of the beach. The marks were small, as of those left by a child, except no child had walked there, or none that Parker had noticed; yet when he looked up from his book, the evidence was before him. Bare feet: he could discern the marks of the toes, and the rounded indentations of the soles and heels. The footprints ended within a few yards of the tree against which he sat, as though the visitor had regarded Parker for a time before moving on.

But the prints progressed only in one direction, and seemed to ascend from the sea: an emergent ghost, arrived unnoticed, come to bear witness in silence.

Parker removed his glasses, cursing—not for the first time—the necessity of them. His optometrist had suggested progressive lenses, which struck Parker as just a fancier name for bifocals. It was an error she was unlikely to make again, Parker regarding progressives as a short step from adopting a pince-nez, or wearing spectacles on a gold chain while smelling of cheap sherry. Now, non-progressive lenses in hand, he looked left and right, but it was an instinctive response and nothing more, because he did not really expect to glimpse her: this lost daughter, this revenant being.

"Jennifer."

He spoke her name aloud, and let the wind carry it to her. He wondered what had drawn her here. She would not have returned to him without cause.

He closed his book and stood to brush the sand from his trousers. He was reading Louis L'Amour's *Education of a Wandering Man*, and thought he might have enjoyed meeting the writer. He had devoured L'Amour's Westerns as a boy, because his grandfather's shelves were filled with copies, but he hadn't returned to them in the years since. Parker supposed he'd underestimated L'Amour because of the nature of his novels, and their associations with the games of cowboys and Indians played when he was young, or the TV shows that had once obsessed him: *The Virginian*, *Casey Jones*, *The Adventures of Champion*. Now it turned out that L'Amour had read more of the great works of literature than anyone Parker had ever before encountered, either in life or in print. He had spent time as a hobo on the Southern Pacific, as a deckhand on Atlantic vessels, as a boxer, as a writer, and always with a book close at hand. Parker felt as though he had encountered a kindred spirit in L'Amour, albeit one much wiser than he would ever be.

The fall leaves were turning, the woods slowly transforming from green to red and gold, their colors like a smokeless conflagration. A chill had gradually crept into the air as the day progressed:

14

not so much as to make sitting by Ferry Beach uncomfortable, but sufficient to rouse a man from his reading and cause him to seek shelter at last.

But Parker did not want to leave, not yet. He experienced a familiar, unsettling sense of dislocation. The traffic sounded wrong to him, as though heard through fog. The light was smoked in sepia, the smell of the sea now heavy with decay.

And his dead child had come.

Parker recalled the night his mother passed away. He had been sitting with her at the hospital before returning to the house in Scarborough that they shared with his grandfather, and in which they had lived together since the death of Parker's father. His mother was sleeping when he arrived, and sleeping when he left, neither speaking nor moving for the duration of his visit. It was dusk as he departed, and he remembered thinking that the world appeared oddly skewed, its angles and the disposition of its structures no longer true, so that he had to concentrate hard on his driving for fear he might sideswipe another vehicle, or mount the curb while turning. He had made himself a sandwich in the kitchen with some leftover beef, and poured a glass of milk. He ate just a few bites of the sandwich, and then out of necessity rather than appetite. The pleasure had disappeared from food as soon as his mother entered the hospital; now he, like she, survived largely on fluids. His grandfather was dozing in an armchair by the living room window, and had not heard him return. He did not wake the old man, who needed his rest. Those on a deathwatch do not sleep well.

When the call came shortly before midnight, summoning his grandfather and him to the hospital because his mother's time was running short, he was not surprised. He had known it was near, even as he held her hand earlier that evening. He could see it in her face, hear it in her breathing, and smell it on her skin and breath as he kissed her goodbye. She seemed to be growing smaller in the bed, her life essence evanescing, diminishing her as it went, and in her withering she exuded a chemical rot.

She was dead by the time they reached the hospital. He thought she might already have been dead when the nurse called, or close enough to make no difference, and the woman had decided not to break the news over the phone, but instead let them remain a father and a son for just a little longer. His mother was still warm when they arrived, and he and his grandfather each held one of her hands until she grew cold.

At the time, Parker was seeing a girl from Scarborough, and while his grandfather spoke with a doctor in the corridor, he found a pay phone and used it call her. She answered on the third ring, even though he'd expected her father to pick up at that time of night. She told him that she hadn't been able to sleep, but couldn't understand why. She'd been sitting on the stairs when the phone rang.

He had always loved her for that. Sometimes, he thought, a person could intuit.

Like now.

He decided not to linger, leaving the beach and the footprints behind. Perhaps he wasn't the only one to have sensed the approach of wrongness. Whatever trouble was circling had also drawn his daughter, come to see what might be brewing, come to protect him. Vehicles passed him on the road, but all were unfamiliar to him, and he recognized none of the faces behind the wheel.

He reached the house. The external security light clicked on as he neared the front door, but he headed around the side to enter from the kitchen. He had grown into the habit of using this entrance because the house often felt too big, too empty, when he came in through the hall. Even the attempt on his life that had almost killed him—the shooters approaching from the trees, using the darkness as cover—had not caused him to alter this routine, although the additional safety systems installed in the aftermath of the attack probably contributed to a certain peace of mind, however belated it might be.

He placed his book on the kitchen table, turned on a lamp, and sat. He followed the movements of the sun as it altered the pattern of light on the salt marshes, and listened to WBQA, Maine Public Classical. Eventually he resumed his reading, and when the phone rang he was almost grateful, because he sensed the source of the shadow was about to reveal itself at last. He picked up, and a voice, unchanged, spoke to him from down the years.

"Mr. Parker?"

"Yes."

"This is—"

"I know. It's been a long time."

"It has. I hoped we'd never have to speak of this again. I'm sure you felt the same way."

Parker did not reply, and so the man continued.

"I thought you should know," he said. "They pulled a body from the Karagol."

The past shadows us.

The past defines us.

In the end, the past claims us all.

THEN

CHAPTER
II

The Karagol was both lake and stream, the former temporarily consuming the latter, although the outlet flow was a feeble, shallow extrusion that soon became lost in mud and marsh, as though to hide itself in shame. Unlike so many bodies of water in the region, the Karagol took its name not from any indigenous tongue, nor from the homeland of some European settler, but arose out of a combination of Greek mythology and Turkish geography: the mountain lake of Karagöl, in Izmir, was associated with the myth of Tantalus— Tantalus the cannibal, the filicide, the thief—whom the gods punished for his crimes by forcing him to stand in a pool of water from which he could never drink, sheltered by a tree, the fruit of which he could never eat, and threatened by a massive boulder that hung forever over his head.

The literal translation of *karagöl*, in its Turkish form, was "black lake," an appellation with which few who looked upon its Arkansas incarnation were likely to take issue. It seemed to consume light, and was one of the few watering holes given a wide berth by local children, even in the worst heat of summer. Occasionally, some boy would dare another to dive into it, or attempt to submerge himself beneath its surface for a count of ten, but the wiser ones refused to accept the challenge, and the dumber came to regret their decision. The lake was always cold, the kind of algor that penetrated skin and flesh to take up residence deep in bone and joint, so that even a brief immersion was enough to set a person to aching for days after. Its color was a result of the dissolution of organic matter from the Ouachita Forest, rendering the water heavily acidic, although those schooled in such matters declared that it should by rights have been deep brown, not black, but could not explain the disparity, for the little stream that ran from it grew lighter the farther it flowed from its origins.

The Karagol, then, resembled less a lake than an oil spill, an impression given greater force by the viscosity of its contents, which clung to the limbs of anyone unfortunate enough to come into contact with it, as though the waters, having lured at last a warm body, were reluctant to release it again. Nothing lived in its depths, or no entity worthy of the description. A professor from the University of Arkansas—Go Razorbacks!—had traveled to the Ouachita some years earlier to study the lake, and claimed to have discovered in it a form of algae worthy of further study. The academic spent a week immersing himself in the Karagol, sometimes wading as deep as his chest, despite local injunctions to seek an alternative means of making his name in scientific circles. He later fell sick from septicemia and died, and nobody from the university ever felt compelled to go paddling in the Karagol again.

Technically, the Karagol and its surrounds weren't actually part of the Ouachita National Forest, or the Arkansas National Forest as it was formerly known. It stood at the forest's southeastern boundary, but for some reason— either an administrative error, or some quirk of Roosevelt, Coolidge, or Hoover—it failed to make the grade as a succession of executive orders created, and then extended, the preserve. Perhaps, as more than one Arkansas native had suggested over the years, someone from Washington had taken the time to view the Karagol, and decided, quite sensibly, that the U.S. government had better things to be doing with its money than protecting what looked like nature's own cesspool.

This neglect didn't affect the Karagol much either way. Nobody dumped in it, because the surrounding land to the east and south was marshy, and transporting anything heavy across it wasn't worth the effort or risk; and the forest on its western and northern sides was inaccessible by road, in addition to consisting of protected rare pine, and so was preserved by law. Much of the Karagol stood on what everyone agreed was probably county land, known locally as the Karagol Holding, even if the county wasn't rushing to claim it, and it wasn't too clear what the county might have done with this territory had it decided to exercise its right of ownership to begin with.

So the Karagol was left alone.

Well alone.

• • •

If the lake was named Karagol, and the stream also, then one might have expected the town to be similarly denominated. This had actually been the case until the 1880s, when a meeting of local worthies concluded with a decision to alter the town's name to Cargill, on the grounds that it was easier to pronounce and spell while retaining some connection to the original nomenclature, which was certainly true, and was the way most people pronounced "Karagol" anyway. It was also believed that a settlement named Cargill might attract more residents and businesses than one called Karagol, which turned out to be mildly delusional. A century and change later, Cargill still didn't amount to a great deal of anything: a couple of pleasant buildings from the twenties and thirties, a whole bunch of average ones from the decades after, and a few thousand souls, including the coloreds, because they were God's children too.

Cargill sat at the heart of Burdon County, the smallest and least prepossessing county in the state of Arkansas. The next-smallest, neighboring Calhoun, had a population 10 percent larger, of which half could barely rustle up two nickels to rub together. In Burdon, by contrast, nobody rubbed two nickels together, not unless he had a friend, and particularly one he could trust not to steal his nickel. The county had known poverty and hard times, but little else.

Timber had been Cargill's wealth, relatively speaking, until the last big mill closed in the 1980s. Since then, the town appeared to have been inching its way toward oblivion, with little prospect of rescue. Folks prayed for the coming of the Savior, mostly to put them out of their misery, until—lo!—their better prayers were answered. A savior appeared, and he even resembled the guy on the church walls by virtue of being a white male who smiled a lot. William Jefferson Clinton, the son of a traveling salesman out of Hope, Arkansas, became the forty-second president of the United States, which meant that some federal manna was bound to come the Bear State's way. And while Burdon County might have been right at the bottom of Bubba's list, at least it was *on* the list.

Now all folks had to do was wait.

Because, miracle of miracles, Bubba had come through for them.

CHAPTER
III

The Cargill Police Department wasn't much to look at from the outside, which meant it had the good grace not to stand out from the rest of town. It shared offices and facilities with the fire department, the mayor's office, and the council, and a parking lot with Ferdy's Dunk-N-Go, a popular doughnut store, diner, and appliance repair center. The department numbered a chief, three full-time patrol officers, and a handful of part-timers, all of whom were at least as good as Cargill deserved, and some far better, in large part because Chief Evander Griffin had recruited most of them himself once he'd managed to get rid of some of the dead wood during his first year in the job. He had fired one officer, convinced another to accept a retirement bonus of $2,000 to go live with his daughter in Tacoma, and an automobile accident had saved him the trouble of dealing with a third. Fortuitously, Kel Knight, the only full-timer left standing after that cull, was the sole officer Griffin would have chosen to retain anyway. He had immediately offered Knight a sergeant's stripes—well, after they'd buried what was left of the previous holder of those three stripes, the automobile accident being a bad one involving a tree, a fire, and a combination of accelerants, namely gasoline and all the alcohol in the victim's system.

But rebuilding and expanding the department after years of neglect was a struggle. Griffin had only recently managed to secure funding to replace what had passed for their best patrol car—a used Crown Vic without heating or air-conditioning, and troubled by a seat stuck in a semi-recumbent position—with a means of transport that permitted a driver to sit up straight, and not risk hypothermia in winter or suffer dehydration in summer. He'd raised salaries to the maximum the town could afford, and used his own money to buy some vests that might potentially stop a bullet, or at least slow its progress. The mayor and council had been as supportive as they could, given their limited resources, because the alternatives were to amalgamate with one of the neighboring townships, all of which were worse off than Cargill; rely solely on the state police, who already had their work cut out; or strike a deal with the Burdon County Sheriff's Office, and Griffin would rather have resigned than do that. So in order to retain its chief, and provide a functioning police service, Cargill had ponied up.

But it was also in the town's interests to invest in law enforcement, because decisions were being made in Little Rock and Washington, D.C., that might yet prove to be its salvation. Sometimes, one had to spend money to make money . . .

On this particular evening in downtown Cargill, Griffin was finishing up some paperwork, and contemplating the possibility of getting home in

27

time to consume a leisurely dinner, followed by an hour in front of the TV with his wife. He caught sight of his reflection in the window as he glanced into the night, and concluded—not for the first time—that his wife ought to have found herself a younger, better-looking mate. He was grateful that she had not, and was so far resisting any inclination to trade him in for a superior model, but Griffin was a modest man with, he felt, much about which to be modest. He was approaching fifty, and had recently been forced to purchase a new belt for his pants due to an insufficiency of holes in the previous cincture. He still retained much of his hair, which was a blessing, but the dark luster of youth was a distant memory. Napping had become habitual to him, and his feet often hurt. Wherever he looked, downhill beckoned.

Griffin had relocated his office from the back of the building because the view was depressing him. Tornadoes had begun to shift east in recent years, so that Tornado Alley—once the preserve of Texas, Oklahoma, and Kansas—now covered regions of Arkansas, including Cargill. The first of the year's twisters had struck a couple of weeks ago, leaving a trail of wrecked homes and ruined lives. Griffin had discovered the remains of a mongrel dog stuck up a bald cypress. The dog was trapped in the topmost branches and was entirely undamaged—apart from being dead, which, Griffin supposed, was about as damaged as a dog could get. The equipment wasn't readily available to remove the dog, so its body had remained in the tree for days. By an unfortunate quirk of fate, Griffin's office window had provided a direct line of sight to the dead dog. When it was eventually retrieved, he could still see the tree, and picture the animal, so he moved his office because it wasn't as though he didn't have enough to feel depressed about.

Griffin was currently reading a government memo relating to the threat to law enforcement posed by the Y2K problem. With a little less than three years to go to the new millennium, the worrywarts were prophesying a version of the End Times, with planes falling from the sky and computers exploding because no one had thought about what might happen once all those nines turned to zeroes. Griffin wadded up the paper and threw it in the trash. He hated flying, which meant his only worry on the Y2K front was ensuring that he wasn't under any malfunctioning planes as they dropped, and the department's sole computer was so old that it ought to have come with a key attached in order to wind it up. The computer would be doing him a favor if it went up in smoke, because Griffin couldn't use the damned contraption anyway.

Kevin Naylor, one of the full-timers, appeared at his office door. Griffin liked Naylor. The kid was barely into his twenties, but brighter than any three members of his extended family put together, and was somehow managing to combine his obligations to the department with a course in public administration. But he was supposed to be off duty, and should by rights have been home studying, or even just resting that big brain of his for a while.

"Kevin," said Griffin. "What can I do for you?"

"I think we might have a problem."

"What kind of problem?"

Naylor chewed his bottom lip, as he tended to do when troubled. Griffin had spoken to him about it because he felt it made Naylor appear unsure of himself, or possibly mentally deficient, neither of which was desirable, but it was a habit the boy was struggling to shake.

"Someone," said Naylor, "is asking questions about Patricia Hartley."

Cargill boasted six bars—if "boasted" was the right term, which it probably wasn't; "could fess up to" might have been more appropriate—of which three were unspeakable, a fourth was tolerable as long as one didn't eat the food, another was functional at best, and the last might just have managed to keep its head above water even in a town with a greater range of more acceptable drinking and dining options. That establishment was Boyd's, which was clean, served average food in above-average portions, and was generally untroubled by outbreaks of alcohol-related violence, which meant that Griffin regarded it with a tolerant eye. Boyd's took its name from Boyd Kirby, who had opened its doors back in 1972, and departed to wipe down that great counter in the sky in 1991. Since then, Boyd's had been in the hands of Kirby's widow, Joan, who ran the place much as her husband had done, minus the swearing, Boyd Kirby having regarded the spaces between every syllable of a word as an opportunity to exercise the range of obscenities at his command, which had been considerable.

Boyd's was quiet when Griffin and Naylor arrived, Thursdays, Fridays, and Saturdays being the days when Joan made the majority of her money, the rest of the week representing pocket change. The bar had a well-stocked jukebox, although light on soul and R&B, which meant none at all. It was currently playing something by the Eagles, because somewhere in town was always playing something by the Eagles, and it might as well be Boyd's as anyplace else. Griffin counted a dozen customers, of whom he could have named eleven. The twelfth was sitting in a corner booth with his back to the wall and a window to his left. From this vantage point, he could watch the parking lot, the bar, its clientele, and the door. A copy of the *Washington Post* was folded before him, next to a slightly diminished roast chicken platter and two glasses, one half-filled with soda, the other with water. As Griffin approached, the man placed his hands flat on the table, where they could clearly be seen. Naylor hung back by the main door, and joined everyone else in watching Griffin, just in case anything more interesting than the Daytona previews might be about to unfold.

The stranger was in his early thirties, Griffin guessed: not tall, and of medium build. His hair was dark, fading prematurely to gray at the sides. He was wearing a blue cotton shirt that hung loose over his jeans, and a dark T-shirt underneath. Naylor hadn't been able to tell if he was armed, but Griffin thought he looked like the kind of man that might be. It was the way he held himself as the chief approached. He didn't appear nervous to be the object of police attention, which meant he was used to it. That made him police, criminal, or a private investigator. Police would have had the manners to introduce himself before asking question about Patricia Hartley, and private might have had the good sense to do the same.

Which left criminal, and the closer Griffin drew to him, the more this showed signs of being the likeliest possibility. His eyes burned very bright. There was rage in them, and something approaching agony. Griffin had seen a facsimile of it in the gaze of bereaved parents, and those driven to take revenge on tormentors. If this man were not in possession of a weapon and a grudge, Griffin would have been very surprised to hear it.

"Evening," said Griffin.

"Evening," said the newcomer.

"Mind if I sit?"

"Not at all."

He was smiling slightly, more in resignation than good humor, as though this intrusion upon

32

his evening had been anticipated, even as he might have hoped to avoid it.

"My name is Evander Griffin. I'm the chief of police here in Cargill."

"I know."

Griffin felt unease keeping pace with curiosity. Were this man's hands not so visible, Griffin might well have had him under a gun by now.

"That's usually the cue for someone to offer his name in return," said Griffin, "or I could ask you to produce some identification, but I find a plain exchange of appellations to be more civilized."

"My name is Parker."

"And where are you from, Mr. Parker?"

"New York."

"What do you do there?"

"I'm currently between positions."

"Unemployed?"

"By inclination."

"So what was your previous vocation, before you became inclined to divest yourself of it?"

"I'd prefer not to say."

Griffin grimaced. The man hadn't done anything wrong—or not so far as anyone could tell—beyond asking questions that the majority of people in the county would have considered unwelcome. He hadn't broken any laws, but the chief was used to a degree of cooperation from those who strayed into his orbit, because it contributed to the smooth running of the town. If knowledge was power, ignorance was powerlessness. There were gradations of both, but Griffin preferred to remain firmly in credit with the former.

"What happened to your hand?" he said.

The knuckles of Parker's right hand bore traces of lacerations, now almost healed.

"The jack slipped while I was changing a tire."

"Looks like you were punching the tire, not changing it."

Parker glanced at the limb and stretched the fingers. The action made him wince, and his eyes assumed fresh traces of pain both actual and remembered.

"I might have lost my temper," he said, almost vacantly.

"You do that a lot?"

"I try not to."

"That seems wise. What's your interest in Patricia Hartley?"

"None."

"But you've been asking about her."

"I have, but I'm done asking now."

"And why is that?"

"Because I thought her death might be relevant, but it isn't."

"Relevant to what?"

"To another inquiry."

"Which inquiry?"

"A personal one."

"Are you a private investigator, Mr. Parker?"

"I told you: I'm between positions."

"Yes, you did tell me that. The investigation into

Patricia Hartley's death is ongoing, and therefore it's of interest to me when someone comes along to check on its progress."

"Is it?"

"Is it what?" said Griffin.

"Ongoing? Of interest? Both?"

"Are you trying to be funny?"

"Not at all. It just strikes me that if there is an investigation into the girl's death, it hasn't made much progress at all, which begs the question: Just how interested are you?"

"I don't think I appreciate your tone."

"I hear that a lot."

"I'll bet you do. Did you know Patricia Hartley?"

"No."

"Or her family?"

"No."

"This your first time in Burdon County?"

"First time in Arkansas."

"You can prove that, I suppose?"

"Would I have to?"

"You might, if you were the suspect in a killing."

"What killing would that be?"

"The killing of Patricia Hartley."

"I'm confused."

"And why is that?"

"My understanding is that Patricia Hartley's death was determined to be accidental, but you've just described it to me as a killing."

"Mr. Parker, I'm starting not to like you. You appear averse to transparency."

"Patricia Hartley's body was discovered on December tenth of last year. If I have to, I can prove where I was on that date."

"And where would that have been?"

"New York."

"Were you in employment at that time?"

"I was."

"Doing what?"

"Am I under arrest?"

"No."

"Good, because I thought I might have missed part of the conversation."

"I know the feeling," said Griffin.

"If I'm under arrest, you're obliged to Mirandize me."

"I'm aware of that."

"And offer me access to a lawyer."

"I'm aware of that, too."

"Then you'll also be aware that I don't have to answer your questions. I'm going to reach for my wallet now, so I can pay the check. I'd prefer if you, or the gentleman by the door, didn't shoot me. Is he one of your officers?"

"He is."

"I think I've seen him around. He has a good eye."

"I'm sure he'll be flattered to hear it. Where's your wallet?"

"In the pocket of my jacket."

The jacket was hanging from a hook beside Parker's head.

"If it's all the same to you," said Griffin, "I'll ask my officer to retrieve it for you, just in case."

He raised his left hand, summoning Naylor.

"Mr. Parker's wallet is occupying a pocket of his jacket. I'd be obliged if you'd find it for him."

Before he reached for it, Naylor asked if the pocket held any sharp objects, or anything else of which he should be aware. That was how he said it, Griffin noted: "of which I should be aware." The boy really was wasted in Cargill.

"No," said Parker.

"Are you armed?"

"No."

Which was a pity, Griffin thought, because Boyd's was a bar, not a restaurant, which made it illegal to carry a firearm on the premises. It would have been sufficient justification for placing Parker in a cell overnight while Griffin tried to figure out the Hartley angle.

Naylor found the wallet and handed it to the chief, not Parker.

"Don't mind if I take a look, do you?" said Griffin.

"Would it matter if I did?"

"I'll take that as permission."

He didn't find much: cash, a pair of credit cards, and a New York State driver's license in the name of Charles Parker. There was also a small photograph of a woman and a young girl, both blonde, both beautiful. Griffin held it up so the man could see it.

"Your family?"

The alteration in Parker was momentary, but profound. The rage was gone, and only grief remained in its place.

"Yes."

"Did something happen to them?"

No reply.

"I asked you a question," said Griffin.

With that, the rage returned. It was bridled, but only barely.

"I'm done answering your questions," said Parker. "Arrest me, or give me back my wallet and let me be done with your county, your town, and your dead girls."

Griffin didn't surrender the wallet.

"Dead girls," he said.

"What?"

"You mentioned dead girls. Patricia Hartley was just one girl."

Parker stared at him, and Griffin stared back.

"Officer Naylor," said Griffin, "arrest Mr. Parker for obstruction of justice. And be sure to read him his rights."

CHAPTER
IV

Griffin let Naylor take care of searching and cuffing Parker, and placing him in the back of the patrol car. Parker didn't try to resist, or make any objection to his treatment, which confirmed to Griffin that the man was familiar with the mechanics of the process. He drove Parker to the station house in silence, Naylor following in his own vehicle, and there relieved him of his belt, shoelaces, wallet, and watch before placing him in a holding cell for the night. He figured Parker had eaten, even if the size of the portions at Boyd's had defeated him, but he did offer him a cup of coffee, which was declined. By then Kel Knight had arrived to take over the night shift, and the fourth full-time officer, Lorrie Colson, had returned from a domestic disturbance call. One of them would have to be at the station at all times while Parker remained in custody, but Naylor lived only a block away, and said he would be willing to pull on a coat and boots to provide cover if the need arose.

Griffin took Kel Knight aside once Parker was safely behind bars. Knight was a rawboned, balding man who had never been known to raise his voice above conversational levels, and had yet to fire a weapon at anything other than a range target during his eighteen years in law enforcement, first up in Clay County, then down in Cargill. He had returned to this, his hometown, to care for his ailing parents, both of whom had died within months of his arrival, which didn't say much for his abilities as a nursemaid, although admittedly his folks were already circling the drain by the time Knight arrived.

He had served in Vietnam, which might have explained his reluctance to shoot at anyone again, Kel Knight having endured a superfluity of carnage in Southeast Asia, and thus exhausted his interest in the taking of lives, Asian or otherwise. Also, like many servicemen who had served in that conflict, he retained no hostility toward his former enemies. When twenty-five thousand South Vietnamese men, women, and children were settled at Fort Chaffee, Arkansas, Knight was among those who tore down the GOOKS GO HOME signs that began to sprout like toadstools in the vicinity of the base. He had no time for those who professed hatred toward the refugees, the ones that whispered of leprosy and venereal disease, and complained about the incomprehensibility of the newcomers' language, the smell of their food, and the undoubted criminal aspect of their character, these Russos and Mullers and Reillys, these Nowaks and Campbells and Karlssons, each themselves only a generation or two removed from the immigrant ships, and whose parents and grandparents had been forced to endure similar slurs in this once strange land.

If Knight had a flaw, it lay in the asceticism of

his mien. He didn't drink, smoked only a pipe, and had never sworn within earshot of Griffin or, quite possibly, anyone else. He was a father to four teenage boys, which meant he must have had carnal relations with his wife at least four times, but it wasn't clear that he'd enjoyed the experience, or was in a hurry to revisit it now that his wife's childbearing years were behind her. He was a hard man to get to know, and a harder man to like. But Griffin had done both, and was now as close to a friend as Kel Knight possessed.

"What did this Parker do?" Knight asked.

"He irritated me," said Griffin.

"If that was enough to put a man behind bars, half the town would be cluttering up our jail."

"God preserve me from your sensitivities. If it's more amenable to you, his actions and behavior gave me grounds for reasonable suspicion, and I decided to place him under arrest until the nature of his character could be established. Does that sound better?"

"It *sounds* better. You still haven't told me what it means."

"He's been asking questions about Patricia Hartley—Kevin says he was over by her old place earlier today, trying to establish where her people might have gone—but declined to elaborate on why."

Knight didn't bite. He'd made clear his position on Patricia Hartley in the past, and no good could come from going over the same ground again, not

41

with his boss in the kind of mood that had already seen him lock up one person for invoking her name.

Griffin showed him Parker's driving license.

"New York," said Knight. "Huh. You figure him for a reporter?"

"He's no reporter. And why would a New York reporter be interested in a dead black girl from Burdon County, Arkansas? She barely made the papers out of Little Rock."

"Then what is he?"

"That remains to be seen."

Griffin glanced back at the cells through the plexiglass screen in the door. Parker was sitting against a wall with his eyes closed. Griffin could almost sense him listening, even though there was no way their voices could have carried to him, so quietly were they speaking.

"You're confident that a night in the guest suite might lead to an improvement in his attitude?" said Knight.

"Even if it doesn't, it'll give us time to find out more about him."

"Has he asked for a lawyer?"

"He hasn't asked for anything at all." Griffin picked up his hat. "It's already after ten in New York, so it's unlikely we'll get much joy until tomorrow, which gives us an excuse to let him cool his heels. You find yourself with a few free minutes, run him through the databases, but morning should suffice."

Kel Knight wasn't any more competent than Griffin when it came to computers, a fact he continued to do his best to conceal, even though it was common knowledge to all. Each man carefully avoided calling the other on his ignorance, and thus they contributed to the smooth running of the department.

"Morning it is, then," said Knight.

"He's not going anywhere," said Griffin, "and I've already put in a longer day than any sane man should."

He left Knight and Colson to it, and headed to the parking lot. Kevin Naylor was leaning against his car, smoking a cigarette. He wasn't in uniform, so Griffin couldn't really discipline him for it, but he'd still have preferred the boy to resist the urge. Griffin checked his watch. If he were lucky, his wife would have left his dinner in the oven. If not, she'd have fed it to the dog. Then again, if she'd made meat loaf, it was the dog that could consider itself unlucky.

Naylor watched him approach.

"Chief."

"Kevin."

He could see that Naylor was troubled, and he knew by what: the same itch that was bothering Kel Knight—and bothering Griffin, too, truth be told, although he chose to scratch it only in private.

"You got something you want to say?" asked Griffin, in a tone that made clear his total absence of any desire to listen should this be the case.

"No, sir."

"Then go home. And Kevin?"

"Chief?"

"Don't smoke in the goddamned parking lot."

Naylor put the cigarette out against the sole of his shoe, and almost flicked the butt into the night before thinking better of it. Instead, he dropped it into one of his pockets, and kept his eyes fixed on the ground as Griffin got in his car. He knew what had been done to Patricia Hartley. They all did.

And still, they'd abandoned her to her fate.

They'd left her to be forgotten.

CHAPTER
V

Kel Knight looked in on the prisoner. Parker's eyes were now open, but otherwise he remained in the same position as before.

"You need anything?" asked Knight.

"Something to read, if you have it."

"We got the Yellow Pages."

"I hear it starts strong, but tails off toward the end."

"I'll see what else I can find." Knight began to move away, then paused. "You know, Chief Griffin is okay."

"Is he?"

"I wouldn't have said so otherwise. You could have saved yourself a lot of trouble by answering his questions."

Parker shifted position to lie down on his bunk.

"This?" He took in the cell and—by extension—the station house, Cargill, and the rest of the county, if not the world entire. "This isn't trouble, and I'll be gone by morning."

"You seem very sure of that."

"I am, because I'm not your problem." He turned his face to the wall. "Your problem is dead girls."

Evan Griffin didn't head straight home, despite the lure of it, but first stopped off at the Lakeside Inn. The Lakeside wasn't actually located near the

Karagol, which represented a sensible planning decision on the part of the original owners, because in summer the mosquitoes swarmed over the black water, and it exuded a stink of vegetal decay. If a person stood on the roof of the motel, it might have been possible to glimpse the lake in the distance, although only after someone had cut a swath through a plenitude of evergreens, and it wouldn't have been worth the effort. The Lakeside was run by the Ures, Thomas and Mary, but the bank held the paper on it, and the bank, like most everything else in the area, owed its existence and continued survival to the Cade family. The Cades had been in Arkansas, and more particularly Burdon County, for a long, long time. Their history was embedded in its earth, like the roots of the oldest trees, like the Karagol itself.

Thomas Ure appeared from the office as Griffin pulled into the lot. Ure wasn't usually on duty so late, and was dressed for an evening on the town, as long as the town wasn't Cargill. Here, people dressed up only for baptisms, weddings, funerals, and court appearances.

"Is there a problem, Evan?" he asked.

"There might be, unless you forget you saw me here."

"I never did have a good memory for faces," said Ure, "or names."

"I always liked that about you," said Griffin. "Room twenty: single or double occupancy?"

"Just one guy."

"Thanks. You can go back to being forgetful now."

He waited for Ure to return to the lobby before removing the motel room key from his pocket. He'd found it among the possessions of the man named Parker, although it wasn't exactly a surprise: Cargill had just two motels, and the Lakeside was the more salubrious. The other, the Burdon Inn, was as damp and cheerless as it looked, and it was said that the bedbugs were as big as a man's fingernail. Griffin didn't know what they were subsisting on, because it sure as hell wasn't guests. The Burdon Inn only stayed open to give Bill Gorce a project on which to waste his time and retirement money. When Gorce eventually died, the Burdon Inn would expire with him, or vice versa; if the Burdon Inn collapsed to the ground tomorrow, Griffin was sure that Bill Gorce would founder at precisely the same moment. But Gorce didn't appear likely to depart this world anytime soon. He was holding on for better times, like everyone else in the county. They'd been holding on like that for a long time, but now they had hope.

As long as they stayed quiet and pretended that nothing bad was happening.

As long as nobody asked questions about dead girls.

A quarter of the rooms at the Lakeside were currently occupied, judging by the lights behind the windows and the vehicles in the lot. The majority of the cars and trucks bore out-of-town plates, and looked like they had heavy miles on them, except for one newer Ford Taurus sitting alone at the end of the block to the right of the office. Griffin would have made the Ford for a rental even without the company sticker in the corner of the windshield.

Griffin stopped outside Parker's room. Technically, he should have gone to a sympathetic judge, such as old Lew Hawkins over in Boscombe, and asked for a search warrant, but even a soak like Hawkins might have balked at signing off on a warrant based on nothing more than a man's intransigence. Griffin wasn't overly concerned, though; he could justify the search as incident to the arrest, which gave him the authority to scrutinize areas within the arrestee's immediate control. A man could throw a stone from the door of Boyd's and hit the Lakeside Inn, which Griffin chose to interpret as falling under "immediate control." Anyway, it wouldn't make much difference unless the examination of Parker's motel room turned up evidence of the commission of a crime, in which case Griffin would work back and set about bolstering the reasons for the arrest before securing a warrant. But that wasn't the main purpose of entering the motel room. He was curious about Parker, and his interest in Patricia Hartley. An inspection of the contents of his room, and perhaps also his rental car, might provide Griffin with some answers.

Despite Ure's assurance that Parker had checked in alone, Griffin took the time to knock hard and identify himself before inserting the key in the lock. He heard the mechanism click, and shifted his right hand to the butt of his gun before turning the knob and opening the door.

"Hello?" he called again. "This is the police. Anyone in there?"

No one answered. He saw a single lamp burning between the twin beds, but that was all. The TV was off, and the clock radio was unplugged. Griffin closed the door behind him, locked it, and secured the dead bolt. Like all motel rooms, this one smelled of stale cigarette smoke and cheap air freshener, and the décor and bedclothes hadn't been renewed in a decade. The two beds didn't look as though they had even been sat on, never mind slept in. A single black case, small enough to be carried on a plane as hand baggage, stood on the metal rack, and the bathroom contained a black leather toiletry bag. Otherwise, the room showed no signs of occupancy.

The Lakeside Inn did not offer safes, which meant that anything valuable or incriminating would be contained in the suitcase. Griffin tested it, but it was locked. He took out his pocketknife and used it to bust the catches. If Parker turned out to be the Zodiac Killer, or was keeping his victims' fingers as souvenirs, well, Griffin would have a lot of favors to call in from Lew Hawkins.

He opened the suitcase to reveal a gun.

CHAPTER
VI

Exercising the right of seniority, Kel Knight sent Lorrie Colson out into the night to do a couple of circuits of the town before holing up on a side road by the Gas-N-Go at the southern limits, there to keep an eye out for drunks, hired assassins, and bank robbers, but mostly drunks. The Gas-N-Go was part of the Ferdy Bowers empire of "N-Go" businesses, which also included the Wash-N-Go, the Dunk-N-Go, and the short-lived Mow-N-Go, a mower servicing and garden maintenance company that had barely survived a single summer, most local homeowners being content to take care of their own lawns when the need arose, and also sufficiently skilled to repair their own mowers, too, thank you very much, without paying a premium to Bowers and his people for performing the service. Ferdy Bowers was one of the few businessmen in Burdon County not beholden to the Cades, although until recently he'd been smart enough to tick along with them, and not interfere with their affairs beyond a certain level of acceptable competition. But lately Bowers had started smelling money in the air, and relations with the Cades had deteriorated as a consequence.

Knight left the door between the cells and the main body of the station open, just in case the prisoner called out, before stepping into the parking lot and lighting his pipe. Evan Griffin might not have tolerated the smoking of cigarettes in the station house or by his officers while in uniform, but he gave Knight a pass on the pipe, if only in the lot, since it served to enhance the quiet authority of his sergeant—or so Knight had informed him, and Griffin had been too bemused to argue. This impression of competence was aided by Knight's passing resemblance to the late actor Lee Van Cleef, who, despite making a decent living starring in Westerns, had no affection for horses. Knight wasn't sure how a man who didn't like horses ended up as a Western star, but stranger things had happened in the world, and would undoubtedly continue to happen until that same world came to its inevitable end.

Knight's radio beeped, and Colson's voice said, "Kel, you there?"

"Where else would I be?" he replied, because wherever he went, there he was.

"Company's coming," she said. "Jurel Cade just drove into town."

Griffin pulled on a pair of plastic gloves before removing the gun from its shoulder holster. It was a Smith & Wesson 1076, chambered in 10 mm, the kind issued to FBI agents after two of them were killed in a shoot-out in Miami-Dade County in 1986 because their weapons at the time lacked sufficient stopping power. The original shitty plastic grip on Parker's S&W had been replaced with one that looked custom-made, and the weapon was clean, oiled, and in good order. Alongside it was a New York State permit, which would be honored in Arkansas under reciprocity agreements. The weapon was unloaded, although the nine-round single-column magazine in the corner of the case was full.

Griffin restored the gun to its holster and laid it to one side.

"Huh," he said.

He got down on his knees between the two beds and felt beneath their frames. Within seconds, his fingers touched another gun, taped to the underside of the bed on the right. Carefully, he eased it free. This time, he was looking at a .38 Colt Detective Special, so old that the prancing pony badge on the left side of the butt was worn almost smooth, and the frame was pitted and scarred. Yet, as with the S&W, it was in prime working condition; unlike the S&W, it was fully loaded.

Griffin returned it to its hiding place and resumed his examination of the case. Without disturbing the contents more than was necessary, he established that it contained a couple of changes of clothing, a pair of black Timberland boots—freshly waterproofed, judging by the smell—and a thick sheaf of papers and photographs held in a blue pocket file secured with a pair of elastic bands. Griffin removed the bands and opened the file. He took one look at the contents, closed it again, and restored the bands. He put the S&W back in the case and managed to get one of the catches to lock again, but not the other. With the file under one arm, he left the room, closed the door behind him, and drove home.

He wasn't angry. He wasn't even disturbed.

In fact, he was almost relieved.

Kel Knight continued smoking his pipe until a pair of headlights appeared from the south, approaching slowly up Main Street. The street lighting wasn't great at that end of town, and a couple of the bulbs were also busted, which meant the vehicle didn't become completely visible to him until it neared the lot—not that Knight needed the illumination to make an identification, not after the warning from Colson.

The colors of the Burdon County Sheriff's Office were yellow and brown, an unfortunate combination that had led the less respectable elements of county society to dub it "Shit-N-Shitter," which made it sound like another business misfire from the mind of Ferdy Bowers. Not that anyone would have uttered that description within earshot of Jurel Cade, a man who smiled a lot but never laughed.

Cade unfolded himself slowly from the interior of the car, like some predatory insect emerging from its lair. He topped out at six-five in his stockinged feet, but favored heavy work boots with deep soles and heels that added at least another inch to his height. There was no fat to him, none at all, and in

53

proximity he radiated heat, so that the windows of his patrol car were permanently fogged, winter and summer, because the vents didn't work worth a damn, the sheriff's office being no more flush with funds than any other branch of law enforcement in the county. The Cades were generally tall and rangy, males and females both, so that family gatherings resembled a collection of blades or farm implements arrayed side by side. They all had the same eyes too: deep blue and hungry, like cruel seas. They weren't bad, the Cades, not exactly— no family could be entirely ignoble—but they were greedy, and protective of their own. They had been the dominant force in the social, political, and economic life of Burdon County for as long as anyone could remember, and longer still, and seemed destined to remain so into the future given the absence of any significant rivals, the ambitions of Ferdy Bowers and a handful of other holdouts notwithstanding.

"Evening, Kel," said Cade, although it was now well into the night.

"Evening, Jurel," said Knight. "Social visit?"

No love was lost between these two men and each knew it, but Knight had been prepared to accommodate a level of grudging respect for the younger man until Patricia Hartley's death. In the aftermath, he saw no cause for any but the most superficial of niceties.

"I heard Evan was up to Boyd's earlier," said Cade. "Made an arrest."

"That's right."

"Anything I should know about?"

"Northern boy. Had a little too much to drink, and proved disrespectful of the chief's authority. We thought we'd accommodate him in a cell, and give him the opportunity to contemplate the error of his ways before we put him back on the road."

Jurel Cade absorbed this information without any change in expression. Knight might as easily have been addressing himself to a statue. Cade's hair was thick and black, with a natural curl that he tried to hide by keeping it cut short most of the time. In winter he let it grow a shade longer, with the result that the kink was currently at its most obvious. Some in the county liked to speculate— although again not in the immediate vicinity of Jurel, or any other member of the Cade clan—that he could have a little Jew in him from up the line, but Knight didn't think that likely. The Jews might have helped to open up parts of the state in the nineteenth century through their trading ventures, as was the wont of the Semitic race, but they had long been in general decline in Arkansas, a couple of pockets of Judaism excepted, and Cargill wasn't Bentonville or Little Rock. The Jews who ventured as far as Burdon hadn't lingered, and Knight couldn't recall ever meeting a Jew native to the county in all his born days, nor did he believe that his father or mother could have boasted the acquaintance of any. He had nothing against them as a people; they simply did not figure in his life or

55

memory, and the same could likely have been said for that of the Cades.

There was another possibility for the kink, of course, one that even the most daring or foolhardy of commentators chose to leave unspoken. The Cades, like a fifth of all families in antebellum Arkansas, had owned slaves. In a period when the ownership of even a dozen slaves would have been regarded as significant, the Cades had a hundred in their possession, many of whom they hired out to plantation owners and farmers. Who was to say that, back in the day, a little darkness hadn't crept into the Cade bloodline?

"Way I heard it," said Cade, "your guest was drinking soda at Boyd's. Hard to rate that as much of an intoxicant, not unless the bubbles went to his head."

Knight wondered who at the bar had made the call to the sheriff's office. It wouldn't have been Joan Kirby, because she and the chief got along like gangbusters. Knight decided that he'd talk to Kevin Naylor the next day, and Joan also, with a view to establishing the identities of those in attendance when Parker was arrested. He might have to pay someone a visit, and remind them that Jurel Cade didn't live in Cargill, while Kel Knight most assuredly did, and a certain level of loyalty toward the local police department was not only appreciated, but also expected.

"He was trying to sober up," said Knight.

He didn't know why he was lying to Cade.

Actually, he did know, and it wasn't to protect the man in the cell. Even had he been upfront with Cade about Parker's interest in Patricia Hartley, he didn't think it likely that the county's chief deputy would get more out of the prisoner than Griffin. But Knight and Cade had conflicting agendas when it came to the Hartley girl—just as, on a different level, Knight had issues with the chief's handling of the matter—and he wasn't about to feed Parker to the Burdon County Sheriff's Office until more had been learned about him.

"Uh-huh," said Cade. "You mind if I look in on him?"

"I believe he's sleeping."

"Won't take long."

Knight could hardly refuse. He stepped aside and directed Cade with his pipe.

"Take as long as you want."

CHAPTER
VII

Evan Griffin got home to discover that his wife hadn't made meat loaf but chicken casserole, and had neither thrown it out nor fed it to Carter, the dog. It was late for him to be pulling up to the table, but he was so hungry that he knew he wouldn't sleep unless he ate. He carefully divided the portion of casserole in two, fed a little to Carter by hand, and heated the rest in the microwave. He took an O'Doul's from the refrigerator and popped the cap. He'd long ago fallen into the habit of having a beer when he came home, regardless of the hour, and one sometimes became two, although rarely more. It started to rankle with him—Griffin was distrustful of dependencies—so he'd switched to O'Doul's because it was more a matter of having a bottle in his hand, and something approximating the taste of beer in his mouth, than the alcohol itself. When the microwave pinged he set the plate on the table, his beer and a glass of water beside it, and the file from the motel room above the plate, being careful not to get any food on the pages. So engrossed did he become in the contents that he didn't hear Ava come down the stairs, and wasn't aware of her presence until her shadow fell across the table, and she said:

"Is that Patricia Hartley?"

Griffin saw no point in denying it, now that

she'd seen the photograph. It was a picture from Patricia's high school yearbook, the same one that had been placed on her coffin. Behind it were more graphic images of her body, visible as fragments behind the main photo: a leg here, an arm there. Had he been forewarned, he would have closed the file before Ava arrived: not out of any great sensitivity to her feelings—they'd been married too long for that, and she'd seen and heard too much—but because Ava, like Kel Knight, had also made known her feelings about the death of Patricia Hartley, and he didn't want to give her an excuse to rake over the ashes of that particular subject, because they never seemed to cool.

"Yes," he said.

"You find out something new?"

"No. There is nothing new for me to find out, because it's not my case."

"Don't take that tone with me."

She cuffed him gently across the back of the head as though he were a child, even though he had a dozen years on her. The blow barely ruffled his hair, and was more loving and possessive than an actual rebuke, but he had to make an effort to hold his temper nonetheless.

"And this isn't my file," he continued.

"Then whose is it? Sheriff's office?"

"Nope."

Which begged the question of how Parker had come by these images. They looked like Tucker McKenzie's handiwork, being perfectly framed and in focus, even though they were copies of pictures that had been taken with an instant camera. McKenzie was the forensic analyst most frequently dispatched by the state crime lab to this part of Arkansas, but as far as Griffin was aware, Hartley's death hadn't been referred to the lab. McKenzie had been briefly present at the scene, but not in any official capacity. Griffin hadn't seen these particular prints before, so how had they come to be in Parker's possession? It was another subject to be explored with him in the morning.

"You know I don't like it when you try to be enigmatic," said Ava. "I didn't marry you so I could spend my time guessing what you were thinking, or no more than should be obligatory with a man."

"I arrested someone this evening," said Griffin. "That's how come I was late for dinner. He had this file in his possession."

"All those papers, just for Patricia Hartley? That's more than the law has accumulated."

The little jab again.

"He has details of other killings in there too."

"Others like her?"

"No, but a similar level of badness, or worse."

"Worse than what was done to that girl?"

"There's lots worse than what was done to that girl. I've seen some of it with my own eyes."

"Not in this county."

"No, I guess not."

Griffin wasn't about to contradict her. For every

60

case he shared with his wife, he kept another to himself. Had he not done so, he would have been forced to choose between his job and his marriage, because the latter would not have survived its infection by the former. Once, when he was still an innocent, Griffin had believed that evil in its purest form was a property of the universe that predated mankind, and upon which the worst specimens of humanity might draw in only the most extreme cases of malignance. He no longer viewed his species in such terms, and had since concluded that some men and women came into this world with a profound and terminal rancor embedded in their DNA. They nurtured it inside themselves, and evinced only pleasure in its parturition.

"And who is this man?" asked Ava.

"His name is Parker. He's from New York."

"Is he a reporter?"

"That's what Kel suggested, but I don't think so."

"You didn't ask him?"

"I asked. He just didn't answer."

"Which is why you locked him up?"

"I regarded his reluctance to cooperate as a deliberate provocation."

"You planning on asking him again tomorrow?"

"I am, although by then we should know more about him, on account of our inquiries."

"You think he could have killed some of the girls in that file of his?"

"I didn't get that sense from him."

"What sense did you get?"

The question was sincerely meant. Ava trusted her husband's instincts. She wouldn't have married him if she didn't, given that one of those instincts was, presumably, that she might make a good wife, and perhaps also a good mother, although that hadn't happened, not yet. They were trying, which was fun, but desperation was starting to creep in, which wasn't. The doctors said it wasn't him, but her, so it might be that her husband's instincts, while trustworthy, had not been flawless.

And yet, and yet . . .

No, she thought. *Best to wait. Best to be sure.*

"That he knows his way around the law," said Griffin. "And he's angry, which means he might be dangerous."

He pictured Parker sitting in Boyd's. He had a picture of a woman and a little girl in his wallet, but he wasn't wearing a wedding ring, so he could be divorced or was never married to the woman to begin with. Either way, he was carrying grief for them—of that much, Griffin was certain—so they might be dead. He owned one gun associated with federal agents, and another old and worn enough to have been inherited from a previous generation, a weapon favored—although not exclusively—by detectives back in the day. He was looking into killings of women, deaths notable for their brutality, their strangeness, and—Griffin searched for the right word—the *theatricality* of the crime scenes. He had access to police reports, photographs, and autopsy findings.

"I think he might be police," said Griffin. "If not now, then not so long ago."

"Then why didn't he say so?"

"I don't know."

Ava reached out a hand, and her fingers hovered for a moment over the photograph of Patricia Hartley as though to comfort the ghost of the girl.

"And what will Jurel Cade have to say about this?" she asked softly.

"Best he doesn't find out."

"I hope he does. I hope this man has come to cause him all the trouble in the world."

"What's trouble for Jurel may also be trouble for me."

She kissed the crown of his head, just where his hair was beginning to thin.

"No, that's not true," she said.

"Why not?"

"Because you're nothing like Jurel. You always try to do what's right."

"I didn't do right by Patricia Hartley."

"You will, down the line, when the opportunity presents itself. Perhaps this man represents an opportunity."

"You have a lot of faith in me."

"And patience. I was just waiting for you to come around."

"To your way of thinking?"

"To our way of thinking. We're the same, you

and I. That's why we're together. But sometimes, it takes a while for one of us to catch up with the other."

She rubbed her right hand through his hair. Her left hand rested on his shoulder, and he took it in one of his paws. He had massive hands. It was a Griffin family trait. When he and Ava began courting, he had been reluctant to hold her fingers too tightly for fear that he might break them.

"You really think the coming of this man is a sign?" he said.

"I don't hold with portents, but you've met him and I haven't."

That's right, thought Griffin, *and on one level I wish he'd never stopped in Cargill, because life would have been simpler had he kept moving. But now that he's here, I'm not sure I want him to leave, not if my feeling about him is right.*

"It seems like the whole county wants the memory of Patricia Hartley to be obliterated," he said.

"Not the whole county, just the wrong part of it. She had family and friends, people that cared about her."

"The future of thousands is hanging in the balance right now. Everyone's boat will rise with the tide."

"Not Patricia Hartley's."

"No, not hers."

She kissed him again.

"How much longer do you plan to keep reading?"

"I'm done. I've discovered all I'm likely to for now."

"Good. Don't bother clearing up. I'll take care of it in the morning."

She patted the dog and waited for her husband to get to his feet, just in case he was tempted to reconsider. Griffin walked with her through the house, and released her hand only as she entered the bedroom, while he continued to the bathroom. He took care of his business and brushed his teeth. When he spat the toothpaste into the sink, it came away bloodied. He washed the redness away until the porcelain was spotless again.

Evan Griffin sat on the edge of the bathtub and thought, as he did each day, about Patricia Hartley—and Estella Jackson, too, because her picture had been in Parker's file alongside Hartley's. These were the dead girls. The majority wished them to be forgotten, but the dead, in his experience, preferred to be remembered.

And sometimes, they refused to allow the living to forget.

CHAPTER
VIII

Jurel Cade looked at the man hunched over the stainless steel toilet in the cell, retching drily. Kel Knight stood behind Cade, impassive.

"Doesn't look like he's sleeping now," said Cade. "Was he like this when you brought him in?"

"I told you," said Knight. "He'd been drinking to excess."

Even though Parker had been brought to the cell soberer than Knight himself, and that was saying something, since Kel Knight had been an abstainer since his twenties, which came from being the son of an alcoholic. Knight wondered how much Parker had heard of the conversation with Cade. Enough, Knight decided, to put on a show in order to corroborate the tale spun about him. The more he saw of this Parker, the more puzzled Knight became.

Cade tapped at the bars with his right foot.

"Hey, you okay in there?" he said.

Parker raised a hand, seemed to recover himself, and released his hold upon the toilet bowl to sit back against the bunk. He wiped his mouth and rubbed his face.

"I've been better."

"You're a long way from home."

"I'm traveling."

"For what purpose?"

"I'm hoping to pick up work."

"What kind of work?"

"Security."

"In Burdon County?"

"I took a detour."

"To what end?"

"I got tired of looking at highways."

Cade didn't register happiness with this explanation. He tapped at the bar again, and contemplated the toe of his boot, as though imagining the harm it might do to this man were he permitted time alone with him.

"Where are you headed?"

"Louisiana, maybe."

"Maybe?" Cade smiled at the use of the word. "You got people down there in Louisiana?"

"Contacts."

"Contacts. Is that so?" Cade wagged a finger at Parker. "You know, I don't believe a word that's coming out of your mouth. Cargill PD will run you through the system. If they come up with wants, you'll be sorry you found your way to my county."

My county. Knight stifled a sigh. The arrogance of the man.

Wants were outstanding warrants, or pickup orders from a judge. Knight noticed that Parker didn't ask for a clarification of the term. Neither did he respond to Cade's goading. He rubbed his mouth again, climbed back onto his bunk, and closed his eyes. Cade appeared to be on the verge of saying more to Parker, before deciding that it would probably be a waste of both their time.

Cade and Knight headed for the door, the latter dimming the lights upon leaving as a courtesy to the prisoner. No point in torturing the man with bright bulbs if he wanted to rest.

"Sometimes I think we ought to put a sentry box on the roads in and out of this county," Cade remarked.

"To stop people from leaving?" said Knight.

"You hate it so much here, you could always go be a pain in the ass someplace else."

"You might think so, but nobody's recruiting pains in the ass."

"My conclusion is that there's always a surplus."

"That would also be my reasoning, based on the available evidence."

Cade cracked the knuckles in his hands, as though girding himself for bloodshed.

"You're testing my self-restraint, Kel."

"I'm sure trying, Jurel."

Cade requested a look at Parker's ID, and Knight watched him take down the details in a notebook. Had it been a different hour, Cade might have taken it upon himself to delve deeper into the reasons for Parker's presence in Cargill. Had he done so, it wouldn't have taken him long to establish that Parker had been asking questions about Patricia Hartley. Cade might yet discover this, which could cause problems for Knight and Griffin down the line, although both would stand by the story about Parker being drunk and mouthing off, because at least 50 percent of it was true and the rest couldn't be disproved, which made it true by default.

Cade looked back in the directions of the cells. "That man didn't smell much like a drunk to me."

"You ought to have been here earlier."

"Yeah, I kind of wish I had been," said Cade. "I think I'll be about my business."

"Justice never sleeps," said Knight.

Cade paused at the door.

"I can't always tell when you're being sarcastic, Kel," he said.

"My wife says the same thing."

"You figure she'd know by now. I guess you're a conundrum to her."

"That must be it."

"To her, possibly," Cade continued, "but not to me. I had you pegged a long time ago."

"We understand each other, then."

"We probably do, at that. Don't fuck with me, Kel. You ought to know better." He used the profanity deliberately, and with relish. He was well aware that Knight didn't hold with swearing— didn't hold with much at all, not that Cade could see. He found Knight's self-righteousness aggravating, not least because, if Knight and his kind had their way, the whole county would be doomed. As far as Jurel Cade was concerned, the needs of the many outweighed those of the few, and being forced to live with the implications of that conviction was one of the burdens of public service.

"As for our friend in there," said Cade, "if he comes up dirty, I want to hear about it, and if he comes up clean, I want him expelled from this locality. You have a good night, now."

And with that, he was gone.

When Knight returned to check on him, Parker was lying on his back in the shadows, contemplating the ceiling of his cell.

"That was quite the performance you staged," said Knight.

"I heard you talking to Chief Deputy Cade. I thought I should back up your story."

"Why would you do that?"

"For the same reason you lied to him in the first place, I suppose."

"And what would that be?"

"Because the less he knows, the better."

"Knows about what?"

"About anything."

Knight tamped fresh tobacco into his pipe. "Just who are you?"

"You know my name."

"That's not what I meant. If you were more open, it might serve to enhance your general likability."

"It wouldn't make any difference what I said. Most of the details you won't be able to check until morning. And I'm starting to grow fond of this cell. It has character."

Knight relit his pipe. Griffin wasn't around, and the smell would most likely have faded by morning.

"There's a fresh pot of coffee," he said, "if you want some."

"I'm good, thank you. If no one else is likely to be kicking at the bars for the next few hours, I'll try to get some rest."

"You do that. We'll pick you up some breakfast from Ferdy's come seven. By the time you've scraped your plate clean, we should know more about you."

But Parker didn't reply, and Knight left him in peace. He chatted with Colson, who had just returned, and began catching up on paperwork. He was halfway through the first report when he realized that Cade had never introduced himself to Parker, yet Parker had known him by sight.

Knight looked at the clock, and decided that morning, and answers, couldn't come quickly enough.

CHAPTER
IX

Despite what he'd told Knight, Parker did not close his eyes. He had some zaleplon back in his motel room, but he wasn't about to ask someone to go get it for him. In any case, he worried about growing dependent on it, and used it only when even a series of disturbed nights failed to make him tired enough to rest well—which, for Parker, meant dreamlessly.

Who are you?

I do not know. I can only say what I was.

And what was that?

I was a husband, a father.

And now?

I am neither of those things. I am a widower. I do not know if there is a name for one that has lost a child. If there is, there should not be. It is unnatural.

What do you see when you close your eyes?

That's easy.

I see red.

CHAPTER
X

Evan Griffin's phone rang shortly after 5 a.m. He heard Ava, still half asleep, start to complain as he dived for the receiver to stop the noise. She'd never wanted a telephone in the bedroom, but Griffin was a heavy sleeper, and the phone downstairs could have sounded until Doomsday without waking him. He turned his cell phone off at night and left it in the kitchen. He'd heard stories about radiation, and decided the device properly belonged with the microwave.

"Hello?"

"Evan, it's Kel."

Kel Knight rarely called him Evan. The last time was when Griffin's mother died. He sat up as Ava came fully awake beside him.

"What is it?"

"We have another body."

Parker opened his eyes. Dormancy, or some version of it, had come to him eventually, but now he'd been woken by sounds of activity in the station house. After a few minutes Naylor, the young officer who'd put the cuffs on him back at the bar, appeared, dressed in full uniform. Parker asked what was happening, but Naylor gave him the cold eye before leaving again, once he'd established that the prisoner still appeared to be in one piece.

Parker listened closely, trying to pick up some clue as to what might be happening, but the door connecting the cells to the main body of the station was firmly closed, and any conversations between the officers were muffled and unintelligible.

Parker hadn't liked the look on Naylor's face. It suggested that trouble had not only arrived but was unpacking its bags for a long stay, and might well find a way to involve him, if it hadn't already. He glanced at the damaged knuckles of his right hand. He should have kept driving, he thought, and never have left the highway for Burdon County.

Patricia Hartley, like the town of Cargill itself, was a dead end.

The girl lay naked on her back among dwarf sumac, her arms and legs splayed. Her body bore evidence of multiple piercings from a blade. A partially stripped branch had been jammed into her mouth and forced down her throat, while a second was buried deep enough in her vagina to have hit bone. Griffin surmised this without the benefit of an X-ray, because Estella Jackson had been violated in a similar way, and probably Patricia Hartley as well, although the worst of her injuries had not featured in any newspaper or autopsy reports and were therefore the subject of base rumor and conjecture. Jurel Cade, meanwhile, had warned all those with knowledge of the facts to keep their mouths shut, even around husbands and wives, fathers and mothers.

Like Jackson and Hartley, the girl was black, and probably no more than sixteen or seventeen years old. Griffin didn't recognize her, even allowing for the disfigurement, but then, he couldn't have named more than a handful of the colored kids around town, and then only the ones who had crossed his path for the wrong reasons. But no child deserved this, no matter her color, her disposition, or her place in the hierarchy of the county.

He asked Kel Knight who had found her.

"Tilon Ward."

"What was he doing out here?"

"Claims he was heading into the Ouachita to check on his raccoon traps."

"Before five in the morning?"

"He said something about early birds."

Tilon Ward purportedly lived on welfare, but like many such individuals, he found ways to supplement his income. One of them was hunting, both in and out of season. The other, it was strongly suspected, involved the production and distribution of methamphetamine, which sold for about $100 per gram in Little Rock, Fayetteville, and Fort Smith. Here in Cargill, locals got a discount, because good deals made good neighbors. Ward wasn't a bad guy as suspected meth manufacturers went, but that didn't make him a good one. Residents of the state were currently being sentenced at three times the national rate for methamphetamine offenses, which wasn't a statistic to make anyone proud. Even the dealers didn't need the kind of attention those figures would inevitably attract. Griffin had tried speaking informally to Ward about his activities in an effort to encourage a reconsideration of his life choices, but hadn't got anywhere. Eventually, he knew, Ward would end up dead or behind bars, and neither of those solutions to the problem he represented would give Griffin any pleasure.

There was history between them, these two.

"You want to talk to him?" said Knight.

"In a few minutes. Did he call 911?"

"No, he got in touch with the station house direct."

"Huh," said Griffin. That was another thing about Ward: he wasn't dumb, and didn't allow wax to build up in his ears. He was fully aware of the tensions in the region, and the whispers about Patricia Hartley. Ward was setting down a marker by electing to inform the Cargill PD about the body, and not Jurel Cade, who was chief investigator for the county. Ward liked Griffin a whole lot better than he did Jurel Cade, and perhaps trusted him to do what was right by the town—although what that might be, Griffin himself had yet to determine. All he knew for sure was that he now had a second body with which to contend—or even a third, depending on how one counted Estella Jackson, and there was only so long a man could allow such a state of affairs to endure.

"What about clothing, or possessions?" he asked.

"Nothing nearby," said Knight, "but we'll wait for better light before we start the search."

Griffin forced himself to look again at the girl's body, but without anger or sorrow. They would serve no purpose here.

"We won't find anything, not unless he was careless, and this doesn't look like the work of a careless man."

"Indeed it does not."

In the beam from his flashlight, Griffin could see some blood on the ground between the dead girl's legs, and some more around her mouth, but not a lot of it. She'd likely been killed elsewhere, and the branches inserted after her death. The latter was a small mercy. She'd endured enough pain at the end.

"Any idea who she is?"

"No, but I've sent Lorrie Colson to fetch Pettle."

Reverend Nathan Pettle was pastor of the Cargill African Methodist Episcopal Church. He also ran an outreach program for the poor of all denominations, and was the main point of contact between the black and white communities in Cargill. Pettle was their best chance of identifying the girl quietly and quickly.

"What about forensics?"

"Tucker McKenzie is on his way."

Which Griffin was glad to hear, because he had questions for McKenzie about the photographs of Patricia Hartley contained in Parker's file.

"Who's at the station house?" said Knight.

"Naylor."

Joshua Petrie, one of the part-time officers, was

standing nearby, keeping an eye on Tilon Ward, who was sitting on the rear fender of his truck, smoking a cigarette and looking sallow, even allowing for the cocklight, as Griffin's English grandmother used to call this time of morning. If it wasn't for Parker, Griffin could have had Naylor here as well. Then again, it might be that Naylor was no longer guarding some drifter from New York, but a killer.

Griffin wondered how long he could get away with keeping the fact of the body's discovery from Jurel Cade: just a few hours, probably. Loyd Holt, the coroner, wasn't actively corrupt, but he was ineffectual and wouldn't be disposed to making an enemy of the sheriff's office. His handling of the Hartley case was confirmation of that, if any were needed. Burdon was one of only three counties in the state in which coroners were appointed, rather than elected to two-year terms. In practical terms, this meant Loyd Holt served at the pleasure of the Cade family. He was their creature.

Tucker McKenzie, on the other hand, didn't give a rat's ass whether Jurel and his kin liked him or not, because they didn't pay his salary, so Holt was the weak link. With some arm-twisting, he might be willing to hold off for a while on informing Jurel Cade. Holt received $2,500 a year as county coroner, and for that he was required to be on call 24/7. On the other hand, he possessed zero medical qualifications, had only been elected because he was a chronic insomniac—which meant he was usually wide-awake when the night calls came through—and was additionally the third-best undertaker in the county.

Of three.

"We're not equipped to handle a killing like this," said Griffin. "We need more people, and a level of expertise that's beyond us at our best."

"We could let Parker go," said Knight. "It would free up Naylor, at least."

"The hell we will. We don't even know for sure who he is yet, and now we have a dead girl, and a stranger in custody who was asking questions about other dead girls."

"If you really think he's a suspect, I can tell you for nothing that he didn't kill this one."

"How do you figure that?"

"The body's dry. It rained last night from midnight until two, which means she was dumped here after the rain stopped, when we had Parker locked up tight."

"What about the trees? They could have sheltered her."

"Not enough to keep her completely dry."

Griffin conceded the point. Oddly, he was relieved to have Parker cleared of suspicion, although he could not have said why.

"You didn't find out anything from searching his motel room?" said Knight.

Griffin reddened. "Why would you ask that?"

"I saw you palm his key."

"You ought to be a detective."

"I like to think I'm helping to keep you straight. Well?"

"If I had examined his room—which I'm not admitting I did, because that would be an illegal search—I might have found two guns: an old thirty-eight Special, and a ten milli Smith and Wesson, a weapon that, last time I checked, was in the arsenal of federal agents."

"If he was a fed, he'd have told us so. They don't take well to being locked up. You think he could have stolen those guns?"

"He was too relaxed for a man hoarding illegal firearms, and he's in possession of a permit. He also had a file containing graphic photographs, along with autopsy and police reports relating to the murders of women and children, material on Patricia Hartley and Estella Jackson among them."

"So if he's not a criminal . . . ?"

"I didn't say he wasn't, but he might also be more than that."

"Police?"

"Perhaps once. Not now."

"So why not just say that? Why let us lock him in a cell?"

"Because he didn't seem to care what we did," said Griffin. "Whatever he was looking for down here, Jackson and Hartley weren't it. Still, I want to know more about him before we give him back his liberty, not to mention restoring his access to those guns. Now I'm going to talk to Tilon over there, see what he has to say for himself. I want you to wake Billie"—Wilhelmina Brinton, or just plain Billie to everyone who knew her, took care of secretarial duties for the department—"and tell her to get to her desk as soon as she can. I'm good for the extra hours. She can free up Kevin to join us, because we're going to need extra pairs of hands and eyes."

Billie Brinton was no pushover, and knew how to handle a weapon, and herself. Griffin wasn't anticipating any trouble from Parker, but you never knew. He was on his way to speak with Ward when Knight spoke again.

"This one is going to be different, right?"

But Griffin did not reply.

CHAPTER
XI

Tilon Ward was in his mid-thirties, but like so many of those born in this impoverished place, he could have added another ten years to his age and no one would have blinked. As far as Griffin could tell, Ward subsisted on one square meal a day, if that, supplemented by coffee, cigarettes, and the occasional Coors Light. If he was involved in the production of methamphetamine, he was smart enough not to use it himself.

"Tilon."

"Evan."

"You okay there?"

Ward nodded, but looked as though he wanted to throw up again. He'd already done so once, according to Knight, although he'd had the good sense to puke far from the dead girl.

"Never seen a body before," he said, "or not one like that."

"You want to tell me how you came to find her?"

"Like I told Kel, I was on my way to check my traps. I smelled something bad, went to investigate, and there she was."

"You always go after bad smells? Might have been a dead animal."

"I know how dead animals smell. This was different."

He had a point, Griffin knew. There was something distinctive about the emanations from human mortality.

"Did you touch anything?"

"Nothing. I saw her, retraced my steps, and made the call."

His cell phone stuck out of the side pocket of his jacket. Coverage was scratchy out here, and Ward had been forced to drive a ways back toward town before he picked up a signal.

"Traps, huh?"

"That's right. Coon traps."

Ward met the chief's gaze. If Griffin wanted to make an accusation, the look said, he'd better have the evidence to back it up, because Ward wasn't about to admit to anything unless he had to.

"How often do you inspect them?"

"Most days."

"You take the same route each time?"

"Mostly."

"When did you last come through?"

"Yesterday."

"Could the girl have been here then?"

Regardless of what Knight had said about the rain and the trees, Griffin wasn't entirely dismissing the possibility that the girl might have been killed elsewhere a day or two earlier, with the body subsequently being relocated to the sumac grove.

"I don't think so."

"Why not? From the looks of her, she's been dead for two days at least."

"Because almost as soon as I smelled her, I saw her. I got good eyes. Didn't have to take more than a couple of steps to make her out."

"Meaning?"

"I'd have noticed if she'd been there yesterday, even without the smell. Like I said, I got good eyes."

"Even in the dark?"

"It's not dark. It's just a different light."

And he was right about that as well. It was all a matter of texture. This was a fairly remote stretch of road, for now, but the girl's remains hadn't just been dumped; she'd been laid carefully on the ground, and the branches had probably been put inside her once she was in position. It would be hard to transport a body with two branches wedged inside, and that was before carrying it down a slope and arranging it just so among the trees.

"Can you think of anyone else who comes this way into the woods?" said Griffin.

"I've seen people around, but not many."

That was set to change, though. Almost within sight of where they stood was a fenced-off area of land, partially cleared: a Cade property, waiting for construction to commence. Two metal poles had recently been erected beside the gates, and word was that a banner was ready to be hoisted from them, trumpeting a new start for the county.

"And there are easier ways into the Ouachita, since—"

Ward bit his tongue. He'd almost made a

mistake. The reason most folk chose not to explore certain parts of the woods was because they might stumble across a meth lab or those involved with it. Encountering Tilon Ward was one thing, but dealing with some of his associates was another. All this Griffin surmised from Ward's hesitation. Ward's truck contained a big lockbox in its bed, and Griffin wondered what he might find inside if he searched. But to do so he'd need a warrant, and Judge Hawkins would require a semblance of probable cause before signing off on Tilon Ward.

But Griffin wasn't about to fight that battle now. It was coming down the line, and then he and Ward would have a reckoning, whatever their history, but the pressing issue was dead black girls.

"And who might those folks be?" said Griffin.

Ward gave him a few names, but reluctantly. This was a small town, and just as nobody wanted the police knocking on the door asking about murders, so too did no one wish to point a finger at others. It was a surefire way to have one's tires slashed, or worse. But none of the men identified by Ward struck Griffin as the murderous type, or at least not the kind to kill a young woman. He could see a couple of them falling back on a gun or their fists owing to an inherently hostile disposition and a paucity of patience and common sense, but not engaging in this level of sadism and defilement.

"If I was you, Tilon," said Griffin, "I'd stay out of the woods for a while."

Ward did not appear particularly enamored of

85

this suggestion. Griffin figured the meth wasn't going to make itself, and the meth addict customer base was not noted for its loyalty. Also, while Ward might have been involved in manufacture and distribution, Griffin didn't have him pegged as the guiding force behind the operation, although he had his theories about that as well.

"What about my traps?" said Ward.

"You catch a coon in one of them, it's not going anywhere."

Griffin knew that Ward, like most of those in the county who trapped raccoons, used live traps rather than foot ones, if only to stop the animals gnawing off a limb to escape. The raccoons might lose some weight before Ward came to kill them, but that was about the worst he could anticipate, assuming any of this was about traps to begin with.

"I'll take it under advisement," said Ward.

"Do you even know what that means?"

"It means I don't plan to stay out of the woods. It's a free country."

"It hasn't been a free country since the *Mayflower* landed, and this particular expanse of it is about to get a whole lot less free."

Ward lit another cigarette from the butt of the first. He almost threw away the dead soldier before spotting the look on Griffin's face, and instead stored it in one of his pockets once he'd snuffed out the last of the burning tobacco. Griffin was immediately reminded of Kevin Naylor, who had performed the same action the night before, and under similar pressure. It sometimes felt to Griffin that he was destined to spend much of his life attempting to inculcate better habits of behavior in the young.

"Less free because of . . . her?" said Ward.

Griffin picked up on the pause, but didn't ascribe any significance to it.

"Among other reasons."

"It won't matter, not if Jurel Cade has his way."

"You see Jurel here?" said Griffin.

"Not yet, but I will if I stick around long enough."

"Then you'd best be about your business, unless you have an urge to discuss your activities with him."

Ward didn't. The only reason the forces of law and order in Burdon County hadn't moved en masse into the Ouachita to investigate reports of meth production was because there were too many trees and not enough police, but that situation remained fluid, and change was coming.

Ward jangled the keys of his truck as a prelude to departing, and Griffin said, "Tilon."

"Yes?"

"I appreciate your making the call to us first."

Ward glanced over at the body.

"You ought to have a woman officer out here," he said. "It's wrong to leave her like that, surrounded only by men."

"You're right, but we can't do anything until the scene has been photographed. We'll cover her up soon as we can, and Lorrie Colson will be back before long."

Ward nodded.

"I guess I'll be hearing from Jurel about all this," he said, "whether I stay around or not."

"Most likely."

"Better be worth the vexation."

He got in his truck and drove toward town, leaving Griffin to reflect on the strange forms that goodness and morality sometimes assumed. He'd do his best to remember this moment, and another, when the time came to take down Tilon Ward.

A white 1981 Pontiac Phoenix SJ coupe rattled down the road toward Griffin, slowing as it came. Loyd Holt, the coroner, might not have been the only man in Arkansas still driving the '81 Phoenix, but he was certainly the only one to give every impression of continuing to enjoy the experience. He had added blue racing stripes to his vehicle, and whitewall tires, which was like putting lipstick on a pig—a pig, that is, with an eighty-four-horsepower engine. Griffin could almost have understood someone holding on to the '82 Phoenix, which could outaccelerate a Trans Am in its day, but not the '81. Even relative poverty didn't excuse it, and it was even more unbecoming as a mode of transportation for a coroner.

Holt brought the Phoenix to a halt, which took some time. He'd probably learned many years before not to slam on the brakes, as this caused the rear wheels to lock. Even if he'd had the problem seen to, Griffin thought, the memory of the experience would undoubtedly have remained with him.

Holt was a small, rotund man in his forties, his avoirdupois being a product of his insomnia, which caused him to eat at odd times of the day and night, and made him unsuited to most forms of physical exercise. He was single, and had never been married, although it was not for want of asking. Griffin doubted that there existed a single, divorced, or widowed woman in Burdon County between the ages of twenty-five and fifty who had not, at some point, found herself the object of Loyd Holt's attentions, but he was never unpleasant or untoward, and moved on once it became clear that his feelings were unlikely to be reciprocated. He was just lonely, with a hint of desperation to him. Someday he might find a fellow insomniac to keep him company, and his life would be happier as a consequence. He was an unlikely occupant of the highest-ranking law enforcement position in the county, even if only nominally, but thus had the Arkansas constitution been framed.

"Where's the body?" Holt asked, once he'd emerged from the Phoenix.

"Over by that dwarf sumac."

Griffin led the way to the scene, Kel Knight watching. Holt knew only that a body had been discovered, but he had not been informed of the precise nature of that discovery. As he looked down at the dead girl, a weight appeared to descend on him.

"Jesus," he said. "Has Jurel been informed?"

"He will be," Griffin replied, "just not right now. Tucker's on his way. Once he's documented everything, I'll make the call. Are we clear, Loyd? I'll make the call."

The implication was beyond misunderstanding: if Holt went running behind Griffin's back to Jurel Cade, Griffin would do his utmost to ensure that Holt's already problematic existence descended into outright misery.

"He's not going to like it."

"Frankly, Loyd," said Griffin, "I couldn't give a damn what Jurel likes or doesn't like."

But even as he spoke, he heard his own bluster, and Holt heard it too.

"It's on your head," he said.

"If these girls keep dying, it'll be on all our heads," said Griffin. "And Jurel's will roll just as easy as yours or mine."

CHAPTER
XII

The woman named Billie hadn't introduced herself to Parker, but he'd heard the younger officer, Naylor, use her name before he left. She appeared at the bars with a cup of coffee shortly after 6:30 a.m., and placed it on the floor for him to take, being careful to instruct him to remain where he was until she'd stepped away. He wondered if someone had tried to throw hot coffee over her in the past. If so, it wouldn't have ended well for the prisoner involved, given that Billie was built on substantial foundations and wore a holstered gun on her belt. It behooved a man to mind his manners in such company.

"You mind if I ask what's happening?" he asked.

"They found a girl's body, just out of town."

"Like Patricia Hartley?"

Billie squinted at him. She'd been told nothing about the prisoner beyond the fact that he'd mouthed off to the chief, and she should keep her distance until they found out more about him. But if she'd come across him in a bar, she thought she might have spoken with him. He didn't raise her hackles or give her the creeps, not like some of the men she'd encountered during her years with the department. He just seemed sad—and angry, because the two often went together.

"It's a body. That's all I know. Breakfast may

take a while, because it's just you and me here for now."

"I'm in no hurry to eat, but thank you anyway."

"You didn't kill her, did you?"

"No."

"I guess you would say that, though, even if you had killed her."

"I guess so."

"But if you've done something bad, I'll be disappointed in you."

A flicker on the man's face: a smile attempting to construct itself from underused muscles.

"I wouldn't want that," he said.

"No, you wouldn't. You need anything else?"

"I have a book to read, but it's kind of you to ask."

"I'll be back to you later with that food."

"Thanks."

Billie left him, increasing her pace as she heard the phone begin to ring. She picked up and listened as the caller identified himself. She wrote the name CHARLIE PARKER in block capitals across the top of a fresh page, and began taking notes.

Christ, she thought, as the lines began to fill with her handwriting, *Kel and the chief need to get back here, and fast. They need to let this man out of his cage before he has a mind to break out of it himself.*

Tucker McKenzie was everything that Loyd Holt was not: tall where Holt was short, slim where he was fat, confident where he was not. McKenzie also slept like a baby, and had given up asking women to marry him after the first one said yes. He was now carefully walking the scene, camera in hand, his equipment bag hanging from his shoulder. Griffin and the others left him to it, not wishing to obstruct or distract him while he was getting his bearings. Once he was done, he joined Griffin, Knight, and Holt.

"What do you think?" Griffin asked.

McKenzie gave him a look before continuing, and Griffin gathered that two conversations would be required between them, the first public and the second more private.

"It looks clean, at first glance. She was set down after the rain stopped, so we might luck out on boot or shoe prints, but I wouldn't get my hopes up. I saw some smears in the dirt beside the body, so whoever left her there may have been smart enough to obscure any tracks. When the light improves, I'll take a closer look at those branches, see if anything might have snagged on them. What I can tell you now, you already know: she wasn't killed where she lies, and there's evidence of torture."

"Torture?" said Griffin.

"Some of those wounds are shallow. I reckon whoever did this tormented her for kicks before he got around to killing her. Also, those branches inside her didn't originate here. They're black hickory, and I don't see any of that nearby.

We'll need to figure out where they might have originated, and search those areas. Until the branches are removed, I won't be able to tell for certain if they were scavenged or cut for purpose. As for the cause of death, I wouldn't like to speculate, but if you forced me, I'd say that one or more of those stab wounds might have been sufficient to put an end to her."

"All right," said Griffin. "Soonest started."

McKenzie began checking his camera. "You have a name for her yet?"

"No. We got a couple of missing persons, including two colored women, but the ages don't match. We're going to consult Reverend Pettle, see if he can't help us identify her."

"Uh-huh." McKenzie clicked off a shot and rolled the film on. "Loyd, can you give us a minute?"

Holt made an effort to object, if only for form's sake. "I'm the coroner. Whatever you got to say, I should hear."

"Loyd," said Griffin, "how badly do you want to have to lie to Jurel Cade when he arrives?"

"I don't want to have to lie to Jurel at all."

"Then perhaps you ought to take a walk."

Holt didn't bother to protest. In fact, to Griffin's eyes, he appeared pleased to be asked to absent himself from proceedings, which was worrying.

Burdon County, Griffin thought, was about ready for a new coroner.

CHAPTER
XIII

Kel Knight kept an eye on Loyd Holt while Griffin and McKenzie conversed out of earshot. Like the rest of the department, Knight now owned one of those cursed cell phone gadgets, although he sorely wished it were not the case, Kel Knight being of the view that if he wanted to be contactable at all hours of the day and night, he'd pitch a tent outside Ferdy's Dunk-N-Go, and leave a light on so folks could find him in the dark. Admittedly, one couldn't travel far from the heart of town without losing coverage, but it was scant succor for someone who valued his privacy the way Knight did.

Even though Holt had moved some distance away, and believed himself to be unobserved, Knight could see him discreetly checking his phone, moving it here and there in an effort to pick up a signal. When he failed, he began painstakingly typing out a text message, presumably in the hope that it might be sent as soon as the bars on the phone appeared again. If the recipient were anyone other than Jurel Cade, Knight would have been shocked to learn it. In his view, Holt's fear of the chief deputy almost certainly outweighed any obligation the former might have felt toward Evan Griffin, the Cargill PD, and the requirements of law and justice. He wondered how long it would take Holt to find an excuse to leave the scene. Not long, as it turned out.

"I'm going to head home for a few minutes," Holt told Knight. "I didn't dress warmly enough, and there's a dampness in the air."

"I keep an old coat in the trunk of my car," said Knight. "Never know when a man might require another layer."

"All due respect, Kel, you got six inches on me, and I got at least twelve on you around the waist. I don't believe one of your coats is going to do me much good. I'll pick up coffee and doughnuts from Ferdy's on the way back, and some bagels, too."

"If you're sure," said Knight.

"I am."

Knight watched Holt get into his crappy Phoenix and start the engine. Just as he was about to pull away, Knight made a roll-down-the-window gesture.

"What is it?" said Holt.

"You're running on a flat, Loyd."

"What?"

"Left rear. Doesn't look like you're going anywhere until you get it changed."

Holt leaned out the window and took in the deflated tire.

"Aw, goddamn."

"Won't take long to fix. I'll give you a hand. You got a spare?"

"In the trunk."

"You want to pop it open?"

Holt did, and a jab with Knight's pocketknife put paid to the spare tire just as assuredly as it had the left rear.

"Right," said Knight, "let's get started."

McKenzie watched Kel Knight lift out the spare tire as Loyd Holt struggled with the jack. He'd noticed Knight kneeling by Holt's car a few moments earlier. Now he understood why.

"Seems like Loyd has a problem with a tire," said McKenzie.

"That's unfortunate, but Loyd doesn't know from problems," said Griffin. "Talk to me."

"I could see a puncture at the base of the girl's skull when I knelt beside her. Didn't need to lift her head to spot it, but I thought you'd prefer to be made aware of it before Loyd was."

A deep injury to the base of the skull, a killing wound. Griffin returned in his mind to the photographs in Parker's file, and one in particular: a girl lying naked in a pool of water, the red hole of a penetrating skull fracture clearly visible, dried blood around her ears and eyes.

Patricia Hartley.

Evan Griffin had not been permitted to view Patricia Hartley's body. The little he knew about the circumstances of its discovery came from Tucker McKenzie, who had heard on the grapevine about the body while he was over in Hot Springs working on another case, and had swung by the scene on the assumption that he would eventually be needed one way or another. When he arrived, Loyd Holt was parked within sight of the corpse, along with a couple of sheriff's deputies, but Holt was reluctant to let McKenzie get to work, not without Jurel Cade's permission—and Cade, said the coroner, had briefly left the scene to make a call. McKenzie had convinced Holt that it might be wise to have some pictures, if only to cover Holt's own back in the event of any questions, because rain was coming. Holt, who was so committed to watching his own back that he might have been part owl, acquiesced.

McKenzie had only just commenced work when Jurel Cade returned and instructed him to get the fuck away from the body. Cade also ordered him to hand over any film from his camera, but Tucker McKenzie was too old and ornery to play that game, and a standoff occurred. Finally, though, McKenzie was forced to surrender the film to Cade, partly because he was not on the scene in any official capacity, and in theory the pictures might prove useful to Cade in his own inquiries; but mostly, Evan Griffin now believed, because McKenzie had discreetly taken a series of snaps of Hartley's body with an instant camera, copies of which were now in the possession of the prisoner named Parker.

"She needs to be sent to Little Rock for autopsy," McKenzie had told Cade, as he prepared to depart—if, he assumed, only temporarily.

"No," said Cade, "she doesn't."

"You want to explain why?"

Cade looked to the coroner.

"Tell him, Loyd."

"I believe it's an accidental death," said Holt.

"You've got to be fucking kidding me," said McKenzie. "That girl has one stick jammed in her mouth and another in her vagina. This is a killing."

"You the coroner now, Tucker?" said Cade. "Last time I checked, Loyd had the honor of holding that position."

"She stumbled, and fell down that slope behind," said Holt. "Lot of sticks and stones on the ground here."

But he wouldn't look at McKenzie as he spoke.

"This is wrong," said McKenzie.

"It's Loyd's decision to make," said Cade. "And mine," he added, "as chief investigator for the county. I can't afford to waste resources on an accidental death."

McKenzie wanted to say more, but he held his tongue. He saw what was happening, and why. This was about the future of Burdon County, and the fortunes of the Cade family.

This was about money.

Much of this McKenzie later shared with Griffin over a beer at Boyd's. It was McKenzie's opinion, based admittedly on only a brief sight of the body, that Patricia Hartley had suffered an injury to the base of her skull, just below the bump known as the inion. It looked as though a blade might have caused it, but McKenzie couldn't be certain because a puncture from a sharp stone might equally have been responsible. The effect had been to sever the brain from the brain stem, shutting down her nervous system. Death would have been almost instantaneous.

And now here was another naked dead girl, with what might be a similar wound to her head, but with more injuries to her body than Patricia Hartley had suffered.

"I can see no signs of disturbance," said McKenzie, "not like there was with Patricia Hartley. Where she's resting, that's where her killer wanted her to be found."

"Anything else?"

"She's missing two fingernails from her right hand. The ME will be able to tell for sure, but I'd say it looks like they weren't removed, but broke off, possibly during a struggle. The hands are real clean. I'd suggest they were washed before her body was dumped, which means she may have clawed her killer. Finally, for now, you surely noticed the marks on the decedent's wrists. They're rope burns, and they're deep. The skin is broken, which means the victim attempted to free herself. It also means that we should be able to pull fragments of the binding material from the wounds. They'll be useful if you ever get as far as a prosecution, and can find the original rope."

Griffin finished writing down everything he'd

learned. He would have no trouble remembering what McKenzie had said, but he was a meticulous man. If this was to be handled right, it had to begin now. He wasn't about to let this girl go the way of Patricia Hartley.

A sorry sun was scattering sickly light through pallid cloud, but it wasn't making much difference to the temperature. And there was, as Loyd Holt had noted, a dampness to the air: Griffin could feel it penetrating his clothing, digging deep.

"How long are you going to need?" he asked McKenzie.

"A couple of hours, but I'll aim for less. What are you going to do about Loyd in the meantime, apart from sabotaging his vehicle? I sense his spine may be weakening, and it was made of Jell-O to begin with."

"I may have to be more forceful with him. I'm not sure his loyalties lie where they should."

"If Cade comes, he could try to seize the evidence."

"I know that," said Griffin.

He considered raising the subject of the pictures in Parker's file before deciding to leave it for another time. He didn't want to risk alienating McKenzie. They needed him on their side.

"So?"

"So get moving, Tucker."

Tucker McKenzie got moving.

101

CHAPTER
XIV

Parker finished his coffee before dozing as the sky grew lighter. It sometimes came on him this way: a restless night would be followed by exhaustion, and he would sleep until late in the morning, or even into the afternoon. He tried to fight it as best he could, because he feared a time when he might be reluctant to leave his bed at all, but he was a man unmoored and his obligations were few. They could, in fact, be boiled down to one: to find the one who had taken his wife and child from this world and tear him apart.

Sometimes he dreamed, and in his dreams he was permitted to view Susan and Jennifer, but only at one remove. They passed through vistas detached from the reality of their previous existence, and their movements were the slow, final struggles of drowning victims. On occasion, his dead family assumed other forms, the essence of them inhabiting new bodies, as though seeking to remain connected to a realm that would, in the end, erase them entirely from its cognizance. He would hold on to them as long as he could. He would hold on to them until death came for him, too.

But even now, barely months after their murders, he was struggling to keep all of those memories intact. With each day that passed, he seemed to lose one more. He could almost feel them fading, the details of faces and gestures, of words spoken, of touches given and received, falling away, color draining from them like photographic images too long exposed to light.

I want to be with you again. I do not want to live in this world without you.

But I have to stay.

I will find him, the one who did this, and when I am done with him, I will search for you both. I will leave this place, and I will travel to where you are.

Wait for me.

Listen for me.

I will come.

CHAPTER
XV

Loyd Holt might have been a poor excuse for a coroner, but he wasn't a total dullard. A puncture to one tire might have been regarded as unlucky, but damage to two, including the spare that had sat unused in the trunk for so long, smacked to him of a conspiracy. This impression was reinforced when nobody would give him a ride back to town, make a call over the radio for someone to come out and pick him up, or even provide or secure a replacement tire. It was confirmed when he started walking, only to find Evan Griffin blocking his path.

"I know what you're doing," said Holt. "You're keeping me here because you think I'm going to call Jurel."

"No," said Griffin, "I'm keeping you here because I *know* you're going to call Jurel. I need more time, Loyd. Tucker's not a man to rush, which is only right."

"And I need this job, Evan. The money makes a difference to me."

"Then do it properly."

"Don't talk to me like that. I've always performed my task to the best of my abilities."

Which was, in Griffin's view, part of the problem, Loyd Holt's best being the very definition of bare adequacy.

"I realize that," said Griffin. "I'm trying to do the same, but it's going to become difficult for me from the moment you get in touch with Jurel."

"Jurel Cade is the chief investigator for the county. I have a responsibility to inform him of what's occurred."

"You can inform him just as soon as Tucker has finished with the scene."

Holt practically danced on the spot with frustration.

"But by then it'll be too late!"

"Too late for whom?"

"For Jurel."

"You don't serve at his favor."

"No, I serve at the favor of his entire fucking family. So do you, Evan. You may not believe you're a political appointee, but you are. If the Cades want you gone, you're gone, and Cargill will just have to swallow its sorrow before finding someone to take your place."

"You mean someone who'll do as the Cades tell him?"

Holt quit dancing. His eyes met Griffin's, and the chief saw the native cunning concealed behind a clown's demeanor.

"Someone who'll do right by the county," said Holt.

"We have dead girls, Loyd."

"No, we have poor dead colored girls, Evan. That's not the same thing. I'm sorry for what happened to them, truly I am, but we got to think of the needs of all the people in this county. We're a couple of signatures away from a new beginning, the one we was promised, and that'll be good for everyone, black and white."

And how often had Griffin heard those three words over the last year? *We was promised. Better times are coming. You just have to hang in there. They're on their way, you can bet your house on that, because we was promised.*

We was promised, we was promised, we was promised.

"Not much good to that girl back there," said Griffin. "Not much good to Patricia Hartley."

"They're both dead, Evan, so I'll tell you this for free: they're beyond caring. Now get out of my fucking way, or I'll have you up before Judge Hawkins for obstructing me in the commission of my duties."

Griffin gave it a few seconds, for dignity's sake, before yielding the road to Holt. The little man went tramping toward Cargill, cell phone in hand.

Griffin's radio spoke. It was Lorrie Colson. She was with Reverend Nathan Pettle, but had held off on bringing him to the scene until Tucker McKenzie's work was complete. But Pettle, unsurprisingly, was growing impatient. If a member of his congregation was dead, her people needed to be informed.

"Tucker?" Griffin shouted, as Knight came over to join him.

"Five minutes."

Loyd Holt had already reached the top of the nearest rise, and was now descending the other side, vanishing from sight. It looked like the ground was swallowing him up, which would have been preferable to the alternative. In a couple of minutes, if that, Holt would be on the phone to the county sheriff's office, and Jurel Cade would come running.

"Help Tucker to pack up," Griffin told Knight. "Make sure you secure everything he has, put it in the trunk of your car, and take the long road back to town."

Knight started moving.

"And Kel?"

"Yes?"

"You cover that girl. I want her nakedness concealed before the reverend gets here."

CHAPTER
XVI

Tilon Ward had not driven very far. He'd parked his truck on a side road, amid a smear of trees on a hill, giving him a clear view of the police activity while concealing him from sight. There he sat in the driver's seat, smoking a cigarette and thinking that, as fucked up as life could sometimes be, the possibility always existed that it could get fucked up a whole lot more. He felt a tickling on his cheek. When he scratched at it, his finger came away wet. He had not even realized he was crying.

Tilon could have told Evan Griffin a great deal about the dead girl. He could have shared with him her identity, and where she lived. He could have described her body in intimate detail, and the sounds she made during sex. He could have offered up the taste and smell of her, and the way she spoke his name, with the emphasis on the second syllable instead of the first, because she thought it was fun to pronounce it differently from others, and by individuating him she made him more her own.

Tilon didn't think anyone knew about him and the girl. He'd warned her not to share the fact of their relationship with anyone, because it would stir up a world of hurt for both of them. To some, it might have resembled a commercial exchange—sex for money—but he had never really considered it to be thus, and he did not believe that she did either, because he sensed her affection for him was real, and he had begun to reciprocate in kind. Oh, he still gave her cash whenever they met, because she and her mother didn't have much of their own, but it was more in the manner of a gift than payment for services offered and received—or so he told himself, and told her as well, although the truth was more complex than that, and he might have been fooling himself just as much as he was fooling her.

Yet how odd it was that he should have been the one to discover her body, as though some force beyond human comprehension had intended it to be this way. Tilon had even briefly considered abandoning the remains, leaving them for someone else to find. By involving himself, he would inevitably draw police attention, and if the investigation uncovered the association between him and the girl, he would become a suspect. While he maintained a grudging respect, even trust, for Chief Evan Griffin, he retained none at all for Jurel Cade. The latter was looking for an excuse to move against Tilon, and if he could pin some killings on him, he would—especially these killings, because making an arrest would take a lot of the pressure off the county. But Tilon Ward knew this much: he hadn't killed this girl, or Patricia Hartley, or anyone else, which meant that locking him up wouldn't put an end to whatever was happening.

Unless, of course, it did. What if the killer decided to make use of a patsy and went to ground after the arrest, leaving Tilon to suffer the consequences? The state of Arkansas had the death penalty, and wasn't shy about sticking men with the needle. It was also, in its callous way, color-blind when it came to capital punishment, which was almost admirable unless you happened to be the white man strapped to a gurney while fingers probed for a suitable vein.

So common sense dictated that Tilon should have kept his mouth shut and let someone else find the dead girl. But whatever feelings he'd had for her, combined with a semblance of common decency, impelled him to make the call. He was part of it now, but he supposed he'd been part of it from the first time he took her to his bed.

He heard the sound of vehicles approaching from the direction of town, and moments later a Cargill PD cruiser headed for the scene, closely followed by a Country Squire station wagon in dirty winter white. Ward recognized the car: it was Reverend Nathan Pettle's, which meant the police were only minutes away from identifying the body. At the same time, another Cargill PD cruiser was leaving the scene, Kel Knight behind the wheel.

Ward was tempted to use the arriving and departing cars to mask his own withdrawal—sound carried oddly around here, and he had no desire to attract further attention—but he was also worried about taking to the road before all the players were on the field. He'd witnessed the interaction between Loyd Holt and Evan Griffin as a dumb show, followed by Holt's slow trot toward town, and figured out what had probably occurred. It wouldn't be long before Jurel Cade made his appearance, and Ward didn't want to run into him.

So he lit another cigarette, watched, and waited.

CHAPTER
XVII

Kel Knight pulled into the parking lot of the Cargill PD at almost the precise moment that Reverend Pettle was being led by Evan Griffin to the body. As ordered, Knight had taken a circuitous route back to town because he, like Tilon Ward, was anxious about crossing the path of Jurel Cade or any of his deputies. In the trunk of Knight's cruiser was a box containing the evidence collected by Tucker McKenzie at the scene, along with all the film from his camera. Usually McKenzie would have taken the film away to be developed, but on this occasion he was content to relinquish everything to Kel Knight once Knight had signed all the relevant paperwork.

Knight removed the box from the trunk and headed inside. The box didn't weigh much, but that didn't make its contents potentially any less valuable. Billie Brinton emerged from behind the reception desk as he appeared, brandishing a sheaf of faxes and handwritten notes. She'd been tempted to call Griffin at the scene to inform him of what she'd discovered about Parker, assuming she could even raise him on his cell phone, before deciding that he and the rest of the officers had enough to occupy them with a murdered girl.

"Kel—" she began, but he quickly cut her off before she could proceed.

"One minute," he said. "I need you to witness this."

The department didn't have an evidence locker per se. What it did have was a big old safe from the turn of the century, manufactured by the Victor Safe & Lock Company of Cincinnati, Ohio. It had previously formed part of the furnishings of the Arkansas Loan & Thrift Corporation, a notoriously fraudulent operation that left more than two thousand investors, including a number of churches, out of pocket to the tune of $4.2 million when it collapsed at the end of the 1960s. No one was entirely clear on how the safe had finally come to reside in Cargill or, more particularly, with the town's police department, but it served a useful purpose on occasions such as this, which was all that mattered.

Kel Knight and Evan Griffin were officially the only members of the force with access to the safe, and Billie made a show of turning away while Knight fiddled with the combination, even though she knew the numbers by heart. Once the door was open, Knight showed her the itemized evidence list from Griffin, including the rolls of film, and asked her to countersign each item as it was placed in the safe, with the exception of the film canisters. These he entrusted to Billie herself: her son Craig was an amateur photographer, and made some money on the side taking pictures at local weddings, retirements, and sporting events. Craig had his own darkroom, and—having learned well on his mother's knee—knew how, when, and why to keep his mouth shut.

"You want me to take them over to him now?" she asked.

"I do, just in case Jurel Cade comes calling."

"We got to talk first."

"We don't have a lot of time."

"It's about the prisoner, Mr. Parker."

Knight noticed the addition of the honorific.

"What about him?"

She thrust a bundle of papers at him.

"I think you ought to let him out. And fast."

Reverend Nathan Pettle stood over six feet tall, and had formerly weighed more than 300 pounds before his physician advised him to lose weight or die. He now tipped the scales at 160, having shed the equivalent of a person in the last two years. But a man who loses that kind of mass in his fifties is likely to end up with a certain quantity of skin surplus to requirements, and so Nathan Pettle had become a creature of creases and folds, with a wardrobe of old clothes that had been heavily nipped and tucked to fit in a manner that, had he been vainer or wealthier, might profitably have been applied to his integuments as well. His hair had been gray for as long as anyone could remember—it was gray in his wedding pictures, and they dated from the early seventies—lending him an air of dependability and wisdom that, depending on one's opinion of the preacher, either accentuated or belied reality. For his part, Griffin had always considered Pettle a weak, unimpressive individual, one who relied on the inherent dignity of his position, rather than any notable personal qualities, to bolster his leadership credentials among his flock, aided by the absence of any significant competition. But Pettle was useful at election time, representing a block vote that could be courted by candidates, and he monitored his community closely.

Now Pettle stood over the body of the dead girl and whispered a prayer.

"Do you know who she is?" said Griffin.

"Her name is Donna Lee Kernigan. She lives—lived—over on Montgomery Road."

"She have people?"

"A mother, Miss Sallie, and a grandmother, Miss Imogene."

"Where's the father?"

"Long gone. I don't believe Donna Lee ever even knew his name."

Griffin looked puzzled. "We estimate that she's been dead at least two days," he said. "Strange that no one should have reported her missing."

"Miss Imogene is in the hospital. She got the emphysema. Miss Sallie, well, she works, but she's unsettled."

"What does that mean?"

"I believe she abuses alcohol and narcotics."

"What about the daughter?"

"She was a good girl. Miss Imogene always said so, and she wouldn't lie about such matters."

"Where does the mother work?"

"Paper mill over by Malvern. She cleans there."

Malvern was a good thirty miles away.

"How does she get to work?"

"She drives. She got herself a little Toyota."

"Does she come home each night?"

"Mostly." Pettle let this hang. "Donna Lee attended school. She didn't go hungry."

Which was more than could be said for a lot of kids in the county, black or white.

"Is the mother at home now?"

"I couldn't say, but I assume she's on her way to work by this hour."

Griffin would send Colson to check. Maybe Pettle could go with her as well, just in case.

"Anything else you can tell us?"

Pettle shook his head.

"These are just children," he said, and Griffin knew that he was referring to both Donna Lee Kernigan and Patricia Hartley. "Who would do something like this to a child?"

Pettle's eyes were growing wet with tears. He took out a large red handkerchief and used it to wipe them away.

"I don't know," said Knight. "Who would do something like this to anyone?"

"We can't stay quiet any longer. If these were white girls . . ."

"I hear you."

Pettle looked hard at him. "Do you?"

Griffin stared back. "We're going to find whoever is responsible."

"Who's 'we'?"

"Our department."

"Not the state police?"

"They may become involved, but that won't be up to me."

"And who will it be up to?"

"You know the answer to that question."

Which was when, from over the rise, Jurel Cade appeared.

Billie Brinton was gone, leaving Kel Knight alone at the station house. He was rereading the faxes, and Billie's notes, for the third time, and contemplating the pain that colored some men's lives. If it had been his call, he'd have released Parker immediately, apologized for the misunderstanding, and offered his condolences. But releasing him would be Evan Griffin's decision, and Knight thought the chief might first wish to speak with the prisoner again, especially in light of the morning's events. And it still wasn't clear what had brought Parker to Cargill, although Knight guessed that he was trying to establish, and rule out, connections to his own loss.

Knight set the papers aside and walked down to the cells. Parker was lying on his bunk, one arm over his eyes, the remains of his breakfast on a tray beside him; Knight had instructed Billie to pick up food from the Dunk-N-Go before heading out to deliver the rolls of film to her son.

"You still doing okay?" he asked Parker.

"I finished the book." Knight had dug up a battered copy of Shirley Jackson's *We Have Always*

Lived in the Castle for Parker to read. "So unless you can promise me a library card, I'm about ready to leave now."

"I have to wait for the chief to get back. I can't let you go before then. But we know who you are, and I'm sorry you've ended up in that cell. You could have helped yourself more, but I'm not going to question your reasons for remaining silent. We'll get it all straightened out when Evan returns."

Parker still hadn't changed position or even glanced in Knight's direction.

"I hear you have another body."

"That's right."

"You might not, if someone had looked more closely at the others."

"I agree with you."

"I'm sure," said Parker, "that your agreement will be a source of great easement to the dead girl's family."

Knight took out his pipe and tobacco, and began filling the bowl. He'd long ago acknowledged that it had become a tic for him when under stress. Sometimes he'd just work at filling and tamping, and not even bother lighting the tobacco.

"I got to reiterate that you're hard to warm to," said Knight.

"Me and this town both."

"Well, it'll be behind you soon enough."

"Thanks for breakfast," said Parker, and he turned again to face the wall.

CHAPTER
XVIII

Tucker McKenzie had met a lot of lawmen like Jurel Cade in his time, but never one quite as fully developed in his failings as much as his strengths. Cade's particular essence was not entirely venal, yet he was rotten at the extremities, and like all such corruption, his was progressive and incurable. It was hard to rise to a position of authority in a county like Burdon without being compromised to some degree, but impossible to continue in that office without becoming fatally perverted. At the same time, Cade was committed body and soul to Burdon, and his level of tolerance for domestic violence, sexual abuse, theft, assault, and murder was generally low. In that sense, his behavior in the case of Patricia Hartley might have been considered out of character, were it not for the larger context. Where Jurel Cade was concerned, in any conflict between the county and the individual, the individual must lose—unless the individual in question was wealthy and powerful, in which case what was best for them would probably also be best for Burdon. This worldview, though, might have been ordered and colored by the fact that Cade's own family was the wealthiest and most powerful in the region.

Now McKenzie watched while Cade and Griffin prepared to go at it before an audience that also consisted of one of Cade's deputies, two members of the Cargill PD, Reverend Nathan Pettle, and Russell Sadler, the local mortician contracted to deliver human remains to the state medical examiner in Little Rock, despite Loyd Holt's best efforts to wrench the contract from him. Beside Sadler stood his daughter Mary Ann, who was being groomed to take over the business once her father was himself planted in the ground. Already there were mutterings of discontent in the county about this proposed succession, a significant section of the population being of the opinion that God had not intended women to be undertakers, members of the female sex being perceived as lacking the requisite dignity and solemnity. Since Mary Ann Sadler had never yet been known to smile, and was reckoned to have emerged from the womb already dressed in black, solemnity didn't appear likely to be a problem, and it all came down to a general resistance to change. Russell Sadler was of the opinion that people would come around in time, and probably sooner rather than later, given the necessity of seeing to their dead and the absence of any multitude of choices. It was either the Sadlers, the Ryans up in Toving— who were Catholic, and therefore suspect as far as the roadside churches were concerned—or Loyd Holt, who overcharged and underperformed, and had once dispatched the wrong corpse to a church, the error being discovered only at the end of the service.

Sadler had already taken a look at the remains, and he and McKenzie had agreed that it might be best if the branches lodged in the body were cut before she was placed in the hearse. Sadler had a small electric saw that would do the trick without causing excessive movement or vibration, thereby avoiding further internal damage. He was about to start work when Cade arrived, and all labor ceased. Now it was a question of seeing which side would prevail in the dispute over jurisdiction.

"The fuck is going on here, Evan?" Cade asked.

"You might want to modify your language," Griffin replied, "or else we're going to start this conversation with a falling-out."

Cade took a deep breath.

"Take it as done," he said, "but the question stands."

"We have another body, mutilated like the Hartley girl."

"I can see a body, but I don't know about the rest. Why wasn't I informed? Why'd I have to wait to hear about it from Loyd Holt?"

"We'd have informed you in due course, as a professional courtesy. For now, we're still busy documenting the scene."

"The hell with professional courtesy: I should have been told the moment you found that girl."

"Jurel, this land falls under the jurisdiction of the Cargill PD, not the sheriff's office. If we require assistance, we'll ask, but any investigation will be conducted by my department."

121

"We're beyond the town line here," said Cade. "This is part of Botile Township."

"Which has contracted Cargill to provide police services."

"I would dispute that interpretation, Evan, and also advise you to be less confrontational in your manner."

"I'm not being confrontational." Griffin kept his tone even. "I'm simply stating the facts. This is our case."

Cade turned from him and addressed McKenzie.

"How far have you got, Tucker?"

"We're done, Jurel, or good as."

"You address your questions to me, Jurel," said Griffin quietly.

Cade ignored him. "And the evidence you've processed?"

"I said," repeated Griffin, louder now, "you address your goddamned questions to me!"

Cade redirected his attention to Griffin, but with all the obvious reluctance he could muster, and with his anger barely contained.

"I think we ought to conduct this discussion somewhere more private," he said.

"Happy to do it, once I've finished here. That girl's body is going to Little Rock to be autopsied at the state crime laboratory. When she's gone, you and I can sit down over coffee, and see if we can't arrive at some agreement on how best to proceed."

Cade was coming to the conclusion that this particular phase of the battle was lost. He returned to the remains and lifted the plastic sheet that was covering them. What might have been sorrow clouded his face, although the precise source of it, in Griffin's view, could have been the potential ramifications of the murder as much as, if not more than, the fact of it.

"You identify her yet?"

Griffin had already warned Pettle to stay silent, and so had no fear of being contradicted when he answered that they were not yet certain of the victim's identity. He saw Pettle look to the ground, and decided that the reverend would have made a shitty poker player, so it was just as well that his church frowned on gambling.

"That true, Reverend?" asked Cade.

After only the shortest of pauses, Pettle nodded. "It's true," he said.

Griffin figured Pettle could make his peace with God later, and the lie contained a modicum of truth: no official pronouncement would be offered until a member of Donna Lee Kernigan's immediate family had made a positive identification of the body.

Cade knew he was being played, but he was outnumbered, and arguing further would only make him look bad. So he took the softer option: he retreated, knowing that ultimately, as chief investigator, he still held most of the high ground. If Griffin insisted on investigating the killing, Cade would do his damnedest to block the involvement of any outside agency, aided by his family's contacts in Little Rock. For now, Griffin and the Cargill PD were operating alone.

"I look forward to that coffee," Cade told Griffin. "Deputy Arkins here will stay at the scene, in case you need any assistance. Call it professional courtesy."

Griffin didn't wait for him to drive away. He gave Cade his back, and went to help Sadler and his daughter ready Donna Lee Kernigan for her journey to Little Rock, and a meeting with another blade.

CHAPTER
XIX

There was no response when the police knocked on the door of the Kernigan residence, and Colson and Naylor saw no car in the drive. The house was a single-story dwelling, with a kitchen and living room at one side of the hall, and two small bedrooms at the other, with the bathroom in back. Like most homes in Cargill, it could have done with more TLC and some serious repairs to the shingles, but a fresh coat of paint wasn't as essential as putting food on the table, and plastic patches to the roof had managed to see it through winter.

This section of Cargill was officially known as Eastville, but it wasn't uncommon to hear it referred to as Blackville. It was home to more than a thousand people, of whom 95 percent were black, the remainder being whites and a handful of Hispanics living on the periphery.

The arrival of a pair of police cruisers inevitably attracted attention, and one of the neighbors confirmed to the officers that Sallie Kernigan had not been seen at the house over the weekend, or at least her car hadn't been parked there, which meant she probably hadn't returned to town after work on Friday. When Colson asked if this was common practice for Kernigan, the neighbor just shrugged. His name was Thomas Wesley Grant.

That was how he identified himself: not as Thomas Grant, or Wesley Grant, or any diminution of either, but Thomas Wesley Grant. Colson vaguely recalled his face from around town, but couldn't have put a name to it. After all, Thomas Wesley Grant had never been in trouble with the police, or come to them for aid, plus Colson had been with the department for only a year and was still getting to know the people she needed to know, which was mainly the criminals, the malcontents, and the lunatics. The rest, she had decided, could wait for more opportune circumstances.

"What about her daughter?" asked Naylor. "Have you seen her around?"

Thomas Wesley Grant scratched at the stubble on his chin. "She the one you found?"

Colson had resigned herself to the fact that no amount of discretion was going to prevent the dissemination of the news of another killing. The whole town would know about Donna Lee, by and by. She checked her watch and wondered what was keeping Pettle. He should have been with them by now, because they'd all left the scene at more or less the same time.

"Can you just answer the question, sir?" said Naylor. "It's important."

Thomas Wesley Grant thought for a while, his eyes fixed on the Kernigan house across the street.

"No," he said at last, "I can't say that I have."

"Do you recall when you last saw either of them?"

126

"I saw Miss Sallie go to work shortly after seven on Friday morning, and I saw Donna Lee leave for school not long after. I eat my breakfast at the same time every day, and my table overlooks the street, which is how I know."

"Did you see Donna Lee return that afternoon?"

"No, but I was out for most of the afternoon. I only know about the morning for sure."

"And did you notice anyone else come by the house?"

"No, sir."

"Do you have a key to the Kernigan residence?"

"No, sir, but I believe the Howards might. They live on the right. Mrs. Howard and Miss Imogene, Donna Lee's grandmother, are cousins."

They thanked Thomas Wesley Grant for his time. Colson used her cell phone to get a number for the La Salle Paper Company in Malvern, and called to check if Sallie Kernigan had reported for work that morning. After some back and forth, a woman who sounded like she smoked sixty a day before gargling the ashes confirmed that Sallie hadn't shown up yet, and was now nearly two hours late.

"Is she often late?" Colson asked.

"People who are often late get fired," said the woman.

Colson thanked her, left a number for the Cargill PD, and requested that the secretary call should Sallie Kernigan appear.

While Colson was on the phone, Naylor was checking with Hindman High School to find out

127

if Donna Lee had made it in on Friday, and if so, when she had left. Hindman was the only high school in Cargill. Its student body was black by a small majority, even though the school was named after Thomas Carmichael Hindman, an Arkansas congressman who commanded the Trans-Mississippi District during the War of Northern Aggression—incurring the dislike of the state's citizenry in the process because of his methods—but was guilty of a tactical error at the Battle of Prairie Grove that effectively resulted in Arkansas falling to Union forces. Hindman subsequently fled to Mexico, and was murdered upon his return to the state, probably by a former Confederate. All things considered, Naylor thought, the institution's founders could have come up with a better eponym. But Hindman was a good school, and generally untroubled by racial tensions. It was only when its students traveled farther afield, usually for sporting events, that color became an issue and its players were subjected to taunts.

Naylor got through to the school principal, Mr. Quarles, and informed him of Donna Lee's death, although he stressed that they were still waiting for a family member to make a formal identification. Quarles passed Naylor to the school secretary, Mrs. Huson, who confirmed Donna Lee Kernigan's attendance the previous Friday, and also noted that the girl had band practice after class—she played the flute—and so had stayed until after 6 p.m. The secretary didn't know how Donna Lee got home, but she checked with the music teacher, who informed her that he'd seen Donna Lee waiting at the corner and being picked up by someone in a truck, although as the evening was dark he didn't notice the make or the color, nor could he have identified the driver.

Once the officers had concluded their calls, Colson called Griffin to update him. The chief was on his way back to the station house, and told them to get the key to the Kernigan residence from the Howards and check it out, but to wear gloves and try not to disturb anything. Tucker McKenzie was grabbing some breakfast, but he'd be over there within the hour to conduct the forensic examination.

Mrs. Irene Howard was an elderly, stooped black woman, with a similarly stooped black husband. Colson thought they looked like characters from a fairy story. Like Thomas Wesley Grant, they hadn't seen any sign of Donna Lee or her mother since Friday, but Mrs. Howard was more vocal in her disapproval of Sallie Kernigan's lifestyle.

"She drinks too much," she said. "She makes Miss Imogene worry for her."

"Uh-huh," agreed her husband.

"Does she have a boyfriend?" Colson asked.

"She has lots of boyfriends," said Miss Howard.

"Uh-huh," said her husband.

"Anyone you might know?"

"According to Miss Imogene, they's mostly over in Malvern, or that's where she sees them," said Miss

Howard. "And they ain't those kind of boyfriends."

"Uh-uh," said her husband, shaking his head.

Naylor appeared confused.

"Then what kind of boyfriends are they?" he asked.

"The temporary kind," said Miss Howard.

"Temporary," said her husband.

"How temporary?"

"They pays by the hour."

"By the hour," agreed her husband. "They's whoremongers."

Colson and Naylor made a cursory search of the Kernigan home, but saw nothing to indicate signs of a struggle or abduction, and certainly no indication that Donna Lee might have been killed there. The cottage was tidy, with the exception of the smaller of the two bedrooms, which had clearly been Donna Lee's. This was messy in the way that only a teenager's room could be, so much so that Naylor, who had been a scrupulous child, thought it might have been burgled, until Colson—who had three sisters, two brothers, and a comfort with disarray—assured him it was normal for a teenage girl. They decided to wait for McKenzie to arrive before embarking on a more thorough search.

The refrigerator was stocked with the kind of foodstuffs that offered satiation for minimum outlay, albeit by sacrificing a certain amount of nutritional value. In a closet by the sink they found four bottles of Everclear grain alcohol, along with a couple of bottles of cheap wine and some malt liquor. One of the bottles of Everclear was half-empty, and the refrigerator contained two unmarked bottles of liquid, one clear and one that smelled like Hawaiian Punch. Colson guessed that Sallie Kernigan was mixing the Everclear with water to make a form of cheap vodka, and adding the Everclear to the Hawaiian Punch for special occasions.

Sallie Kernigan's nightstand contained headache and indigestion tablets, birth control pills, an open pack of Trojans, a six-inch knife, and an Astra Terminator pistol: a .44 Magnum with the barrel chopped down from six inches to just under three, the rear sight melted and the frame recontoured. Colson picked it up in her gloved hand, feeling the weight of the gun. It wasn't a typical woman's weapon, and she wondered how Kernigan might have come by it. She unloaded the Astra and bagged the ammunition. Finally, at the back of the nightstand, and hidden in a copy of the Bible that appeared to have been partially hollowed out for this particular purpose, she found four small plastic baggies: two containing white powder, one containing pills, and the fourth containing clear, chunky crystals. She waved them at Naylor. They both knew meth when they saw it. One couldn't serve in law enforcement in Burdon County and not be able to identify the drug, whatever its form.

"Nothing like variety," said Naylor. "She can smoke it, snort it, inject it, or add it to the hooch in the refrigerator. Happy times."

Colson ran her fingers over the bag of rocks. This was pure crystal meth, created without contaminants. Its manufacturer knew his trade.

They went back outside and tossed a coin to determine who would stay and wait for McKenzie. Naylor lost, so Colson headed back to the station. Along the way, she passed Reverend Pettle and signaled for him to stop, pulling up alongside his car.

"What kept you?" she asked.

"I needed a moment to compose my thoughts. It's not every day you have to tell a mother that her child has been butchered and sodomized."

Colson replied only to let Pettle know that Sallie Kernigan wasn't at home or at work, so he could save himself a trip. Later in the day, someone would have to visit Donna Lee Kernigan's grandmother, Miss Imogene, and inform her of the girl's death, but it didn't seem wise to do that before Sallie Kernigan had been told. Nevertheless, if Sallie didn't show up before too long, they'd have to speak with Miss Imogene in the hope of locating her daughter through her. Pettle confirmed his willingness to help at any time, and Colson thanked him before driving off. Pettle didn't immediately follow, but instead remained in his car by the side of the road, contemplating the morning's events.

Reverend Nathan Pettle knew that a lot of people in Cargill regarded him as substandard material, even certain members of his own congregation. He wasn't the best preacher, nor the most sagacious or patient of pastors, and he found his faith was tested regularly by the realities of human existence. It was also the case that a black man learned to show one face toward whites and another to his own people. If he did that often and long enough, even he might become confused about his own identity, and risk becoming that which he pretended to be.

But Pettle cared about his faithful, and tried his best to do right by them. There were those among his flock who said that he should have gone to the newspapers when the investigation into Patricia Hartley's death came to an end before her body was even consigned to the flames. Pettle knew Jurel Cade wouldn't have stood for that; and besides, if any reporters had cared enough about Patricia Hartley, they'd have come calling without his prodding. Nobody wanted to rock the boat in Burdon County, not with so much money riding on its future. But now there were two dead black girls—three, if you counted Estella Jackson from way back—and even Jurel wouldn't be able to put a pattern like that down to a series of accidents. If he tried, Pettle would have to defy him—for the sake of the victims and his own position in the community. If Pettle rolled over again, any authority remaining to him would vanish.

Yet he, like many others, had been promised so much. If he made an excess of noise he would lose it all, and everyone—including his own churchgoers—would suffer for it.

So Reverend Nathan Pettle closed his eyes and asked God to give him the wisdom to determine the value of a single life—and, most particularly, this life, because he had known the girl, and knew her mother.

Oh yes he did.

CHAPTER
XX

Colson returned to the station house, where she arrived just as Griffin was pulling into the lot. The priority now was to trace Sallie Kernigan—not only to inform her of her daughter's death, but also to establish her movements over the course of the weekend. While no one at the Cargill PD wanted to believe she might have killed her own daughter, it was possible that Sallie had crossed paths with whoever was responsible. Kel Knight came to join them, so Colson went through the details once again for his benefit, describing the discovery of the pistol and meth in Kernigan's nightstand, and sharing the music teacher's account of a truck picking up Donna Lee Kernigan after band practice on Friday.

"If she was using meth, she might have been getting it from Tilon Ward, or one of his people," said Knight.

"Ward's people don't have a monopoly on meth," said Griffin.

"They do around here."

"Maybe, but my understanding is that while Tilon may be involved in its manufacture, he leaves the problem of supply to others, especially when it comes down to teener bags."

"But Ward also drives a truck," said Knight, "and Donna Lee was last seen getting into one."

"Half the county drives a truck," said Griffin, "and Tilon was the one that called us to say he'd found Donna Lee's body. He looked to me to be in shock, and that's hard to fake, especially when your skin turns gray."

"I'm not saying he killed her," said Knight, "only that he may know more than he's sharing."

"Then we'll talk to him again," said Griffin. "In the meantime, I want people down at Hindman High interviewing the kids from the band, the music teacher, the custodian, and anyone else who might have been around when Donna Lee got into that truck. For now, that's the last sighting we have of her."

Colson said that she'd take care of the school business once she'd had a chance to use the restroom and freshen up. Griffin told her to get something to eat, and she assured him she'd grab a breakfast bagel from the Dunk-N-Go, and wolf it down in the car on the way to Hindman. Griffin gave her a nod of approval. Colson was the first female officer in the history of the Cargill PD, an appointment that had not been greeted with universal approval in the town. She was also a rarity by the standards of many police departments in the state, unusual enough to have featured in newspaper and TV coverage. Griffin had worried about her in the beginning, but stopped after she ruptured Donnie Stark's right testicle and busted two of his ribs when he made a grab for her outside Boyd's one Friday night.

Once Colson was out of earshot, Knight asked Griffin if he could have a word.

"It's about Parker."

Tilon Ward lived with his widowed mother on a property to the east of Cargill. He'd moved back in with her after his divorce, initially recolonizing his former childhood bedroom while he worked on converting an old stable building into suitable accommodation for himself. He now had his own kitchen and living area, and a large, comfortable bedroom in which he could enjoy female company without inconveniencing his mother. She was a tolerant woman by any standards, but Ward saw no reason to parade his conquests before her, especially when they were younger than was appropriate for a man in his thirties—or when they were black, his mother's sufferance of her son's vices not extending to miscegenation.

Seated at his kitchen table, Tilon flipped his cell phone open and closed, open and closed. The instrument had revolutionized his business, but he now had fewer excuses for being out of contact with his partners. Dead zones apart, he was on call 24/7.

Tilon's employer would want to know about his relationship with Donna Lee Kernigan, but Tilon's view was that it wasn't yet an issue, and would only become so were it to be discovered by the law. First up, he needed to get in touch with Sallie, offer his sympathies on the loss of her daughter, and make sure she wasn't about to land him in a cell through whatever she might have to say to the police. Even amid her grief, he was confident she could be made to understand the necessity of discretion, particularly if she wanted to keep the supply chain open, for both herself and others. Unfortunately, Sallie didn't possess a cell phone, and when Ward tried to call her at work, he was told she hadn't yet arrived. He declined to leave a message, because his mother hadn't bred a simpleton.

He mused for a while on who might have wanted to kill Donna Lee. If the rumors were true about what was done to Patricia Hartley, then the same person or persons responsible for her death had also murdered Donna Lee. Unless the two girls were connected in some way—and Ward couldn't see how, given that the two weren't even friends—it looked like the police were dealing with a random sex killer, maybe even the serial kind about which his mother liked to read in her true crime books, and possibly the same one that had done for Estella Jackson, back when Tilon was still married and looked to have escaped Cargill forever.

In which case, thought Ward, at least Donna Lee's death wasn't personal.

CHAPTER
XXI

Griffin sat at his desk, Kel Knight opposite him. The office was small, barely spacious enough to accommodate the desk, two chairs, and a selection of mismatched file cabinets. The walls were decorated only with official notices, Griffin being reluctant to advertise his personal or professional history in the form of commendations and photographs. Those that needed to know about his past already did, and the opinion of the others did not concern him.

Griffin had just finished talking on the phone with the mayor, Joe Haines. Cargill, in common with the rest of Burdon County, utilized a weak-mayor system, in which the mayor had no formal authority outside the council, and lacked the power to hire and fire, or veto council votes. This suited the Cade family, which was why the system had been instituted to begin with. Haines, who owned the town's sole auto dealership, was a conscientious man, and honest to boot, which made him a lousy car salesman, and not much better as an Arkansas politician. Griffin had listened as Haines engaged in ten types of hand-wringing over the discovery of another body, before finally hanging up on him.

Now, his coffee going cold, Griffin was reading a litany of Parker's pain: his father, a detective, lost to suicide after a fatal shooting involving two teenagers; and his wife and child taken from him by a killer unlike any Griffin—or, it appeared, most everyone else—had ever encountered. Mother: dead. Grandfather, a retired state trooper up in Maine: dead. Griffin thought that he had never before encountered a man so alone. He felt both guilt at his own treatment of Parker, and anger at him for permitting the situation to have arisen in the first place through his obduracy. Occasionally, depending upon the page he was reading, Knight would offer information not included in the document, but mostly Griffin was permitted to read in silence. When he was done, he returned to the murder of Parker's wife and child: blinded, partially skinned, and left for him to discover in the kitchen of his own home. Griffin didn't know how the man was still walking upright, let alone functioning on any identifiably human level.

"Billie got all this?" asked Griffin, when he was done.

"The majority of it."

"What about the rest?"

"I made a call."

Knight's sister-in-law was married to Jack Kavanagh, a police lieutenant in Brooklyn. He and Knight met only at weddings and funerals, but a contact was a contact, especially when it came to police.

Griffin saw that Knight was playing with his damn pipe again.

"If you've got something to say," said Griffin,

"then say it, but you're still not going to ignite that contraption in here."

Knight restored the pipe to his shirt pocket before speaking.

"Parker was regarded by some in the NYPD as a blue flamer"—"blue flamer" was police slang for a rookie who wanted to change the world—"and by others as a Jonah. He was carrying baggage for his old man, and the killing of those two kids, so he probably felt he had something to prove. He made detective in three years, and scored some good busts, but didn't seem set on winning popularity contests. According to Jack, Parker wasn't cut out to be police. He was too solitary, and too troubled. He took chances with his safety, which meant he also took chances with the safety of his partners. He joined to do penance for his father's sins, but he was always going to burn out, or get himself or someone else killed. What happened to his wife and daughter, no one would have wished on him, but . . ."

"If it was going to happen to someone," Griffin concluded.

"Yes."

"Is that it?"

"No." Knight looked over his shoulder, instinctively checking that no one was nearby. "Those almost-healed cuts on his knuckles."

"What about them? I never believed they came from an accident with a car tire."

"Someone killed a guy named Johnny Friday in

141

a Port Authority restroom up in New York a while back. Beat him to death, and left his body cuffed and gagged in a stall."

"Who was this Friday?"

"A pimp, predator, and sexual torturer. He worked the waifs and strays at bus stations while handing out miniature Bibles and religious literature. He'd feed the kids drugged soup, and then they'd vanish. Later, someone would spot one of them in a pornographic photograph or film, but most were never seen again."

"You're telling me that Parker killed him?"

"I'm telling you that Parker was spotted at the Port Authority in the hours before Friday died, and it looked as though he might have been watching Friday for a while. But nobody witnessed the attack, because whoever killed Friday timed his move well. The restroom was almost empty, apart from a junkie who'd locked himself in one of the stalls and wouldn't have woken if the walls fell in around him. The janitor had given up monitoring his clientele during the Carter administration, and his radio was playing at full volume to discourage loitering. Finally, nobody wanted to know, because to know would be to get involved. It was only when the blood started flowing that someone saw fit to tell the janitor, and he did the smart thing and went to find a cop. A man was seen leaving the scene, but it was cold, so he had a scarf over the lower half of his face, and the hood on his jacket was raised. By the time the uniforms arrived, he was gone."

"Was Parker questioned?"

"Not until a few days later. He admitted to being at the bus station, but said he was waiting for a contact that never showed."

"Did they ask him about those cuts?" said Griffin.

"Accident with a car jack, more or less the same as he told you."

"And they bought all this?"

"No witnesses, and no prints. Jack says the Port Authority Criminal Investigations Bureau thinks the killer might have taped his fingertips, because one of the witnesses saw what looked like plastic on the suspect's hands. There was some talk of getting a warrant and looking for bloodstains on Parker's clothing, but they didn't think they had enough to satisfy a judge, and it could be that the will wasn't there, not after what happened to Parker's family. And no one was weeping for Johnny Friday. If Parker did take him out, certain parties might have chosen to regard it as an act of public service."

"But there's no evidence that he did?" said Griffin.

Kel Knight wasn't sure that he liked the look on Griffin's face. It bore definite signs of contemplating expediency.

"None, beyond circumstantial. Why?"

"Just get him out of that cell," said Griffin. "I want to talk to him."

CHAPTER
XXII

Tucker McKenzie was working his way through the Kernigan residence, but had so far found nothing to suggest that Donna Lee might have been abducted from her home. Still, he had dusted for prints, and suggested to Naylor possible avenues for investigation, although it was Naylor himself who spotted the obvious.

"Where's her school bag?" he asked.

He was right: there was no trace of Donna Lee's bag. If she had returned home at any point over the weekend, the bag should have been in the house, teenage girls, in McKenzie's experience, being reluctant to carry textbooks around unnecessarily; and the small desk in Donna Lee's bedroom, at which she presumably studied, bore no traces of schoolwork.

Colson was already at Hindman High. Naylor called and asked her to check if Donna Lee had been carrying her school bag when last seen. Colson said she'd get back to him, which she did five minutes later.

"She had the bag with her," she said.

It was therefore possible that Donna Lee Kernigan had never returned home following band practice, making it all the more important to identify the driver of the truck that picked her up.

Which was precisely what Colson was currently attempting to do.

• • •

The three girls seated before her had all been crying, but one had obviously been crying more than the others. Her name was Vernia Crane. Her eyes were heavily swollen, and she clasped a wad of tissues in her left hand so that they resembled, to Colson's eye, a white flower. The two remaining girls, Lashaye Jenkins and Shari Hill, looked nervous and sad, but Crane's grief was of another magnitude entirely. According to the school, and the three girls themselves, they had been Donna Lee Kernigan's closest friends.

Colson started slowly, asking about their routine that morning, and how and when they'd heard about Donna Lee's death. She then progressed to the nature of their friendship with the deceased girl, how long they'd known her, and the kind of person she was. Colson was gentle throughout, permitting them the latitude to digress, trying to keep the conversation as informal as possible under the circumstances. Crane spoke less than her peers, but contributed when questioned directly. Gradually Colson worked her way around to Friday night's band practice, at which two of the girls, Crane and Hill, had been in attendance. Colson asked if Donna Lee had appeared troubled or distressed that evening, or earlier in the week. Had her behavior changed lately?

At this, Crane reacted. It was the slightest of responses—a tensing, a movement of the eyes— but Colson picked up on it, and she thought the other girls did too. Colson didn't immediately pursue it, though, and instead asked if any of them had been present when Donna Lee was collected by the truck on Friday evening. All three said they'd left before Donna Lee, which had already been confirmed by the music teacher, but already it was clear that the dynamic in the room had altered. Whatever Colson might learn, it would have to come from Vernia Crane. Colson tossed a few more softball questions, and received assurances that none of them had seen or heard from Donna Lee since Friday, before thanking them for their time and informing them that they could leave.

But as they stood to go, Colson asked Crane to remain for a moment. Crane visibly sagged, like a prisoner who had, for an instant, believed she might yet escape the gallows. She returned to her chair, but kept her eyes on the floor.

"How close were you and Donna Lee?"

"We were best friends," said Crane.

"Were you closer to her than Shari and Lashaye were?"

"I guess."

"Did you share a lot?"

Crane nodded.

"Everything?"

"No, not everything."

"What things didn't you share?"

"Stuff."

"You must know, Vernia, that we're anxious to speak with whoever was driving that truck. The

146

driver may have been the last person to see Donna Lee alive."

She didn't add that the driver might also have killed Donna Lee. She didn't have to, because Vernia would have to be dim-witted not to have come to that conclusion without help, but neither did Colson wish to voice an accusation that might cause Crane to protect this unknown party.

"I know that," said Crane.

"Then do you also know who was driving the truck?"

She shook her head.

"Are you sure?"

"I'm not lying."

"I wasn't implying that you were," said Colson, although she kind of was. "But if you even had a suspicion, or a thought of who it might be, that would be a help."

Crane assembled and disassembled the tissue rose in her hand. She had very long fingers. According to the music teacher, she was already a skillful pianist, helped by an analytical mind and a natural inquisitiveness.

"It only started recently," she said at last.

"What started recently? A relationship?"

"Yes."

"How recently?"

"A couple of weeks. Might be a month."

"Was it sexual?"

"I think so. Donna Lee talked about being on the pill. The guy didn't like to use rubbers."

"And this relationship, was it with the driver of the truck?"

"I don't know. She didn't tell me his name, and the first I heard about a truck was this morning. But I got the impression, from things she said, that he was older than her, and—"

Colson waited.

"And could be he was white," Crane finished.

"Why do you say that?"

"Maybe 'impression' isn't what I mean. She told me he was older. The white part I just assumed. It was in the way she was acting, and some of what she said about him and what he liked."

"Liked in what sense?"

"This song came on the radio, and Donna Lee said that she was sick of hearing it, that he played it all the time, but then she caught herself and wouldn't say anything more."

"Do you remember what the song was?"

"I think it's called 'Night Moves,' but I couldn't swear to it."

"Bob Seger?"

"Yeah, that sounds right. I'd recognize it if I heard it again. I mean, the song is okay, but, you know . . ."

"It's kind of white."

For the first time that morning, Vernia Crane managed a smile. It was malformed, and died shortly after birth, but it was something.

"Yeah, very white."

"Did you know Patricia Hartley?"

"Just as a face around town."

"Or Estella Jackson?"

"No."

"Did Donna Lee?"

"I don't think so."

Crane frowned. She stared at Colson, even as Colson realized her error in connecting Patricia Hartley's death with Donna Lee Kernigan.

Because Crane had heard the rumors about what was done to Patricia Hartley, and now she knew what had befallen her friend.

Vernia Crane fell from the chair to her knees, lay on the floor, and curled herself into a ball of pain, and all Colson could do was hold her and say, "I'm sorry, honey. I'm so, so sorry . . ."

CHAPTER
XXIII

Kel Knight freed Parker from captivity before escorting him back to the Lakeside Inn to shower, shave, and change his clothes. Parker noted that his wallet and car keys had not been returned to him, and pointed this out to Knight as they drove down moribund streets.

"Chief Griffin would like to talk to you before you make any decision about leaving Cargill," said Knight.

"That decision has already been made," said Parker. "Keeping my possessions from me isn't going to make me change my mind."

"Well, he'd still like to talk with you."

Parker decided that he didn't have a lot of choice in the matter, not unless he planned to depart Cargill on foot and without a nickel to his name. Knight turned into the parking lot of the motel and pulled up in front of Parker's door.

"You may find," said Knight, "that your bag has been opened, although its contents remain intact."

"That," said Parker, "was impolite."

"We're hoping you might decide to overlook the discourtesy, just as we'll elect to ignore the armaments in your room."

"They're licensed firearms."

"Maybe you'd like to sit around in a cell some more while we try to confirm that."

150

Parker didn't reply, but got out of the car, entered his room, and closed the door behind him. He got the impression that Knight's attitude toward him had altered, and not for the better, but he was untroubled by the change. He'd been in Cargill for thirty-six hours, and so far hadn't met anyone he would be sorry to forget. He noted the busted lock on his case, and opened it to check on the Colt and his document file. Neither was exactly as he had left it, and the contents of the file were additionally disordered. He knelt on the floor and saw that the .38 was still in place, but the pencil mark he had made beside the barrel was now obscured. Even had the Cargill police been subtler, and Knight not alluded to guns, plural, Parker would have known that his room had been searched.

He showered, put on fresh clothing, and changed his footwear. Knight was still sitting outside in his patrol car. Parker was tempted to make him wait some more, but the more he delayed, the longer he'd be forced to spend in town. With no other option, he headed back out, locking the door behind him.

"Hardly seemed worth the effort to lock up," he said, as he got in the car, "but old habits die hard."

Knight looked at him. "Do you have *any* friends?" he said.

"If you're applying for a vacancy, you're out of luck."

"When I'm that desperate, I'll shoot myself."

He reversed out of the parking spot.

"You won't have to," said Parker. "I'm sure you'll have no trouble finding someone to do it for you."

And they returned to the station house in sour silence.

CHAPTER
XXIV

Tucker McKenzie dropped by the Cargill PD to consult with Griffin once the examination of the Kernigan home was complete. He didn't have a great deal to add to what they already knew, but had pulled a variety of prints, including a number from the bedrooms of both Sallie Kernigan and her daughter. He told Griffin that he was going to return to the site of the body dump, and conduct a further search of the land with assistance from one of his fellow forensic analysts and a couple of staff out of Little Rock.

"I have a question for you," said Griffin. "Do you know a man named Charlie Parker. He's ex-NYPD."

"Charlie Parker," said McKenzie, "like the jazz musician?"

"Probably the same spelling."

"No, I can't say that I do."

"We had him in one of our cells last night."

"Why?"

"He displayed an aversion to providing straight answers."

"Do I detect an edge there, Evan?"

"Parker was in possession of Polaroids of Patricia Hartley's body, pictures with which even I was unfamiliar until last night. I know you sometimes use an instant camera as backup."

"I do."

"Did you take instant photographs at the Hartley scene?"

"I did."

"If these are the same pictures, did Parker get them from you?"

"He did not."

"Any idea how he might have come by them?"

"None," said McKenzie. "Is there an accusation coming?"

"Not from me, and this conversation is strictly private. I just need to know the truth: Did you circulate those pictures?"

McKenzie saw no reason to obfuscate. He had done nothing wrong.

"Not widely, but some people up at the state crime laboratory are familiar with their contents. After that, they made their way to the FBI, or so I understand."

In addition to the field office in Little Rock, the FBI maintained satellite offices, known as resident agencies, in six other locations throughout the state. The El Dorado agency was responsible for Burdon County, but none of its agents had been in touch with Griffin about Hartley's death. If they had contacted Jurel Cade, the chief deputy had not seen fit to share this information with the Cargill PD.

"How interested are the feds?"

"Officially," said McKenzie, "or unofficially?"

"The first I can answer for myself. The second is more relevant."

"They have no reason to involve themselves, but they're aware of what's been happening."

"And?"

"They don't like it any more than we do, but pressure to look the other way is being applied right across the board, and it's coming from on high."

"How high?" said Griffin.

"From Washington. Maybe not from Bubba himself, but close."

The liberals might have been patting themselves on the back when Clinton ended twelve years of Republican rule, but only the most naïve of souls could have mistaken him and his team for sentimentalists. This was the man who, as governor of Arkansas, had sent Ricky Ray Rector to the death chamber in '92 just to prove to presidential voters that he was tough on crime, but old Ricky Ray had lobotomized himself during a failed suicide attempt in '81, leaving him so mentally impaired that he set aside the slice of pecan pie from his last meal so he could eat it after his execution.

"Jesus," said Griffin.

"They don't want a murder investigation down here," McKenzie concluded. "But we knew that already."

Griffin felt the lassitude begin to descend. It would be easier to surrender the case to Jurel Cade, and permit him to produce a simulacrum of an inquiry. Maybe there would be no more dead girls.

Perhaps whoever killed Donna Lee Kernigan had sated himself with her. But instead Griffin said:

"To hell with what they want or don't want."

"My sentiments exactly. What about this Parker?"

"I'm going to do my best to convince him to stay."

"Why?"

"Because," said Griffin, "I think he knows a lot about killing."

CHAPTER
XXV

Parker sat in Evan Griffin's office, occupying a chair that rested unevenly on the floor, although whether through a fault in the chair or the surface, he could not say. His wallet, phone, and car keys lay on the desk in front of the chief. Griffin had risen to shake Parker's hand after he was escorted into the office by Knight, and invited him to sit, but had said nothing else since then. He remained slouched in his chair, his hands folded over his small paunch, his right index finger tapping a slow regular cadence, carefully regarding the man opposite him. If he expected Parker to break the impasse, or begin showing obvious signs of discomfort—the foibles of the chair or floor apart—he was destined to be disappointed. Parker had grown used to stillness and quietude, and days could pass without his conversing with anyone but the dead. All his turmoil was within.

Finally, Griffin spoke.

"Why didn't you tell us who you were?"

"I did."

"I think," said Griffin, drily, "that you might have expanded a little further on the subject."

"And what would I have said?"

What indeed? Griffin had not considered the question in his way. How could this man have explained to a stranger the nature of the tragedy that had befallen him? Would he even have wanted to do so? In his position, Griffin thought perhaps that he, too, would have opted to say nothing at all.

"I don't know, but enough to avoid spending a night in a cell."

"I had to spend the night somewhere," said Parker, "and your cell was less depressing than my room. Incidentally, were you the one that searched it?"

"Yes."

"If you're going to make a habit of it, you ought to learn how to pick a lock."

"I'll add it to the list of life skills I haven't yet managed to acquire, including forbearance."

Parker watched a truck pass, its semi-trailer loaded with logs. Fragments of bark spilled into the late morning air before falling to earth like dying moths.

"I'd really like to leave your town now," he said.

"Why did you come here in the first place?"

"You read the file in my room. I think you understand."

"Either you're on a crusade," said Griffin, "or you're trying to find whoever killed your wife and child. My guess is the latter. You're interested in murders involving mutilation and display, which is what drew you to Cargill, and the Hartley case."

"Not only hers, because there was also Estella Jackson to consider. But yes, that's about the size of it."

"You're aware that we found another body this

158

morning, murdered in a similar fashion to those two young women?"

"I heard. If someone had investigated the Hartley killing properly, the latest girl might not be dead."

Griffin noted the phrasing of the reply, its avoidance of any explicit ascription of blame, even if the imputation was clear.

"Do you understand how things work in this county?" he said.

"As far as I can tell, nothing works in this county."

Griffin didn't bother to contradict him. Burdon County functioned, but not in a fashion comprehensible to outsiders, or those who failed to appreciate the relationship between poverty and pragmatism.

"Jurel Cade, whom you've met, is the chief investigator for the Burdon County Sheriff's Office, and therefore also for the county itself," said Griffin. "He decides what cases get investigated and prosecuted, aided by the coroner, Loyd Holt, who's in Jurel's pocket, and does whatever he's told. Any request for outside assistance—such as from the state police—has to go through the sheriff's office. This department has autonomy to conduct inquiries of its own, up to and including cases of homicide, but it doesn't have the resources to mount large-scale criminal investigations. We don't even have a detective. Patricia Hartley's body was discovered beyond the jurisdictional boundary of the Cargill Police Department, and therefore her case devolved to the sheriff's office, and Jurel Cade."

"Who then did nothing about it."

"That's not entirely correct. I believe Jurel may have asked a question or two about Hartley's movements, and signed off on some paperwork."

"My mistake," said Parker. "I meant to say 'less than nothing.' "

Griffin let it go. Arguing with this man would do no good, especially when all that he was saying was accurate.

"As of this morning," Griffin continued, "we have another victim, same M.O. The girl's name was Donna Lee Kernigan. She was seventeen years old. This time, it's definitely in our jurisdiction. Jurel may continue to dispute that, but he'll be wasting his breath. So we intend to investigate, and try to find the one that killed her."

"I wish you luck," said Parker. "Now I'm going to take my possessions and continue on my way."

"We need assistance," said Griffin. "Cargill has suffered just eight homicides in the last fifteen years: three of them were domestic, one was the result of a mistimed punch in a bar fight, and one was a hit-and-run. In each of those last five cases, the culprit was apprehended within twenty-four hours. In two of them, he was still at the scene when our officers arrived, and the investigative process didn't take much longer than the killings themselves. The other three murders remain unsolved. One of them is that of an elderly woman named Lucille Vail at her home about four years ago. Her husband, Gene, went missing at the same time, and later turned up hanged from a tree. He was our only suspect. The second is the death of Estella Jackson, of which you're aware, since you had a copy of her case file among your possessions. The third is Donna Lee Kernigan."

"What about Patricia Hartley?"

"Patricia Hartley's death was officially determined to be accidental."

"By whom?"

"The county coroner."

"She had sticks inserted into her mouth and vagina."

"She was found at the bottom of a rocky slope. The corner decided that any injuries she received resulted from her fall."

"She was naked."

"It was speculated that narcotics might have been involved, but the coroner decided that, on balance, this was unlikely."

"Did the autopsy results suggest that?"

"There was no autopsy. The coroner has the authority to decide whether or not an autopsy is required. In this case, deeming the death to be accidental, he saw no cause to send the body to Little Rock for examination. Also, had he accepted the possibility of narcotic ingestion, it might have required him to authorize a proper investigation."

Parker stood. He removed his possessions from the desk.

"You ought to find another job," he said.

"Actually, a lot of people in this county ought to find another job, starting with the coroner."

"You won't hear any disagreement from me about Loyd Holt. Speaking for myself, though, I'm too old to retrain."

"What about the third killing?"

"Estella Jackson. That was five years ago."

"There are similarities."

"The nature of what was done to her was widely known in this county, and a lot of time has elapsed since then. Similarities don't mean it's the same culprit."

"So nobody considered a link between her and Patricia Hartley, or saw fit to question the coroner's decision?"

"Nobody in a position of authority wants any of these killings investigated. They'd prefer whatever happened to Patricia Hartley—and, by now, Estella Jackson also—to be buried or burned along with the bodies. But you can change that. You have expertise that we don't possess. I'm asking for your help, Mr. Parker."

"I'm sorry," said Parker, "but this isn't my problem."

Griffin considered all the objections he might offer, all the efforts he might make to persuade this man otherwise, but uttered none of them. He thought he understood. Who was to say that, in a similar position, he would have behaved any differently? Parker had lost nearly everything. The least he could be left with was his hope of revenge.

"No, I don't suppose it is," said Griffin.

"So I can go?"

"I don't see any reason for you to stay."

Parker got to his feet. His eyes drifted away from Griffin, his gaze already elsewhere.

"Before you leave," said Griffin, "I'd be interested to learn how you came by the material on Jackson and Hartley contained in that file of yours, especially the Hartley pictures."

"There are men and women in law enforcement who feel as though they owe me something," said Parker. "They don't, but I'm not about to refuse their help."

"That may be true," said Griffin, "and the Jackson material could have come from anywhere, because there are copies of it up in Little Rock. But even I hadn't seen some of those pictures of Patricia Hartley. I believe they might have been taken by Tucker McKenzie, our local forensic analyst."

"I don't know the name, but not everyone in this state is prepared to turn a blind eye to murder on the say-so of a deadbeat coroner."

"Perhaps not," said Griffin. "But some of us are now trying to do the right thing."

"It's too late."

"I choose to differ. And I hope you find him, the one who did this to you and your family."

"I will, or he'll find me. Either way, I'll face him in the end."

"I'll ask Kel to give you a ride back to the motel," said Griffin.

"I'd prefer to walk."

And he did.

From the office window, Griffin and Knight watched Parker cross the street and head west toward the motel.

"You're letting him go?" said Knight.

"You're the one that didn't want him to stay to begin with."

"I may have been mistaken. I don't have to like him to work with him, and we need help."

"We'll just have to do what we can without him."

Griffin thought of the dead girls. They deserved better, but he would try his utmost, for their sakes.

"What next?" said Knight.

"We talk."

"To who?"

"To everyone."

CHAPTER
XXVI

Tilon Ward always kept a heavy-duty canvas bag packed and ready, just in case everything ever went to hell and he needed to run. The bag contained clothing, toiletries, a Beretta 9 mm, and just under $15,000 in cash, along with two 1908 twenty-dollar Double Eagle gold coins that had been given to him by his father as a wedding gift, and were now worth about $3,000, give or take. The bag was usually stored under the bathtub, but right now it was sitting on Tilon's bed, because he was thinking that the time might have come to leave town for a while.

He should never have slept with Donna Lee Kernigan, not in a community like Cargill. He'd been careful, and it wasn't as though her momma had objected—if nothing else, Sallie Kernigan was a practical person, and viewed her daughter's dealings with Tilon Ward as an adjunct to a business relationship—but there were no secrets in a town this size, especially not when a teenage girl was involved. Tilon had always enjoyed a taste for younger women, although not so young as to be illegal, because he wasn't a deviant, which was where he differed from his father, Hollis. The difficulty was that, while Tilon was growing older, the age of his women was staying more or less the same. He supposed that eventually he'd have to acquiesce to reality, and start sleeping with women in their late twenties or—God forbid—even older, but he wasn't about to throw in the towel until he had to. Also, one of the advantages of being a meth dealer was that your product was always in demand, and often by those who didn't mind paying for it in something other than hard cash.

He held the Double Eagles in the palm of his right hand. His old man hadn't left him much, apart from the coins—well, the coins, and an unshakable belief that the system was designed to fuck men over, and therefore the smart ones found a way to fuck it in return. He had no idea how his father had come by the Double Eagles, except that he probably hadn't acquired them legally, Hollis Ward living by the conviction that only a fool paid ticket for anything, and the mark of a clever man was to pay as close as possible to nothing at all.

But Hollis was gone now.

Tilon's truck had a full tank of gas. He could put three hundred miles of daylight between him and Cargill before he had to stop for a refill. From his bedroom window, he saw a red Ford Pinto pull up in the yard. His mother got out and removed a bag of groceries from the trunk. Somewhere in there would be chicken thighs, because she always made fried chicken on Mondays, with beans and mashed potatoes. She moved more slowly now, he noticed. She'd taken a bad fall a year earlier, and it had shaken her confidence.

He restored the Double Eagles to the bag, and

the bag to its hiding place behind the tub, just as he'd done countless times over the last few years. He couldn't run, not yet, because if— or when—his relationship with Donna Lee was discovered, his absence would be construed as guilt, and Jurel Cade would as happily see him locked up for murder as for the manufacture of methamphetamine. Even to leave town so soon after coming across Donna Lee's body would draw suspicion. But he also had obligations here: to his customers, and more particularly to his employer.

At that moment, as though his thoughts had invited the scrutiny of that very consciousness, his phone rang. He checked the number and decided it would be unwise to ignore this call.

"Randall," he said.

"I hear they found another dead colored girl."

Tilon decided not to clarify that "they" hadn't found her, but he had. He should have just come clean, because Randall Butcher would learn the truth soon enough. For the present, though, Tilon had decided on a policy of not admitting anything to anyone.

"That's right."

"Did you know her?"

Careful, careful.

"I knew her mother. Professionally speaking."

"Which means you also knew the girl."

"In passing."

The silence from Butcher was troubling. Tilon wouldn't have dared attempt to lie like

167

this to his face. Randall Butcher was a naturally distrustful individual. It was a depressing personal characteristic, one of Butcher's many.

"Do we need to worry?" Butcher said, once he was certain that the lull in the conversation, and the possible reasons for it, had registered with Tilon.

Only about whatever Sallie Kernigan has left of her stash, thought Tilon, *which I supplied, and maybe about the gun I gave her after she said someone tried to break into her house one night, and also about whatever she might have to say to the police once she discovers her daughter is dead, which means whatever she might have to say about me . . .*

"No, we don't need to worry," said Tilon.

"Good. Because when you didn't show up this morning, like we'd discussed, I have to say that the possibility of worrying did cross my mind."

"Well, now you got no cause to."

"I guess not."

"I think we should lay low for a few days."

"Why is that?"

Because there's been a murder, dumb-ass. Not even Jurel Cade can cover up this killing.

"There'll be an investigation," said Tilon.

"There won't be no investigation, not a real one. There wasn't last time."

"But now there are two bodies to add to Estella Jackson's. They can't let that slide."

"How long have you lived in this county, Tilon?"

"Somewhere between too long and far too long."

"Then you ought to know better. A lot of money is coming down the pipe, more than even dead *white* girls would be worth endangering. And why are you bringing up Estella Jackson? That's ancient history."

Tilon realized he should have admitted to Randall his role as discoverer of Donna Lee's body, because then he could have explained his reasons. He'd witnessed her injuries, and looked upon the branches forced into her body, which sounded a lot like what Estella Jackson had endured back in the day. Instead, Tilon now had to double down on the first lie, because a confession would cause Butcher to speculate on what else he might be hiding.

"I hear Kernigan had sticks put inside her, or so they're saying. That was what was done to Estella Jackson."

"Among other things," said Butcher. "There's whispers that Patricia Hartley might have been butchered that same way, no matter what Loyd Holt says."

Tilon had heard this too, although no one could swear to it.

"But if I was you," Butcher continued, "I wouldn't be mentioning Estella Jackson in the same breath as Donna Lee Kernigan, not with your family history."

Which received no argument from Tilon, although he hadn't considered this further complication until Butcher mentioned it.

"I still think we should wait," he said.

"We have customers," said Butcher.

"Just for a few days."

"Shit." He could almost hear Butcher's gears clicking as he carried out the risk-benefit analysis. "Forty-eight hours. After that, we get back to work."

Tilon's palms were sweating. He forced himself to relax.

"Forty-eight hours," he echoed. "I'll call you."

"You do that. And Tilon?"

"Yes?"

"Were you fucking that dead girl? I mean, before she was dead, although I wouldn't put it past you to try her cold. I know what your family's like. You got some aberrations in you."

"What? No!"

"You better not have been. I wouldn't want to have to cut you loose. That wouldn't be salutary for you."

No, Tilon understood, that certainly wouldn't be salutary for him. They wouldn't just cut him loose. They'd shoot him in the head and inter his remains in a hole in the woods.

"I hear you," he said, but Butcher had already hung up. Tilon stared at the bathtub, and what lay hidden behind it. He stayed like that for what seemed to him like an age, before walking to the main house to check on his mother.

CHAPTER
XXVII

Parker drove east. Cargill receded in his rearview mirror—its cracked sidewalks, its boarded-up storefronts, its FOR LEASE signs—until the environs finally disappeared from view. His destination was Belzoni, Mississippi, where a woman named Eliza Tarp had been crucified against a tree some six months previously, a crown of honey locust thorns impaled on her head, and a wound opened in her right side that appeared to have been inflicted by a harvest sickle.

He should have gone straight to Belzoni, he thought. He had wasted valuable time in Arkansas. The manner of the deaths in Cargill had always seemed to him cruder than the actions of the one he sought, and nothing he had learned in the interim had caused him to reconsider, but they were among the killings in the cache that had been provided to him, and by ruling them out he was narrowing the parameters of his search, if only marginally.

Cargill, he reflected, was a miserable town, in a miserable county, and therefore a miserable place to die—not that it would have made much difference to Patricia Hartley, Donna Lee Kernigan, and Estella Jackson. Dying was dying, and the only mercy came at the end.

The sky was a turbulent gray. More rain was coming. Ahead of him he saw a gas station, with a diner attached. He wasn't hungry, even though he had consumed just a few mouthfuls of the breakfast supplied to him in his cell. Perhaps it would have been truer to say that he felt no great desire to eat, but desire and necessity were not the same. He had not enjoyed a meal in many months. He ate because he had to. Food was fuel, and nothing more.

He pulled up at a pump, filled the tank, and moved the car to a space near the diner. By the time he had paid for his gas at the register, the first drops had already begun to spatter the glass, so he entered the diner through a connecting corridor beside the beer fridges, its walls decorated with framed Bible quotations, including one from Proverbs outside the restrooms that read, "There are those who are clean in their own eyes but are not washed of their filth."

He ordered the chicken salad sandwich, but when it arrived he found himself unable to eat. He was no longer in a diner in southwestern Arkansas. He was instead in a restaurant in Rehoboth Beach, Delaware, and seated across from him was the woman who would later become his wife. Rain was falling, and Susan was laughing at something he had said on this, their first evening together; the beginning, the initial step on a path that would lead to marriage, a child, and finally a house in Brooklyn awash with blood.

But it had not been raining during that meal. He remembered it clearly. It was an unsullied evening, because he had met her as the sun shed the last of its gold on the boardwalk, having noticed her around town over the previous days. He could not recall much about burying his wife and child, could not bring to mind anything but clouded, fragmentary recollections of the days between their deaths and the closing of their graves, but his first date with Susan was vivid in every detail.

Sometimes he believed that he saw them, his lost wife and child. He caught glimpses of them in the shadows, or smelled their scent. He conversed with them, and heard their responses. It was not uncommon, he knew, this conjuring of the dead by the living. It was an illusion, but who was to say what was real and what was not? If nothing else, it was a bulwark against the final forgetting.

Now Susan was before him again, although her features were strangely blurred. Her laughter faded away, but a little of the smile remained. Her eyes grew sad, as though she were conflicted in her affections for him. The shadow of the rain drew dry tears on her face. The rivulets were dark. They looked like blood.

where are you going? she said. Her voice came to him from far away and was broken by static.

"Southeast," he said.

why?

"I'm trying to find him."

but not for us, not for our sakes

Jennifer was suddenly seated by her mother, her face also unclear to him. She was not looking at her father, but toyed with an unseen plaything in the air. He wanted to reach out and take her in his arms, but she was not there, not truly, and he feared that if he tried to touch her, even this phantasm might vanish like smoke.

"For whom, if not for you?" he said.

don't lie

you were always a bad liar

"Was I?"

perhaps only where i was concerned

i saw through you, though

i always could

"I was happy for you to do it."

so why are you looking, if not for us?

He heard the distant crash of surf breaking, or it might have been truck wheels passing on the wet road. He could no longer be sure, and he did not care. For the moment, those he had lost were here with him.

"For me," he said. "For my own sake."

yes

Susan, both absent and present, stroked Jennifer's hair.

but why stop?

"To eat."

but you're not hungry

"For gas."

but your tank was almost full

"To rest."

but you are not tired

He pictured a woman being crowned with thorns,

the garland digging into her scalp, the barbs tearing at hair, skin, and flesh. He watched a man kneel over Patricia Hartley and Donna Lee Kernigan in order to defile them with sticks.

The seat across from him was empty, as it had always been, as it would always be. He stared at his hands, and the scars upon them.

Unknown dead voices called his name.

CHAPTER
XXVIII

Reverend Nathan Pettle entered his home through the back door. He slipped off his shoes and placed them on the mat bought by his wife for that purpose, printed with the words SHOE INN, which Delores had found funny. The house was quiet. Delores would be down at the small community center next to their church, where she hosted a social group for seniors every second day from noon. Her car was still outside, because Delores preferred to walk whenever the opportunity arose. She had started to put on weight and was embarrassed by it. He assured her that he had not noticed, but she did not believe him because he had given her no cause to. She no longer believed anything that he told her.

Pettle took a seat at the kitchen table, facing the image of Christ the Redeemer brought back from a business trip to Kenya by one of his parishioners. Pettle liked it because this Christ was noticeably dark-skinned, and had the build of a laborer, someone who could cut and carry wood, and worked with his hands. This was Pettle's Christ, not some fragile Caucasian figure marked as a victim from birth, doomed to die an emaciated death on a cross.

Pettle closed his eyes, clasped his hands before him, and tried to pray. When he opened his eyes again, Delores was standing by the kitchen sink. She was barefoot, but so lost had he been to his own thoughts that he doubted he would have noticed her approach even had she chosen to alert him to it. His wife was a plain woman, and he had first been attracted to her by the strength of her character as much as the depth of her faith. It was she who had been the true rock in the early days of his ministry—no, *their* ministry—when he preached to his flock beneath spreading trees or in the living rooms of their homes, accepting payment in the form of food offerings: bread, eggs, once even a whole deer, which had sustained him and his family through a long winter and spring at the start of the decade, until at last Delores became so sick of the taste of venison that she vowed never to eat it again. Hers was a practical, implacable Christianity, one wanting in warmth. She helped where and when she could, and made a positive difference to the lives of others, but her husband's congregation looked elsewhere for words of comfort in times of distress. That was not her way, and none judged her for it.

She stared at her husband, her expression unreadable.

"Is it true?" she said.

"Is what true?"

"That it was Sallie Kernigan's girl they found out in those woods."

"Yes," he said, "it's true."

Delores Pettle took a single long step toward her

husband, drew back her right hand, and slapped him hard across the face.

The rain was down for the rest of the day. The patch of woodland on which Donna Lee Kernigan's body had been discovered remained taped off, with signs posted advising that this was a crime scene, and any attempt to trespass upon it would be met with the full force of the law. Evan Griffin had arranged a roster of officers to stay at the scene. It was tying up valuable resources, but he knew it was necessary.

Griffin had wanted to conduct a massive fingertip search of the surrounding area, with Tucker McKenzie supervising, but he didn't have the manpower to do it properly, not without the assistance of the sheriff's office, and that was unlikely to be forthcoming until after the meeting with Jurel Cade—and possibly not even then, depending on the outcome. Instead, McKenzie had done what he could with his own people, making the best of not very much at all. Already Griffin was starting to feel the investigation slipping away from him, and it had barely commenced. He was out of his depth. The only lead was the truck that had picked up Donna Lee. He had already set his officers to interviewing those living and working in the vicinity of the school, just in case someone might have noticed the truck or the driver, and could remember the license number, or the color of the driver's hair, anything.

Jurel Cade had left a message to say he'd been delayed, and their meeting would now have to take place later in the afternoon. Griffin guessed that Cade was working out his next move, trying to find a way to limit the damage should the Cargill PD prove unwilling to back down or reach an acceptable compromise. Evan Griffin knew that he wasn't very popular with the Cade family. Soon, he wouldn't be popular with most of the population of Burdon County.

He took his coat from the stand in his office and picked up his car keys. He wouldn't do anyone any good sitting behind his desk. He told Billie he was going to join Kel and the others over at the school, but only once he'd run by the Kernigan house to take a look at it for himself. He might swing by the crime scene as well, just to check that everything was copacetic.

As he was about to leave, a man appeared in the doorway of the station house. The rain dripped from his head and clothing, and the light in his eyes made Griffin suddenly fearful, as though he had erred gravely by invoking this presence, by adjuring it to remain in this town, this world.

"You forget something?" said Griffin.

And Charlie Parker replied: "Perhaps."

2

A small town is automatically a world of pretense. Since everyone knows everyone else's business, it becomes the job of the populace to act as if they don't know what is going on instead of its being their job to try to find out . . . In a world like this, news is not welcome . . .
—Jeanine Basinger, *A Woman's View: How Hollywood Spoke to Women, 1930–1960*

CHAPTER
XXIX

The people on this earth can be divided into two groups, for the most part: those who want to leave a place, and those who want to stay in it. The rest simply haven't made up their minds yet. The smaller a place, the greater the pressure to pick a side, although one doesn't have to stick with one's choice. Circumstances may alter; life gets better, life gets worse.

Generally, though, life tends to stay the same.

For much of the twentieth century, Cargill was the kind of town in which people resided because they didn't have the resources—financial, familial, or psychological—to go anywhere else. Even if curiosity about other lives, or existential unease at their own situation, caused some citizens to look farther afield, the majority elected to extend their gaze no farther than the boundaries of their own state—or perhaps, in exceptional circumstances, those of contiguous states—in which case they discovered little that struck them as an improvement on their present condition; it was another series of crossroads, except with a heavier dusting of strangers. After a time, the larger part just stopped looking, and tempered accordingly their expectations and those of their offspring.

But Cargill was changing. Prosperity was on the way. It had been promised, and the populace had elected to believe that promise. They had invested themselves and their futures in it, and nothing could be allowed to get in its way, not even—or most particularly—dead girls, which was why a lot of folk in Cargill and its environs were angry at Patricia Hartley and Donna Lee Kernigan for getting themselves killed to begin with. Oh, they were also angry at whoever had killed the girls— they weren't monsters, and only the most ignorant or self-deceiving had chosen to believe the lies about Hartley's death—but for now the individual responsible for the murders remained anonymous and unseen. It was the evidence of his activities, in the form of bodies, that was potentially damaging to the town, the county, and their own prospects. Any public acknowledgment of murder risked drawing unwanted attention from outside, hence the level of discontent at Hartley and Kernigan's failure to exit this world in a more considerate fashion. (Estella Jackson was a different case, her passing having being consigned to bygone days, and thus dating from a time before any augurs of prosperity.) This unhappiness was not expressed openly, or in so many words, but it was present nonetheless, evinced mainly in the form of a quiet callousness, a careful constraining of compassion, and even in the commonly held belief, predominantly among whites, that this could well be the work of a black man, one who had chosen to take his rage out on his own people but, by doing so, was causing collateral harm to all.

But to pretend the killings were not happening meant they might continue, which would make outside interference not only more likely, but inevitable.

It was a quandary, and no mistake.

CHAPTER
XXX

Griffin sat with Charlie Parker at a table in Boyd's. The bar rarely opened before late afternoon, the widow Kirby holding that the class of person who might drink in a bar prior to this hour was not someone she wished to have on the premises. She chose to make an exception for the chief and the man with him on the grounds that (a) they wanted only coffee; and (b) it paid to stay on the right side of the police. If it struck her as curious that Chief Griffin was now engaged in a seemingly civil conversation with someone he had arrested at that very booth the previous night, she elected not to remark on it, understanding without being told that her discretion was to be relied upon in this instance. After all, the only reason the chief might have come knocking on her back door, requesting ingress and hospitality, was because he didn't wish for this meeting to be noticed or overheard. So Joan Kirby served them coffee, and some fresh brownies to take the bare look from the table, before positioning herself out of sight and earshot, the first step toward forgetting their presence entirely.

"Here's what you have to understand," said Griffin. "This county has been poor for as long as anyone can remember, and it didn't look as though that situation was likely to change anytime soon.

Even when other parts of the state started to do better, Burdon stayed stuck in the dark ages.

"Then Clinton got into the White House, and suddenly circumstances took on a whole new complexion. He'd made promises to the men and women of this state, and it was expected that they'd be kept. Arkansas was already beginning to see an influx of aerospace and defense contractors, on account of how we're cheap, low-tax, anti-union, and don't ask too many awkward questions, but under Clinton that process is accelerating. William Faulkner was right: Our economy is no longer agricultural; it's the federal government. Aerospace and defense represent a fresh start for the state, a better future, and Burdon County has a chance to benefit, because Cargill is on the verge of becoming the new Huntsville, Alabama."

Huntsville represented the New South in extremis. Back in 1950, it had been a town of 16,000 people, subsisting on cotton revenues. By the mid-1970s, its population had grown to more than 140,000, thanks to the presence of the George C. Marshall Space Flight Center, nineteen command centers including Army Missile Command and the Ballistic Missile Defense Systems Command, and plants operated by IBM, Chrysler, Lockheed, and others.

"You ever hear of Kovas Industries?" asked Griffin.

"No," said Parker.

"Kovas makes missile components and guidance systems, but it's also investing heavily in high-tech armaments, robotics, pilotless aircraft—the kind of stuff you only see in movies. It's looking to open a new research and manufacturing facility in the South, beginning with four hundred employees but expanding, over five years, to fifteen hundred. Because the work is so hush-hush, Kovas has very specific requirements: basically, it wants to turn somewhere into a company town. Kovas will invest in housing, schools, new businesses, all with the aim of creating a secure environment not only for itself and its employees, but also for the other companies that will follow, because the new facility is just the first of five that Kovas plans to build, and those plants will need their own support structures. We're talking tens of millions of dollars, and long-term prosperity for wherever the company elects to settle. The choice has come down to Arkansas or Texas, and Little Rock is pressing Clinton hard to put his finger on the scales and tip the balance in favor of the home team. Right now, Cargill is leading the field as the preferred site for the key build. We've had Kovas executives and their security consultants carrying out all kinds of surveys for the past two years, and the word from Little Rock is that they like what they see—not just here, but in the whole county, because we're prepared to hand it over to them lock, stock, and barrel, just as long as their money is good."

"And how do you feel about that?" said Parker, because Griffin's tone suggested a certain ambivalence.

"I may be less enthusiastic than most, although not so much that I'd want to see Texas benefit over us. Still, I have my reservations."

"Because you won't be the law in Cargill any longer," said Parker. "Kovas will, and your department will exist to serve the company's interests first, and those of the community second."

"It's been suggested that those interests are one and the same."

"But you're not convinced?"

"Not completely."

Parker sipped his coffee. It tasted like coffee in bars everywhere, which meant it wasn't good enough to justify a second cup. He took in Boyd's shabby décor, and the smell of old grease and spilled beer. It was about what one would expect from the best bar in a town like Cargill. But if Kovas moved in, Boyd's would have to change, just like the other businesses in town. Money would transform the bar, even to the point of rendering it unrecognizable, because money would transform the entire region.

"And Jurel Cade?" said Parker.

"The Cades are the major landowners and property developers in the county. They stand to benefit more than most if Kovas decides to locate here."

"Which is why Jurel Cade buried the investigation into Patricia Hartley's death."

"As chief investigator, Jurel is entitled to make any such calls," said Griffin, "including whether or

189

not to seek the assistance of the state police. But in this instance, I believe the powers that be in Little Rock would have approved of his decision to leave the state police out of it. Unofficially, Little Rock may even have been involved in making that decision. Nobody up there wants to see the Kovas deal endangered. If that means filing away a black girl's possible murder as an accidental death, then so be it."

"What about Patricia Hartley's family?"

"What about them?"

"When I was asking around—before you locked me up—I struggled to find any trace of them. Someone said they'd moved away."

"That's right: a mother and two young sons. They left town not long after the funeral."

"Why was that?"

"Their house burned down. As a gesture of goodwill, and in light of the loss they'd already suffered, the Cades secured alternative accommodation for them in Lucedale, Mississippi."

"Lucedale is a long way from Cargill."

"Hell of a long way. You can see the Gulf of Mexico from it, or good as."

"What about the fire?"

Griffin shrugged. "These things happen."

"Do they?"

"They do around here."

"What about the Kernigan girl? Did she have anyone?"

"A mother and grandmother. We're still trying to trace the mother. She works out of town, and hasn't been seen since Friday morning."

"Maybe she got offered a place in Lucedale too, and accepted it to save someone the trouble of burning down her house."

"I couldn't rightly say."

Parker was back to wishing he'd kept on driving. It seemed as though Evan Griffin was one of a handful of people in the state of Arkansas with any interest in solving these killings, or one of the few with even a semblance of the power required to investigate them. And this was alien territory for Parker: he didn't know the South and, truth be told, didn't want to know it. The majority of its population didn't think like him or share his views. How William Jefferson Clinton had emerged from them, he couldn't say, except that Clinton was probably more like the rest than he appeared to be. A man didn't get to be called Slick Willie by his home electorate for nothing.

"You can't investigate these killings without Jurel Cade's help," said Parker. "Whatever evidence exists is held by his office."

"There is no evidence in the Hartley death," said Griffin, "beyond scraps."

"Why? Even if the coroner signed off on an accidental death, the sheriff's office would still have been obliged to document the scene and file paperwork."

"It all got left in a sheriff's office cruiser that

was run through a car wash. Their vehicles have at least as many holes as ours. The contents of the boxes were destroyed, including the file, or what passed for it."

Parker stared at him for a time, but did not speak. Words were redundant.

"You'll still need to talk Cade around," he said, finally.

"That could be difficult."

"Perhaps not as difficult as you might think," said Parker.

"Why do you say that?"

"Because you now have three dead women in Burdon County, two of them murdered in the last three months alone. Whatever the reason for the hiatus between the first and second deaths—because it makes no sense to rule out a link—the killing has now resumed with a vengeance, and it's going to continue. Estella Jackson, the first, was a cold case, and Cade and the coroner managed to write off the second death, but Donna Lee's Kernigan's murder represents a pattern, and patterns mean publicity. It may be that Kovas Industries has so far accepted Jurel Cade's assurances that the situation is under control, but this most recent death is going to change that. The only thing worse than a series of unsolved murders is a series of unsolved murders that's ongoing. If Burdon County is to retain any hope of securing that investment, it lies in finding whoever is responsible for these deaths. Burying your heads in the dirt won't work any longer."

Griffin checked his watch.

"I have a meeting with Cade in about an hour's time. I think you should ride along for a more formal introduction."

"I can hardly wait."

"In the meantime, there's something I'd like to show you. It's on the way."

"And what would that be?"

"First of all, the place where Patricia Hartley's body was found. And then," Griffin added, "the place where I think it was meant to be found."

CHAPTER
XXXI

Jurel Cade prowled his father's study, the silence broken only by the ticking of the Newport tall case clock in the corner, one of just seven known to have been signed by the eighteenth-century clockmaker Thomas Claggett. Jurel had always regarded the clock as too big for the room, and thought it more rightly belonged in the hall, but his father was not to be reasoned with on this subject—or any other.

Delane Cade—or "Pappy" to those who knew him best, including persons beyond his own immediate family—was now in his eightieth year, and displayed few signs of mental decline. His three children all bore his imprint, although his younger son, Nealus, had more of their dear departed mother in his temperament, which revealed itself, in Pappy's view, as a tendency toward sensitivity that veered frequently into sullenness. His daughter, Delphia, by contrast, displayed comparatively few of those traits that Pappy considered typical of, or even integral to, the female sex, either as manifested previously by her mother or by anyone else of her gender; she remained a troubling anomaly to him, like a hermaphrodite or androgyne. Yet it was to Delphia that Pappy had entrusted the day-to-day running of the family's business concerns, though he had seen fit to ensure that all three of his offspring would receive a generous share of the Cade wealth in the event of his demise, thus avoiding any costly and unseemly wrangling over the succession.

Until recently, the promise of such a bounty might have held only marginal appeal, given that the Cades were rich in property and assets but less well endowed with hard cash. But for the past two years, Pappy, assisted by his daughter, had been intimately involved in luring Kovas to Arkansas—more particularly Burdon County, and specifically those regions of Burdon County owned and controlled by the Cade family. Only that morning, Pappy had been in conversation with three state senators regarding further modifications to the tax deal on offer to Kovas, and had scheduled a meeting with one of the governor's fixers to ensure that 1800 Center Street would row in behind any such agreement. Pappy was still finding his feet with Mike Huckabee, who had replaced Jim Guy Tucker as governor following the latter's conviction for conspiracy and mail fraud over Whitewater. (Which was another fuckup, one that, for a time, had threatened to derail the Kovas deal, until someone close to the Clintons gave assurances to Kovas executives that the independent counsel could look into Whitewater until his eyes bled without finding enough to indict the president. Pappy could only be grateful that he had declined to involve himself in the development of those vacation rentals on the White River. If only Slick Willie and his wife had been similarly prudent . . .)

And now, with Kovas on the verge of signing on the dotted line, someone was dumping dead girls almost within sight of land earmarked for the company's construction projects. If this went on, Pappy would soon be reduced to burying the damn bodies himself, and praying that no one noticed the smell.

Pappy took in the figure of his older son. Jurel's problem, Pappy thought, was that he held too much rage inside him. It made him unsuited to diplomacy. Pappy had hoped that the sheriff's office might be a proving ground for Jurel, knocking some of the rough edges from him before he commenced the ascent to higher office. Instead, it appeared that his son was committed to remaining what he was, where he was: another small-time lawman in a small-time county. Pappy, however, had not lost faith in his ability to mold his middle child into a more evolved specimen. Whatever the outcome, Jurel would still be useful when Kovas moved in, because the company could be assured that the law was on its side in Burdon County, and would do everything in its power to guarantee prosperity and security for all. Unfortunately, this would be difficult for Kovas to swallow if girls kept getting themselves murdered around Cargill.

"Sit down, Jurel," ordered Pappy. "You're making me nauseous."

Jurel sat, but his left foot maintained a nervous tapping on the floor.

"This Donna Lee Kernigan," said Pappy, "you sure she died like the last one?"

"A stick at each end," said Jurel, "like a spit roast."

"My God," said Pappy, although it wasn't clear whether he was reacting to the nature of the crime, his son's analogy, or both. "And there's no question about it being in Cargill's jurisdiction?"

"We could argue geography, but Griffin won't listen. We might lean on him. He has a mortgage, among other debts, and one of our banks holds the paper on his home. Plus, he wants to keep his job. He loves it, just as I love mine."

"Lean on him to what purpose?"

"To encourage him to hold off on any formal investigation until Kovas has committed to the county. Once we have contracts signed, they can't pull out, right?"

"They can pull out anytime they please," said Pappy, "especially if it emerges that information pertinent to their final decision was concealed from them. I think serial murders might qualify in that regard. We could end up in court until the Second Coming."

Pappy dropped another peppermint Tic Tac into his mouth. He sucked on them continuously, ever since his cardiologist had ordered him to give up smoking and cut down on his drinking. Pappy kept boxes of Tic Tacs in his office drawers, the glove compartment of his car, and the pockets of his clothing. Like a skeleton, he rattled when he walked.

"If there's an investigation, and publicity," said

Jurel, "they won't have to pull out because they'll already have opted for Texas."

Pappy crunched down hard on the Tic Tac.

"When are you meeting Griffin?"

"In about an hour."

"Tell him to come here."

"Are you sure?"

"If I wasn't, would I have said it? Evan Griffin's a reasonable man. He wants what's best for the county. There might be a way we can make this work for everyone."

Jurel understood by his father's tone that this part of the conversation was now concluded. He stood again, and walked to the french windows to stare out at the garden beyond. It was in a poor state, even for the time of year. His mother had always tended it well, but Pappy took no interest or joy in plants and flowers, and with his wife's passing it had fallen into disrepair. A yard service came in during the summer to keep the lawn trim, and clean up the leaves in the fall, but any suggestion that Pappy might like to add some color to the beds fell on deaf ears. It was possible, Jurel considered, that only his father's affection for his departed wife prevented him from paving over the garden entirely.

Not that the house itself was in significantly better condition. Ever since Nealus had moved to his own place—although one, by mutual agreement between the siblings, on their father's land, and within summoning distance of the family home—

the dwelling appeared to have grown darker and dustier, despite the efforts of Miss Quinnett, who took care of cooking and cleaning for Pappy. He wouldn't allow her to disturb the rooms he used regularly, and claimed the vacuum cleaner gave him a headache. He also preferred dimness to brightness, and eschewed any illumination stronger than lamplight. The whole property bore a miasma of mortality.

And was that such a surprise? For all his apparent haleness, Pappy was catching glimpses of the Reaper. His mind was still alert, but his body was ailing. His enduring legacy would be the Kovas deal, and the consequent transformation of Burdon County's fortunes. Already he had arranged an endowment for a new library in Cargill to be erected in his name after his death, even though he'd never read a book for pleasure in his life. But he'd also ordained that, should he die while the current governor remained in office, he didn't want him to turn the first sod, or any other such nonsense, on the grounds that "fucking Huckabee will just fill the whole place with Bibles." Pappy wanted Jim Guy Tucker to do the needful instead. Jim Guy might have been a crook, but at least he wasn't always bothering Jesus with his shit.

"Jurel?"

His father's voice brought Jurel back.

"Yes?"

"You still think a Negro killed those girls?"

Jurel considered the question.

"I believe it would be for the best if that was the case," he said.

Which wasn't really answering the question.

"You have any suspects?"

Yes, he had suspects. The county wasn't short of coloreds with criminal records, some of them violent—wasn't short of white people with records either, but that was beside the point.

"Some."

"Well, leave me to reflect on how we might progress with that."

Jurel didn't make any objection, didn't attempt to point out that he was the law in the county, not some old man sucking on Tic Tacs because he was too scared to smoke. It wouldn't have been true anyway. Power and money determined the law, and justice, like beauty, was in the eye of the beholder.

Jurel left Pappy's office, closing the door behind him. From the kitchen he heard the clattering of Miss Quinnett. She'd been a fixture in the house for as long as he could remember, back when she was in her thirties and he was still a little boy. She'd never married. He'd never thought to ask why, except that he thought she loved his father—not in a sexual way, or as a dog might love its master, but as a mother loves an errant child that has grown into an equally errant adult. Even though she was younger than Pappy by fifteen years, she seemed to Jurel to be much older, as though this house had stolen the years from her.

Miss Quinnett was to be looked after in his

father's will, but with a percentage, not a set sum. She, too, would benefit from Kovas's arrival in Burdon County, if only so that she might pass on her employer's largesse to various brothers and sisters, and assorted nieces and nephews. But even in this simple way, so many lives would be improved.

Jurel opened the front door. A man was approaching the house, his build so thin that he seemed almost to pass untouched between the raindrops: Nealus, youngest of the clan. Behind him, a Mercedes was pulling into the drive, a woman behind the wheel: Delphia, arriving. The Cades were closing ranks, securing their future and that of the county.

Jurel wondered if Nealus had been watching for his sister. They had always been intimate, these two, eldest and youngest siblings respectively, and more so since the death of their mother. Jurel, the middle child, had been equally distant from both, like the apex of a long, narrow triangle.

Wreathed in the crepuscular light of home, he waited to admit them.

CHAPTER
XXXII

Parker and Griffin stood on an escarpment, the result of some tectonic shift in the landscape many thousands of years earlier, with forest behind and sparser growth below. The slope was a mixture of exposed stone and thin grass; it wouldn't be too difficult to descend, but less risky when the ground was dry. They'd already been forced to walk from the road to this point, and Parker had accepted the offer of a raincoat from Griffin. It wasn't doing much to keep his head dry, but a man took his comforts where he could.

Griffin pointed toward a stand of pines below, where the remains of crime scene tape still fluttered.

"That's where Patricia Hartley's remains were discovered," he said. "We can take a closer look if you like, but there won't be much to see. We think she rolled down the slope before coming to rest at the foot of those pines. Even Loyd Holt doesn't contest that; he just elects to believe she was still alive when she started falling. She had abrasions all over, and the branch in her"—Griffin paused, and settled for "lower body"—"had snapped. We found the other half of it about halfway down the slope, right about where that big boulder juts out."

Parker didn't bother hiding his puzzlement. In the context of what Griffin had told him about the placement of Donna Lee Kernigan's body—and what he knew about the murder of Estella Jackson, in the event that she had been murdered by the same individual—it made no sense for the killer to have dumped Patricia Hartley so carelessly.

"What am I not seeing?" he asked.

"You can't see what you don't know to see," said Griffin. "Where you're standing is federal land. Down there is private property, owned by the Ingram family. The edge here marks the boundary."

Parker took in the woods, both around and below, and the distant hills. He was moderating his opinion of Griffin and the Cargill PD by the minute, because the odds had been stacked against them from the start. He squatted, and noted that the ground inclined slightly as it reached the edge, but he detected no sign of any collapses. Patricia Hartley's body could only have been pushed over the edge intentionally.

Unless . . .

"Any indications of animal damage?"

"None," said Griffin. "We have black bears, and they'd certainly be capable of moving a body, but they'd chew on it first. Patricia had been dead for less than a day when she was found; to a predator, her meat would still have been considered fresh. Bears don't go in much for rotten meat, not unless they're starving. Had an animal been involved, we'd know about it."

"So your opinion is that someone moved Patricia Hartley's body so it wouldn't be discovered on federal land, because that would have meant involving the FBI?"

"It is."

"You have anyone in mind?"

"Patricia was found by a woman named Wadena Ott. She's lived a harder life than many, and gets by on food stamps, whatever she can catch in her traps, and bottles of seventy-proof cherry brandy. Like a lot of folk barely holding it together, she has a fear of the law, but everyone tries to be as understanding of her needs as they can, including the sheriff's office. She called them as soon as she got home. Jurel Cade was first on the scene."

"Do you know that for sure?"

"He told me so himself."

"And what does Wadena Ott have to say about all this?"

"Whatever Jurel told her to say, which is that she found the body at the bottom of the slope, not the top."

Parker envisioned Jurel Cade, his foot against the naked body of Patricia Hartley, using the sole of his shoe to give her one final push over the edge.

Where have I come to? What manner of place is this?

He took a small notebook from his pocket and added Wadena Ott's name to it. Rain speckled the page. He discerned smoke rising in the distance from a fire that was either being smothered by the rain or was refusing to yield to it.

"Tell me about the Cades."

Griffin did, giving him a truncated family history, but concentrating principally on those that remained, namely Pappy and his brood: Delphia, Jurel, and Nealus. Parker listened without interrupting, all the while regarding the woods; the rocky slope that had damaged Patricia Hartley's body still further, inflicting injury upon injury; and the Karagol standing like a great pool of tar to the east of his vantage point. If this was the Cades' kingdom, they could have it.

"So," said Griffin, when his monologue was concluded, "what do you think?"

"I'm wondering," said Parker, "if anyone in this county has a regular first name."

"You're named after a jazz musician."

"No, I'm not."

"You're telling me it's a coincidence?"

"My parents didn't listen to jazz," said Parker. "The name came from elsewhere. My grandfather didn't leave a great deal of value to my father, except for a brass match dispenser and a spectacle case, both made by the Charles Parker Company of Meriden, Connecticut, in the nineteenth century. They're very collectible, or so I hear. When I was a child, my father would take them out and show them to me. He liked to claim they'd been made for me, which was why they had my name on them. I even believed him, for a while. When he died, they passed to me, as he'd always promised. I still have them somewhere, but I haven't looked at them in a long time."

The pause before "died" was barely detectable, but Griffin picked up on it. He still elected not to reveal his knowledge of Parker's own troubled family history, a legacy that amounted to far more than nineteenth-century trinkets.

"So you were named after a match dispenser?" he said at last.

"Or the spectacle case," said Parker. "Take your pick."

"I'd go with the musician, or claim your folks just liked the name."

"Some people used to call me Bird. It was a running joke."

"Your tone suggests you never found it funny."

"Like I said, it was based on a misconception. I went along with it. It was easier than trying to correct them. I even caught myself using it, which was odd."

Griffin's radio crackled into life. It was Billie Brinton, informing him that the venue for his meeting with Jurel Cade had been changed from the sheriff's office to Pappy Cade's residence.

"Is that usual?" said Parker.

"Nothing about the Cades is usual, but it means that Pappy is already trying to turn the screws on the investigation."

"You think he can find an extra chair for me?"

"You may have to remain standing. The Cades' brand of Southern hospitality is predicated on an affinity with the host, and Pappy doesn't put out the welcome mat for bluecoats, not unless they have money to spend. He still believes the Mason-Dixon Line ought to have a wall along it."

"The more I discover about this county, the unhappier it makes me," said Parker.

"It grows on a person."

"Not if he doesn't stand still for long enough."

"Mr. Parker, I think you may be a misanthrope."

Griffin began to lead the way back to the car. They took a more circuitous route than before, bypassing areas where the rain had made the ground treacherous. Parker counted three hunting stands: bow hunters for deer, most likely, given the time of year.

"Are you from around these parts?" said Parker.

"No, I was born and raised in Osceola. That's Mississippi County, up in the northeast. It's not so different, though."

"Sorry to hear that."

"You don't give up, do you?"

"I like to think it's one of my better qualities."

"Well"—Griffin sounded dubious—"if you say so." He checked his watch. "We got some time. I'm of a mind to check on Tilon Ward. He doesn't live far from here."

"He's the one that found Donna Lee's body, right?"

"He is. He's also, if in the absence of conclusive evidence, involved in the manufacture of meth-amphetamine, a quantity of which was discovered in Sallie Kernigan's bedroom."

"Is he the only source in town?"

"If the stories are true, he's strictly a maker, not a purveyor. He leaves the sale and distribution up to others. But he's not the brains of the operation, although it's not for want of intelligence."

"So who does he work for?"

"I don't know," said Griffin, "but I have my suspicions."

"Which are?"

"Which are my own, for the time being." He patted Parker on the arm, and continued walking. "I wouldn't want to overburden you with information so early in our relationship."

"God forbid," said Parker.

CHAPTER
XXXIII

Parker and Griffin arrived at the Ward property just as Tilon Ward was preparing to leave in his truck. Ward didn't look surprised to see them, but he didn't appear pleased either. Griffin introduced Parker, describing him as a detective from New York who had offered to assist and advise the Cargill PD in the current investigation. For a police officer dealing with a suspected meth cook, Griffin struck Parker as less adversarial, and Ward as less defensive, than might have been anticipated, even as Griffin raised the subject of the meth found in Sallie Kernigan's home.

"You wouldn't happen to know where that came from, would you?" said Griffin.

Tilon Ward's expression remained neutral.

"No," he said, "I wouldn't."

Griffin nodded, as though Ward had answered in the positive rather than the negative.

"Because if you did know, that might lead me to suspect you were familiar with the Kernigan family. Are you telling me you weren't? Because you looked real shook up this morning."

"I'd just found a dead girl impaled with sticks. Maybe you're inured to such sights, Evan, but I'm not."

Evan: Parker registered Ward's use of Griffin's first name.

"No, I can't say that I am," said Griffin. "But you must know Sallie Kernigan. You drink at the Rhine Heart, and she used to work there."

Ward shrugged. "I knew her to order a beer from."

"No more than that?"

"No more than that."

"And her daughter, you ever speak with her?"

"Denny doesn't permit minors in his bar."

"That wasn't what I asked."

"If I'd known who Donna Lee was, I'd have told you when I found her body."

"I'd like to believe so, Tilon. I'd be discontented with you otherwise."

A woman in her late sixties emerged from the house and walked across the yard to one of the outbuildings. Griffin raised a hand in greeting, but she did not return the gesture.

"Must be awkward sometimes," said Griffin.

"What?" said Ward.

"A man your age, living in his mother's pocket. Hard to keep your business private."

"We each have our own space. It's not so bad."

"That would make life easier, I'm sure. You got a woman, Tilon?"

"No one special."

"How about someone not-so-special?"

"Not even that. If you think I was sleeping with Sallie Kernigan, you're wrong. You can hook me up to one of those lie detector machines, and it'll confirm the truth of it."

"That seems like a definitive declaration."

"It is. You find her yet?"

"Who?"

"Sallie Kernigan."

"Why do you ask?"

"Because her daughter's dead, and I was the one that discovered the body."

"Which gives you a proprietorial interest in developments?"

"Which means I give a shit."

"No," said Griffin, "we haven't found Sallie yet. Should we be worried about her?"

"I don't know. Should you?"

"I'm starting to be. It's a hell of a thing, Tilon."

"It is. A hell of a thing."

Ward shook his car keys.

"We keeping you from something?" said Griffin.

"I got some errands to run in town."

A silent exchange passed between the two men. It ended when Ward looked away.

"Then you'd best be about them," said Griffin. "And drive carefully, Tilon. You've had a shock."

They stayed behind Tilon Ward as far as the outskirts of Cargill, where Ward took a right while they drove straight on.

"So?" said Griffin.

"I don't know him as well as you do," said Parker, with deliberate ambiguity, but Griffin didn't bite.

"Feel free to speculate."

211

"He's hiding something, but not a sexual relationship with Sallie Kernigan."

"A business one?"

"If that was the case, isn't it likely that he would have crossed paths with her daughter?"

"Unless Sallie chose to keep any dealings with Ward distinct from her home life," said Griffin.

"But what dealings? You said yourself that Ward might cook the product, but he doesn't sell it."

"There are always exceptions."

"So why make one for Sallie Kernigan?" said Parker.

"Assuming Tilon did make one."

"Assuming that."

Griffin chewed at his lip, then caught himself doing it. He was catching his officers' bad habits. Next thing he knew, he'd be buying a pipe.

"One of Sallie Kernigan's neighbors suggested she might be whoring."

"In town?"

"No, we'd have heard. Over in Malvern, where she works."

"Does it sound likely?"

Griffin mulled on it. "No, or not habitually. The older generation is not above indulging in a rush to judgment, and I wouldn't contest that Sallie has a wild streak. We'll make inquiries, though. Malvern has a population of about ten thousand. Not much easier to keep a secret there than here."

Parker made another note. Griffin noticed that the pages of the notebook were heavily annotated.

He had not come across it during his search of the motel room, and it had not been on Parker's person when he was arrested. He must have concealed it well.

"You know," said Griffin, "I was hoping you might have figured all this out by now, what with you being a detective from New York and all."

"Former detective."

"Still."

"Sorry to disappoint you."

"Yeah," said Griffin. "I think the TV shows lied."

CHAPTER
XXXIV

Tilon Ward parked his truck behind the Rhine Heart, and entered through the rear door that sat between what passed for the kitchen on one side, and what qualified as restrooms on the other, both bearing only a tangential relationship to the requisite hygiene standards in either case. If Boyd's represented the closest to upmarket dining that Cargill offered, then the Rhine Heart was its opposite. It took its name from a play on the owner's surname, Rhinehart, and served hot dogs and schnitzel if the proprietor was in the mood. Mainly it offered beer, liquor, and pretzels, which amounted to three of their five-a-day for a considerable section of its clientele.

But the Rhine Heart was also where a man could go if he wanted to find out what was happening in Cargill without being called on his curiosity— or more pertinently, where Tilon Ward could go, since Denny Rhinehart's premises offered a safe, nonjudgmental environment in which Tilon sometimes conducted his business affairs, with Denny receiving a sweetener in return for his facilitation.

And Denny also knew Sallie Kernigan. As Griffin had so recently pointed out, she had formerly tended bar at the Rhine Heart, until a disagreement with Denny over where his hands should be permitted to wander caused her to seek employment opportunities elsewhere. Tilon had offered to intervene on her behalf, but she didn't like working at the Rhine Heart anyway, its patrons sharing a similar mind-set to its owner when it came to feeling up the staff. By then Sallie didn't need the extra money, since she was earning enough from the meth she was selling. Tilon had helped her to establish herself by advancing a thousand dollars' worth of product on trust, and in return Sallie hadn't objected when Tilon began sleeping with her daughter.

Tilon was still shaken from his encounter with Griffin and the stranger, Parker, who hadn't spoken beyond the initial greetings, but only listened and watched. By this point, Tilon was having trouble keeping track of all the lies he was being forced to tell. Once more, he wondered if he should have come clean with Griffin the moment he stumbled on Donna Lee's body, but that would have brought its own difficulties. And he hadn't been thinking straight. How could he have been? Now he had to live with his falsehoods, and hope that the damage from them could be contained.

Denny Rhinehart was working the bar alone, which meant using a dishcloth to redistribute the dirt on the glasses while watching some shitty comedy rerun on the ancient TV set high in a corner. Tilon counted four other patrons, two of whom greeted him by name, and two of whom ignored him, Cargill being a small town in which people nursed grudges the way regular human beings cultivated houseplants. Tilon took a seat at the bar as far from anyone else as possible, and ordered a beer. Denny deposited it before him, the bottle wrapped in a paper napkin, and told Tilon it was on the house.

"I heard what happened," he said, "about how it was you that found the Kernigan girl."

Tilon looked Denny in the eye, but could perceive no intimation of duplicity. Denny didn't know about Tilon's relationship with Donna Lee.

"Yeah, it was."

"That's bad," said Denny. "I always liked Sallie."

Tilon resisted the urge to break the bottle against Denny's nose, if only because he'd have damaged his own hand. *If you liked her so much,* he wanted to ask, *why couldn't you have kept your fucking hands to yourself?* Instead he said, "Any of her friends been in?"

The Rhine Heart might have been many things, filthy not least among them, but it welcomed anyone with money to spend, regardless of creed or color, and Denny had no tolerance for racist talk. Even after she'd quit her job behind the bar, Sallie Kernigan had continued to drink at the Rhine Heart once or twice a week.

"No," said Denny, "but I wouldn't be surprised to see some of them later." He wiped the bar with the same cloth he'd used on the glasses, the same cloth he probably used for everything, and had for days. "But Kel Knight was in here asking after her."

"When?"

"An hour ago. Seems Sallie doesn't know about her daughter yet. Cops are trying to track her down." Denny squinted at Tilon. "You wouldn't be able to help them, would you? I mean . . ."

Denny trailed off. Even in the comparatively sympathetic surroundings of the bar, some subjects were better off not discussed aloud. Denny might not have been aware of Tilon's relationship with Donna Lee Kernigan, but he'd noticed that Tilon was tight with Sallie, and it wouldn't have been beyond him to speculate on meth being the source of their bond, Sallie Kernigan having a fondness for a good time.

"If I knew, don't you think I'd have told them?" said Tilon.

"Yeah, sure. Sorry." Denny poured himself a glass of water, more as an attempt to distract from whatever offense he might have caused Tilon than anything else. "That's two young women, though. Three if you count the Jackson girl, although who's to say that killing has anything to do with what's been happening lately."

"The present is history's child," said Tilon.

"You read that somewhere?"

"No, I just made it up."

"You believe it?"

"Only a fool wouldn't."

Denny, who might have been about to argue, decided against it, not wishing to appear a fool before Tilon Ward.

217

"What's going to happen?" said Denny.

"They're going to investigate."

"Who is?"

"Evan Griffin. The Cargill PD."

"You really believe that?"

"You asked me. I told you."

Denny twisted his glass on the bar, creating hollow circles of moisture on the old wood.

"But what if the Kovas people hear about it?"

"You think Jurel Cade can keep this one quiet?"

"He managed it with Patricia Hartley, no matter what Loyd Holt might have to say about her death being an accident."

"That was before they had another body," said Tilon. "And Griffin is different."

Griffin *was* different. He was a straight arrow, and because he came from outside the county he wasn't as beholden to old ties of friendship or family. He didn't accept favors, and didn't do many either, although he had always cut Tilon a lot of slack. But any obligation Griffin might have felt toward Tilon was about used up by now, and whatever remained of it had probably drained away following this afternoon's exchanges.

Once again, Tilon told himself that he hadn't done anything wrong in the eyes of the law. Donna Lee Kernigan was seventeen—okay, sixteen when he'd started sleeping with her—which made it legal under the Arkansas Code. True, some people in town might have frowned on a relationship between a teenage girl and a thirty-six-year-old man, but last time Tilon checked, he hadn't signed any morals clause. His only error lay in not admitting to knowing Donna Lee when he notified the police about her body.

And what good would that admission do him now? *None at all,* was the answer. He didn't know anything that might help the investigation, so he'd just end up drawing heat, and Randall Butcher wouldn't like that. Worse, Tilon might find himself in a prison cell if he couldn't provide an alibi for his movements over the weekend, because one surefire way of putting an end to any concerns about Kovas and its future in Cargill would be to identify a suspect and keep him locked up until all the paperwork was signed. The case could take years to come to trial, and in the meantime the real killer might suffer a heart attack and die, thereby providing further circumstantial evidence of the patsy's guilt. No, to hell with it: Tilon could do more good roaming free than warming a cot in a cell, and who knows what he might learn if he kept his eyes and ears open, and his mouth shut?

He took a last swig of beer, leaving the bottle half-full. He didn't even know why he'd ordered it. Force of habit.

"You hear anything, you let me know," he told Denny.

"Always."

And Tilon departed.

CHAPTER
XXXV

Reverend Nathan Pettle sat alone on the couch in his living room. Delores had finally departed to tend to her seniors, although the reverend's cheek still bore the red mark of her wrath. It was just like a woman, Pettle thought, to ambush a man unsuspecting—and in his own home, while he was still reeling from the trauma of being forced to gaze on the ruined body of a young girl; a girl he knew, a girl he'd watched grow up, a girl that, in another life, he might even have been permitted to raise as his own.

All men had moments of weakness, and all women, too. It was part of the human condition, but what mattered was that one sought the Lord's forgiveness for one's trespasses and endeavored not to sin again. And he'd done that: he'd gone down on his knees before God after sleeping with Sallie Kernigan for the first time. He had prayed for absolution, and promised not to transgress in a similar fashion in the future. He'd wept for himself and his sinful state.

Admittedly, he'd also decided against sharing with his wife the fact of his unfaithfulness, both in order to spare her any pain and to ensure the continuation of their marriage. After all, he reasoned, he'd seen the error of his ways, and whatever his failings—and they were, he felt, relatively few, and mostly minor—once Nathan Pettle made a decision, he stuck with it. He had never intended to stray. Sallie had been struggling, both financially and psychologically, with raising a daughter alone, and had turned to him for advice and compassion. She had broken down in his arms, and he'd held her and—

Well, you see how it was, and how easily a man might waver. Let he who is without sin . . .

Mind you, he might have struggled to justify the subsequent encounters, and the intensity and variety of them, but he'd been blinded by lust and had fallen prey to the schemes of the Father of Lies, because there was nothing Satan enjoyed more than bringing low a man of God. In a way, the fact that Pettle had persevered in his calling, even after so many stumbles, might have been regarded as testament to his inner strength.

Finally, though, he had vowed never to sleep with Sallie Kernigan again, and meant it. He was helped in this regard by his wife's discovery of the affair—if it could even be dignified with such a description, given its brevity—and the domestic humiliation and uproar that followed, but he liked to believe he'd have resisted any further temptation, even without Delores's intervention. Not that his wife had chosen to perceive it that way. God might forgive, but woman did not. Three years had passed since then, and Delores still showed no signs of extending absolution to her husband.

Pettle slipped to his knees from the couch. He gripped his hands tightly together, bowed his head, and prayed for Donna Lee Kernigan, and her mother, wherever she might be. Principally, though, he prayed for himself: for the strength to lead his flock at this difficult time, for the wisdom to choose the right path for all.

And for the continued concealment of his subsequent errors, that they might remain buried and undisturbed, now and forever.

Amen.

CHAPTER
XXXVI

Denny Rhinehart spoke quietly into the bar phone, the one that sat beneath the bags of peanuts that might or might not still be within their use-by date, the Rhine Heart's patrons being less than particular about such niceties. From this vantage point, Rhinehart could see Tilon Ward sitting in his truck, the smoke from his cigarette winding into the afternoon air. The rain had stopped, but it was likely to be a temporary respite. The elements weren't done with the county yet.

"Yeah," said Rhinehart, "he just left. No, he's outside, smoking. You want I should get him?" He listened. "Okay, okay. I just thought you should know that he was asking about her."

He hung up the phone and opened a bag of nuts. Sallie Kernigan: Denny Rhinehart had always entertained a jones for her, and her daughter, too—once Donna Lee had become legal, of course, because he wasn't a pervert. He'd seen her on the road a couple of evenings back, as she was walking home from school, her bag swinging and her hips swinging along with it, because she'd filled out in a healthy way this last year. Denny, being a good Samaritan—almost a friend of the family, you might say, seeing as how the wages he had until recently paid her mother probably bought some of those clothes Donna Lee was wearing—pulled over and offered her a ride.

Donna Lee turned him down. She did it with a smile, but Denny could tell that she was wary of him. He didn't know what tales her mother might have been spreading about him, but he hadn't liked Donna Lee's attitude.

No, Denny thought, he hadn't liked her attitude one little bit.

CHAPTER
XXXVII

Parker waited in the public area of the Cargill Police Department while Griffin went into conclave with his officers to inform them of his decision to co-opt the newcomer into the investigation. After five minutes, Parker was invited to join them. No one displayed obvious resentment at his presence, with the exception of Kel Knight. Griffin had warned Parker this might be the case, explaining that Knight was Cargill born and bred, and therefore preternaturally disposed to being suspicious of those who were not.

The truth was more complicated. Kel Knight was a man of deep moral and religious convictions, and had become a police officer because he believed that justice was not solely the prerogative of the Divine. Decades of exposure to the realities of law enforcement, and the accompanying explorations of the shadows behind the Magnolia Curtain, had served only to strengthen him in this position; but it had also resulted in a hardening of his attitudes, an inflexibility that rendered him intolerant of human failings. Now he was being forced to confront a situation in which the outcome he desired—the investigation of a series of killings, and the apprehension and punishment of the culprit—might necessitate the involvement of someone whom he adjudged, if only on the basis of hearsay, to have blood on his hands. For the present, Knight was debating the nuances of the issue on an internal level. How long that might continue, and what the results might be, would likely depend on Parker's behavior.

In order to ensure that the new arrival had the requisite powers required to aid the investigation, Parker was sworn in as a volunteer officer and temporarily provided with a badge and department ID. Griffin didn't bother offering him the use of a gun: the man was already well supplied, and it wasn't as though the department was running a superfluity of firearms and ammunition. As it was, most of the officers paid for their own weapons.

When all this was completed, Parker and Griffin took their leave and drove toward the Cade homestead in Hamill, southeast of Cargill.

"I have a question to ask," said Griffin at last, as they passed the diner and gas station at which Parker had made his decision to return. He took in the windows, but no woman and child stared back at him.

"Only one?"

Parker watched the landscape roll by: trailers that had become permanent residences out of necessity and were now nearing the end of their natural lifespan; houses that were hardly more prepossessing, their greater resilience excepted; stretches of woodland that were not being stewarded, encroaching on fields cultivating only weeds; and failed businesses standing alongside those battling the same fate. It reminded Parker of parts of rural Maine, where he had spent his adolescence and young adulthood following the death of his father. Poverty knew no accents, no natural boundaries; it was depressing in its uniformity. The only difference in Burdon was the evidence of tornado damage, like the wrath of God made manifest through crushed homes and uprooted trees.

"A weapon in your possession might be the kind issued to FBI agents, or am I mistaken?" said Griffin.

"There's an agent named Woolrich," said Parker, "down in Louisiana. The gun was a gift from him. He's an assistant SAC in the New Orleans field office, but until recently he was working out of New York. I've known Woolrich for a few years, and he's okay. We became friendly, even close. He came to the funeral. When I chose to resign from the force, he offered to provide information, within certain limits. I'm looking for motifs, listening for echoes, because my wife and daughter weren't the first. What was done to them was too consummate for that. The one who killed them had practice, so where did he start?"

Griffin said nothing. He was in awe of the younger man's focus: the clarity of his rage, and the purity of his desire for vengeance. He found it hard to envisage Parker losing control to the extent required to beat another human being to death, but neither was Griffin so foolish as to believe him incapable of it. In the confines of the car, Parker's very restraint drew attention to what was being suppressed: power, violence, and wrath. Perhaps Kel Knight was right to be doubtful, even fearful, of him.

"Not in Burdon County," said Griffin, finally.

"No, but someone did, back in '92, with Estella Jackson. She may be the key to what's happening here. Was Jurel Cade the chief investigator?"

"No, that would have been toward the end of Eddy Rauls's time."

"Is Rauls still around?"

"Oh yeah."

"You say that with feeling."

"Eddy Rauls will outlive us all. The man is mostly nails and granite. He kept a paper shredder under his desk for the tickets, fines, and summonses he chose to destroy in return for money or favors, and a blackjack and ball-peen hammer as cures for intransigence and recidivism. Looked at from a certain angle, you could say he kept the county running smoothly, and spared the courts a lot of time and trouble. From another angle, it might be argued that he engaged in acts of gross illegality, and viewed the sheriff's office as his personal fiefdom."

"So he was the sheriff?"

"No, he was happy to work from the shadows. Eddy didn't hold with politics, or the democratic process. He was the power behind the throne as chief deputy, and bent a succession of sheriffs to his will."

"Will he talk to us?"

"He might, if he's in the right mood. He's no fan of the Cades. He might still be chief investigator now if Jurel and Pappy hadn't encouraged him to retire early."

"How did they manage that?"

"Eddy got careless and left a paper trail," said Griffin. "Then his friends began to desert him, or just upped and died. Same for any allies he might have cultivated in Little Rock, so he couldn't rely on the attorney general's office to give him a pass, especially once Jim Guy Tucker became governor in late '92. By then Pappy Cade was already laying the foundations for outside investment in Burdon County, with the active support of Little Rock, and nobody needed Eddy Rauls arriving with his hand out and an empty grocery bag for the cash. So Eddy received a quiet ultimatum: leave with a pension or be indicted. Naturally, he chose the pension, and he's been nursing a grudge against the Cades ever since."

Parker added Eddy Rauls to his list of names.

"Anyone else I should know about," he asked, "while we're on the subject of people holding grudges?"

"If you mean against the Cades, that's a complex issue. Ferdy Bowers has no love for them, and he's had his nose bloodied by Pappy in business dealings over the years, but he stands to gain from Kovas, if not as much as Pappy and his brood. That disparity remains a source of resentment for him, but the lure of enrichment keeps a civil tongue in his head. And then there's Randall Butcher."

"Who's Randall Butcher?" said Parker.

"You asked me earlier if I knew who Tilon Ward might be cooking for. I'm not alone in feeling that it might be Butcher. He owns a chain of strip clubs across the state, and is currently appealing a decision by a Burdon County judge denying his application for a five-thousand-square-foot building off Linseer Road, just inside the Cargill town limits. Butcher wants to develop it as the jewel in his empire of the flesh. The site is zoned C-Three Commercial, which means that no sexually oriented business can open within seven hundred and fifty feet of a school, church, or residential neighborhood. Butcher is arguing that the church in this case is disused, and two houses don't constitute a neighborhood. He wants his club up and running before work starts on any Kovas facility, so he can reap the benefits of horny construction workers with money burning holes in their pockets."

"And how do the Cades feel about this?"

"The Cades are among those opposing the application, mainly because they don't own the site—Butcher acquired that land behind their backs—and also because they might be hoping to invest in a similar, marginally classier establishment down the line. So Butcher is trying to drum up local support to persuade the Alcoholic Beverage Control Division to review his application, and the Cades are doing their best to discourage all concerned.

"Just to complicate matters further, the disused church, and the land on which it stands, was donated about a year ago to the Cargill African Methodist Episcopal congregation. Their current house of worship is already too small for their needs, but if the population expands, they'll have to look elsewhere, and that old church would be perfect, assuming they can raise the funds for repairs. If they do decide to relocate, Randall Butcher's strip club will be dead in the water. Last I heard, he was trying to convince Reverend Pettle to sell up in return for another site. Trouble is, Randall doesn't have another site to offer right now, because everyone that owns property is sitting on it in the hopes the Kovas deal will produce a windfall. Plus, the majority of development land is in the hands of the Cades."

"It sounds like the Cades have bet everything on Kovas," said Parker, "and other people are following their lead. If it goes bad, the family will have made a lot of enemies."

Griffin glanced at him.

"You think these killings might be a way of getting at the Cades by sabotaging Kovas?" he asked.

"It's possible," said Parker, "assuming you're right, and Patricia Hartley's body was originally left on federal land in order to draw in the FBI. But why not do the same with Donna Lee Kernigan, and how does it all connect back to Estella Jackson, who died long before Kovas even appeared on the radar? Also, it seems to me that most people in Burdon County, including the Cades' rivals, will benefit from Kovas, so blowing up the deal in order to hurt the Cades would involve a suicidal degree of self-harm."

He paused for a moment.

"And killing is hard," he said, finally.

Griffin didn't comment. He had never killed anyone, and intended for that situation to endure until he was laid in his grave. He didn't doubt the truth of Parker's words, but retained some hope that, whatever the rumors about Johnny Friday, the assertion was not based on Parker's personal experience.

"What was done to those young women involved planning, and viciousness," Parker continued. "It wasn't enough just to take their lives: they had to be violated after death, and their bodies displayed."

"Meaning?"

"It shows real hate, and that hate is growing stronger."

They were nearing the outskirts of Hamill, the county seat, even though it was smaller than Cargill. Nevertheless, Hamill resembled the latter, right down to the crumbling strip mall on the edge of town. It was as though the two men had come full circle and arrived back at their point of origin. Parker had the uncomfortable sense that he might never be permitted to leave Cargill, and had somehow wandered into a hell of another's making.

Griffin turned off the main road. They drove for another mile, until they came to a lane on the right signposted PRIVATE. Griffin turned again, and followed a trail marked by stunted trees to a cluster of four dwellings, three of them new, and one, the largest, of older vintage. Made of dark wood and darker stone, it spread over three floors, the boundary marked by a low wall that circled the property. Four cars were parked in the driveway, one of them a Burdon County sheriff's cruiser.

"The big house is Pappy's," said Griffin. "The others theoretically belong to each of the kids, although Delphia now spends most of her time in Little Rock, and Jurel has a place of his own in town."

"Nothing like a close-knit family," said Parker.

"True," said Griffin, as they came to a halt. "And the Cades are nothing like a close-knit family."

CHAPTER
XXXVIII

Any number of people might have been on the list of those who Tilon Ward didn't wish to see waiting at his mother's property when he returned from driving around Cargill and its surrounds, half-hoping to catch a glimpse of Sallie Kernigan or her vehicle, and all the time thinking about Donna Lee. High on that list would certainly have been Pruitt Dix, and not just because, even in repose, Dix possessed the demeanor of a man who got off on smothering infants. His malignant singularity made him also a fixture, if only in the abstract, on the lists even of those who had yet to encounter him, like a nightmare waiting to be lent flesh.

Dix was Randall Butcher's enforcer. Butcher maintained two faces. The first he displayed to the organs of federal and state government, including the Arkansas Alcoholic Beverage Control Division, the IRS, and anyone in possession of a badge. When Butcher wore that identity, he accessorized it with a suit and tie, and the genus of Little Rock lawyer that didn't need to advertise on highway billboards.

Randall Butcher's other face, the one with which Tilon was more familiar, was very different, typically complemented by jeans, a check shirt, the threat of violence, and its instrument in the guise of Pruitt Dix. But Dix rarely made house calls, and when he did, it was usually with an eye to ensuring that someone's health took a turn for the worse. Dix wasn't a big man, but God had packed a lot of meanness into that small space. Dix kept his head and face completely shaved, his dark eyebrows excepted, wore no earrings, and eschewed tattoos or other markings. Neither did he smoke or drink. His only vice was hurting people, and since this was how he made his living, it had assumed the status of a virtue.

Dix was leaning against a 1970 Chevy Chevelle LS6 in forest green. The paint looked as though it could have done with some work, but this neglect was deliberate. Beneath the shabby exterior, the body was pristine, and it boasted a 7.4-liter engine to make a dead man weep. The car stereo was playing some classical music that Tilon recognized from the meth labs, because Dix always determined the soundtrack while they worked.

Tilon could see his mother peering out through the kitchen window. He hoped she hadn't called the police. He could understand the impulse, but it would be better for all concerned if she resisted. He parked his truck alongside Dix's Chevy and got out.

"Pruitt," he said. "What brings you here?"

Dix didn't answer directly, but instead inclined a thumb toward the house.

"I told your momma I was a friend of yours. I didn't want her to become concerned."

His voice held just the faintest of lisps. It was the

kind of speech defect that children and ignorant men were tempted to mock and imitate. No one had done so in Pruitt Dix's presence for a very long time.

"No, we wouldn't want that," said Tilon.

"Maybe you ought to wave to her, just to confirm my bona fides."

Tilon waved a hand with all the enthusiasm of a man who fears having his fingers shot off. The drape on the window fell, and he could see his mother no longer.

"She seems like a nice lady," said Dix.

"She is."

"You think she still has urges?"

"What?"

"Needs—of a sexual nature."

"I don't know, Pruitt. I try not to speak of such matters with her."

"Just curious. Because your poppa's been gone a long time, right?"

"He has."

Dix had not blinked once since the conversation began. His eyes were yellow-green, like those of certain cats, and Tilon could not recall ever witnessing the dilation of their pupils. The neutral expression on Dix's face rarely changed, even when he was causing pain to another, and so it was difficult to know when one was being baited by him—with predictable consequences if one rose to it—or if one was merely engaged in an exchange with an entity that did not think or reason as other humans did.

"I would not be inclined to fuck her myself, you understand," said Dix. "It was by way of being a general inquiry into the physical appetites of her gender in the mature years."

Tilon had no desire to pursue the topic. He could not conceive of the workings of Dix's mind, but a day that had started as badly as a day could begin, short of his own extinction, now appeared intent on deteriorating still further.

"You still haven't told me why you're here," said Tilon.

"I'm here because you lied to Randall."

With Dix, it was important not to react. His placidity was only skin-deep, and he associated excessive displays of emotion with insincerity.

"I don't know what you mean," said Tilon. "I wouldn't lie to Randall about anything."

"You lied by omission. You neglected to inform him that it was you who found the Kernigan girl. He's curious as to why that might be."

It was fortunate for Tilon that he had already prepared himself for this eventuality. He had just not expected it to arrive so soon, although its inevitability was entirely a product of his own actions.

"I was in shock. It didn't seem to matter who found her, only that she was dead."

"Randall doesn't believe that was your call to make, under the circumstances."

"These aren't ordinary circumstances."

"Which is why he'd like to see you."

"When?"

"Now."

"I'm busy, Pruitt."

"Not so busy that you couldn't take time out for a beer at the Rhine Heart."

Tilon mentally ran through the faces at the bar in an effort to establish who might have ratted him out, unless Dix had been following him since this afternoon, which was unlikely. It could have been any one of the customers, but Tilon had the feeling it might have been Denny Rhinehart himself, which meant that Denny and Randall Butcher were closer than Tilon had believed. This realization did not make Tilon happy.

"I've been trying to find Sallie Kernigan before the cops do," he said. "I thought Denny might know where she was."

"Why? You want to console her in her time of loss?"

"She works for us."

"Does she?"

"She sells."

"I wasn't cognizant of that."

"It's a recent development."

"And when did you start taking such a direct interest in distribution?"

"We're going to need people on the ground when this Kovas business kicks off. I considered it advisable to begin cultivating contacts we could trust. Sallie has a good manner. People like being around her."

"Do they now?"

He sounded skeptical. Pruitt Dix didn't like being around people, with the exception of Randall Butcher. Enjoying the company of others was an alien concept to him.

"She might work for you," he said, "but *you* work for *us*."

"I work for Randall," Tilon corrected.

Dix's right hand jerked, as though he had only just restrained himself from inflicting an injury on the man before him. Tilon wondered how many others had been less fortunate, and ended up being deprived by Dix of the use of a limb, or blinded in one eye. And Dix had done worse than that: he'd buried bodies in the Ouachita for Randall Butcher.

"You do enjoy walking close to the edge, Tilon," he said.

"We have that in common, Pruitt."

Dix danced his fingers on the body of his car, permitting some of his anger to leach away through the action. Tilon would not have been shocked had the paintwork bubbled beneath Dix's touch.

"I can't go back without you," said Dix. "It would look bad."

"I'm asking for a few hours more. I'll be with Randall soon enough."

Dix mulled over this before nodding his acceptance. He slid behind the wheel of the Chevy in a single graceful movement, the action bequeathing a trace of his scent to the air. He smelled like the sediment in a vase of dead flowers.

"Were you fucking her, Tilon?" he asked through the open window.

The question threw Tilon.

"Who?" said Tilon, which was the wrong answer, and Dix let him see that he knew.

"Sallie," he said. "Who else would I be asking about?"

"No," said Tilon, "I wasn't fucking her."

Dix shrugged.

"Good-looking woman," he said. "I could understand it if you were. What about the daughter?"

"Randall asked me that already."

"And what did you say?"

"I told him 'No.' "

"I guess that clears it up. Shame about the girl, though. I hope they find Sallie soon. A mother has a right to know the fate of her child."

The car started with a growl, but Dix didn't gun it. That wasn't his style. Tilon watched him drive slowly away before returning to his apartment. His mother intercepted him in the yard.

"You ought to be more careful in your choice of friends," she said.

"He's not my friend."

"He said he was."

"He lied."

Tilon tried to pass around her, but she gripped his arm.

"Erma Glass called. She says the talk around town is that you found the Kernigan girl."

"That's right."

"You ought to have told me so."

"Why, Momma?"

"Because I got a right to know. I shouldn't have to wait to hear about it from the likes of Erma Glass."

Tilon's temper broke.

"What do you want me to tell you?" he shouted. "You want to know what was done to her? Is that what you want to hear? The one who killed her, he stuck branches in her, jammed them in her mouth and her privates, same as was done to Patricia Hartley and Estella Jackson. He fucked Donna Lee with a stick. He fucked her. With a *stick*. You happy now? You satisfied?"

His mother's face crumpled, and he took her in his arms.

"Jesus Lord," he said, and then he was crying too, and the sobs shook him so hard that he couldn't stay on his feet. He sank to his knees, and his mother descended with him.

Because she knew. God, she knew. She had eyes to see and ears to hear.

"What will I tell them if they come asking questions about her?" she whispered.

"Nothing," said Tilon. "Tell them nothing."

241

CHAPTER
XXXIX

Parker and Griffin were shown into a wood-paneled office that was too dark to be anything but depressing, and smelled like the lobby of an old folks' home. Four people were waiting for them: one woman and three men. None appeared particularly enthused by their arrival, but Jurel Cade looked more resentful than the rest.

"What's he doing here?" he asked Griffin, pointing the toe of a boot in Parker's direction.

"I could ask a similar question about your family," Griffin replied. "Last time I checked, none of them was an officer of the law."

"Just answer the damn question," said Cade.

"He's assisting us with our investigation. He's been sworn in as a volunteer member of the Cargill Police Department."

"Really?" said Cade. "Because last time I saw him, he was behind bars."

"That was a misunderstanding."

"Get him the fuck out of here, Griffin. I don't know—"

"Wait!"

The voice came from the man seated behind the desk. He was older than the others, and his presence, even seated, was imposing. Only the slightest tremble of his hands gave any obvious indication of infirmity, but Parker guessed he was in his early eighties, and the lineaments of his skull were clear to see beneath his skin, so that he might bear witness to his own impending mortality each time he looked in the mirror, and force all those who met him to do likewise.

This, then, was Pappy Cade.

"Who are you?" he said, addressing the question to Parker.

"My name is Charlie Parker. Chief Griffin asked me to assist with the investigation into the murders of Donna Lee Kernigan and Patricia Hartley, and I agreed."

"Patricia Hartley wasn't—" Jurel Cade started to interrupt, only to be quieted again by a look from his father.

"And what brought you down here to begin with?" said Pappy.

"I wanted to get closer to nature."

Pappy's washed-out blue eyes regarded Parker for a time before his death's head split, exposing gravestone teeth.

"Well, ain't you a character. Is that New York humor?"

"No, that's not humor at all."

Pappy's eyes flicked to Griffin.

"What would happen if I were to object to this man's involvement?"

"It wouldn't make much difference," said Griffin, "beyond disimproving my mood."

"I thought you might say that. Jurel?"

"Chief Griffin is entitled to hire and fire as

he sees fit. The county sheriff isn't obliged to cooperate, though, if he believes the appointment runs contrary to the best interests of law and justice."

"Did you just make that up?" said Parker.

"Fuck you."

"Because it sounded made up."

"I said—"

"Yeah, I heard you."

Griffin held up a hand. *God preserve me,* he thought, *from young hotheads.*

"I'd be obliged if we could discuss this in a civilized fashion, because I think we all have the best interests of the county—and law and justice—in mind."

The woman spoke for the first time.

"I agree," she said. "We should be more hospitable toward our new guest."

She appraised Parker openly, stopping just short of checking his dentition. "My name is Delphia, by the way, seeing as how we're to be spending time together. This is my younger brother, Nealus. Jurel, you've met. And our father, Delane, although he answers to Pappy."

Delphia Cade was as lean as her siblings, but her face was fuller, softening the ravenous look that was a family trait, so that being in their company was akin to confronting a pack of wolves. She was undeniably attractive, if only in a way that promised a great deal of trouble in return for only the barest of efforts. Her fingers were unadorned by rings, and she wore a single gold chain around her neck. Her hair was brown, and had been styled to disguise the fact it was thinning. Parker wondered if it might be stress, because as she rose to shake his hand he saw that the skin around her neck and ears was raw and irritated. Her grip was very firm, and she held his hand for slightly longer than was comfortable between strangers, so that he felt she was releasing him almost reluctantly. He resisted the urge to count his fingers when she was done.

Nealus didn't get up, but waved from his chair. He resembled a softer version of Jurel and Pappy, but was more of a clotheshorse than either. He was dressed in a blue blazer and tan pants combination more suited to an older man, and his shoes were brown slip-ons. He lacked only a monocle and a cocktail glass to complete the picture.

The woman who had shown in Griffin and Parker reappeared with coffee and pastries on a tray, and Nealus roused himself sufficiently, if only at his father's instigation, to source an extra chair for Parker once it became clear that the latter had no intention of absenting himself from proceedings. The woman poured the coffee, added milk and sugar as required, then left.

"I still think he has no cause to be here," said Jurel, this time without even indicating that Parker was the subject of his complaint. "This is police business—*local* police business."

"If it was just police business," said Griffin,

245

"we wouldn't be meeting in your daddy's study."

Parker noticed that he didn't look at Jurel when he spoke. His attention was fixed principally on Pappy, but his eyes did divert briefly toward Delphia. Here, then, was where the true Cade power resided, and none of it was being wielded in defense of Jurel. Griffin had slapped him down, and the others had permitted it to go unremarked.

"Your objection is noted, Jurel," said Pappy, "but we'll be moving along now."

An additional "there's a good boy" remained unspoken, but everyone heard it anyway. Jurel bristled, but held his tongue.

"So," said Pappy, "Donna Lee Kernigan. I believe that was the young woman's name."

"Correct," said Griffin.

"A terrible thing to have happened."

"Again," said Griffin.

"I'm sorry?"

"A terrible thing to have happened again, given that she now appears to be the second victim of the same killer, possibly even the third if we include Estella Jackson."

"There's no cause to connect Jackson to the other two," said Jurel.

"Are you now accepting that, in the case of Patricia Hartley, the coroner may have erred in his decision to declare her death accidental?" said Griffin.

"I'm not disputing the coroner's decision. I'm just saying."

"There are similarities among all three deaths," said Griffin.

"But with years separating them. And the details of Jackson's murder have been common knowledge for all that time. Half the county knows she died with sticks inside her."

"Are you suggesting a copycat?" said Pappy.

"I'm not suggesting anything, because I don't have the evidence for it," said Jurel. "It's the chief here who's jumping to conclusions."

"Eddy Rauls failed Estella Jackson," Griffin told Jurel, "and you and Loyd Holt failed Patricia Hartley. It's about time someone roused himself to do more than sit by and let this brutality continue."

"Jesus Christ," said Pappy, "it's like listening to dogs yap." He glanced at Parker. "You're keeping very quiet."

"Maybe I just like dogs," said Parker.

"Son, you seem hell-bent on riling me."

"With respect, I'm not your son."

"And with respect, I'm grateful. I have trouble enough with my own curs."

Pappy reached for his coffee. The cup rattled against the saucer, spilling some of the liquid, but he didn't seem to notice or care. He slurped noisily, but only Nealus reacted with discomfiture.

"Chief," said Pappy, once he had restored the cup to its resting place, "let me explain where we're at. Three Kovas executives, including the CEO, Rod Elvin, are due here next week for a final survey of sites in Cargill and Hamill, followed by a meeting with all interested parties in Little Rock to nail down the tax agreement. If everything goes well, we'll have signatures on the first contracts before the end of the month. This is a delicate point in the negotiations, and we need to avoid negative publicity, or anything that might cause Kovas to turn tail and run for Texas."

"We have girls dying, Mr. Cade," said Griffin. "That can't be ignored."

"I'm not asking you to ignore it, Evan."

Parker noticed that Pappy moderated his tone whenever he addressed Griffin directly. Here was a clever man, one used to getting his way, and as happy to use blandishments as threats. "I'm asking if any investigation can be . . ."

"Postponed?" Nealus suggested.

Pappy brightened, and smiled at his youngest offspring with delight, even a degree of surprise.

"Yes, postponed," he said. "But only until we have the deal locked down."

Griffin looked to Parker.

"You're the expert," he said. "You got an opinion on anything other than dogs?" There was a glint in his eye.

"Hold on," said Jurel Cade. "What kind of expertise are we talking about here?"

"Seven years with the NYPD," said Parker, "four as detective."

"Seven years?" said Jurel. "Hell, I got ten under my belt."

"In Burdon County," said Parker.

"Yeah, in Burdon County," said Jurel. "Crimes don't just happen in New York."

"Which is why we're here," said Parker. He addressed Pappy. "Look, Mr. Cade, police prioritize the first forty-eight hours in any criminal investigation for a reason. If we don't have a lead in that time, the chances of solving the crime halve. Unless we proceed quickly, Donna Lee Kernigan will join Patricia Hartley and Estella Jackson on the cold case list."

Parker decided to throw Jurel Cade a bone. He might not have liked the chief deputy much on initial acquaintance, but they were going to have to work together nonetheless, and Parker would have to ensure that any obstruction was kept to a minimum. If Griffin was correct, this was someone capable of interfering with a crime scene by pushing the naked body of a dead girl down a hill.

"The chief investigator here may be right to remain cautious about connecting the two latest killings with that of Estella Jackson," Parker continued, "but the fact remains that you've had two linked murders in the space of a few months, unless you're intent on persisting with the farce that Patricia Hartley's death might have been accidental."

Jurel seemed ready to do exactly that, but Parker saw Pappy Cade shake his head slightly, which was enough to settle the matter.

"That raises a number of possibilities," Parker continued. "Either the person responsible for the murder of Estella Jackson has returned to the area, and picked up where he—and it is a male, in all probability—left off; or an individual familiar with his activities has decided to imitate them: a copycat, as has been suggested.

"Two killings in that space of time represent fast work. These aren't the actions of someone who is cooling down for long between victims, which means either he's compulsive or he's enjoying it. Whichever it is, he's not going to stop, and the likelihood is that the gap between the murder of Donna Lee Kernigan and his next victim will be shorter still. He wants attention, but he's not getting it."

What Parker had to say next depressed him. It was necessary, if only to shock Jurel Cade and his father out of whatever remained of their torpor, but it went against all that he believed as a detective and a human being.

"Or he's not getting it," Parker concluded, "from killing young black women."

That changed the mood in the room, but only temporarily. The first words came, again unexpectedly, from Nealus Cade.

"My brother is of the opinion that these killings represent black-on-black violence," he said. "Isn't that right, Jurel?"

Once again, Jurel Cade was looking at his father, waiting for some cue, a signal to proceed, but it didn't come. Pappy was too busy recalculating the odds in the light of Parker's pronouncement.

"Jurel?" Nealus repeated.

"Yeah, that's what I thought," said Jurel, but he sounded distracted.

"On what basis?" said Parker.

"On the basis that it would be hard for a black man to abduct and kill two—three, whatever it might be—white girls in a small county like this, but easier for him to take women from his own community."

"What about a white man taking black girls?"Jurel was like a boxer, unused to taking hits, suddenly finding a soft fight turning into an ordeal.

"Yeah, well, that might also be easy," he conceded, "if he knew his way around."

"It requires a lot of rage to inflict that kind of damage on young women, Mr. Cade," said Griffin.

But before Pappy had a chance to respond, Delphia intervened.

"Mr. Parker, why are you so certain that a man is responsible?" she asked.

"I'm not," said Parker. "It's just more likely to be a male, for a whole bunch of reasons: the sexual component, for one, and the extreme violence, for another. Mostly, though, it's because that's just what some men do."

"You have a dim view of your own sex."

Parker didn't bother replying. He was already tired of her. Her every utterance came with a slight upturn of the lip, as though she found the world just amusing enough for a sneer and considered any effort to improve this existence, or moderate its injustices, to be a fool's errand.

"Delphia," said Pappy, "why don't you and Nealus go take a walk in the garden?"

"It's cold and damp outside," said Nealus.

"Then wear a coat."

"What about Jurel?" said Delphia.

"Last time I checked, he had a badge. You don't."

"You asked us to be here, and I have a right to stay. I'm the who's one up in Little Rock protecting our interests."

"And I'm the one that got us there!" said Pappy, slapping his right hand hard on the desk. "I asked you to leave us alone. Don't embarrass yourself further by inviting a forcible removal."

Nealus stood first.

"Come on, Phi," he said softly. "You're smarter than them all put together, so it's their loss."

Delphia didn't argue further. She took her cigarettes and a cell phone from her bag, and left without undue haste, only the faintest trace of redness to her cheeks betraying her sense of humiliation. Her father waited until she and her younger brother were gone before resuming the conversation.

"You really think he'll switch tracks?" he said to Parker. "That he'll start on white girls?"

Parker reminded himself that this might be the New South, but the old one lingered in the shadows, and whispered in the ears of men as long-lived as Delane Cade.

"He's not burying the remains, which means that part of the pleasure for him lies in their discovery.

There are men who kill for decades, and get away with it because they hide the evidence well. Every victim is an assemblage of clues, because the victim is the point of contact with the transgressor. If you don't want to be caught, the first step is not to leave a body."

"Wait: you're saying this man *wants* to be caught?"

"Not to the extent of giving himself up, but he probably accepts that his time is finite, which means he'll seek to do as much damage as he can before the net closes on him. So far, he's killed at least two young women, with an increase in sadism between the first and second, but with little return from his perspective in terms of exposure. It means he has to up his game. By his logic, the deaths of young black women may not appear to be of sufficient interest to the police, or even the media. If that's the case, he'll have to find a victim that might be."

"Why is he doing this?" said Pappy.

"That's a very good question. As I said before, compulsion or enjoyment—or a combination of both, because they're not the same thing."

"What I mean is, why now?"

Once again, Parker thought that Pappy Cade was a very shrewd man.

"You're wondering if it might be connected to Kovas," said Parker.

"Aren't you? You're the expert talking about finite periods."

"It had struck me as a possibility, although an extreme one."

"Like the chief here said, whoever did this has a lot of hate," said Pappy. "Well, there's a lot of hate in this county, and no small amount of it is directed at our family."

"Why?"

"Because we're wealthier than most. We have a degree of power."

"That typically fuels resentment, not outright hatred."

"Which is a very fine distinction, and one on which I would be reluctant to bet a life."

"Kovas's arrival will bring prosperity to this region," said Parker. "From what I've heard, even those with cause to dislike you and your family will start making money."

"I've met men who'd sacrifice the prospect of wealth if it meant their enemies suffered as a consequence."

"Are you that kind of man, Mr. Cade?"

Beside him, he heard Griffin draw, and hold, a breath. Pappy nodded, as though Parker's words had confirmed a suspicion, and this knowledge might have to be acted upon in the future.

"No, I always valued money more," he said. "But I've done my share of harm to others in the course of my life—harm, and more than harm. That's all in the past, though. I decided it wasn't much of a legacy to bequeath."

"If you could compile a list of those who haven't

made similar moral and philosophical progress, I'd be interested to see it."

"I can give it to you now: Ferdy Bowers, Randall Butcher, and a handful of politicians up in Little Rock, but I don't see any of them cutting up young girls."

"Not even Randall Butcher?" said Parker.

"His name isn't his nature," said Pappy. "Randall Butcher is a man of low breeding, but he aspires to respectability."

"Will he achieve it?"

"Not in this state. He'll have to go where people don't know him, to a place where his lineage is not a source of contempt, even among those born to the shoeless."

"He might be worth talking to anyway, regardless of his breeding," said Parker.

"So does this mean we have accepted the necessity of a proper investigation," said Griffin, "one in which we can rely on the cooperation of the sheriff's office?"

Jurel Cade had remained silent throughout this exchange. He saw that the dynamic had altered, and was waiting to learn how it might affect him. Now, with his father's agreement to supply information, the contours of the new landscape had become more apparent.

"Jurel?" said his father.

"We don't involve the state police," Jurel replied. "We keep it between the Cargill PD and the sheriff's office."

255

"The state police have expertise and resources that we don't," said Griffin.

"But they don't understand the county like we do," said Cade. "And you have your expertise sitting next to you. You told us so."

Griffin looked at Parker, who shrugged. It wasn't his call to make. He and Griffin were conducting a negotiation, and their priority was to emerge from it having gained more than they lost.

"Agreed, reluctantly," said Griffin.

"Anything else?" said Pappy.

"Nobody talks to the newspapers or TV," said Jurel, "beyond what's required for the dissemination of vital information."

"Hard to keep a lid on murder," said Parker.

"We'll manage," said Jurel. "We've done it before."

"Yes," said Parker, without admiration, "you have."

"Aided by the fact that we own the *Burdon County Courant*, and five other papers across the state," said Pappy. "We got a share in one of the TV channels too. As for the others, I can make calls if required. They all have eyes on the Kovas tit."

"I have some demands too," said Griffin.

"Go on," said Pappy.

"Complete access to all sheriff's office records relating to Patricia Hartley and Estella Jackson."

Parker knew there would be little or nothing relating to Hartley, but the Jackson material might prove important.

"Agreed," said Pappy, before Jurel could answer. He waited. "What else?"

256

"Cargill PD takes the lead on this, not the sheriff's office. No decisions are taken, no moves made, without my approval."

"Not happening," said Jurel.

"Agreed," said Pappy.

"Wait a minute—" said Jurel.

"It's done, son," said Pappy. "Learn to live with it. Is that all?"

"That's all," said Griffin.

"It's not much."

"It's more than I had before."

Pappy Cade stood and extended a hand to each of the visitors. He didn't bother asking to be kept apprised of progress. His son would take care of that, but Pappy was shrewd enough to realize that if Griffin and Parker were intent upon keeping any details from him, then asking them not to do so at this juncture would be like pissing into the wind. Yet he was convinced that Evan Griffin was an honorable man. It was one of the chief's weaknesses. As for Parker, Pappy was not yet in a position to speculate.

"I'm sure you three have a lot to talk about," he said, "but I'd appreciate a moment alone with the chief investigator before you begin."

Griffin and Parker moved toward the door, but it opened before they could reach it, and the housekeeper arrived to escort them to the anteroom. Either she'd been listening at the keyhole or Pappy Cade had a silent button on his desk.

Once they were gone and the door had closed

behind them, Pappy leaned back in his chair and let the trembling seize him in earnest. He could control it for a time, usually by pressing down on a hard surface, or holding one hand in the other, but when he finally gave up, the shakes returned in spades.

"Your feelings wounded?" he said to his son.

Jurel Cade stared at the floor. Were this any other man, Jurel would have had a grip on his throat by now.

"Why allow me to be present at all," he said, "if your intention was to demean me?"

"Is that what you think was done here?"

"What else could it be?"

"Think, Jurel. What have we given up?"

"My authority in the county, or did I just mishear?"

"Words. Lip service. You proceed as you always have, and let Griffin believe what he wants. He won't solve these killings. He doesn't have the manpower or the skill. If he finds out anything useful, we'll know soon enough, but you decide what should be shared with him and what needs to be held back."

"And Parker?"

"Find out everything you can about him," he said. "And hear me, Jurel: I want whoever is slaying these girls to be dead or behind bars within a week."

Pappy closed his eyes.

"Preferably dead."

CHAPTER
XL

Parker and Griffin drove back to Cargill. They'd spent a further fifteen minutes outside with Jurel Cade going over the particulars of how the investigation should proceed. Now that he had his father's imprimatur on progress, Jurel was more conciliatory than before, but it remained to be seen how that might reveal itself in practical terms.

By now the day was almost done, and the light had taken on a funereal tone; bare deciduous trees smeared the sky, and the forest was like an encroaching darkness on the land. Parker felt a familiar lassitude begin to descend. Evening and night were hardest for him. That was when he missed Susan and Jennifer most, and in a way different from morning. Waking, that dawning recollection of loss, was like the reopening of a wound, ferocious in the suddenness of its pain; night, by contrast, was a slow, dull ache that ended only fitfully with sleep, there to mutate into visions of the dead, dreams in which his wife and daughter spoke to him in a language he could not understand, and died over and over in ways that bore no relation to the truth of their passing. They drowned, they burned, they suffocated behind plastic, all the time their lips moving, enunciating words that had meaning only for them, as though in leaving one world for another they had inherited a new dialect, an idiom unintelligible to the living.

Yet in daylight, when he talked with his dead wife as he drove, when he addressed his lost child as he shaved, they were entirely comprehensible to him, and he to them.

But he feared that the latter discourse might be less real than the former.

Griffin spoke, tearing him from his meditations.

"What?" said Parker.

"I said that you never told me why you came back."

Parker barely gave the question thought.

"To distract myself," he said.

Griffin chose not to ask him from what. He had no need.

"Is that all?"

The briefest of pauses.

"Yes."

"Well, I never expressed my gratitude."

"Save it till later. Even then, you may not have cause to thank me when we're done."

Griffin tried to speak lightly—"You of a mind to cause trouble?"—as Parker's thumb explored the grazed knuckles of his fingers.

"It doesn't matter whether I am or not. Either way, it'll come once we start asking questions. The Cades won't be able to prevent it, and neither will you, even if you had the motivation."

"Why do you say that?"

"Because you're using me. If this investigation stirs people up, or endangers the Kovas deal,

260

you'll be able to blame some of the fallout on me. I provide an element of deniability—not much, but enough for you to survive if it all goes bad. I can also rattle cages that you can't, and if anyone complains, you'll be empowered to make sympathetic noises and promise it won't happen again."

"That's a hell of an accusation to make."

"Feel free to deny it."

Griffin didn't bother. He might never have expressed it in those terms, or even have admitted it to himself, but now that Parker had come out with it, he knew it to be true. He could only hope to make the local population understand that it was a question of degree: the potential harm this inquisition might cause to their hopes of prosperity versus the certain damage that would follow if another young woman died.

"And the Cades," said Parker, "are doing the same with us. That's why Pappy acceded so quickly to your demand for control of the investigation. He believes you'll fail, and any harm you cause will rebound on you and your department. In the meantime, he'll reassure Kovas in an effort to protect the deal."

This, too, was unworthy of argument from Griffin. Pappy hadn't conceded anything to them that he hadn't already written off long before they arrived at his door.

"What did you think of the Cades?" Griffin asked.

261

"I don't like any of them."

"It's a reasonable response."

"Is it the wrong one?"

"That depends on what you require of them, but I'll admit that none is without specific failings. Pappy is a pragmatist, but genuine in his desire to vouchsafe affluence to the county, if only for the sake of his own vanity. Jurel can be an astute investigator, and he's been good for the sheriff's office, more or less, but he's his daddy's instrument, if you hadn't already noticed. He's also selective in his inquiries, and immoral in his methods.

"Delphia is her father's eyes and ears in Little Rock, and takes care of the day-to-day running of the family businesses, but has no kindness in her, and is incautious about making political enemies. She's the only one that's married—to the Cade family lawyer, or one of the lawyers, although he tomcats around on her, and she cuckolds him in turn, so rumor has it. His name is Branstetter, but she never took it. There's talk of a divorce on the horizon, with Branstetter currently calculating the price for his silence."

"Silence?" said Parker.

"Nothing down here is straight. Draw a line with a ruler, and it comes out crooked. Branstetter isn't only a lawyer: he's also a bagman. He's smoothed out a lot of problems on the Kovas front, aided by a logroller named Charles Shire, who's been looking after Kovas's interests down here. Spousal privilege meant that the Cades had some protection should federal investigators have shown an interest in the more irregular specifics of the negotiations—unlikely, given that Arkansas owns the White House, but one can't be too careful. I mean, look at Whitewater: no one is entirely safe, not even behind locked doors on Pennsylvania Avenue. The Cades have supported the Clintons since Bubba ran for the House against Hammerschmidt in '74, and Pappy is owed favors in return, some of which he might have called in for Kovas. But if Branstetter were to roll over in the event of a divorce, well, there's no telling where the indictments could end. So he'll earn himself a nice payoff for all those years spent sharing a bed with Delphia Cade, and be thankful that he emerged at the end with his cock and balls still attached to the rest of him."

"And Nealus?"

"Doesn't look like much, does he?"

"No, I can't say that he does."

"Oddly, he's the only Cade that the majority can abide without equivocation. He cared for his mother in her final illness, and now sits on the board of a couple of charities related to cancer and Parkinson's, because Martha Cade suffered from a combination of both. He's also heavily involved in environmental causes, not entirely unrelated to the fact that it annoys his sister and his old man. He might even qualify as a moderating influence on his father, if such a thing were possible."

"The Cades' mother had Parkinson's?"

"That's right."

"Interesting," said Parker.

"Why?"

"I think Pappy may also have it."

"Yeah, I saw the twitches. If that's true, he's keeping quiet about the diagnosis."

"Perhaps he doesn't want to admit to weakness, not with his precious accord so close to completion."

"That could be it."

They passed the town line, and shortly after entered Cargill itself. Griffin drove Parker straight to his motel.

"I had Billie make up a dossier for you," he said. "It should be waiting at the reception desk. It's got local maps, a list of names of some of our more noteworthy citizens, phone numbers, whatever she felt might be useful. You think of anything else you require, you just have to ask. Keep receipts for expenses, and we've cleared a desk for you at the station house in case you want to use it. Tomorrow we can figure out a division of labor, but I'll be guided by you as far as possible. After all, you've done this kind of thing before."

"And Jurel?"

"He won't be actively obstructive. Like his daddy, he's ultimately a pragmatist."

Parker pictured Patricia Hartley's body, battered and broken by a slope of stone and scree.

"Yes," said Parker, "I suppose he is."

CHAPTER
XLI

Randall Butcher wasn't a man to hide how he made his money—or not the money he made by legal means; he felt it was better to remain more discreet about the funds that had accrued from methamphetamine, heroin, and a quantity of cocaine for the high-fliers. It gave him pleasure to watch congressmen, state senators, and even the odd preacher tramp across the parking lot of the Gilded Cage, the first—and, so far, finest—of the gentleman's establishments that formed the backbone of his entertainment operation. They might have liked to pretend that they were superior to Butcher, their shit smelling of rose petals, but when they required money for their campaigns, or cash to keep God's work going, he ensured that they or their representatives had to travel to his principal place of business to ask for it. A little dose of reality wouldn't hurt them, a reminder that they were just like other men, and if they wanted to stay awhile and enjoy the show, he'd comp them a couple of drinks and a plate of ribs.

The Gilded Cage wasn't on a par with the better clubs in Miami, or even New Orleans—this was Burdon County, Arkansas, where most strip joints claimed to be high-toned if you didn't find cigarette ash in your drink—but it had professional lighting and sound systems, two bars, four seating areas, including a VIP room, and televisions for every eyeline. More pertinently, it also boasted dancers men would drive long distances to see naked, women who could carry on a conversation without making a patron want to scour his ears out after. The food was prepared fresh, and the price of drinks was just high enough to dissuade the impecunious. It had a dress code—no shorts, no wifebeaters—and a strict no-touching rule in both public and private sections. The Gilded Cage, insofar as any strip club could be, was a clean house.

Butcher was a blond man of average height, soft in some of the wrong places and hard in most of the right ones. He'd run with a rough crowd in his youth, yet somehow had avoided any convictions or jail time. When a couple of those old friends came calling later in life, he'd put them to good use in the more caliginous regions of his realm, while keeping them far removed from his clubs, because he didn't want his legitimate interests tainted by any association with criminals. A few years earlier, Butcher had even been feted at the annual Gentlemen's Club EXPO, the industry's national convention and trade show, narrowly missing out on a nomination for Club of the Year. (Or so he'd been informed: Randall Butcher might have been clean, but he wasn't *that* clean.)

With the combination of income streams from flesh and drugs, Butcher should have been living high on the hog. The fact that this wasn't the case was largely down to a run of bad investments, and a mistaken belief that he knew better than his financial advisors, a conviction unaltered by his growing losses. Increasingly, he required drug income to subsidize his speculations and atone for the bad advice picked up from business magazines, crooked accountants, disbarred lawyers, fortune-tellers, homeless guys at bus stops—wherever it was that Butcher acquired his immaculately misguided financial nous.

The impending touchdown of Kovas Industries in Burdon County promised a way for Butcher to dig himself out of debt—and not only in the form of the Gilded Cage II, his proposed club in Cargill, currently blocked by shortsighted zoning regulations. Through an intermediary, Butcher had also quietly put money into two construction companies that had barely been getting by in recent years, on the grounds that each had been promised subcontractor roles as soon as the ink dried on the Kovas paperwork. A third contractor was ready to move in and demolish the old church at the center of the planning dispute and raise the new club in its place, with the intention of having it up and running before Kovas's construction workers even got their boots dirty. His lawyers assured him that the zoning difficulties were slowly but surely being dealt with, which left only the problem of Reverend Nathan Pettle and his congregation.

Butcher had visited the reverend personally in an attempt to reason with him. He regarded Pettle as a fundamentally benign but misguided man, as evinced by the image of the black Jesus that hung on the wall of Pettle's home, since everyone knew Jesus was Caucasian—or at worst tanned, like a white man who'd spent too long working in the sun. But Pettle wasn't shifting on his conditions: in return for ceding the site to Butcher, he wanted a location of similar size within the town limits, and a cash sweetener, both of which presented difficulties because, so far, Butcher had neither the site nor the cash.

From the window of his office in a small two-story block behind the Gilded Cage, he took in Tilon Ward's slow approach across the lot. Butcher had known Tilon's father, which wasn't much in the way of a boast, Hollis Ward having been a sexually incontinent man of base predilections. His disappearance had been the best outcome for all concerned, Hollis himself perhaps excepted, depending on his ultimate fate. The son had inherited certain of the father's skills without the vices that went with them, or so Butcher had believed, but recent developments now required a reconsideration of their relationship.

Behind Butcher, Pruitt Dix shifted in a chair. Butcher could see him reflected in the glass. There was a doglike aspect to Dix, he thought: his loyalty, his stocky muscularity.

Also, he liked burying things.

CHAPTER
XLII

Parker entered his motel room to find a message asking him to contact the front desk. He made the call, and was informed that the Cargill PD would be covering the bill for the duration of his stay, and he was being upgraded to the motel's honeymoon suite. He could pick up the key at his convenience, along with an envelope dropped off by Billie Brinton. Parker packed his bag and retrieved the .38 from under the bed. He had never entirely reconciled himself to his father's gun, yet neither could he relieve himself of its burden. It had become a symbol of the past, a physical expression of the weight of his history.

In the silence of his room, he hefted the Smith & Wesson before pointing it at the shadows gathered in one corner.

"Come out," he said. "Show yourself."

From the darkness he conjured up the figure of a man, with a blade in his hand and blood on his skin, but faceless as his victims. Parker wondered how often this creature had watched him, both before and after stealing away his wife and child. He was aware of the taint of the killer's regard, like a fingerprint upon the soul. Somewhere, he was waiting to see how Parker might respond. He might even be here in this town, another traveler passing through, studiedly anonymous, staring at the closed drapes in the window of a cheap motel room, imagining the life of the man behind them, in all its devastation.

Parker lowered the gun, stored it in the bag, and replaced it with the holstered 10 mm. He slipped it onto his belt, and positioned the weapon under his jacket so that it was barely visible. Now that he was attached to the Cargill PD, he felt more comfortable about carrying concealed. Once all this was done, he gathered his belongings, left the room, and locked the door behind him. Only three other vehicles sat in the lot, and all were empty. He was the object of no one's attention, or none that he could see, and the evening air smelled of burning.

Evan Griffin's bones ached. He intended to run a bath when he got home in order to soak away the day's events, but first he wanted to talk to Kel Knight and establish what progress, if any, his officers had made in his absence.

Tucker McKenzie had finished his work at the Kernigan house and at the scene of the body's discovery, and was promising a full report by morning. According to Knight, the house search had produced little of note beyond the meth and the gun. If Donna Lee had been seeing someone—an older white man, if her school friend was to be believed—he had left no trace of his presence in her daily life. A canvass of the neighborhood around the school had so far served only to

270

confirm that none of the residents interviewed had noticed the truck that picked up Donna Lee after band practice. The police would continue trying to establish her movements from that moment on, but for now it remained the last time anyone had seen her alive.

And still no trace had been found of Sallie Kernigan, although Malvern PD confirmed that there was no record of her arrest on charges of solicitation, nor did any Malvern gossip suggest she had engaged in acts of prostitution, as intimated by some of her neighbors. Naylor had also driven out to her place of work, but had returned with no new information other than that Sallie appeared to have been well liked by her co-workers. She'd had some trouble with men "taking liberties," according to one of her fellow cleaners, a woman named Bobbye Osborne, who reminded Naylor of a younger version of his mother, but she'd learned to deal with it.

"You have to, when you're a woman," said Bobbye Osborne, "and more when you're a black woman."

Naylor hadn't disagreed.

Then Griffin told Knight of the meeting with the Cades, and the promise of cooperation from Jurel Cade and the sheriff's office.

"What about Parker?" said Knight.

"At first, Jurel wasn't pleased to learn of his involvement, but he mellowed in the end, relatively speaking."

"Because Pappy ordered him to?"

"Perhaps 'advised' would be more appropriate, for the sake of appearances."

"So what next?" said Knight.

"We see what evidence hasn't been lost or destroyed from the Jackson and Hartley killings, and work on establishing connections between those women and Donna Lee."

"What if they were just random victims?"

"It's of no account. The same man likely killed at least two of them, and he's either local or has passed through here on occasion, enough to know the lay of the land. By tomorrow we should have more names to add to the list of people we need to talk to."

Before leaving the Cade compound, Griffin had asked Jurel to help compile a record of known sex offenders in the county, along with those residents whose racism veered toward the extreme. Billie Brinton had already done the same for Cargill and the surrounding area, regardless of whether the individuals in question had ever been convicted of, or even charged with, any crime. It was, the chief decided, depressingly long for a small town.

"Anything else?" he said.

"Only that the discovery of the meth in the Kernigan house, along with the unregistered firearm, has got me thinking again about Tilon Ward."

"He knows more about the Kernigans than he's telling us, I'll grant you that," said Griffin.

"Tilon Ward is a criminal," said Knight. "All criminals are, by nature or proclivity, dishonest."

"I still don't make Tilon for a killer."

"I'm not suggesting he is, only that his secrecy could be an impediment to progress."

Knight wanted to say more, but did not. It was not for him to remind Griffin that he had no obligations toward Tilon Ward, no matter what Ward might have done, or tried to do, for him in the past.

"You may be right," said Griffin. "You want to take a run at him, see if you can succeed where I couldn't?"

"I already dropped by his place. According to his mother, he left an hour or so earlier, and she couldn't say when he'd be back."

"Did she tell you where he went?"

"She claimed not to know."

"Claimed?"

"I was reluctant to believe her."

"We can try again come morning. Who's on duty tonight?"

"Petrie and Giddons." Two of the part-timers. "And I'll hang on for a while, just in case. I took a nap earlier, so I'm good to go."

Which might or might not have been true, but Griffin didn't object. He wanted time at home, and not only to eat and bathe. He required space to think.

"Did Billie clear that desk for Parker like I told her?"

"Over by the window."

"You could look happier about it. We have an investigation in progress, and some of the expert help we needed."

"This is me looking happy."

"If you say so." Griffin headed for the door. "But that'll teach you to be careful what you wish for."

CHAPTER
XLIII

The motel's honeymoon suite wasn't exactly somewhere a bride would choose to spend her wedding night, not unless she'd been around the block a few times and was happy to settle for a roof over her head and a kitchenette with a toaster oven. It did come with a seating area: a couch that erred on the side of firm, and a pair of easy chairs that weren't noticeably easy at all. Parker spread his notes over the burn-scarred coffee table, along with a detailed map of the county, and commenced drawing up a rough plan of action for the days to come. He'd have to wait until morning to see if Billie Brinton could find contact details for the family of Patricia Hartley down in Lucedale, Mississippi, since Jurel Cade claimed to be unable to help. According to Jurel, the Hartleys weren't actually staying in a property owned by the Cade family, and he wasn't sure if they even had a telephone.

Parker realized that he hadn't eaten. Although he was tired, the prospect of spending the evening in his new accommodations seemed both dispiriting and pointless. The murder of Donna Lee Kernigan was likely to be the main subject of discussion in Cargill that evening, and if a man sat quietly in a bar, pretending to mind his own business, he might learn a lot, assuming the news about his appointment to the local police department had not yet circulated too widely. To combat his tiredness, Parker changed his shoes, an old trick he'd learned from his days on the force, and picked up the novel he'd been trying to read for weeks: *Ivanhoe* by Sir Walter Scott. He had wanted something entirely removed from his own experience, and in which he could lose himself when he chose, but had not been able to concentrate on a book in weeks. His thoughts kept drifting to the dead, and their voices called to him from a past that now belonged to another man. He folded the novel inside a copy of the *Burdon County Courant* that the motel had provided free of charge. He'd attract less attention with reading material before him, although he supposed that depended upon the nature of the bar in which he ended up. There were drinking establishments in which a man with a book would draw the kind of interest more usually associated with dancing bears and snake charmers on the basis of novelty value alone.

He left his room, and stood for a time watching cars and trucks roll by. Music drifted from Boyd's: Townes Van Zandt had usurped the Eagles, however temporarily, which could only be considered an improvement. A brand-new Lumina pulled into the motel's parking lot: a classic rental car, confirmed by the Hertz rental agreement visible on the dash as it pulled into a space close to Parker. Two men emerged, both dressed in business suits, but only one of them looked like a businessman. The other was textbook private security, from the bristles on his mustache to the gun in the shoulder rig that his too-tight jacket failed to disguise. Lack of concealment was probably the point, Parker thought, because this did not strike him as a man who cared to hide his worst aspects. He carried himself like one permanently poised to inflict violence, and who would require scant cause to do so, if any cause at all. His gaze, as it drifted over Parker, was like being showered with effluent.

Parker waited for the two men to head into the motel lobby before taking a stroll past the car. The seats were empty and clean, but the rental agreement on the dashboard bore the name Charles Shire, and the corporate discount came from Torviva Industries, S.A. From Griffin, Parker knew that Torviva, registered in Switzerland, was Kovas's parent company. He wondered whether the visit was bad timing, or if all of the Cades' efforts had been for naught and Kovas had sent Shire, its fixer, to find out exactly what was happening in Cargill.

CHAPTER
XLIV

A similar question regarding events in Cargill, although less politely expressed, had just been posed in Randall Butcher's office. Unfortunately, Tilon Ward didn't have an answer, or none that Butcher wanted to hear.

"Another killing," said Tilon. "That's what the fuck has happened."

"Are you trying to be funny?"

"No, Randall," said Tilon, and he wasn't. The fact that he was in Butcher's office, with Pruitt Dix hovering in the background, was an indication that the situation was about as far from funny as one could get without blood and weeping. Only under exceptional circumstances did Tilon Ward find himself in these surroundings, Randall Butcher, as has already been established, being minded to maintain degrees of separation between his legal and illegal activities.

"Why didn't you tell me it was you that found the body when we spoke earlier?" said Butcher.

"I was in shock."

"You never seen a dead body before?"

"Not a young girl's naked body, and not one impaled with sticks."

"Is that all?"

"I don't know what you mean."

Tilon heard movement behind him and sensed

that Dix had drawn nearer. He didn't turn to look, though. He didn't want to see Dix's eyes, or have Dix stare into his.

"I think you do," said Butcher softly, "and if I were you, I'd be very careful how I answer the next question, because I'm already unhappy about having to ask it again: Were you sleeping with her?"

Tilon wasn't careful.

"Who?" he said, and a second later Pruitt Dix sliced at Tilon's right ear with an ivory-handled pocket blade, neatly splitting the lobe. The injury instantly began to bleed heavily, soaking Tilon's shirt and jeans and releasing droplets to explode on Butcher's wood floor. Tilon screamed in pain and cupped his right hand to the wound, the blood dripping through his fingers and tears springing from his eyes.

"The next time," said Butcher, "I'll let Pruitt take the whole ear. Now, were you or were you not fucking Donna Lee Kernigan?"

How did he know? Tilon wondered. *We'd been so careful.*

"Yes," he said. "I was fucking her."

Butcher smiled at Dix, still hovering over Tilon. "See, I told you so," he said. "He has his old man's taste for tender meat."

He returned his attention to Tilon.

"Pruitt here was sure you were sleeping with the mother, but I informed him he was mistaken. The apple don't fall far from the tree, and your daddy always did have a problem counting the years when it came to women."

Butcher dug a cloth napkin from a container in the corner of the office, where he kept the better tableware for the club's VIP area, and handed it to Tilon, who pressed it against his ear.

"Did you kill her, Tilon? Was it you that left her out there with a stick at each end?"

Tilon stared at the floor.

"No, I didn't kill her."

"You sure?"

"I cared about her."

"Yeah, you're a regular romantic, sleeping with girls young enough to be your daughter. Do the police know?"

"No."

"They will, soon enough. If I could figure it out—and I don't even live in your godforsaken town—then others will too, and that little girl probably talked to her friends about you."

"She didn't. I told her not to."

"And you think she listened to you? She was a teenage girl. If she could keep anything to herself, she wasn't human. What about the mother? Did she know about you and her child?"

Tilon didn't reply.

"Jesus, Tilon. Was that why you was asking after Sallie Kernigan at the Rhine Heart, so you could make sure she kept her mouth closed?"

Tilon nodded. He'd have serious words with Denny Rhinehart once all this was done. If a man couldn't trust his bartender, whom could he trust?

"What did you give Sallie: some freebies, a discount?"

"Both, like I told Pruitt."

He decided not to mention the gun. It would only enrage Butcher still further.

"You told Pruitt you were cultivating her as a dealer."

"That too."

"Bullshit, or near as. And in return for your largesse, she let you sleep with her daughter? That's some good parenting right there."

Butcher sat against his desk. The beat of the music was barely audible from the club next door. He'd largely ceased to notice the noise, but when he did, he found it annoying.

"When did you last see the girl?" Butcher asked.

"Early Saturday morning. I took her to my place Friday night. My momma was visiting her sister in Dumas. She has cancer."

"I'm sorry to hear that. Still, to every cloud. So Donna Lee stayed over?"

"Yes."

"And then you drove her home next day?"

"No, I dropped her off on Vervain."

A number of the roads in Cargill were named after Arkansas wildflowers: Vervain Street, Indian Paintbrush Lane, Goldenrod Way. It made them sound prettier than they were.

"Not many houses around there. You really didn't want to be seen with her, did you, Tilon?"

"No, but it was close enough for her to be able to walk home. You the police now, Randall?"

"You want Pruitt to even up your earlobes?"

"No."

"Then shut up and answer my questions. What time was that?"

"Before seven, maybe. It was still dark."

"You check to make sure she got back okay? You call or anything?"

"No."

"Doesn't say much for your solicitude. You might have cared about her, but you didn't care enough. You figure she's dead because you didn't drive her to her front door?"

Tilon didn't reply.

"Answer me, goddamn you."

"Yes," said Tilon softly.

Butcher eased himself from his perch and squatted before Tilon.

"You know, Tilon, I was seriously considering having Pruitt take you into the Ouachita and let you dig your own grave, all the trouble you risk bringing down on us because you share your daddy's appetites, but it would likely have caused more problems than it solved. Also, right now you cook the best meth in the state, and I'm in need of the cash flow generated by your expertise.

"But Jurel Cade has a hard-on for you, and old Pappy might see a way of using you to get at me, because that old bastard could hear a coonfart in a thunderstorm, and nothing in Burdon County stays hidden from him for long. All things considered, it might be better if you were to disappear for a while. I have a place you can stay before you head back into the woods and get to cooking."

"Won't that make the police suspicious?"

"You got an alibi for the rest of the weekend?"

"Mostly I was home. I sat up late Saturday with my momma watching movies on cable. She has trouble sleeping."

"Police know this?"

"I believe I told them so, or near enough."

"There you are. You got nothing to worry about."

Tilon wasn't certain of that. He slept in quarters away from the main house, so it wouldn't have been difficult for him to slip out without his mother noticing, apart from the noise of his truck. He therefore remained vulnerable to suspicion.

Butcher stood, and began moving papers around on his desk. The conversation was clearly drawing to a close.

"What about my momma?" asked Tilon.

"Pruitt will swing by, let her know you're safe, if that'll put your mind to rest."

It wouldn't, but Tilon let it slide. He wasn't in a position to argue.

"In the meantime, we'll start assembling the ingredients," said Butcher. "We're short on muriatic, but that won't take long to fix."

Muriatic—or hydrochloric—acid could be bought in most hardware stores, especially those with a pool section. But locals weren't doing much with their pools in February, and large purchases risked drawing attention. Butcher had a couple of tame suppliers, but he'd also been stockpiling industrial-sized buckets of drain cleaner, just in case.

"And lye," Dix added. "We're going to need lye."

Lye was used to neutralize any excess acid in the manufacturing process, but it served other purposes as well. Tilon returned to an incident a year or so earlier, when Dix had asked him to take a look at a stainless-steel cylinder out by one of the cookhouses because he thought there was something hinky about it. Tilon had opened it up and caught the smell at the same time as he saw the syrupy brown mix, and picked out what was left of the skeleton poking from the fluid. He could still hear the echo of Dix's laughter as he threw up.

Dix placed his hands on Tilon's shoulders.

"No hard feelings," he whispered into Tilon's uninjured ear.

Tilon shook his head, and wished he'd run when he had the chance.

CHAPTER
XLV

Reverend Nathan Pettle stood before his congregation, his wife seated in the front row alongside their daughter, Melissa, who was in the year below Donna Lee Kernigan at Hindman High, and had known her by sight. The Pettles' only son, Robert, was an electrical engineering major at the University of Arkansas up in Fayetteville. He'd offered to come down and lend his support to the community, being that kind of boy, but his father had instructed him to stay where he was. Pettle had been assured of a place for Robert at Kovas after his graduation, a small acknowledgment from the company of the reverend's support for its endeavors, and the last thing he wanted was for Robert to be in any way associated with the fallout from Donna Lee's murder. Robert had a conscience, which was good, but had yet to learn when it was appropriate to speak truth to power, and when it was better to keep one's mouth shut in order to determine which way the wind was blowing. Right now, that wind was blowing the stink from Donna Lee Kernigan's corpse straight into Nathan Pettle's face.

Robert was also better than his younger sister at gauging the relative health of his parents' relationship, so the increased tension between husband and wife was unlikely to escape him.

Even Melissa's teenage self-absorption had been pierced by the barely concealed rancor in the family home, although she hadn't yet raised the subject. In any case, she was more likely to broach it with her mother than her father, and Lord knew how Delores might answer, especially in her current mood.

And there *was* Delores, glaring up at him, wishing she could expose him for the hypocrite he was, imagining herself standing before these fine people, her husband's flock, and announcing that he, their shepherd, had fucked the mother of the girl they were gathered here to mourn, fucked her like the low-life animal he was. Maybe he'd have to exercise both his husbandly and pastoral authority once they were alone, and remind her that, regardless of the resentment she persisted in harboring toward him for his failings, a young girl was dead, and she ought to set aside her bitterness and weep for this lost life, and possibly shed a tear for Sallie Kernigan, wherever she was. Yes, he might just do that.

Or, he thought—because Delores's face seemed in that instant to grow hard, as though she were eavesdropping on his musings—he might not.

The choir reached the conclusion of "Little Innocent Lamb." Pettle had made the hymn selections himself, and the assembly had already been treated to "There Is a Balm in Gilead" and "Jesus Lay Your Head in the Window." Even if he was a sinner, Pettle knew how to put together a service.

The last notes faded, but he allowed a moment or two longer for the silence to bed down. Just as he was about to speak, the rear door of the church opened, and a man appeared, a single white face among the black.

And Pettle had to bite his tongue to stop himself from swearing aloud.

CHAPTER
XLVI

Evan Griffin had taken his bath and changed into fresh clothes. He'd also instructed Kevin Naylor to attend the hastily convened service at Reverend Pettle's church, and take note of what was said, and who was in attendance—as well as who might be absent, because that could be interesting too. Naylor was technically off duty, but this was a time of crisis. He was also the only black officer in the department, and Nathan Pettle's congregation was entirely non-white.

Kel Knight called while Griffin was buttoning his shirt, and confirmed with him the wording of the statement to go out to the local press. Jurel Cade might have preferred a full media blackout, or its closest equivalent, but the death of a young woman and the disappearance of her mother couldn't be ignored entirely, so a compromise had been reached. The statement acknowledged the discovery of Donna Lee's body and an ongoing police inquiry into the circumstances, but not much else. Still, at least they'd be circulating a picture of Sallie Kernigan, and requesting that anyone in the vicinity of the discovery site over the weekend, or by Hindman High on Friday evening, should come forward, even if they didn't believe they'd seen anything of importance.

Griffin padded barefoot to the kitchen, where

his wife had already placed the evening meal on the table. He noticed that she'd put out the good silverware and was using the plates they kept for parties and Thanksgiving. She had also lit a candle. He experienced a brief surge of panic at the possibility that he might have forgotten their anniversary, before remembering that it wasn't for another week. He counted the days on his fingers, just to be sure, before taking his seat.

"This is all very elegant," he said, when she joined him.

"I know it might seem strange, after what happened today," she said, "but I had some good news. Well, *we* had some good news."

"And what might that be?" he asked.

He saw that she was drinking water. Usually, she treated herself to a small glass of wine with dinner. It was one of her few vices. He felt time stop. He wanted to ask, but was afraid. Then she said the words, and even as he stood to take her in his arms, and even as they kissed, and even as he cried and she cried, he knew that in return for this blessing he would forever know fear.

He held his wife, the mother of his unborn child, and tried to force from his mind the images of Patricia Hartley, of Donna Lee Kernigan.

Of Charlie Parker and his dead.

CHAPTER
XLVII

In a darkness suffused with decay, the man responsible for the murders of Patricia Hartley and Donna Lee Kernigan—and others besides—kept vigil with the dead. He held in his right hand a charm bracelet once owned by the Hartley girl, and in his left an earring taken from Donna Lee. He was not worried about keeping the items. The police would track him down eventually, he knew, but just in case anything should befall him unexpectedly, he wanted there to be no doubt about his culpability. He didn't want to have gone to all this trouble for nothing.

His only concern was that a small part of him had enjoyed killing Donna Lee. The Hartley girl had been more difficult, and he hadn't been convinced of his ability to persevere with his plan in the days immediately after her death—because he smelled her upon himself, and not pleasantly—but Donna Lee had been easier. It was in the way she'd struggled, wriggling under the weight of him. He'd liked that. He'd liked it a lot, and his excitement had made him want to hurt her more. He was now looking forward to the next girl, which briefly caused him to consider the possibility of a different outcome.

Suppose he could somehow achieve his aims without being caught?

Suppose he could keep on taking girls?

Why, that would be just lovely.

Difficult, but lovely.

CHAPTER
XLVIII

Parker's search for food was delayed. He discovered that he had left his wallet in his room, and as he returned from retrieving it, he noticed Charles Shire and his goon conversing in the parking lot. Out of curiosity, Parker tried to eavesdrop on them, but their voices were too low. Finally, Shire returned to his accommodation and the goon drove the rental car out of the parking lot, after which Parker decided to drop by the reception desk.

The motel lobby was excessively warm and smelled of cheap coffee and old doughnuts. Parker asked the desk clerk, Cleon, about local bars and restaurants. Cleon was in his late twenties, prematurely balding, and worked most evenings, often while listening to light opera on the stereo system and sketching lavish costumes for stage shows. He was the cousin of one of the owners, and was taking a distance-learning course in design studies. If he wasn't the gayest man in Arkansas, he was closing in fast on the front-runner.

"Boyd's is nearest," said Cleon, "and the food's not bad."

"I've been."

"How did you like it?"

"Not a whole lot. I got arrested."

This news didn't faze Cleon.

"That's funny," he said. "Most people get arrested at the Rhine Heart. It doesn't happen so much in Boyd's."

"The Rhine Heart it is, then," said Parker. "What's the food like?"

"Fine, as long as you don't swallow it."

"I'll bear that in mind."

"Happy to have helped. How's the honeymoon suite?"

"Homely."

"That's what we're aiming for. Lavish wedding accommodations on the first night set up unrealistic expectations for the years to come. I think I read that somewhere, or perhaps I made it up. Either way, it has the ring of truth."

"You should put it on the door."

"I'd get fired, so perhaps I will." He set aside his pencil. "Is it true that you're helping the police investigate the Kernigan girl's murder?"

"Did someone tell you that?"

"Sergeant Knight told the owners you were assisting the department when he came by to negotiate a rate for your room, and the Cargill PD doesn't need assistance with anything else right now."

"Then it's true."

"Patricia Hartley's death also?"

"Yes."

"Good."

"I'm not sure that's the general attitude."

"Probably not, but who cares?"

Parker glanced at the guest information form by Cleon's right hand. He could see Charles Shire's name.

"Kovas might," he replied, "and a lot of people waiting for that ship to come in."

"I think Kovas, their ship, and this town can all go to hell," said Cleon.

"You don't like Cargill?"

"No, and Cargill doesn't like me, but the town started it."

Cargill didn't strike Parker as a good place to be gay. He wondered why Cleon had stayed as long as he had. Money issues, possibly, or family ties. Escaping from small towns was never easy. They buried their hooks deep.

"How discreet are you, Cleon?"

"More than you might think."

"That's just what I would have guessed. How often does Charles Shire stay here?"

Cleon cocked an eyebrow.

"Mr. Shire? He's been a frequent visitor in the last six months. This is already his fourth visit this year. He's some kind of liaison between Kovas and the state. Everyone has to be nice to him."

"And the man who arrived with him this evening?"

"He hasn't stayed here before, although I've seen him around. I usually like men with mustaches, although I don't think he's on the market. Then again, that might be for the best. He doesn't seem like the tender kind."

"Does he have a name?"

Cleon lifted Shire's reservation to display the one beneath.

"Leonard Cresil," he said. "He carries a gun."

"I noticed."

"You're carrying one, too."

Cleon, it was emerging, had very sharp eyes.

"But I'm one of the good guys," said Parker.

"That's what I'm hoping. If I hear anything I shouldn't, I'll be sure to let you know."

"I'd be grateful."

Parker buttoned his jacket and headed for the door. Cleon resumed his sketching.

"If you don't mind me asking, Mr. Parker," he said, "why did they turn to you for help?"

"I was a detective once. I have some experience."

"Of killings like these?"

"No, not exactly like these, but close enough."

Cleon contemplated the reply.

"How do you do it?" he said.

"Do what?"

"Look upon the results of that kind of violence."

"You make it sound like there's a choice."

"Well, you could look away."

Parker opened the door and was welcomed by the night.

"I tried that," he said. "It didn't work."

CHAPTER
XLIX

Reverend Nathan Pettle washed his hands in the small bathroom at the rear of his church, with its cracked sink and toilet that dated back to the building's previous incarnation as a VFW post, before the natural attrition of mortality, aided by a schism in the local organization, had resulted in its dissolution. Pettle had done his best to make the premises resemble something approaching a house of worship: he'd added a cross, for starters, and put cheap stained glass in a few of the windows, but the acoustics remained poor, and the floor still bore marks from the removal of the post's bar. Yet it was his church, and he was proud of it. That didn't mean he wanted to stay in it forever, but he'd done his best with what was available to him, and the Lord couldn't ask for more.

He dried his hands and stared at his face in the mirror. He had always been lousy at hiding his emotions. That was how his wife had confirmed the affair with Sallie Kernigan, transmuting base suspicion into the shining gold of truth through the simple expedient of asking her husband directly. As soon as she confronted him, Pettle had confessed. There had been no point in doing otherwise. God had cursed him with the inability to perjure and obfuscate. *Lying lips are an abomination to the Lord, but those who act faithfully are his delight—*

Proverbs 12:22. Pettle was not so hypocritical as to attempt to convince himself that any substantial difference existed between deceit and lying—he had deceived his wife by sleeping with another woman, and hiding his unfaithfulness, which constituted a form of untruth—but he reminded himself that he had fessed up at the first opportunity, and by then the affair was already at an end. *Do not lie to one another, seeing that you have put off the old self with its practices*— Colossians 3:9. He had indeed put off the old self, and refused to lie. He had tried, in the end, to be a better man.

Appallingly, he now wished that someone other than Donna Lee had been found dead that morning. No other fatality, barring that of Sallie Kernigan herself, could have caused such problems for him: not at home, not with Kovas, and not with the police, because Delores was pressuring him to step forward and inform them of the nature of his relationship with the girl's mother. If Delores had guessed the truth of it, she informed him, others were capable of doing likewise. Sallie could have told some of her friends about it, or her workmates. Even Donna Lee herself might have seen or heard something, Delores advised.

And as she spoke, Pettle had witnessed the disappointment and distrust in her face, and glimpsed a future of continued coldness and estrangement. He knew then that whatever damage he might have inflicted on their marriage by his infidelity paled beside what she had done to it by doubting his essential goodness. He had fallen temporarily from grace, like all good men inevitably do, but he had refused to let it define him. His wife, on the other hand, appeared intent upon doing just that, and now he feared that deeper reservations about his character had begun to cloud her mind.

Donna Lee might have seen or heard something.

And what then? Suppose Donna Lee had taken it upon herself to confront the good reverend with her knowledge of his sexual relationship with her mother? What if Donna Lee, unlike Delores, had found herself unable to stomach his sanctimony, and threatened to reveal it to his congregation, to the whole town? In that case, what would become of his dreams of a new church, of his hopes of becoming a figurehead in the rejuvenated Cargill? What would happen to the money promised him by Kovas for mobilizing his flock, for encouraging them to write to their congressman, to state senators and local representatives, to the governor himself, in order to ensure that Kovas, these harbingers of wealth and change, should be facilitated in every way? What would happen to the promised career for his boy? And what would happen to Pettle himself? Men had killed to protect less.

Then there was Sallie Kernigan herself, because she remained missing. Already the talk around town was that Sallie, like her daughter, could well be dead. Whoever killed Donna Lee might have been forced to deal with the mother first in order to get to the girl, or to take Sallie's life in the aftermath so that she could not speak of what she knew. But who would have cause to commit such acts? Who might benefit from ensuring the silence of mother and daughter?

This, Pettle feared, was the sum of his wife's suspicions about him: the husband who had cheated on her was now a man who might have killed to escape the consequences of his licentiousness.

God, he was weary. Earlier that afternoon, he had driven to Hot Springs with Lorrie Colson, the young policewoman, in order to visit with Miss Imogene, now grandmother to a dead child and mother to a missing one. The old woman could no longer breathe unassisted, a lifetime of smoking having rendered her lungs useless, and stage 3 emphysema would soon take her from this world. Already she was virtually without speech, but she'd understood what they were telling her. He'd wiped away her tears and held her hand, until eventually she'd lapsed into unconsciousness. Speaking to her, breaking her heart at the end of her life, was one of the hardest duties Pettle had ever performed, yet he had taken on the burden of it willingly, even as he wondered: *Does Miss Imogene know? Does she, like my own wife, believe me to be capable of this crime?*

"But what about Estella Jackson?" He heard himself speaking aloud, addressing his reflection. "She died the same way as Donna Lee, and I had no cause to kill her. Same with Patricia Hartley."

But everyone was aware of how the Jackson girl died, with branches rammed deep into her—Patricia Hartley too, no matter what lies Jurel Cade and Loyd Holt had elected to tell, the same lies they had convinced Pettle to accept, because to do otherwise would have brought devastation down on the county, impoverishing them all. It wouldn't be hard to replicate killings like that, wouldn't be hard at all. A man would only need a couple of sticks . . .

He should not have colluded with Cade and Holt. That had been one of his mistakes. He should have demonstrated that he was a man of principle. Yet there was so much at stake here for everyone. Pettle wanted to see his people enriched. He wanted them to be able to afford better homes, better food for their table, a better education for their children. Only Kovas offered that hope. So he had chosen to swallow the Hartley lie, and ignore the enforced exile of her family. He had embraced complicity in one sin to avoid visiting harm on generations of families. He had prioritized the needs of the many over the few.

But that would no longer suffice. The members of his flock hadn't just been in mourning tonight: They'd been angry. They'd wanted justice. None of them had departed immediately after the service ended, not one. They'd called on him to stand up for what was right, and not let the death of another black girl go unremarked and uninvestigated. He'd tried to assure them that Chief Griffin was on their side, and felt as they did. Griffin had called Pettle at home a few hours before the service, suggesting it might be a good idea if he addressed the congregation, but Pettle had demurred, and still believed it to have been the correct decision. Griffin meant well, but he was a white police officer in a county and state in which the old divisions remained visible: geographical, social, economic, racial. The town's black population had no reason to accept that Griffin would be any more effective than Jurel Cade in investigating the butchering of their young women, just as Eddy Rauls, Cade's predecessor, had failed to solve the murder of Estella Jackson. It was up to Pettle to convince his congregants otherwise. He had agreed to let Naylor, the town's sole black officer, attend the service, and from the pulpit had advised anyone with information to speak with the police, but no one came forward. They wanted Reverend Nathan Pettle to be their voice. They were putting their faith in him, and he wished so badly to be worthy of it, but he could not, for so many reasons, one of which was currently waiting for him on the other side of the restroom door.

The reprobate named Leonard Cresil.

CHAPTER
L

A familiar car was idling in the lot when Parker emerged from the lobby of the motel. The engine died as he appeared, and the driver's door opened. Delphia Cade emerged from the dimness of the interior, trailing perfume and the promise of misfortune.

"Mr. Parker," she said, and waited for him to acknowledge her.

"Ms. Cade."

"May I trouble you for a moment of your time?"

"Sure."

"Perhaps we could speak somewhere less open?"

"There's always the lobby," said Parker.

"But you have a room here, don't you?"

"I have more than a room, I have the honeymoon suite."

"How quaint. I wasn't aware that there was such an amenity in this town."

"The name flatters to deceive."

"Even so, we might talk there."

Her lips were very, very red, and her teeth very, very white. The canines were sharp enough to leave holes in a man's throat.

"I was on my way to get something to eat," said Parker. "It's been a long day."

"I could always join you."

"Like I said, it's been a long day."

Delphia Cade made a curious gesture with her right hand. In a distant, less enlightened time, it might have been taken for a conjuration or hex. Whatever one chose to call it, Parker would not have been entirely surprised had he suddenly begun bleeding from the eyes and ears.

"Have I caused you some offense?" said Delphia.

"No, Ms. Cade, but you're the sister of the county's chief deputy, and the daughter of its most powerful citizen. I'm not sure it would be proper for us to be alone without a chaperone."

"My father was right: you are a character."

And like her father, she didn't sound as though she considered this to be a boon.

"If you have anything to share that might be of benefit to the investigation," said Parker, "I'd be happy to listen to it at the station house. We can go there right now."

"I did have something to offer, but not information."

"I don't think I'm in the market for what you're offering."

"Don't be uncouth," said Delphia. "I'm talking about a job."

But her eyes said different: they shone with sun-darts of silver, like fish rising to feed.

"What kind of job?"

"A great many people are intent upon entering into my good graces, although you don't seem to be one of them. They look at me and smell money. Some of them think they can smell more than that.

I find the approaches tiresome, even intimidating at times. I've now reached the stage where I'd be happier with personal security, someone to stand by my side. I thought of you."

"I'm flattered, but I'll have to decline."

"Because I'm a woman, or because I'm a Cade?"

"Because I'm here only to investigate a series of killings. If I were to accept a position from you, I would be unable to continue in my current role."

"The investigation would continue without you."

"Probably, but my absence might be a hindrance to a successful outcome."

"My, aren't you confident."

"No, I'm just an outsider, which means I'm not duty bound to any of you. I'd like to keep it that way. But thank you again for the offer."

Delphia Cade's mouth formed a near-perfect circle of hostility. Behind her lips, the tips of her teeth remained visible, lending her the aspect of a lamprey.

"Did you really think I wanted to fuck you?" she said.

"It wasn't an issue either way."

"Because you're in mourning?"

"It's as good a reason as any."

"I don't fuck the town's hired help."

"Technically, I'm working for a bed in the honeymoon suite," said Parker, "but I accept that it's a minor distinction."

She flicked a finger in the direction of the lobby,

and Cleon, who was doing his best to preten
to be monitoring proceedings, and failing.

"Go back to your fag," she said. "He's wa
for you."

"Cleon's waiting for someone, but not for me.
I believe he'll find happiness long before you or

Whatever Delphia Cade detected in his t
caused her anger to recede slightly, and a meas
of sadness rolled in to take its place.

"You ought to leave here," she said.

"I know that, but I can't."

"Neither can I, but I should have, long ago." Sl
took a long, deep breath of the blue-exhaust air.
understand a great deal about the workings of thi
county. I could probably help you with your work,
but I won't."

"And why is that?"

"Because I believe my father and Jurel are wrong
to cooperate with the Cargill PD. It can only
harm what we're trying to achieve with Kovas.
I've worked hard for this—we all have—and the
investigation risks putting a torch to everything."

Parker returned to the incident in the Cade house,
when Pappy had dismissed this woman in a way
calculated to demean her in a room full of men.
Her reaction suggested that it was not the first
time she had been degraded in this way. No matter
how hard she worked, or what she achieved for the
family, her father would never forgive her for not
being born male.

"Do you know what I think?" said Parker.

"Tell me. I'm curious."

"I think you want the deal to go through so you an use the proceeds to buy yourself out of this county, even this state. Kovas represents your best chance of escape, and no amount of dead girls can be permitted to tip the scales."

"How long have you been here, Mr. Parker?"

"Just a few days."

"Just a few days," she said, "and look how much you've learned. We'll make a native of you yet."

Delphia returned to her car, reversed from her parking space, and headed toward the highway, and Little Rock. She did not once look at Parker again, as though she had already excised him from her memory, even as he recognized the foolishness of hoping for any such absolution.

CHAPTER
LI

Jurel Cade didn't boast personal contacts in New York to compare with Kel Knight's, and the Cade family name held modest sway beyond the Arkansas border, but after being sent from pillar to post for a while by the NYPD, he was eventually referred to an internal affairs investigator named John Breen. Breen was interested to hear that Charlie Parker was in Arkansas, and pressed for further details, but Jurel was too smart to give something away for nothing—in that regard, he resembled his father—so he and Breen traded morsels of information until a portrait of Parker began to emerge. The final picture disturbed Jurel, but at least he was now better informed than before about the interloper.

Jurel Cade wasn't an entirely phlegmatic man. He was engaged to be married to a schoolteacher, and intended to set about starting a family as soon as the nuptials were concluded. He could only pray that he, his future wife, and their children, should the couple be so blessed, would never experience any calamity like the one that had engulfed Charlie Parker. He felt sorrow for the man, but still wished he had decided to indulge his desolation elsewhere. His presence presaged no good.

Cade thought it interesting that Breen had seen fit to share with him particulars relating to the murder in New York of the degenerate named Johnny Friday. This, as much as a certain barely veiled hostility on Breen's side, indicated that Parker was short on friends, which meant that little blowback could be anticipated if any further tribulation were to befall him while he was in Burdon County.

Cade picked up the phone again, called Pappy, and shared with him what he had learned.

"Parker is jinxed," Cade concluded, using the very word that Breen also had chosen. "It could be that he's brought his bad luck down here, and it will count against him."

He waited to see how Pappy might respond. The silence went on for so long that Cade began to wonder if Pappy had fallen asleep. The old man had begun to do this more frequently in recent years, which was why Delphia now preferred Pappy to keep his distance from Little Rock, and show his face only when backslapping needed to be done. Having Pappy nod off during meetings with Kovas would not be conducive to easing any doubts the company might be harboring about the Cades' abilities to fulfill their promises.

"If what you've learned is true, he doesn't need the quantity of his pain increased," said Pappy at last, "or not by us. Our arrangement with him and Griffin stands. You give them all the help you can, and stay with them every step of the way. But when you catch sight of the quarry, you move ahead and bring it down. And do it quick and clean, understand?"

"Yes."

"You're a good boy, Jurel," said Pappy. "Once Kovas gets to building, you'll be looked after. We'll sit down for lunch with the governor and talk rewards, once he's finished saying grace."

This was Pappy's ultimate aim: to extend the Cade influence to the State House, and then Washington, D.C. Delphia didn't have the temperament for it, and Nealus was too flighty. That left Jurel, who was just bright enough to be a contender, but not so bright as to be perceived as a threat by those whose help they'd need if he were to succeed. The subject had come up occasionally in the past, but Jurel had remained noncommittal, which his father chose to interpret as quiet consent.

But Jurel had no urge to spend more time in Little Rock, or trade his sidearm for one of those Filofax organizers that Ferdy Bowers liked to carry around with him because he'd seen hot shots use them on TV. There was more of his father in Jurel than he preferred to admit, even to himself. Like Pappy, Jurel was of Burdon County. It was in his blood, and he loved it, for all its poverty and pettiness. Where others saw ugliness, he saw the potential for beauty; what some called corruption, he called practicality; and in what the ignorant perceived as racism, he identified only the echoes of the past, reverberations that would fade in time but never entirely cease. This county was his birthplace, and eventually it would be his fiefdom. His desire extended no further than to run it as he saw fit, and raise his children within sight of the Ouachita.

Jurel hung up the phone, and from his desk watched the darkness grow deeper. He had erred, he realized, in his handling of Patricia Hartley's death. He had believed himself to be acting in the best interests of the county, but it might be that Griffin and his father were correct, and the balance had now shifted. Jurel did not place the same value upon a black life as he did on a white, just as he accepted that poverty brought with it a diminution of consequence, regardless of color. He was the product of a particular culture and a distinctive set of historical resonances; it would have been foolish of him to pretend otherwise. But to recognize a hierarchy was not the same as to wholly abandon those in its lower reaches. Neither did Jurel wish to inherit a county in which a killer of women might find sanctuary, because that sepsis would ultimately infect the body entire.

He rose from his chair, went to the records room, and began assembling the material that might help identify this despoiler of the women in his realm.

CHAPTER
LII

Parker elected to walk to the Rhine Heart instead of driving. The evening was pleasantly cool, and after the New York winter it was a relief to be able to linger outdoors without worrying about layers of insulation—a relief, too, to be away from that city and its memories. His encounter with Delphia Cade had left him bemused, and the crudeness of her approach caused him to wonder if the future of the Cade family was in the right hands. He could only hope that, for the Cades' sake, Delphia's diplomatic skills improved the closer she got to Little Rock.

The Rhine Heart was exactly as he had anticipated: a blockhouse with log cladding, designed to resemble a faux German bar in some imagined copse of the Black Forest. A dozen cars were parked in the lot, and oompah music was faintly audible. All that was missing were men in lederhosen and a faint nostalgia for fascism.

Parker went inside and took a seat alone at the bar. He ordered a soda and a plate of German potatoes. He steered clear of the sausage, because his neighbor's resembled a meat blackjack and smelled like a drain. His soda came with a free pretzel, which was salty enough to induce a stroke. Parker spread his newspaper before him, flicking through it at intervals, but only to distract from his monitoring of the discourse around him. It didn't take long for him to pick up snatches of conversation about the murder of Donna Lee Kernigan, and references to the disappearance of her mother. The general consensus was that Sallie Kernigan was probably as dead as her daughter; and, if so, the same individual was responsible for both killings, which sounded plausible to Parker. Sallie had enjoyed a wild streak, according to some of those who appeared to have known her from her time working in the bar. A woman like that was bound to get in trouble someday, they said, but it was a shame that she might have dragged her daughter down with her.

Parker picked at his German potatoes, which weren't bad and had arrived with slices of brownish bread, just in case he was suffering from a carb deficiency. Eventually, when there came a lull in service, the bartender stopped by to check that everything was okay, and to interrogate the newcomer. The bartender kept his tone light, but Parker knew that any stranger finding himself in Cargill amid current events would attract interest, even suspicion, from locals. It would be better for all concerned if it emerged that an interloper was responsible for their troubles, some drifter who, having succeeded with one girl—or two—had returned to take another, in the manner of a ravening animal discovering territory rich with easy prey.

"My name's Denny," said the bartender, extending a paw. "Denny Rhinehart. This is my place."

"Parker."

They shook. Rhinehart's hand was greasy from serving food.

"Passing through?"

"No, staying a while."

"What is it you do?"

"Oh, this and that. I'm taking time out to consider my options."

"Is that so?"

Rhinehart seemed set to pursue the matter further, when he was prevented from doing so by a male voice from behind Parker.

"You better watch what you say, Denny. It might be taken down and used as evidence against you in a court of law."

Parker turned. The speaker was in his midforties, and dressed much like nearly every other man in the bar: jeans, a heavy shirt worn loose, and work boots. He was probably four or five inches taller than Parker, and carrying more weight than was advisable, but the base was solid. The tips of the ring and little fingers on his left hand were missing, and the scar tissue on the stumps had not yet fully healed. He didn't have a drink, and carried his coat under his right arm, so he had either just arrived or was about to leave: the former, it quickly emerged, as two more men entered the Rhine Heart and joined the first, unbuttoning their coats as they came.

"I'm not sure I follow you, Rich," said Rhinehart.

"This is the latest recruit to the Cargill Police

Department," said Rich, "all the way from New York City. Isn't that right, Mr. Parker?"

Parker didn't know how the man named Rich had come by this information, but he was hardly astonished. Cargill was a small town, and his involvement in the investigation would soon have become common knowledge. But he didn't like the vibes he was getting from Rich or the men with him. Rhinehart wasn't eager for their business, either. Parker could see the bartender's face reflected in the mirror over Rich's left shoulder, and the expression it bore suggested that Rhinehart dearly wished the right to refuse service, as set in print above the register, was one he had the guts to enforce.

"That's right," said Parker.

"They call you in because of those girls?"

"They didn't call me in. I happened to be in town, and the chief asked if I'd be willing to assist with the investigation."

"And naturally, you obliged."

"I'm an obliging person. Do you have anything helpful you'd like to share?"

"Not with you."

"Then I'll get back to my drink."

"That's a soda, not a drink."

"I have a low tolerance," said Parker.

"For alcohol?"

"For everything."

Belligerent flares exploded briefly in Rich's eyes before fading to embers.

"These murders," said Rich, "they're something we ought to be able to figure out for ourselves. This is a small town, in a small county, and the people that live here know it best. Whoever killed those girls will be brought down by those most familiar with its ways, not by an outlander like you. We have the chief, and the sheriff's office. They know how to handle this kind of trouble."

"Their willingness to involve me would suggest otherwise—that, and an accumulation of bodies."

"Your involvement is an error," said Rich.

"We'll see."

Rich's face was growing redder. Parker could see that their exchange had begun to attract attention, because the bar had grown noticeably quieter.

"Don't patronize me," said Rich. "How old are you anyway, thirty? What do you understand about the world outside New York City? What do you understand about anything?"

"You know," said Parker, gesturing at Rich's mutilated hand, "fingers don't grow back. You ought to be more careful."

It was an unnecessarily provocative remark, but that was the point. Rich tensed to lash out, already signaling the direction of the first blow by the position of his feet and the angle of his body. Parker willed him to take the shot. Even if the punch landed, Parker would ride it, and then he would hurt Rich. The man's friends would intervene, but Parker was confident of dealing with the one to the right even before he could form a fist, because he looked sluggish and half-drunk, which would leave only the last of them to contend with—assuming the rest of the clientele didn't decide to weigh in on Rich's side, in which case the odds would become a lot less favorable.

"Everything okay here?"

A woman positioned herself between Parker and Rich. It was Lorrie Colson. She was out of uniform and held a beer in one hand, but still radiated authority, even though she was a foot shorter than Rich. Griffin had told Parker about Donnie Stark's ruptured testicle, and clearly Rich had heard the story too, because he took a step back and allowed his right fist to unclench slowly.

"Everything's fine," he said. "We were just talking."

"Didn't look like you were just talking, Rich. Looked like you were planning on unloading that big right hook of yours."

Rich didn't try to deny it, so Parker spoke up.

"I might have goaded him," he said.

"Now, girls, you're both pretty," said Colson, and Parker instantly felt about sixteen years old, and mildly ashamed of himself. "But Rich here ought to know better than to be making a nuisance of himself. You got somewhere else you need to be, Rich? Because if you don't, maybe you should find a place."

Rich moved away, his friends trailing in his wake. Colson stayed.

"Making friends already?" she said.

"The welcoming committee needs to work on its presentation."

"Tempers may be running high. A killing will do that to people."

"I'll write that down, just in case I forget."

"My, you are tetchy. Probably comes from eating the food here."

"I was warned against it, but I thought the potatoes might be safe."

"That depends on when Denny last changed the oil. I always err on the side of caution."

Colson took the stool opposite Parker and set her beer on the bar. Around them, people returned to their own business, or gave that impression. Someone put money in the jukebox, and Jo Dee Messina earned a royalty.

"So," said Parker, "tell me about Rich."

"Rich Emory. He isn't the worst of them, although that's a low bar to set. Back in the day, his daddy used to run with Buford Pusser down in McNairy County, Tennessee." Buford Pusser: scourge of the Dixie Mafia in the 1960s, which earned him bullet wounds and a dead wife for his troubles. "When Buford didn't get reelected in '72, Rich's daddy came back up here and signed on as a sheriff's deputy. Rich did the same for a few years, but it didn't take. Now he's the owner of a sawmill."

"Is that how he lost his fingertips?"

"Occupational hazard. He'll lose the mill, too, if circumstances don't improve, but he's banking on the arrival of the cavalry."

"Let me guess," said Parker. "Kovas."

"They'll need lumber for building, and what they don't use, the contractors putting up new housing and stores will. Somehow, Rich has managed to keep most of his employees on the payroll, even if it's short time. You're going to meet a lot like him while you're asking your questions, those who are doing their best to keep everyone's head above water, not just their own. You could try not riling them, see how that works out for you."

"I've found it challenging in the past," said Parker.

"That's unfortunate."

She finished her beer and waved the bottle at Rhinehart, who brought another posthaste, and refilled Parker's soda while he was at it.

"The soda's on the house," said Rhinehart.

"What about the beer?" said Colson.

"I wouldn't want to be accused of bribery."

"Too damned cheap, you mean."

Rhinehart shrugged before heading to the other end of the bar to serve one of the men who had arrived with Rich Emory. Colson tapped her bottle against the rim of Parker's glass.

"Cheers, for what it's worth," she said, then: "You don't drink?"

Parker took time to compose his reply. "I went through a period of excess. It didn't end well."

Colson picked at the label on her bottle.

"Evan told me what happened to your family. I'm sorry. I know you've probably heard that a lot, and hearing it again probably doesn't help much, but I am."

"Thank you."

The last time Parker had kept company with a woman in a bar, it was his wife beside him. It helped that Colson looked nothing like Susan, but Parker still had to fight a lump in his throat. He waited until he had it under control before speaking again.

"How much of that exchange with Rich Emory did you catch?" he said.

"All of it."

"I get the feeling he believes a local may be responsible for what's happening here."

"There's a difference of opinion on the subject," said Colson. "You have those who say it's a drifter, the same man that killed Patricia Hartley come back for more—because everyone knew she was probably murdered, but they preferred to live with the lie. This isn't Hot Springs, or Fayetteville. There's always been an antipathy toward those without roots in the county, and these killings have tapped into it. Even the prosperity that Kovas may bring has to be balanced in a lot of minds with the changes that will follow. The town will fill up with those who don't have any ties to the land, disrupting the natural order. Once Kovas arrives, Burdon County will never be the same again.

"But," she concluded, "however frightening it may be for them to suppose that a stranger is shedding blood here, it's harder yet for them to

319

countenance the possibility that it might be one of their own."

"And what do you believe?"

"He's local," Colson said firmly. "You saw where Patricia Hartley's body was found, and I know the chief told you his suspicions about where it might have been put originally. That's not an easy location to access. You have to know the way to the outcrop. And neither Donna Lee nor Patricia was killed where the remains were discovered, so unless he has a van or an RV, he's working from a base. Even if he's using a vehicle, he needs a safe location in which to park it, where he knows he won't be disturbed. That's local knowledge right there."

And then there was the simple fact that he had made Burdon County his hunting ground, not anyplace else. Even if the killer wasn't native, thought Parker, he had a point of connection with this area.

"And Estella Jackson?"

"That was different. She was tortured to death and left in a shed. But it might be best for you to read the report first, and not have me prejudice your thinking."

Colson abandoned her beer and stood to leave.

"You staying?" she said.

"No, I'm done."

"Are you parked in the lot?"

"I came here on foot."

"I'll give you a ride back to the motel."

"I can walk."

"I'd feel better if you accepted the escort."

"Because Rich Emory might be about to resume the argument?"

"No, Rich has said his piece now, and he's not dumb. But there are others who are better at keeping their emotions hidden, and they'll be watching you as well. Evan says you brought your own guns."

"That's right."

"You carrying now?"

Parker moved his shirt to display the butt of the Smith & Wesson.

"Make it more visible. It'll act to discourage any foolishness. By this time tomorrow, everyone will know that getting in your face will be like getting in the face of the chief himself—or worse, Kel Knight."

They made their way to the door. A few people glanced in their direction, Rich Emory and his crew among them. Parker didn't bother to wave goodbye.

"I'm not feeling the love from Knight," said Parker.

"He hasn't warmed to you, I admit. I don't know why."

Parker had his own theories. He wondered how much Griffin and Knight had learned about him from their sources in New York. Whatever it amounted to, they'd probably made the decision not to share all of it with Colson and the other officers.

"It could be a Civil War thing," said Parker, "and I'm just carrying the can for Northern belligerence."

"That must be it," said Colson, as they reached her little Camry. "Fresh wounds, and all that . . ."

Denny Rhinehart watched Colson and Parker leave. Only when the door closed behind them did he relax. He went into the little kitchen where Ivy was cleaning up, now that what passed for food service had ended. Ivy Muntz had been working at the Rhine Heart for six years. She was in her early fifties, and a better cook than the venue, and the quality of its ingredients, deserved.

"You need anything else before I leave?" she said.

"No, thank you."

"You okay, Denny?"

"Fine," he said, "just fine. Hey, Ivy, would you do me the kindness of taking a turn behind the bar for a few minutes. I need to use the restroom."

"Sure."

She stepped through the swing door into the bar. Denny had his own private bathroom beside his office; given the state in which the customers left the stalls of the Rhine Heart, it was an understandable move on his part. He closed the door behind him, pulled the cord on the light, and removed from his pocket a thin length of cloth tied in a bow, strands of dark hair caught in the knot. He'd kept it as a souvenir, but it made sense to

322

get rid of it now. He was about to flush it down the john, but decided instead to burn it, just to be certain.

He lit a match and watched impassively as Donna Lee Kernigan's bright red ribbon turned to black.

CHAPTER
LIII

Nathan Pettle had known men like Leonard Cresil all his life, and his familiarity with such individuals had not enhanced the quality of his existence. Cresil, he knew, had bounced around various police forces during the early part of his career, trailing a reputation for violence and bigotry—his capacity for both being remarkable in scope, extending as it did to anyone who was not Leonard Cresil—before finding a more profitable outlet for his talents in the field of corporate security. Cresil was a native of Chicot County, and his people were steeped in ignorance: he had once informed Pettle, in a rare moment of candor, that his grandfather Vernon didn't realize it was wrong to shoot at black people until he joined the army.

Now here was Cresil, sitting in Pettle's little office, his feet resting on an open desk drawer, cleaning dirt from his fingernails with the folded edge of a Bible pamphlet, the smell of his cologne strangely sweet, even effeminate, for such a man. The pores on his face were excessively large, so that they stored within them the grime of his travels and the sum of Cresil's own discharges. His breathing was loud and irregular, as though he struggled to draw sufficient air into his lungs, even in repose, and his voice at all times held a rattle in its depths. Pettle sometimes wondered if Cresil was ill and if so what his malady might be, but he had never worked up the interest to ask. It might have been remiss of him as a man of God, but was entirely understandable of him simply as a man. When Leonard Cresil eventually departed this life, the next day's sun would rise on a better world.

"I'm disappointed in you, Reverend," said Cresil. He did not look up from his ablutions, but continued to dig at a particularly recalcitrant piece of filth lodged beneath a thumbnail.

Pettle took a seat in one of the two hard chairs facing his desk, reduced to the status of a supplicant. He bore this calculated insult as he had borne so many others throughout his life: with the bitter patience of one who had long ceased to be surprised at the manners of certain white men and women, yet continued to be disappointed that their self-respect should be so dependent on the humiliation of others.

"Why is that, Mr. Cresil?"

"What is the term for the offense where one neglects to inform an individual of information germane to his interests, perhaps in order to protect oneself from accusation or condemnation?"

"I believe it's referred to as a lie of omission," said Pettle, even as he feared that Cresil had somehow become privy to the fact of his fornication with Sallie Kernigan.

"That's it, the operative word here being *lie*. A lie's a sin, is it not, or has church thinking on this matter altered since last I exposed myself to sermonizing? I'll admit that regular religious attendance has been low on my list of priorities in recent years, and doctrine does evolve."

Cresil had finally managed to purge the nail of the last of its crud. He flicked the residue onto Pettle's carpet and threw the pamphlet in the trash.

"No, a lie remains a lie," said Pettle.

"And therefore also a sin?"

"That follows."

"Which is reassuring to know, although it does make a liar of you, seeing as how you neglected to inform me immediately of the Kernigan girl's passing."

"It's been a difficult day, and I had other obligations."

"To your flock?"

"Yes, among similar duties."

"Most of your flock feeds on cheap cuts, but I don't see you wearing sackcloth and ashes and subsisting on welfare."

"I fail to take your meaning."

"Don't play the fool, Reverend, or not to a greater degree than comes naturally to you. Our money trumps whatever responsibilities you might have to anyone else, up to and including God Himself. If you don't share that view, the faucet can be turned off just as easily as it was turned on. We should have known about that girl's body before the bugs found her."

"Is Mr. Shire concerned?"

"He's back in that shithole motel for another night or two, so my guess is, yes, he is concerned."

Pettle was not familiar with every facet, every hidden corner, of the proposed deal to bring Kovas to Burdon County, but he had lived long enough to understand that money didn't flow only in one direction. Shire was Kovas's man on the ground in Arkansas, and his shadow touched all negotiations; but he was also a bagman, and every time he put money in someone's pocket, a little was returned to him, either from the recipient or another source. Demonstrations of goodwill from local and state businesses were required if they were to benefit from Kovas's future presence in the state, and secure for themselves a sufficiently rewarding slice of the pie. Shire would be heavily involved in advising Kovas on the bidding process for contracts, so it didn't just pay to be in his good books: it required payment. Pettle didn't know what Shire was doing with his cut of the money, but if the Kovas deal were to fall through, the fixer's popularity would plummet rapidly, especially if he wasn't in a position to make reimbursements. True, it was not as if those that bribed Shire had been handed receipts, or supplied with cast-iron guarantees, but few would be willing to write off their investments entirely in the event of Kovas choosing Texas over Arkansas. It was therefore a matter of deep personal concern to Charles Shire that any complications should be avoided, or dealt with expeditiously.

"Mr. Shire doesn't have cause to be worried," said Pettle.

"You hear that from God, or someone else?"

"I was speaking to one of Chief Griffin's officers after the service. Jurel Cade and the sheriff's office will cooperate with the Cargill PD, but the investigation will be low-key. Nobody wants a fuss, but everyone shares a desire to see this business brought to a successful conclusion as quickly and cleanly as possible."

Cresil kicked at the desk drawer, and Pettle heard the wood crack.

"What the fuck does that mean? Cade and Griffin, these men aren't trained investigators. They'd struggle to find a fucking cat in a tree."

"Don't swear in my church, Mr. Cresil."

Cresil wagged a finger at him. "And don't you test my boundaries, Reverend."

"Cade and Griffin aren't working alone. They have outside help."

"Outside?" Cresil didn't look pleased to learn this. "State? Federal?"

"An ex-policeman from New York. A detective. Seems he was in the area, and agreed to help."

"Does he have a name?"

"Parker."

"First name?"

"I don't know, but I can find out. Or you could just ask at your lodgings. I believe he's staying there also."

Cresil took this in.

"I guess that must count as progress," he said, finally.

"Of a kind."

"You sound ambivalent, Reverend."

"If white girls were dying—their bodies violated, dumped like trash—we wouldn't be talking about one detective as progress. This town would be alive with police."

"If white girls were dying," said Cresil, "Kovas would already be breaking ground in Texas, and Christ could come back ten times over before you'd see your new church. You got anything else you want to share with me before I leave?"

"No."

"Well, you think of anything, be sure to let me know. Don't make me come asking again."

"I won't."

Cresil stood.

"Did you know the Kernigan girl?"

"I knew the family."

Cresil laughed.

"Is that all? You may lie to yourself, and your wife, but you can't lie to me. I know all about your proclivities, Reverend. I wouldn't be much good at my job if I didn't. There isn't a secret worth knowing in this town that I don't keep close to my chest. I've a notion that your past sin might have reared its head again, and you've returned to the honey pot. You weren't fucking the daughter too, were you?"

"You're a vile human being," said Pettle, the words spilling from his mouth before he could stop them.

Cresil leaned forward, his pupils shrinking to pinpoints of hate.

"I'll let that slide," said Cresil, "on account of how I know you're in turmoil right now, but only if you make it worth my while. Otherwise, I may be forced to distract you from your emotional suffering."

And Pettle saw a future beaded with blood.

"Donna Lee was seeing someone before she died," he said.

"Who?"

"Tilon Ward."

"Now, that is interesting," said Cresil. "Do you think he killed her?"

"I don't know," said Pettle, then: "No."

"Which is it?"

"I never saw that darkness in him, Sallie neither."

Those dark animal eyes regarded Pettle.

"You didn't kill her yourself, did you, Reverend?"

"No."

"I'm glad to hear it. She was a sexy little thing, if that picture in your church is anything to go by. Not to my taste, wary as I am of darker meat, but a damn shame regardless. Any sign yet of the mother?"

Pettle shook his head. He put a hand to his brow, and willed this incubus to be excised from the world.

"If they find her skewered with sticks as well, we're all done," said Cresil. "Even Mr. Shire won't be able to hold the deal together in the event of another body. You'd best pray that doesn't happen, Reverend."

Cresil patted him on the shoulder as he walked to the door.

"Meanwhile, I'll embark on more practical measures."

CHAPTER
LIV

Parker was woken during the night by the ringing of the telephone in his room. The clock on the nightstand showed 4:05 a.m., but when he picked up the receiver, there was no one on the other end of the line. He got out of bed and carefully checked the parking lot from the window, but all was quiet. He went back to sleep.

Shortly before 8 a.m., he wandered down to the lobby to pick up some bad coffee and an apple. Only Cleon was present, working a double shift. He offered to make a more acceptable brew from his personal supply, but Parker thought the desk clerk's manner was off. When Cleon returned with the coffee, Parker asked if he'd put a call through to the room at any point during the night.

"I was the caller," said Cleon.

"I don't understand."

"You were shouting in your sleep. I thought about knocking on the door, but I didn't want to get shot."

Parker tried the coffee. It was good, helped by being served in a proper ceramic mug.

"I'm sorry. Did someone complain?"

"I decided to intervene before that became an issue. I apologize for waking you. I just couldn't think what else to do."

"The apology is mine to make. Did you hear what I was shouting about?"

Cleon didn't reply.

"You can tell me," said Parker. "I think I'd prefer to know."

Cleon's awkwardness increased. "It wasn't so much shouting as crying."

The morning sky was umbrous, and the sunlight had a sickly cast, as though blighted by its passage through the low clouds. Suddenly the coffee didn't taste as good anymore. Parker felt his face grow warm with embarrassment. He had no memory of any of this. Strange to relate, he believed himself to have slept soundly and dreamlessly the night before.

"Do you often have nightmares, Mr. Parker?" said Cleon.

"Only lately. My wife died, and my daughter with her."

"I'm sorry. Was it some kind of accident?"

"No."

Cleon dropped the subject. Parker saw the man named Leonard Cresil appear in his shirtsleeves and walk to the rental car. Cresil had a tattoo along his right forearm. Even from a distance, Parker could see it was the image of a hanged man, the body held suspended by a noose passed through the hollow sockets of the eyes.

"I may be out of my depth," said Cleon.

"That makes two of us," said Parker.

Cresil removed a long box from the trunk of the car. Parker recognized it as the kind used to transport a compound bow. Cresil paused as he prepared to close the trunk again. He looked around, some primitive sense alerting him to scrutiny, until finally his eyes came to rest on the lobby, and Parker. Cresil remained very still for the best part of ten seconds, his gaze never shifting from Parker's face.

"He was asking about you last night," said Cleon.

"What kind of asking?"

"He wanted to know how long you'd been in town, and whether you'd received any visitors."

"What did you tell him?"

"I told him the truth. Did I do wrong?"

"No."

"What if he continues to ask about you?"

"Continue telling."

Cresil looked away at last, closed the trunk, and walked off.

"He said that if I kept my eyes open, he'd make sure I was taken care of," said Cleon. "He left ten dollars on the counter, and told me he'd permit me to service him with my mouth before his departure, if I felt so disposed. Why does Mr. Shire need to keep the company of a man like that?"

"No one needs to keep the company of a man like that."

"But there he is, by Mr. Shire's side."

"Yes, there he is," said Parker. "What's your opinion of Mr. Shire?"

"He always insists on the same room, which we keep for his use alone, and brings with him his own toilet seat."

"Well, a man like that must be clean, right?"

"Or prefers to maintain the impression of cleanliness."

"Which would be more likely."

"Mr. Cresil, by contrast, is definitely unclean."

"In every way," said Parker. "But then he and Mr. Shire are engaged in a dirty business. They're buying your county, so at least one of them has to be willing to get dirty too."

"If I was doing the selling, they could have the county for whatever small change they found down the back of a sofa."

"Then it's lucky you're not on the negotiating team."

"I can't even negotiate a proper salary from my own family," said Cleon.

They watched Cresil disappear into his room.

"Is it still bow hunting season down here?" asked Parker.

"I don't know. I don't hunt."

"It doesn't matter. Mr. Cresil doesn't strike me as a man hidebound by regulations."

He thanked Cleon for the coffee, and asked if it would be okay to return the cup later.

"Just leave it in your room. Housekeeping will take care of it."

Parker headed for the door. Griffin had left a message requesting that he attend a meeting at the station house by 8:30 a.m., and Parker saw no reason to be late on his first morning. He felt a sense of dissociation from all that was occurring, but also a degree of clarity. This inquiry was not personal to him, and so he could view it with some dispassion. Any anger he was experiencing on behalf of the dead women was regulated, and could be directed. But he also resembled a man keeping himself afloat halfway between the banks of a river, drawing breath and kicking water while knowing that he must soon recommence swimming or risk drowning.

And on the land, a presence moved through the undergrowth, waiting for him to come.

"Mr. Parker?" said Cleon. "I want to ask your pardon if you felt I was prying into your affairs, or if I've added in any way to your grief. That was not my intention."

"It never crossed my mind," said Parker.

The Leonard Cresils of this world, he thought, were aberrations, evolutionary anomalies that would eventually bring about their own dissolution, just like the man who had taken his wife and child from him. Men such as Cleon could mitigate the influence on human affairs of such malign entities through the goodness of their own natures, even if they could not make up for it entirely.

"The phone call was a smart idea," said Parker.

"I thought so too."

"I'll see you around, Cleon."

"I look forward to it, Mr. Parker. Very much."

CHAPTER
LV

Tilon Ward woke early, in an unfamiliar bed. The apartment in Hot Springs to which Randall Butcher had consigned him was on the first floor of a building divided into eight units, which was two more than it could comfortably accommodate. The remaining rentals were occupied by the kind of poor white families that provided Butcher with a small but steady proportion of his income, aided by the interest on unofficial payday loans. The interest was high, but not extortionate, as Butcher was reluctant to sow excessive resentment among the masses. His people also supplied some of these tenants with narcotics when required, and Butcher owned most of the local stores that catered for their grocery needs, along with their cigarettes and alcohol. Thus, almost unnoticed, Randall Butcher had enmeshed himself in the fabric of their lives. Without him, their existences would unravel.

Tilon walked to the window and looked out on the cheerless day. Most of the east and southeast was now colored blue on the weather maps, while the temperature had dropped to the low thirties, having been close to seventy only days earlier. Still, Tilon wouldn't have exchanged Arkansas for anywhere else in the country, or not the parts he'd seen of it. He'd spent some time in Boston when he was in his early twenties, having chased the wrong woman to the wrong place, and was convinced his health had never recovered from that single winter in the Northeast. Sometimes, at the memory of it, the tips of his toes stung, like pain in a phantom limb. No, this was the place for him, and he hoped to end his days here, but not in the service of Randall Butcher, and not with the shadow of Donna Lee Kernigan's death hanging over him. He found himself missing her voice and touch. It could never have amounted to anything between them, or nothing more than they already had, but he'd liked Donna Lee a lot more than he had his ex-wife—and he'd married the latter.

Tilon showered under a head from which the water barely trickled, the pressure being kept deliberately to a minimum. He dressed, and ate stale bread from the kitchen cabinet. Pruitt Dix, upon dropping him at the apartment the previous night, had instructed him to sit tight, and Tilon was already growing claustrophobic. He smoked a cigarette in the weed-strewn yard, and exchanged a nod with one of his neighbors but no further greeting. His unit had the unmistakable ambience of a safe house, a place of temporary refuge, and Tilon guessed that the other tenants had learned to mind their own business where its occupants were concerned. He watched TV, and read some of the articles and stories in a pair of ancient editions of *Playboy* magazine, using the blade of a knife to turn the stained pages.

Shortly before 9 a.m., he heard a car pull up

outside. Dix had returned. He had in his possession a black sports bag, which he handed to Tilon. Inside was a selection of Tilon's own clothing, along with some toiletries and a razor.

"I had your momma put it together," said Dix. "I told her not to worry about you, that you'd be back with her soon enough. If anyone came asking, she was to inform them only that you'd gone out of town on business, and she had no way of contacting you. Come on, we're leaving."

"Where are we going?"

"Randall had a change of heart about the cook. He'd prefer you to get started right away."

There was no point in arguing. Tilon got into the car and waited for Dix to join him. The interior was clean and smelled of lemon air freshener.

"You stink of cigarettes," said Dix, as he took the wheel. "You ought to reexamine your lifestyle choices."

Tilon was in no mood for Dix's shit. His ear still ached, and he was sure the lobe needed stitches, because he'd bled on his pillow the night before. For now, the dried blood was holding the wound together. Butcher kept emergency kits at the cookhouses—mostly burn medication and eye baths, but also adhesive bandages and paper sutures. Tilon would tend to the injury once they reached their destination.

"Did they find Sallie Kernigan yet?" he said.

"If they did, they're keeping it quiet."

Tilon had a suspicion that Dix might be looking

for Sallie Kernigan too, and for the same reason as Tilon: to make sure she understood the importance of keeping her mouth shut about her connection to Tilon and meth. Tilon didn't believe Sallie was in any immediate danger from Dix, assuming she was still alive. Ironically, her daughter's murder had guaranteed her safety, if only for the time being. Dix couldn't risk killing Sallie to keep her quiet. If he made even the slightest error, the police would fall on him like wolves, seeking to tie him to Donna Lee's killing, which would then link him to Patricia Hartley, and possibly Estella Jackson, back and back until every unsolved femicide in the state of Arkansas was being hung around Pruitt Dix's neck.

Dix pulled out of the lot and drove east. "You really screwed up, Tilon, fucking the Kernigan girl like that."

"I know it." Tilon thought it was just one more bad decision to add to a lifetime of them. "But you screwed things up more by forcing me to leave Cargill."

"You telling me you had a mind to confess your indiscretion to the police?"

"No, but skipping town means questions will be asked. It'll look bad."

"Well, you can explain the reason for your absence upon your return. You possess a trustworthy face, Tilon, and you'll have time enough to come up with a plausible explanation while you're supervising the cook. You still have Evan Griffin in your pocket?"

"I never had him in my pocket."

"If you say so."

"What about my truck?"

"It's garaged. We'll have someone drive it out to you when your work is done."

But Tilon was barely listening. Whatever was going on here couldn't only be because of his connection to the Kernigans, could it? Randall Butcher didn't ordinarily give a rat's ass who was sleeping with whom, although he made a point of discouraging his dancers from getting involved with customers in his clubs, if only because it rarely ended well—strippers, in Butcher's experience, being prone to lead disorderly lives, which in turn attracted disorderly men.

Then again, it was one thing sleeping with a girl who was barely of age, and another coming across that same girl naked and dead, and then neglecting to mention your earlier intimacy with her to the police. And sure, perhaps a degree of reticence made sense when you didn't have an alibi beyond your own mother, who'd have lied to protect you even if the remains of a dozen dead girls were found stacked in your closet, but those kinds of secrets left a man vulnerable to pressure in the event of arrest, pressure that might usefully be applied to convince him to turn on his sometime employer Randall Butcher, the biggest manufacturer and dealer of meth in the region.

So there was all of that, Tilon concluded, which wasn't helpful to his cause or conducive to his long-term health. Oh, and the skimming. He'd been careful about it, or thought he had. His larceny barely amounted to more than the sweepings from the floor after cooks, but it had added up over time: more than $30,000 squirreled away around the county—closer to $40,000, if you were counting every nickel and dime, which Tilon was.

And maybe Tilon wasn't the only one counting.

He glanced at Dix, whose eyes were fixed on the road while his fingers tapped out the rhythm of some piano concerto from the compilation cassette currently playing on the car stereo. Each piece was only a couple of minutes long, as far as Tilon could tell, which said a lot about the shallowness of Dix's musical knowledge and the duration of his attention span. Dix was a thug with a veneer of sophistication, just like Randall Butcher. Tilon was different. He'd completed most of a chemistry major at Arkansas State. He'd have graduated, too, if the money for his education hadn't run out, and he hadn't subsequently become distracted by the practical application of his skills to the manufacture of illegal narcotics. He was better than Randall Butcher in every way, better than Pruitt Dix. They knew it, too, even as they had become increasingly reliant on his proficiency, which probably explained a lot of their animosity toward him.

He and Dix left Hot Springs behind, the wipers fighting against the rain, the hickories along the roadside standing skeletal in the morning light.

The two men did not speak, for there was nothing more to be said, and in time the ground began to rise, and the clouds hung like dark smoke over the Ouachita.

Trees, and the ghosts of trees; a forest of memories.

They entered, and were swallowed by shadows.

3

The blood-dimmed tide is loosed,
 and everywhere
The ceremony of innocence is drowned . . .
 —W. B. Yeats, "The Second Coming"

CHAPTER
LVI

The Arkansas State Medical Examiner's Office employed a number of forensic pathologists to carry out autopsy work. Of these, the best by far was Dr. Ruth Temple, who was the only one of the state's pathologists to be certified by the American Board of Pathology, the others having decided against taking the one-day exam. This was not to say that her colleagues were unqualified—board certification was not compulsory, and many senior practitioners in the field, including some with decades of experience, declined to bother with it—but Temple's extra year of training gave her an edge. She could have made more money in another medical field, since forensic pathologists traditionally earned less than their medical peers, but she preferred working with the dead. They didn't complain, didn't sue, and occasionally one of them would present Temple with a mystery to which she was able to provide a solution.

Temple had risen early that morning to perform the autopsy on Donna Lee Kernigan. She had specifically requested that the task be assigned to her. Temple had been incensed by the rumors that had emerged from Burdon County following the death of Patricia Hartley, and the possibility that a young woman's murder might have been covered up out of political and financial expediency.

Temple knew all about Kovas Industries, and the lifeline the company potentially represented to a largely impoverished county in a state that regularly figured among the poorest in the Union. She regarded the Burdon County coroner as an imbecile, the sheriff as a political timeserver, and the chief investigator, Jurel Cade, as a dangerous throwback to a time when cynicism and brute force trumped any concepts of legality. But Patricia Hartley deserved better than to have her death consigned to the oubliette, and Temple was damned if Donna Lee Kernigan was going to suffer the same fate. This was a view shared by most of those in the ME's office, who felt a duty to the dead that was as much moral as scientific and judicial, and regarded the handling of the Hartley case as an abrogation of all they held meaningful.

Temple's conversations with Chief Evander Griffin of the Cargill Police Department—including two in the previous twenty-four hours, as well as two more confirmatory discussions with Tucker McKenzie, one official, one unofficial—had convinced her that Griffin felt the same way, and she had agreed, against established procedure, to provide him with a heads-up on the autopsy results before informing the county coroner or chief investigator. Griffin had also suggested to Temple that she might like to refer any additional inquiries from the county sheriff's office about Donna Lee Kernigan directly to him, whereupon he would do his utmost to facilitate the provision of the relevant information. Temple had readily assented, even though it would sour the ME's relations with Jurel Cade still further.

Temple's preferred assistant, Lara Kiesel, was already waiting for her when she arrived to begin the examination. Kiesel, like Temple, had familiarized herself with the older case of Estella Jackson, who was murdered in a similar fashion to Donna Lee. Both Temple and Kiesel had also spoken with Tucker McKenzie about his recollections of Patricia Hartley's remains, and scrutinized the pictures he had managed to take at the scene before being banished from it.

Together, Temple and Kiesel photographed Donna Lee Kernigan while she lay in the body bag, and also X-rayed her in order to record the position of the branches used to violate her. Once these tasks were concluded, they worked together to collect the dirt and foreign bodies from her skin and hair, and opened the smaller carriers in which her hands had been sealed to preserve any residue under her fingernails. Finally, she was removed from the body bag, and her wounds surveyed and recorded, before Kiesel was given the okay to clean her in preparation for the autopsy.

Kiesel thought that Donna Lee Kernigan had been a beautiful young woman—even in death, and with her features brutally disfigured. Her bone structure was very fine, and her skin reminded Kiesel of that Curtis Mayfield song, the one about a people darker than blue. The stump of the branch protruding from her mouth—the upper part having been carefully cut off and sealed as evidence by Tucker McKenzie before she was moved from the scene—struck Kiesel as even more obscene than the branch between her legs. Both represented an effort at degradation, but to Kiesel the defilement of the girl's face evinced an additional element of spitefulness, like the cruelty of a child. Yet somehow the act had failed to erase Donna Lee's essential grace. It was her small triumph over the one who had taken her life.

Kiesel moistened a sponge and began wiping down the body. She had friends who didn't understand how she could bring herself to do this, and more than one man had chosen to absent himself from her life because of where her hands might have been. She didn't care. To her there was something ancient and honorable about this task, and in performing it she was part of a continuum of those who had, for millennia, offered this final tenderness to the dead. Kiesel was not religious, and any doubts she might have entertained about her atheism had been excised by repeated contact with the physical realities of mortality. Her actions came down to dignity and kindness, even to those who had been stripped of the first and could no longer benefit from the other.

She spotted the fingerprint just a second before the sponge would have wiped it away. It was on the inside of Donna Lee's right thigh, just below her groin. It had been concealed from view by a length of ivy attached to the branch lodged in her vagina, or else McKenzie might well have spotted it during his initial examination. As it was, the print could easily have been mistaken for another smear of dirt by a more careless eye than her own.

She placed the sponge in its bowl.

"Dr. Temple?" she said. "I think you should come see this."

CHAPTER
LVII

When Parker arrived at the Cargill Police Department, an unfamiliar face was among those gathered around the table in the meeting room that doubled as a canteen and storage closet. The forty-something visitor was wearing a smaller man's suit, along with the kind of untrustworthy mustache that caused sensible folk to lay a protective hand on their wallets, while his skin bore the floridity of stress, bad diet, and poor health. If he lived to see fifty, Parker would send him a greeting card, but he believed his money was safe. Meanwhile, the expression on Chief Griffin's face suggested that if the visitor lived that long, it would be a poor reflection on God's plan for humanity.

"This is Terry Ridout," said Griffin. "He's the prosecuting attorney for this county."

Arkansas operated a system of prosecuting attorneys, each of whom was assigned a region that might encompass a number of counties, depending upon their size or population, and Burdon County was all Ridout's. The position was an elected one, like so many other judicial positions that Parker had come to believe probably shouldn't have been, which meant that Ridout was answerable to the people, and the people liked results. This, in Parker's experience, was usually the point where the requirements of justice parted ways with those of politics.

Since Ridout didn't rise to greet him, Parker likewise didn't bother offering to shake hands, but took a seat next to Colson.

"Terry here," Griffin continued, "obviously has a professional interest in the progress of our investigation, seeing as how he'll be responsible for prosecuting the case in the event of an arrest."

Griffin waited for Ridout to make a contribution to the conversation, which he duly did.

"It's a fucking mess is what it is," he said.

Nobody made an effort to deny that this was indeed the situation. Parker knew that Ridout had, in all likelihood, signed off on the decision of Jurel Cade and Loyd Holt to ignore the evidence of foul play in the case of Patricia Hartley. But now, following Donna Lee Kernigan's death, he had been placed in a difficult position—an impossible one, even—which was not helped by Griffin's persistence. Unsolved murders wouldn't bolster Ridout's reelection bid or aid his ascent through the ranks. On the other hand, anything he did that might have the effect of harming the Kovas deal would see him prosecuting minor drug busts and cases of sexual activity with farm animals until the end of his career. He was probably already receiving anguished phone calls from Little Rock.

"And from what I hear," Ridout added, "so far you've kicked up nothing more than dust."

"The girl was only found yesterday morning, Terry," said Kel Knight. "And it's not like we're oversupplied with manpower."

"We've done more than kick up dust," said Griffin. "We've interviewed in excess of fifty people living or working in the vicinity of the school, and agreed a way forward with the sheriff's office. Mr. Parker here will meet with Jurel Cade later this morning to examine his files on Patricia Hartley and Estella Jackson in the hope of establishing some point of connection between their deaths and the murder of Donna Lee Kernigan. We're going to continue talking to people in Cargill today, plus we expect the autopsy results from Little Rock by noon. This is a small town, Terry. Someone saw something. They just don't know they saw it, not yet."

"Huh," said Ridout. He didn't sound convinced, and now addressed Parker for the first time.

"I won't lie to you," he said. "I don't like the fact that you're here."

"If it's any comfort," said Parker, "that makes two of us."

"Huh," said Ridout, again. "Chief, would you ask your officers to absent themselves for a moment so I can speak in private to you and Mr. Parker?"

Griffin nodded at Colson and Naylor, and the two part-timers present, Giddons and Petrie. "Kel stays, though," he said. "There's nothing you have to say that he doesn't already know."

Ridout didn't argue, but waited until the door had closed behind the four junior officers before resuming.

"There's a shadow hanging over you," he said

to Parker, "and I don't mean what happened to your family, for which you have my condolences. You're a violent man, and your involvement in this affair strikes me as not far off from giving a wolf the run of the pasture."

So Ridout had made some calls, thought Parker, or calls had been made to him.

"He's police," said Griffin. "Was, and is."

"And we need him." Parker was surprised to hear Kel Knight intervene on his behalf. "Unless you're planning on letting us bring in state investigators."

Confronted with the worse of two bad options, Ridout backed down.

"You know that's not going to happen, not without cause."

"You mean if we find another body, it might?" said Griffin.

"You find another body, and this county will still be poor in a hundred years' time. If you're going to do this thing, Evan, make it count, but my reservations about Mr. Parker stand." Ridout got to his feet. "I think I can file this meeting under 'inconclusive,' " he said, "maybe even 'unsatisfactory.' "

"It's symptomatic of the human condition," said Kel Knight.

Ridout tried to button his jacket, before thinking better of it.

"Save that shit for church."

When Ridout was gone, Griffin went to round up his officers, leaving Parker alone with Knight.

"Thanks for the support back there," said Parker.

"I prayed on the matter last night," said Knight.

Parker checked to see whether he was joking, and decided he wasn't.

"It led me to decide," Knight continued, "that, in the face of moral collapse, we find our footholds where we can."

"When you put it that way," said Parker, "your support doesn't exactly sound unconditional."

"Plus, Terry Ridout's a jerk," Knight added.

He pronounced it "Rid-out," to rhyme with "shout," while Griffin had pronounced it "Rid-oo." Parker raised this point.

"It's 'Rid-out,'" said Knight, "or was, until Terry's old man got pretensions on account of marrying a woman from Richmond, Virginia."

"I've been to Richmond," said Parker.

"That," said Knight witheringly, "does not surprise me."

CHAPTER
LVIII

Faced with what was clearly an exemplary finger-print, Dr. Ruth Temple temporarily suspended any further examination of Donna Lee Kernigan's remains and summoned one of the lab's latent print experts.

"Pristine," said the technician, whose name—thanks to parents for whom Watergate might never have happened—was Spiro Nixon, "particularly for a victim recovered under those conditions."

Changes in body temperature, the actions of weather, and the handling of remains during their removal from a crime scene often militated against getting good prints from human skin.

"That's what I thought," said Temple.

Nixon and Temple exchanged a look that verged on the skeptical.

"What do you think that residue is?" said Temple.

Nixon regarded it under a magnifying glass.

"Charcoal, I'd say. Anything in the forensic examiner's report about a fire nearby?"

Temple checked Tucker McKenzie's notes. "No."

"You find any other prints?"

"Not yet."

Nixon finished photographing the print before carefully lifting it from the remains. "Let's check her out."

Temple and Nixon, assisted by Kiesel, conducted a thorough inspection of Donna Lee Kernigan's body, but discovered no further obvious fingerprints.

"Just that one, then," said Nixon.

"Carelessness?" said Temple.

"It happens. Sometimes you catch a break. We could try fuming, if you want to protect against destroying latents."

Fuming involved heating glue, directing the fumes toward the skin of the victim, and using black magnetic powder to make any latent prints visible.

"Let's do it," said Temple. "But can you run that one first?"

Nixon told her he'd do it immediately, and have an assistant get them set up for fuming in the meantime. Soon after, he called Temple with a hit.

"Hollis Ward," he told her. "Sixty-two-year-old male from Burdon County. Convictions going back to the womb, but mostly misdemeanors, apart from possession of child pornography in '91. That's the good news."

"And the bad?"

"Hollis Ward was reported missing more than four years ago."

"Well," said Nixon, "it looks like he's back."

Evan Griffin struck Parker as being a lot more energized upon his return, Naylor and Colson at his heels. Knight picked up on it too.

"What have you got?" he said.

358

Griffin let Colson do the talking.

"Billie took a call from a Mina Dobbs," said Colson. "She lives near the school."

"Miss Mina," said Knight. "I know her. She's a good woman."

"She noticed a truck near the school on the evening Donna Lee was last seen. She doesn't like seeing vehicles parked with their motors running when school kids might be around. Says it stunts their growth."

"Did she get a license number?" said Knight.

"No, her eyesight's not that strong, but she thought it was a red truck, and kind of new."

"Not many people around here driving shiny new red trucks."

"She said 'kind of,'" Griffin corrected him.

"Still, I can only think of one."

"Tilon Ward," said Griffin. "Damn."

"The same Tilon Ward that found the body?" said Parker.

"None other."

"Could Miss Mina be mistaken?"

"It's possible," said Griffin, "but Kel is right: not many people around here have the cash to drop on a new truck. Most everyone else keeps the old one running until the wheels come off."

"What was Ward's demeanor at the scene?" said Parker.

"He was shocked, but that's not surprising, not after what he found."

"Shocked, or *in* shock?"

Griffin thought about this. "I guess he might have been more than shocked, now that I come to reflect on it. But—"

"Go on."

"I don't contest that Tilon may be involved in narcotics, but he's not a violent man."

"Evan has a soft spot for Tilon," said Knight.

Griffin gave Knight a look that suggested he ought to drop the subject.

"Tilon had a hard upbringing," said Griffin. "His daddy was a deviant."

"What kind of deviant?" said Parker.

"Isn't 'deviant' sufficient?" said Knight.

"No, it's not."

"Hollis Ward was arrested on child pornography charges in 1991," said Griffin. "He did six months in Varner for it. But there was a suspicion that where Hollis was concerned, it might have gone further than looking at pictures."

"Abuse?"

"Rumors, but no proof."

"And where is Hollis Ward now?"

"He went missing about four years back, give or take. Nothing's been heard from him since—or if he's been in touch with his family, they haven't seen fit to share the fact with anyone else."

"Would you?" said Knight.

"Probably not."

Parker was making notes. "If the witness is right, Tilon Ward could be the man with whom Donna Lee was having an affair. If so, that would explain why she wanted to keep it quiet: an older white man and a black schoolgirl sleeping together would raise eyebrows anywhere."

"Or maybe he was seeing Sallie Kernigan," said Colson, "and was just doing her a favor by picking up her daughter from band practice."

"No point in ruling that out," said Parker. "It's a hell of a coincidence for the man who was sleeping with the victim to find her body, but I've come across stranger. And it certainly makes more sense than Tilon having an affair with Donna Lee, then killing her, dumping her body in the open, and reporting it to the police in the hope that he might be able to brazen things out."

"He wasn't around when I dropped by his place last night," said Knight, "and his momma said she didn't know where he was, or when he'd be back."

"Except that woman would lie in her sleep," said Griffin, "especially to protect her boy."

"That's true," said Knight. "She has a tendency to err on the side of untruth."

They agreed to divide up the duties for the day accordingly: Griffin and Knight would tackle Harmony Ward, Tilon's mother; Colson and Naylor would take care of some scut work before continuing the canvass of the townsfolk, aided by Giddons and Petrie; and Billie Brinton would hold the fort at the station. Parker would head to Hamill to see what Jurel Cade had come up with, but he also wanted to talk to Ferdy Bowers, who was one of those reputed to have little love for the Cades; Wadena Ott, who had discovered the body of Patricia Hartley; and the coroner, Loyd Holt, if he had the time. He didn't expect to learn much from any of them, but all represented important pieces in the puzzle, and he wanted to put faces on the names. Ideally, Griffin would have assigned Colson or Naylor to accompany him for the day, but the department was already stretched to breaking, and the next twenty-four hours would be crucial to their efforts.

The other officers departed, but Parker and Griffin stayed.

"I hope you noticed Kel making a stand on your behalf in front of Terry Ridout," said Griffin.

"I thanked him for it. I probably shouldn't have. His reply spoiled the effect. But I will concede that people down here have perfected the art of being impolite in the politest possible way."

Griffin took in his town from the window, drew a breath, and reminded himself that this was a troubled man before him, one who had been through more than any individual, young or old, should have to endure.

"Kel has had experience of dealing with Northern visitors in the past, as have I," said Griffin. "He's had his fill of being patronized, or dismissed as a hillbilly by people who derive their cultural knowledge from *Smokey and the Bandit* and *The Dukes of Hazzard*. It may be that he detects some of that attitude in you, even if you've given him no outright cause to suspect you of it, or it could be that he's preempting what he considers to be the inevitable. But he's also aware of your history and reputation, as am I, which includes rumors I won't dignify by repeating aloud. Terry Ridout is familiar with them too, as he made clear to you this morning, although he didn't hear them from us.

"But just so we're clear: this department doesn't prioritize investigations according to color, and it doesn't employ racists or hillbillies. That's not to say the county doesn't have its share of both, and some other places' share as well, but you won't find any of them working for me. Yes, we nurture ignorance of a most particular stripe down here, but look up north and you'll find its cousin. And while it may seem like we've been left alone to sink or swim because no one wants to frighten off our saviors from Kovas, we have friends in the state police and in the crime lab up in Little Rock, and they don't like what's been happening, or the way it's been handled, any more than we do. They'll help in whatever way they can, but they'll do it quietly, because that's just how it has to be when so many others are of a contrary opinion."

"So it's us against them?"

"And there's more of them. Where this case is concerned, Mr. Parker, you're deep in the Dirty South. You remember that when you get to talking with Jurel Cade."

He opened the door and waited for Parker to walk ahead of him, as though fearful that, if left alone, the detective might waver and consign them to struggling on with their numbers depleted.

"You know, my grandfather was a state trooper up in Maine," said Parker, as Griffin closed the door behind them.

"So I understand."

"I spent a lot of time with him, after my father died. He'd let me ride along with him sometimes. He changed my mind about a great many subjects, just by permitting me to sit beside him in that car."

"Such as?"

"Such as about becoming a police officer, because I didn't want to, not after what happened to my father. But I saw how my grandfather dealt with people, and the obligation he felt toward them. So I didn't follow in my father's footsteps. I tried to follow in my grandfather's."

"And do you see similarities between Maine and here?"

"I do. It's just a divergent shade of green."

"People don't differ much," said Griffin. "Only the scenery changes. But the Cades are both a symptom of a particularly Southern disease and an infection all their own. Don't let Jurel pull the wool over your eyes, because he's all twists and turns. Just watch him. If you have any questions or doubts, and you don't like his answers, we can follow them up later. Is there anything else you need clarified?"

"Can I ask him if he kicked a girl's body down a slope?" said Parker.

"I wouldn't," said Griffin. "But then, I'm not from New York."

CHAPTER
LIX

Ferdy Bowers kept three offices around the county. He bounced among them according to the demands of commerce, including various creditors, of which there were more than he would have liked; and debtors, of which there were, regrettably, fewer, notably debtors of the stripe that might be in a position to make more than nominal payments on their arrears. His assorted business ventures earned him a decent living, but Bowers, like many in Burdon County, aspired to more than that. In his view, a number of factors conspired to thwart this ambition, not least among them the actions of the Cade family.

All this he shared with Parker in his main office, which lay on Cargill's eastern edge and abutted a small strip mall containing a laundromat, Ferdy's Wash-N-Go; a store selling "previously loved" clothing, a description that always made Parker uneasy, for reasons he didn't care to contemplate; and the local video library, which was banking on Chuck Norris movies to make it through to summer.

"He keeps the adult stuff in back," said Bowers. "Some of it has to be illegal. If it isn't, it ought to be. I'm no prude, but Jesus Christ . . ."

Parker didn't ask Bowers how he had become aware of the depths of the video library's depravity.

He supposed only that a man ought to know his neighbors—and, in Bowers's case, his tenants, since he also owned the strip mall. Ferdy Bowers was a short, bullish figure with bright red hair and freckled skin, but he dressed well: his suit was unwrinkled and nicely cut, his shirt a crisp white, and his tie a subdued shade of blue. He was a man who dreamed of better things and, like all such men, was ultimately destined to be disappointed.

"About the Cades," said Parker.

"They run this county. Soon, they'll run the state, or near as makes no difference."

"Because of Kovas?"

"The Kovas investment is important in itself, but also for what it represents: an expression of hope for the future, and a marker for generations to come. If it succeeds—and there's no reason why it shouldn't—it'll attract similar industries, and the kind of federal funding that will permit large-scale infrastructural improvements. Within a decade, this county could be transformed. A lot of people will be better off, and a small few will become very wealthy, all because Pappy Cade had a vision and never deviated from it. He and his family will rise. Whatever they want will be theirs, and whatever isn't offered willingly, they'll be able to buy."

"And where does that leave men like you?"

"Begging for scraps from the table." But Bowers was smiling as he spoke.

"Lucrative scraps?"

"Enough to feed a man and his family well." The

smile faded. "Still scraps, though. A man might wish for more."

"And the Cades aren't the sharing kind."

"They've tried to buy me out over the years," said Bowers. "It's not so much the businesses they're interested in as the land. I've been forced to sell a couple of parcels because the Cades acquired some of my creditors, or pressured them into making me settle my debts. But as of now, I'm secure. I've restructured loans, and closed down operations that weren't profitable. I'll benefit along with everyone else when Kovas comes, and it won't have cost me a dime."

Bowers smoothed his tie and examined the shine on his shoes. His office was filled with pictures of himself, frequently surrounded by men of a similar stripe, grinning, glad-handing. Parker counted only a handful of women, and they were either arm candy or wives that had been dusted off and allowed out for the evening. The walls were freshly painted, and the furnishings new. Even the parking lot outside had recently been resurfaced with asphalt, and Parker suspected that the video library, with its secret cache of pornography, was not long for this world. Ferdy Bowers might not have liked the Cades, but his antipathy toward them was insufficient to cause him to seek his own destruction. He wanted the Kovas deal to go ahead. The murders of young women would not easily be laid at his door.

"Did you know Donna Lee Kernigan?" asked Parker.

"No."

"Or her mother?"

"Sallie I knew."

"May I ask how?"

"She worked for me, for a while."

"In what capacity?"

"She cleaned my home."

"When was this?"

"Many years back. I fired her for being under the influence of narcotics."

"What kind?"

"Not the kind that makes a woman scrub faster."

"But you never met her daughter?"

"Sallie Kernigan was a housemaid, not a social intimate."

"And Patricia Hartley?"

"I wasn't familiar with her, or her people."

"What did you think when you heard she was found dead?"

"I didn't think anything at all. Loyd Holt said that her death was an accident, and I accepted him at his word."

"So you spoke to the coroner about her?"

"I play golf with Loyd, and naked dead girls aren't a usual occurrence in this county—or weren't, until recently. Therefore, yes, the subject came up."

"What about Estella Jackson?"

"What about her?"

"Did you know her, or her family?"

"Only as names. After she died, I tried to acquire

the property on which she was found—it was being sold cheap, for obvious reasons—but someone else got in there ahead of me."

"Pappy Cade?"

For the first time, Bowers became evasive.

"No, a company up in Little Rock. They're using it for timber farming. You seem determined to connect the deaths of those three girls, Mr. Parker."

"All died in a similar fashion."

"Loyd Holt says different."

"Loyd Holt is being willfully delusional. Chief Griffin thinks so too."

"What about Jurel Cade? He's the chief investigator for the county."

"He may be coming around to our point of view."

Bowers looked around his office, at the evidence of his own investments in the future of the county, and could not hide his concern. He envisioned it all slipping away from him.

"The Cades won't stand for an investigation, not right now," said Bowers. "Those negotiations with Kovas are balanced on a knife edge."

Parker thought it an interesting metaphor.

"If another young woman dies," he said, "the negotiations will come to a sudden and permanent end."

Bowers buried his head in his hands for a time before surfacing.

"All it needed was another week, if that," said Bowers. "Now we got Evan Griffin bumbling around, pretending he's a detective."

"And me," said Parker. "I'm also bumbling around."

Bowers scowled at Parker over steepled fingers. His wedding ring was wide and bright, and cast a glow over the framed photo on his desk, which showed him with his arms around three slim, dark-haired women, two young, one older. The girls had inherited their mother's looks, which was fortunate for them.

"It would never have crossed Griffin's mind to do this if you hadn't wandered into town," said Bowers.

"I'm not sure that's true," said Parker, "but we'll never know."

"And if you fuck up our deal with your efforts, what then? You just get to walk away, and leave us to stew in our shit?"

"Probably."

"You're an arrogant man."

"That may be true, but I'm here to help."

"Help who, those girls? They're dead, and this investigation will send the rest of us to join them."

"Or it could save you."

"Don't flatter yourself. You're not here to save anyone, except maybe yourself."

It was an odd remark to make, and threw Parker slightly. Bowers picked up on it.

"That's right," he said. "You're the talk of the town: the ex-cop with the dead wife and child, come south to make up for his failings. You go down to the Dunk-N-Go, you may even find photocopies of the news stories, because they're being shared around. No one wants you in this county, Mr. Parker, and we don't relish our futures being sacrificed at the altar of your grief."

Parker stood to go. As anticipated, he hadn't learned much of use, just enough to know that while Ferdy Bowers might not have been directly involved in any killings, he was complicit in the greater evil that had found a home in this place.

"Thank you for your time, Mr. Bowers," he said. He pointed at the picture on the desk. "You have a beautiful family. I'd keep them close, if I were you."

CHAPTER
LX

Parker made two further stops on his way to meet
Jurel Cade. The first was to the funeral parlor
run by Loyd Holt, the county coroner, but it was
a wasted journey. Holt had little to say, beyond
a recitation of the facts as he saw them, and the
only questions that remained to Parker by the end
of the encounter were how much of Holt's story
might be lies and, of that proportion, how much of
it Holt had by now convinced himself might well
be true. Parker left the coroner's place of business
no wiser than when he arrived, and its proprietor
looked relieved to be returning to the corpse of a
dead infant.

From Billie Brinton, Parker had received
directions to the home of Wadena Ott, the woman
who had discovered the body of Patricia Hartley.
It lay at the end of a dirt road, along which houses
of increasing decrepitude made their stand against
nature and decay. On the seat beside him sat a
bottle of cherry brandy.

He found Ott's property easily enough, because
her name was on the mailbox. He parked in the
empty driveway, facing a similarly empty house.
Even without knocking or entering, he sensed its
abandonment. He picked up the bottle of brandy,
and tapped on the front door without receiving a
response before making a single circuit of the

shack. A covered woodpile in back had recently collapsed, scattering itself on the sparse grass. When he peered in the windows of the house he saw open closets, as though the occupant had left in a hurry. Canned food still sat on some of the kitchen shelves.

Parker returned to his car and drove as far as Ott's nearest neighbor. An astonishingly thin woman of indeterminate age was hanging washing from a line, even though the air was damp. Parker identified himself, and asked the woman, who said her name was Leatrice Wages, about Wadena Ott.

"She left," said Leatrice Wages. A breeze blew her dress against her body, displaying a frame that was virtually sexless. The clothing in the basket by her feet, and on the line by her head, looked as though it had been washed and dried too many times already. Some of it was coming apart at the seams, but would soon be mended like the rest. A fat dog waddled from the house to the porch, and barked once at Parker before waddling inside again.

"When did she leave?" said Parker.

"Yesterday evening. A car came for her, and she packed her bags and went away."

"Did she mention where she was going?"

"I didn't get a chance to ask, not that she would have told me anyway. Wadena is an odd bird."

"Did you notice the license number of the car, or the make?"

"No, but it was one of those black sedans, the

kind that follow a hearse. Two people helped Wadena pack her stuff into it, a man and a woman. I never saw them before."

"Did Wadena look frightened?"

"Just confused, but then she always looks confused."

"Did she ever speak to you about the discovery of a body?"

The shutters came down on the face of Leatrice Wages.

"Do you take me for a fool?"

"No, ma'am, I do not."

"Then don't ask foolish questions."

Parker departed, leaving her with the bottle of cherry brandy.

CHAPTER
LXI

Harmony Ward, mother of Tilon, worked part-time for Ferdy Bowers at the Dunk-N-Go, where she covered the 8 a.m. to 2 p.m. shift four days a week. Bowers employed a lot of older people in his businesses, because he believed them to be more honest than the younger generation. Where Ferdy's Dunk-N-Go was concerned, this applied only to the register, as it was widely known that Shelley Benson ate virtually her own weight in free doughnuts every week, and anyone wishing her to take their order had to cool their heels while she swallowed whatever happened to be in her mouth at the time.

Shelley was at the counter when Griffin and Knight arrived. Harmony Ward was behind her in the kitchen, helping Dean Bowman, the chef and manager, with a backlog of breakfast orders.

"You got time for us, Harmony?" said Griffin.

"We're real busy right now, chief," said Bowman. "Can it wait a couple of minutes?"

Griffin didn't want to wait even a couple of seconds, but there was no sense in riling Dean, who was always willing to make time to feed patrol officers, and had demonstrated considerable generosity in the aftermath of the recent tornadoes—more than Ferdy Bowers might have preferred, or even authorized.

"We'll take a seat," Griffin replied.

Dean instructed Shelley to supply them with coffee, and whatever else they might require. They stuck with coffee. Griffin didn't mind his people accepting a complimentary cup from Dean, but he always made it clear to them that anything more should be paid for. After ten minutes the kitchen managed to get on top of the orders, and Harmony Ward trudged over to their table like a woman on her way to a punishment detail.

"Chief," she said. "Kel."

"If you prefer, we can talk outside," said Griffin, but he was already standing as he spoke, making it clear that Harmony's partialities didn't enter into it. The other diners failed to make even the pretense of not watching them leave. Soon it would be all over town that the police had been talking to Harmony Ward, wife of Hollis Ward, formerly a candidate for the local Chester the Molester, and mother to Tilon Ward, currently high on the list of Residents Most Likely to Be Sentenced to 10–15 Years in Varner on Narcotics Charges.

Harmony didn't bother getting her coat. They walked to the picnic tables on the lawn, and Griffin used his handkerchief to wipe the residue of rainwater from the wood before they sat. Harmony dug in her apron and pulled out a pack of menthol cigarettes and a lighter. From the moment they had entered the Dunk-N-Go until now, Griffin noticed, she had yet to make eye contact with either Kel or him.

"Harmony?" said Griffin.

"Uh-huh." She was still taking in the surrounding buildings, the grass, the trees, and the sky above.

"I'd appreciate it if you'd look at me when I'm talking to you."

"Why is that?"

"It's good manners. It also makes it harder for you to lie."

Now she did look at him. He'd given her an opening, and she took it.

"Are you calling me a liar?"

"No," said Griffin.

"Yes," said Knight.

Harmony was perplexed. Whatever response she'd been anticipating, this wasn't it.

"Well," she said, "which is it?"

"Let's say we're undecided, pending further developments," said Griffin.

"I still don't know where Tilon is at, if that's why you're here."

"I didn't ask you where he was."

"That's what you want to know, though, isn't it?"

"I can't deny that's part of it."

"So there you are. The situation hasn't changed since last time you people came calling. Can I go back inside now?"

Griffin ignored the question. Harmony wasn't going anywhere, or not until she'd finished her cigarette. He arranged his hands before him, and stared at the cross formed by his thumbs, just as he'd been taught to fold them in church. Griffin was one of the few Catholics in Cargill. He and his wife had to drive five miles to worship on Sundays, but he preferred it that way. The distance, and the sprinkling of faces to which he could not put a name, helped him to concentrate on his prayers.

"Harmony," he said, "what does Tilon do with his evenings?"

"What do you mean?"

"Does he watch TV, play video games, read?"

"All those things, I guess. He has his space, and I have mine. Sometimes we watch TV together, but he doesn't like my shows and I don't like his, so it's hard."

"Does he have a girlfriend?"

Harmony sucked on her cigarette and gave a good impression of a grande dame offended by any implication of carnality on her son's part.

"I wouldn't know."

"He's never introduced you to anyone?"

"No."

"How long has he been divorced? Two years?"

"Going on three. I never cared for her."

The feeling, as far as Griffin knew, had been entirely mutual. LeeAnne Estes had hated Harmony Ward the way soap hates dirt. Last Griffin heard, LeeAnne was living up in Juneau, Alaska, which was as far as she could go to get away from the Wards without moving to Russia.

"And all that time he's been living like a monk?"

"I told you: I wouldn't know. It's none of my business."

"None of your business." Griffin laughed, and

378

even Knight cracked a smile. "Harmony, there's not a car or truck goes by your window that you don't notice, and not a word of conversation in the Dunk-N-Go that you don't pick up on and file away. If I thought for one moment that you weren't able to keep tabs on your own boy, I'd begin to doubt that up is up and down is down."

"He's introduced me to a girl or two," Harmony conceded, "but none of them was recent."

"And what about the ones he didn't introduce you to?"

Harmony Ward watched as a breeze plucked the ash from her cigarette and caused the smoke to billow, as though a portal had briefly opened to reveal a world into which she did not wish to step. She had been a good-looking woman in her youth, and held traces of it still, but the two men in her life had stolen all that was best from her, and now two more were trying to take what little she had left.

"I got nothing to say."

"We have a witness who claims she saw Tilon's truck near the school on the evening Donna Lee Kernigan went missing," said Knight, which might not have been entirely true, but was close enough to a possible truth as to make no difference, not here. "Says she saw Donna Lee get in, and the truck drive away."

"That's a lie."

It was said without conviction.

"It's enough for us to look for a warrant to search Tilon's truck," said Griffin. He didn't think

379

it was—and anyway, asking wasn't the same as getting—but that wasn't for Harmony to know. "If we find one hair from that girl's head in there, it won't go well for Tilon. We think he was seeing Donna Lee, but I don't believe he had anything to do with what happened to her. I don't figure Tilon for that order of man."

Harmony glanced sharply at him. He stared back, and saw her face soften, then crumple.

"Don't make me do this," she said, as she began to cry.

"It's for his own good, Harmony. You know it."

"You just want to put someone away for the Kernigan girl's death, because then the money will start flowing into this town."

"No," said Griffin, "I want to see the right person apprehended, because if we make a mistake, more girls are going to die. You know me, Harmony: I'm not about to allow that, not if it's within my power. You don't want it either, and neither does Tilon. If he cared about Donna Lee, he's hurting right now. He's also scared, and probably not thinking straight, but he may know something that could help us. He'll be able to fill in a few of those missing hours, and bring us closer to finding the one that killed her."

Harmony searched in her apron again, and this time came out with a tissue. She wiped her eyes and nose before returning the tissue to its hiding place.

"I'm telling you the truth," she said. "I don't know where Tilon is. He left yesterday."

"And he didn't say where he was going?"

"No. I expected him back last night, but he didn't show. And then—"

Griffin didn't press her, but allowed her to take her time.

"Then a man came by late, and told me to pack some items for Tilon: clothes, toiletries. Enough for a couple of days, he said."

"Did you know him?"

She shook her head. "But he'd called earlier. He and Tilon talked for a while, then he left, and a few hours later, Tilon left, too. I wasn't happy when the man returned and started telling me what to do in my own home. I didn't like him. I didn't like his manner. I think he's morally suspect."

"What did he look like?"

"Small. Bald. Green eyes, but with no light to them, like a dead cat's."

"How did he get to your place?"

"He drove."

"Did you notice his car?"

"It was a crappy Chevy, but it sounded good, like a race car."

"What color?"

"Green, same as his eyes."

"Did you get the license number?"

Harmony rummaged in her apron for the third and final time, produced her cigarette pack again, and opened it. Written on the inside, in pencil, was a license number.

"I think," she said, "that Tilon has been keeping bad company."

CHAPTER
LXII

Leonard Cresil sat in the currently patron-free environment of the Gilded Cage and thought that there were few places more depressing than an empty strip club. On the other hand, Burdon County, like the rest of the state, was unlikely to run out of titty bars that were depressing even when occupied. On his run north, Cresil had passed a club advertising BYOB, Mondays to Thursdays. Cresil didn't know too much about the economics of running a titty bar, but he couldn't see the percentage in letting men arrive carrying their own cooler boxes. Next thing, they'd be consuming their own fried chicken, and getting their old ladies to dance on the stage for free, just so they could view them from a fresh angle.

Cresil had been provided with a cup of coffee by one of Randall Butcher's dancers. She was petite and good-looking, but Cresil seemed barely to register her presence beyond thanking her for the coffee and declining some gravy and biscuits offered in case he hadn't yet eaten. He wasn't a morning guy when it came to his appetites, and this was as true of the carnal as the culinary, but he acknowledged a slight stirring in his groin as he watched the girl walk away. Cresil's urges tended toward the aggressive at the best of times. He lived his life on the basis that any benefit to him had to come at a cost to someone else, and the greater the cost to the other party, the greater the benefit to Leonard Cresil. Ultimately, Cresil wasn't happy unless someone else wasn't happy, and preferably because he'd caused them to be that way. If the Kovas business worked out as Randall Butcher hoped it would—which would be due in no small part to Cresil's own efforts—then Cresil planned to come back to the Gilded Cage some night when he was more in the mood, and claim an honorarium from Butcher in the form of one of his girls, although not that little angel; perhaps, instead, one that was on the slide, and wouldn't be missed too much while her bruises were fading.

Now here was Randall Butcher himself, and beside him that redheaded piece of shit Ferdy Bowers, who had just arrived looking flustered. Cresil had wondered how long it would take for the Cades' two whipping boys to find common cause. He'd known Butcher on and off down the years, and they'd helped each other when it suited them. Bowers he was aware of largely by reputation: the runt of the Burdon County business litter, feeding off whatever remained in the tit once the Cades were done suckling.

The three men shook hands, and Butcher made the formal introductions.

"It's my feeling, Leonard, that you only appear when you have trouble in mind," said Butcher, once they were all seated.

"You know why I'm here," said Cresil.

"The bodies in Burdon County."

"That's right. Mr. Shire is concerned about the activities of the Cargill police."

"I'll bet he is. I hear he's taken money from near half the state, and promised as much again to the other half. Some of that cash in his pocket is mine and Ferdy's."

"Then it's in all our interests," said Cresil, "that a solution should be found to these terrible crimes. Are you feeling all right, Mr. Bowers?"

Ferdy Bowers had shuddered involuntarily. It was a response to the tone of Cresil's voice, and the way his tongue had rolled the word *terrible* around his mouth, as though savoring the taste of it. Leonard Cresil, Bowers thought, was just the kind of man that could spit-roast a dead girl with sticks. It sickened Bowers that he was forced to keep such company, even temporarily. Randall Butcher was bad, but Cresil was a whole other can of worse.

"I'm fine," said Bowers. "It's cold in here, that's all."

"Not to me. It might be that you're susceptible to chills, on account of a constitutional weakness."

"That must be it."

"Get to the point, Leonard," said Butcher. "I got a business to run."

"I'm tired of working for others," said Cresil, "and cleaning the shit from their shoes. I have my eye on a bar in Boca Raton, and figure I may just retire there. If this deal goes through, my bonus, along with a cut from Mr. Shire's end, will set me up for life.

"But Mr. Shire is conflicted: there are risks involved in doing nothing about these killings, and other risks inherent in permitting the police to delve into them. Having slept on the problem, Mr. Shire has come down on the side of no investigation. After all, months went by between the deaths of the Hartley and Kernigan girls. On that basis, the papers will be signed, and the first foundations laid, before we see another body—if we ever do. By then it'll be too late to redline the project, and Griffin and Cade can call in the state police to solve the crime, letting the professionals take care of it. A bunch of amateurs beating around the bushes can only attract the wrong kind of attention."

"And has Shire seen fit to explain this reasoning to Evan Griffin?" said Butcher. "Because my information is that the chief is of a contrary view—a contrary disposition, even."

"Plus, they're not all amateurs," said Bowers.

"What?" said Butcher.

"They're not all amateurs," Bowers repeated. "Griffin has brought in a former detective from New York, a man named Parker."

Cresil eyed Bowers with something approaching interest.

"So I've been led to believe," said Cresil.

"I didn't know about this," said Butcher.

"You've probably been too distracted by pussy

and narcotics," said Cresil. He returned his attention to Bowers. "Have you met Parker?"

"He came to my office this morning. He was asking questions about the Cades, and the dead girls."

"What did you tell him?"

"That he should never have come to Burdon County."

"I could have told him that," said Cresil, "with or without dead coloreds."

"And how does Shire feel about Parker's involvement?" said Butcher to Cresil.

"Mr. Shire hasn't yet been brought up to speed on it," said Cresil, "but I imagine he'll be discommoded when he finds out."

"You could just inform him once the problem has already been taken care of," said Butcher.

"In what way?"

"No Parker, no investigation—or only the imitation of one."

Bowers stood. He might have agreed with the substance of the words—because he had said something similar to Parker's own face—but not their implication.

"I don't want to hear that kind of talk," he said.

"Sit down, Ferdy," said Butcher. "You were in this from the moment you walked through that door."

"Yes," said Cresil, "sit down, Mr. Bowers. I wouldn't want cause to doubt your discretion."

Bowers sat.

"We're not talking about killing," said Butcher, "just derailing."

"If you say so," said Cresil.

"You are incorrigible, Leonard," said Butcher. "You'll make Ferdy here anxious."

"So you'll take care of it?" Cresil asked Butcher.

"I won't even have to use my own people. All it'll cost is a couple of cases of beer. I expect if Shire chose to seek a public vote on his policy toward the investigation, it would receive unanimous support in most quarters. Pruitt won't have trouble finding idle hands for the devil's work."

"So that's one problem solved," said Cresil.

"There are others?" said Butcher.

"One, but it may be both a problem and a solution. I was speaking with Reverend Pettle last night—"

"That preacher and his church are giving me ulcers," said Butcher. "I can remember when he was holding roadside services, and sucking in exhaust fumes along with the fire of the Holy Spirit, and now he wants to go head to head with the Pentecostals."

Cresil didn't like being interrupted. Even after Butcher had finished talking, Cresil allowed silence to accrete, just so Butcher would restrain himself in future.

"Well," Cresil continued, when he judged the moment was right, "the reverend was very close to Sallie Kernigan. He ministered to her needs, you might say, and not just the religious kind."

Butcher seemed about to comment, but thought better of it.

"The affair initially lasted a couple of months," said Cresil, "but came to an end just about the time that the reverend's wife found out about it. Unfortunately, Pettle's flesh is weak, and his spirit isn't much stronger. In recent weeks, he and Sallie reignited the embers of their relationship. That's information you can use right there, Randall. It might convince the reverend to moderate his position on that church business."

"It just might," said Butcher.

"If it does, I'll expect a dividend. I'll leave the amount to your discretion. I know you wouldn't cozen a friend."

Randall Butcher would have cheated his own mother, given the chance, but not Leonard Cresil. Friendship didn't enter into it, only prudence.

"In addition, Pettle told me that Donna Lee Kernigan had been seeing a white man. I think you, Randall, may have an inkling of his identity."

"Tilon Ward," said Butcher.

"How long have you known?"

"We thought it might have been the mother, not the girl, until Tilon yesterday admitted otherwise."

"Even though Ward's daddy had some previous in that regard?"

"Tilon's daddy liked children," said Butcher. "Donna Lee was legal."

"Not by much."

"Enough in the eyes of the law."

"Where's Tilon now?"

"Pruitt moved him out of town."

"Away from the police?"

"And to cook," said Butcher.

"You're taking a chance, cooking meth with all this police attention in the county."

"You pass Bradley's House of Centerfolds on the way over here?"

"That the BYOB titty place?" said Cresil.

"Yep. That's what we're competing with here. I need cash reserves, especially if I'm to start building once Kovas climbs off the fence."

"And once Pettle starts to see sense about that disused church," said Bowers, who was one of Butcher's co-investors in the proposed Cargill titty bar venture.

"If he starts to see sense. That fucking preacher . . ."

Cresil sat back in his chair and folded his hands across his flat stomach.

"If I were the killing kind," he said, "and someone made himself available as a culprit for my crimes, I might take the opportunity to rest easy, and wait for the heat to die down before I started again, assuming I even elected to recommence my activities. It might be that I'd already have gotten such urges out of my system. A passing vice, if you will."

Bowers looked like he wanted to put his hands over his ears, and begin keening to cover the sound of their voices. Instead, he contented himself with looking miserable.

"Are you talking about feeding Tilon to the police?" said Butcher. "What if he has an alibi?"

"Does he?"

"He told me he was home the night Donna Lee probably died."

"He would tell you that, wouldn't he?"

"His momma will attest likewise."

"Then it'll be for the police to establish the truth of it. In the meantime, Tilon will be behind bars, some of the impetus will seep from the investigation, and we can go ahead with confirming deals and making ourselves wealthy."

Butcher tugged at his lip. Cresil's plan didn't quite resemble his own, which was to keep Tilon cooking for as long as was feasible before having Pruitt Dix take him for a walk in the woods. Butcher didn't want Tilon to end up spilling his guts to detectives about the meth operation in order to prove he could be believed on other subjects too, such as the death of Donna Lee Kernigan.

"Or suppose we feed them Tilon, but make sure he's dead when they find him?" said Butcher.

"You know," said Cresil, "that would work too."

CHAPTER
LXIII

Griffin and Knight stood in the parking lot of the Dunk-N-Go, watching Harmony Ward return to work.

"Souped-up green Chevy," said Griffin. "Small, bald driver."

"With dead eyes."

"Sounds a lot like Pruitt Dix."

"An awful lot," said Knight.

"Is he still licking Randall Butcher's boots?"

"Last I heard."

"You think Randall will talk to us?"

"Not without a lawyer, and even if he does, whatever he has to say won't be worth hearing."

Griffin took off his hat and scratched his head. His eczema had begun acting up again. Soon he'd have blood and skin under his fingernails.

"Just when I think this county can't get any more screwed up," he said, "it finds a way to disappoint me."

A similar conversation was also taking place among Dr. Ruth Temple, Spiro Nixon, and Lewis Pickett, the executive director of the state crime laboratory. Pickett wasn't a scientist, but he had progressed through the ranks of the state police and the U.S. Marshals Service before accepting the post of director. The crime lab had previously operated under the auspices of the state police, but it was felt that having an arm of the law processing evidence in a crime might leave a bad taste when it came time to prosecute, so it was now an independent entity. Nevertheless, it helped that Pickett came from a law enforcement background, because it meant he could understand the needs of both the police and the scientists, and manage them accordingly. Alternatively, in times of crisis, it enabled two entirely different groups of people to complain about him simultaneously, thus giving them a target for their ire while the lab went about its business.

Now Pickett listened while Temple and Nixon told him about the fingerprint, and the hit from the system.

"Hollis Ward?" said Pickett. "Well, I'll be damned."

"Do you know him?" said Temple.

"I've had the pleasure down the years, but it wasn't much of one. If you'd asked me about him five minutes ago, I'd have told you he was dead. No chance of an error?"

"None," said Nixon. "It was a very good print."

Pickett caught the implication.

"You're saying it's too good?"

"No, just that if Hollis Ward was seeking to damn himself, he couldn't have gone about it any better."

"And there are no other prints on the body?"

"None from Hollis Ward," said Temple. "We found some bruising to the upper left arm, and got some partials from that. It looks like someone else might have grabbed the victim hard in the twenty-four hours before she died, because the partials don't match Ward's prints."

"Well done on getting even partials."

"We had residue, which helped," said Nixon.

"What kind of residue?"

"I'm guessing grease or motor oil, but I won't be able to say for sure until it's been analyzed. I tried running the prints, but they're not in the system."

Pickett looked again at the hit on Hollis Ward.

"Hollis, Hollis," said Pickett, "where have you been all these years?" He waved the paperwork at Temple. "You been in touch with Evan Griffin about this?"

"No, I thought I'd run it by you first."

"Any reason other than to hamper my digestion?"

"We have a request from the Burdon County Sheriff's Office to copy it immediately on the autopsy results, since the chief deputy is, as you're aware, also the chief investigator for the county, and his office is cooperating with the Cargill PD on the investigation. But Griffin asked that we send all relevant information only to him, and he'd then share it with the sheriff's office. I feel as though I'm tied to a pair of horses pulling in opposite directions."

Pickett didn't have to try hard to look unimpressed. "If Jurel Cade had done his job first time around, we might not be cutting a dead girl. How far into the autopsy are you?"

"Kiesel was about to clean the body when she found the print. We stopped everything."

"Then technically you don't have the full results to share, do you?"

"I guess not," said Temple.

"So call Griffin, tell him what you've found, and then pick up where you left off. When you're done, and you have the report ready, you can deal with the sheriff's office. If Jurel gives you any trouble, just refer him to me."

"Thank you, Lewis."

"Don't mention it, and I mean that in every sense," said Pickett. "I swear, Burdon has got to be the most dysfunctional county in the Union."

CHAPTER
LXIV

Parker drove alone to Hamill, taking some of the back roads to familiarize himself with the land, the browns of branch and earth broken only by the sprouting of new-growth pines. He passed countless iterations of houses of worship—some little more than cabins, others so grandiose that it seemed impossible for them to have any relevance to those who passed through their doors, unless it was to remind them of the distance of their daily lives from the glory of God. Pools of water stood amid the trees where fields had flooded from the recent rains, and here and there lay patches of flattened forest, and the roofless shells of houses, marking where tornadoes had struck. One Pentecostal church had vanished almost entirely, leaving only a sign advertising its former presence and a battered cross that someone had lodged in the earth amid the wreckage. Parker wondered what message the congregation had taken from its destruction. Whatever God was trying to tell them, it wasn't good.

All the businesses he saw were small—bait shops, rock shops, auto shops, storage depots, liquor stores, flea markets—and few gave the impression of flourishing, except perhaps the auto shops and liquor stores. As Parker neared the town limits the latter's number increased. The two adjacent counties were dry, with sales of alcohol banned entirely, which meant that Burdon reaped the benefits.

He arrived at the sheriff's office, where a deputy showed him into a small conference room. Two file-storage boxes stood on the table. Parker was asked if he needed coffee, or anything else, but replied that he was fine. He removed his coat, hung it on the back of a chair, and opened the first of the boxes, the one relating to Patricia Hartley's death. It contained only a single slim folder. Inside was a photostat copy of the original report detailing the discovery of the body, signed by Jurel Cade, and a series of photographs of the scene, taken after Hartley's remains had been removed, all of them replicating pictures already in Parker's possession. The additional photos received by Parker, and not contained in the sheriff's file, had been taken with an instant camera. Parker knew that forensic examiners generally preferred not to use instant cameras because the pictures faded over time, but the results could be useful as *aide-mémoires*, or backups in the event of some disaster with the original records. In this case, any other photographs taken at the scene had been destroyed in the car wash incident, but the instant snaps, as Parker informed Griffin, had eventually found their way to him.

He set aside the photos and moved on to a rough sketch of the area in which the body had been located, with north indicated at the top, and distances carefully and, he thought, accurately delineated, almost certainly to remove any doubt that Hartley had been discovered on county land, not federal. The paper on which the sketch was drawn had suffered water damage at the edges and was stained brown. Finally, there was a crumpled copy of the coroner's report, in which Loyd Holt had recorded a verdict of accidental death.

And that was it: no notes on a search of the scene; no pictures of the body; no account of the discovery of evidence of any kind; no details of the collection and packaging of said evidence, or of control samples; no chain of custody; no witness statements; no interviews; and most of all, no investigation.

Parker made some cursory notes and drew a version of the map, including the distances, but there was little that he didn't already know. He restored the file to its container, put it aside, and went to work on the second box, the one relating to Estella Jackson's murder in the summer of 1992. Here he had better luck. Eddy Rauls, assisted by the previous coroner, and Vester Stanley, at that time the forensic examiner, had worked the scene carefully, conducted systematic grid searches for evidence, and kept copious notes.

Unlike Patricia Hartley and Donna Lee Kernigan, Jackson's body had not been discovered in the open, but in a woodshed adjoining a run-down property about five miles outside Hamill. She had been reported missing six days earlier, but she came from a troubled background and had a history of running away from home, sometimes staying with friends or relatives for days, even weeks, until her domestic situation grew calmer. Typically, though, either Estella or someone else would get in touch to let the family know she was okay. When, on this particular occasion, no word was heard, a sister contacted the county sheriff, which meant that by the time Estella's body was found, she had been missing for nine days. She was located by a party of local men, one of a number of teams assembled by the sheriff to conduct searches of the area. Among them were an uncle and two cousins of the victim. Her father—a dissolute man, and the cause of much of his daughter's misery, according to some of the statements included in the file—was looking elsewhere at the time. Estella Jackson's mother, perhaps thankfully, had predeceased her daughter by two years.

The autopsy concluded that Jackson had probably been dead for a week, meaning she was killed on the second or third day after her disappearance. She had been badly beaten, and the branch found lodged in her mouth had been put there before she died, possibly in an effort to silence her. The branch between her legs was inserted postmortem, but the medical examiner was of the opinion that she had probably been raped before she died, possibly with the same stick.

Parker worked his way through the photographs from the scene. Again, he was familiar with some of them, and the rest didn't add much beyond making him feel depressed. He moved on to the witness statements, and the interviews conducted in the days that followed, most of them by Rauls. They were, Parker thought, more perfunctory than the paperwork from the scene, most amounting to barely a paragraph or two. That in itself wasn't unusual: not every interview carried out in the course of an investigation would prove productive, and the majority involved checking boxes, eliminating suspects, or closing down avenues of inquiry that might otherwise prove wasteful of resources. Only the interviews with Jackson's father extended to multiple pages. From their tone, it was clear that Rauls liked him for the killing, but had no evidence, and no confession, so any suspicions remained just that. No additional paperwork had since been filed.

The door opened behind Parker, and Jurel Cade entered.

"You find our murderer yet?" he asked.

Parker didn't reply, but continued noting the names and addresses on the statements accumulated by Rauls during the Jackson investigation. Cade took a seat and leafed through the Jackson photos.

"You planning on talking to all those people?" said Cade, once Parker had finished writing.

"Some of them."

"Good luck with that. They didn't have much to offer first time around, and at least three of them are dead by now."

Parker thought that Cade's familiarity with their contents meant he'd looked at the Jackson files recently.

"Did you return to the Jackson case after Patricia Hartley was found?" said Parker.

"Out of curiosity."

"And it didn't inspire you to investigate further?"

"I saw no reason to disagree with the coroner's recommendation."

There was no point in raking over those old coals, Parker knew. It would get him nowhere. Jurel Cade's decision had been made as soon as he nudged Patricia Hartley's body over the edge of a hill and watched it tumble down the slope. Everything that followed—including the probable destruction of evidence in a car wash, and the relocation of the Hartley family—was a consequence of that act.

"Why didn't Eddy Rauls call in the state police to help investigate the Jackson murder?" said Parker.

"Eddy always was willful. He'd dealt with enough killings in his time, and solved most of them without outside help. He felt he had this one in hand."

"But he didn't."

"No, but he did have a suspect."

"The father." Parker picked out the relevant statement. "It doesn't seem to have amounted to more than a hunch, in the absence of anything better."

"Aaron Jackson was a violent man. He had that reputation."

"Where is he now?"

"Dead: poisoned himself with alcohol. He's one of the three."

"Who are the others?"

Cade gave him two more names, adding, "But they're of no consequence."

Parker flicked to those statements, and was inclined to agree. One was from a woman named Edith Akin, who was ninety-two years old at the time, lived near the Jacksons, and could only swear to having heard loud arguments and crying from her neighbors' home over the years; and the other came from an interview with a man named James Darby, who had seen Estella Jackson buying candy at the local IGA the night before she went missing.

"I do have another question." said Parker.

"Shoot."

"I count twenty-two statements in the Estella Jackson case, but the covering page lists twenty-three. One is missing. It's a statement from Hollis Ward. Would you know anything about that?"

"No."

"Do you maintain a log of those who access records or evidence from your storage rooms?"

"In theory."

"What does that mean?"

"It means that people are supposed to sign for anything they examine, but our evidence storage includes the space next to the janitor's closet, and a former restroom. We keep them locked, but everyone knows where to find the key."

Parker examined the label on the top of the Estella Jackson box. The last person to sign it out was Eddy Rauls, five months after Jackson's death. Even Jurel Cade hadn't bothered to add his name to the list when he chose to browse the contents after the Hartley killing.

"Was he the same Hollis Ward who was father to Tilon Ward?" said Parker.

"Look at you," said Cade, "keeping up with the local color. Yeah, that's him, but he hasn't been seen around here in years. The general opinion is that he's not coming back anytime soon, either, or not before Judgment Day."

"He's dead?"

"Most likely."

"Natural causes?"

"Most unlikely. He wasn't a popular man. He got charged with possession of child pornography, and did a few months for it, but the story was that he might also have been more hands-on with his vices. When he turned to smoke, nobody was too shocked. They'd be more surprised if he showed up again."

All this Parker already knew, but he was content to let Jurel Cade talk. He'd learn nothing from silence.

"Assuming he's dead, any suspects?"

"The bulk of the county, but I'd be prepared to narrow it down to his wife and son."

"Why?"

"Who knows what went on behind the doors of that home?"

"Abuse?"

"Like I said, hands-on."

Parker took a few moments to think.

"Hollis Ward went missing the same year Estella Jackson died," he said.

"One month after."

"Could there be a connection?"

"I don't know."

"What I mean is this: Was Hollis Ward suspected of involvement in Jackson's murder?"

"I don't have that information."

"But you were a deputy at the time."

"I was, but Eddy Rauls wasn't in the habit of sharing his every thought with mere deputies."

"Or just not with deputies from the Cade family?"

"There you go again, listening to idle gossip."

"The question stands: Was Hollis Ward a suspect?"

"No more than anyone else."

"And his arrest for possession of child pornography didn't cause Rauls to look at him again for the Jackson killing?"

"Getting off on naked children is one thing, and maybe abusing your own son, but raping and killing a seventeen-year-old girl is another. Still, you'd have to ask Eddy Rauls yourself. I couldn't claim to understand his reasoning when I worked under him, and I'm no wiser about it with the benefit of years. Now I have a question."

"Go on."

Cade leaned forward.

"How'd you come by those scars on your hand?"

CHAPTER
LXV

Evan Griffin took the call from the crime lab as he and Knight were discussing how best to handle Randall Butcher.

"Hollis Ward?" said Knight, after Griffin had hung up the phone and shared the substance of the conversation with him. "*Our* Hollis Ward?"

"Unless there's two of him, which would be unfortunate for all concerned."

"That can't be right."

"Fingerprints don't lie."

Knight searched for his pipe, and began filling it with tobacco in order to give his hands something to do while he tried to think.

"You never did believe that Hollis left the county," he said.

"Because," said Griffin, "like most everyone else, I took the view that he was buried somewhere in it. I didn't buy the idea that he'd left of his own volition, because Hollis didn't even like visiting Little Rock, and he only tolerated Hot Springs when the horses were running at Oaklawn. His roots were here, and if a man like that pulls up his roots, he dies."

"Or so you thought."

Griffin watched Knight go through the motion of tamping the tobacco and plucking the loose leaves from the bowl. He knew that his sergeant was aching to light up. Griffin was momentarily tempted to allow it, but knew that if he gave in once he'd never be able to prevent it in the future, and he'd arrive home every night stinking of tobacco, which wouldn't please his wife one bit, especially now that she was pregnant. He'd considered telling Kel about the pregnancy, but decided against it. He and Ava had agreed to wait a while, just until they were sure that everything was okay with the baby.

"Yeah, so I thought."

"Hollis could have gone to ground somewhere else in the state," said Knight, "and replanted those roots in soil that wasn't unfamiliar to him."

"We'd have heard."

"Would we? Hollis could lie low when he chose. All we ever got him for was the child pornography, and even his own lawyer didn't believe that was an isolated incident. And Hollis knew the Ouachita and the Ozarks. He made good money as a guide. It wouldn't have been beyond him to find a place to hole up, even under the nose of the Forest Service."

"But why? He'd served his time."

"Everyone knew what he'd done. Like his lawyer, a lot of them were of the opinion he'd probably done worse, and there was every chance he was going to do it again. Even his wife wouldn't let him back into the house after he was released. Mind if I light my pipe?"

"Yes, I do mind," said Griffin.

Knight looked disconsolate, but didn't argue.

"I'd buy Hollis going to ground for a few months," said Griffin, "but not for years. It wasn't in his nature."

"What if he had no choice about where he went?"

"You're thinking prison?"

"It would make sense."

"No, he had a record. We'd have been informed."

"Mistakes happen, and Hollis wouldn't have been rushing to share details of his previous convictions. Sex criminals do hard time."

AFIS, the federal Automated Fingerprint Identification System, wasn't perfect—no system requiring human input ever was—and it was possible that Hollis Ward might have slipped through one of the gaps.

"Get Billie to put out some terminal requests," he said. "I don't recall Hollis ever using an alias, but tell her to check our records, just in case. Then go smoke your damn pipe outside. I'll give you fifteen minutes."

"What are you going to do?"

"Look for a last known address for Pruitt Dix."

"And Randall Butcher?"

"I know how to find Randall," said Griffin. "I'll just look under the nearest rock."

CHAPTER
LXVI

Parker stretched out the fingers of his hands and heard one of the knuckles crack. Most of the pain was gone from the joints, and he supposed he was fortunate not to have broken any bones.

Fortunate not to be in jail.

But not fortunate to be alive.

No, not that.

"I don't think it's any of your business how I came by them," he said, in reply to Jurel Cade's question.

"I'm just curious, that's all."

"Curiosity is a common ailment. Mortality seems to be the only corrective."

"You have a clever way with words, don't you?"

"There's no point in having any other way with them."

"I made some calls to New York about you. I know Evan Griffin did too, although he and I have differing responses to what we learned. He elected to involve you in his department's business, while I would have escorted you to the county line and told not to come back if you valued your liberty."

"Get to the point, deputy."

"Who was Johnny Friday?" said Cade.

"A pimp. A procurer of children."

"I hear he died."

"He didn't die. He was killed in a bus station restroom."

"They know who did it?"

"Not yet."

"They have any suspects?"

"I'm sure they do."

"Are you one of them?"

"You take your time getting to the point, but you arrive there eventually, don't you?"

"You haven't answered my question."

"Yes, I was interviewed about what happened to Johnny Friday."

"And?"

"I had an alibi."

"Did it hold up?"

"It wouldn't be much of an alibi if it didn't."

"You're being clever again."

"That makes two of us. If you have an accusation to make, you should have the courage to come out with it."

Cade relented, but only slightly.

"When I spoke to New York," he said, "I detected some ambivalence about the fate that befell Mr. Friday. His own mother wouldn't have described him as any loss to the world, and he was always likely to end up prematurely dead or behind bars. Those who take that view probably feel his murder should become a cold case, so it can quietly be forgotten. At the same time, there are still some in the NYPD who cleave to the rule of law, not the rule of the jungle, especially when it applies to one of their own. Just saying."

Parker began to gather his notes.

"You know," he said, "I took a trip out to the location where Patricia Hartley's body was found. I stood on that rise above it, and thought of her remains tumbling down the slope, getting all torn up by those rocks and stones; and that was after what had already been done to her, whatever the coroner and anyone else might have tried to kid themselves into believing.

"I also attempted to interview Wadena Ott, the woman who found Patricia's body, but she left town yesterday in a big sedan, and she doesn't strike me as a person habituated to sedan cars. It's almost as though someone didn't want her talking about what she might or might not have seen, and elected to move her just in case she couldn't be relied on to remember the story she'd been taught."

Parker nudged with a finger the box containing what passed for the records of Hartley's death.

"Those papers, those scraps of fiction, suggest that Patricia Hartley either fell while running down the slope, or else she was already dead when she fell—the coroner speculated on a taste for narcotics, but without any evidence I can see— and her corpse might have been nudged over the edge by an animal. If that was the case, it was an animal that knew the difference between federal and county land, which makes it a very advanced species of predator. I'd be very interested in catching an animal like that. I'd consider it a matter of public safety, because it wouldn't do to have it out there running wild. Who knows what mischief it might get up to if left to roam unchecked?"

Cade had grown very still, and his eyes held pale fires.

"And what would you do with it, Mr. Parker, once you'd found it? Would you kill it? Is that your favored mode of operation in such cases?"

"Only if it left me no choice. I'd prefer to trap it so it could be examined, and an attempt made to determine its nature. After that, people could do with it as they wished. In olden times, villages used to hang the carcasses of wolves from their gates as a warning to the rest of the pack. Metaphorically, I feel there might be an aptness to that."

"You ought never to have come to this land," said Cade.

"I keep being told that," said Parker, "but I'm here now, and I'm not leaving until the man who killed these women has been found. I'll speak with Chief Griffin about what I've learned from the examination of those files. If he thinks you can be of any help in tracing some of the people on my list, I'm sure he'll be in touch."

He was at the door when Cade called his name.

"Men," said Cade.

"What?"

"You told me you weren't going to leave until the *man* who killed these women was found. It's not one man. It's at least two."

"Why do you say that?"

"Whatever might have befallen Patricia Hartley,

Estella Jackson, and Donna Lee weren't killed by the same individual. I was at all three scenes, and you weren't. Jackson's death was different."

"Different how?"

"There was more rage. Her teeth were broken, and her private parts were all cut up by what had been done to them with that branch. The other bodies didn't have that level of damage inflicted on them, not even Donna Lee's."

"Okay," said Parker. He was still trying to figure out how the conversation had taken this sudden turn when Cade decided to answer the question for him.

"I may not like you, Mr. Parker," he said, "but don't mistake that for not giving a shit about those dead girls."

Parker did not reply, but left Cade slouched in a chair, the sunlight reaching for him through the blinds, and wondered at whose hypocrisy might be greater: Cade's or his own.

CHAPTER
LXVII

Denny Rhinehart didn't usually open for business until just past noon, except on weekends. This was not entirely of Rhinehart's own volition. Burdon might have been a wet county, but the Cargill town council, under the influence of various church representatives, had strongly suggested that bars within the town limits should consider serving liquor only after some acceptable portion of the working day was done. This had followed a surge in closures of local businesses, leading to more than a hundred job losses and a concomitant increase in arrests for DWI, minor assault, and domestic violence. While Cargill's drinking establishments were under no legal obligation to abide by this motion, they were given to understand that their responses to it might color any future discussions surrounding the renewal of their licenses.

Rhinehart considered it all so much foolishness, because a man or woman requiring a drink before lunch—or even before breakfast, he who was without sin and all that—could simply look to their own supply at home; or if they were running low, a gas station or liquor store would promptly rectify the situation, within the strictures of the law. Also, if you'd lost your job, and had no prospect of finding another anytime soon, or not anywhere in Burdon County, why not take time to catch your breath, crack open a cold one, and consider your options, however limited they might be? And maybe it would be better to do so in a bar like the Rhine Heart, where a sympathetic bartender could monitor your intake, listen to your problems, and possibly talk you down when you started getting too angry or depressed, than drink alone at home—or worse, not alone but in the vicinity of a partner or spouse who just didn't understand, goddammit, and might become the victim of a regrettable loss of temper.

But Denny Rhinehart had kept these opinions to himself, making only a token objection—and offering a token concession—to what he was assured would be a temporary measure. Once Kovas had broken ground on the first site, these voluntary restrictions could be dispensed with and normal service resumed. Anyway, it wasn't as though he made a whole lot of money before noon. Sometimes it was barely worth opening the place just to serve a dozen beers and a couple of drinks from the well, and even then he had to offer free bacon. But Rhinehart didn't like being told what to do, especially not by the kind of speaking-in-tongues fanatics who comprised the worst of the county's God-fearers, and had more influence on the susceptible than was conducive to easy living. Rhinehart had parted ways with organized religion many years earlier, and with any notion of God not long after. A man had only to gaze on the havoc wreaked on the state by the tornadoes, or take in the slow withering of Burdon County and its people, to come to the conclusion that if there ever was a God, He was long gone from these parts.

So Rhinehart wasn't great pleased when, shortly after 11:30 a.m., Reverend Nathan Pettle entered the bar through the rear door, looking about as uncomfortable as he probably felt, if not more so, Pettle not being a drinking man. Rhinehart and Pettle, like most citizens of stature in Cargill, were on nodding terms with each other, but hadn't exchanged a word since the meeting convened four months earlier to discuss opening hours.

"Reverend," said Rhinehart. "You're an unlikely visitor. I hope you parked out back, where none of your congregation are likely to see your vehicle and speculate on your vices."

He grinned, but Pettle didn't grin back.

"I was hoping to speak with you for a few minutes, Mr. Rhinehart."

There were many residents of Cargill with whom Denny Rhinehart would have preferred not to spend time in colloquy, and Reverend Pettle figured high among them. Whatever had brought the preacher to his door, it wasn't going to lead to an increase in Rhinehart's takings, and might even require him to listen to a sermon.

"To tell you the truth," said Rhinehart, "I came in early to get my paperwork done while things were quiet. If there was a way we could do this another time—"

"I think we should talk now," said Pettle. "It's about Donna Lee."

• • •

Tilon Ward, the bag of clothing and toiletries slung over his shoulder, trudged through the woods, Pruitt Dix following close behind. Randall Butcher operated three meth cookhouses out here in the Ouachita, the two smaller ones in converted RVs for reasons of convenience and mobility, and the largest in a house that once belonged to a family called the Buttrells, although the last of them was set to fertilizing daffodils in 1989. The dwelling subsequently fell into disrepair, and would in all likelihood have been swallowed up by the forest and eventually forgotten, had the body of Estella Jackson not been discovered in the woodshed close to the main house. Such limited appeal as the property might have offered to most prospective buyers immediately turned to smoke after the killing, and nobody thought much about it when a company in Little Rock acquired the Buttrell acreage and commenced planting pine. The more optimistic townsfolk theorized that the company might even make a profit on its investment down the line, although others took the view that it was some kind of tax write-off, because the Buttrell land was hard to access, and any tree farming or logging would require construction of a better road.

As for the families residing on the adjacent land, they had long since ceased to take an interest in what went on there, any inquisitiveness they might once have entertained evaporating following a single visit from Pruitt Dix—although the threat

415

of the stick was balanced with a carrot in the form of an envelope of cash delivered twice yearly, the Thanksgiving payment being slightly larger than the summer one in recognition of the additional demands the season placed on the pockets of the poor.

Now, as Tilon passed through the rising pines, the house became visible, the two RVs already parked in the yard and a handful of men moving between them. Usually Butcher kept the mobile labs away from the Buttrell land, but not this time. He had buyers lined up, and they'd take all the product he could provide. It made sense to bring the three arms of his operation together in one location, which would save on manpower and costs.

Tilon paused. There, to the right, stood the woodshed in which Estella Jackson had died. Out of whatever impulse—simple perversity, most likely—Butcher had insisted on leaving it intact. Pruitt Dix sometimes slept there if he was obliged to spend the night at the property, and the weather wasn't too cold. Dix didn't like sharing intimate space with other people. He preferred to cohabit with the dead rather than the living.

As for Tilon, the Buttrell place still gave him the creeps. Whenever possible, he worked out of the RVs, and when he had to go to the house, he tried to leave before dark.

Dix arrived at his side and patted him on the back.

"Home sweet home."

CHAPTER
LXVIII

Parker was already gone from Hamill when a red Nissan appeared in his rearview mirror, flashing its headlights. He couldn't see the driver clearly because of the sunlight on the windshield, but he pulled over nonetheless, even as his right hand found the butt of the gun under his jacket. He watched as the door of the Nissan opened and a young man stepped out: Nealus Cade, Jurel's younger brother. Parker released his grip on his weapon and rolled down a window.

"Mr. Cade," he said. "Can I help you with something?"

Nealus Cade buried his hands deep in the pockets of his jeans, and looked back at his car. It was a 240SX, a relatively cheap coupe that gave a lot of bang for the buck.

"I wanted to speak with you."

"Speak away."

"Not here." He indicated his car. "I'm afraid someone might notice us."

"If you didn't want to be noticed, you should have chosen a less ostentatious mode of transportation."

"That's what my father says."

Nealus was in his early twenties, but he still resembled a teenager, perhaps as a consequence of growing up in the shadow of his siblings, and of Pappy Cade. Yet the young man had a certain strength of character, judging by the care he was said to have extended to his mother in her final illness. It might have been better for him had he found a way to leave Burdon County after she died, because he now appeared to be trapped in a new cycle of dependency with his progenitor.

"He might have had a point," said Parker. "Hard to stay under the radar in a car like that."

"I have a Dodge too, but it's in the shop. Seriously, I'd prefer not to be seen talking to you by the side of the road."

"Do you have an alternative in mind?"

"There's a diner in Fordham, about five miles east of here, just over the county line. It's called the Dairy Bell. How about I meet you there?"

Parker checked his watch. He wanted to return to Cargill, but he could probably spare a few minutes.

"I can do that," he said.

"Great," said Nealus. "I know I sound paranoid, but give me some time to get ahead of you, okay?"

"Mr. Cade," said Parker, "in case you hadn't noticed, I'm driving a rental Taurus. I doubt I could keep up with you if I tried."

Denny Rhinehart made a pot of coffee and filled two cups from it. He and Pettle sat at a table in the dimness of the bar, the Rhine Heart's windows bearing shutters on the inside that the proprietor kept closed when he wasn't accepting customers. Now, with the doors locked front and back, they

418

served to offer the two men complete privacy. The radio was playing in Rhinehart's back office: KKPT out of Little Rock, one of only two classic rock stations the device was able to pick up. Nobody was ever permitted to change the station for fear it might never be located again, thereby leaving Rhinehart to subsist on a diet of Christian Contemporary, Gospel, and Regional Mexican, until he eventually surrendered to the inevitable and blew his brains out.

Pettle drank his coffee. He took it without cream or sugar, like a penitent.

"I know Sallie informed you about the relationship between her and me," he said, without further preamble. "I wish she hadn't, but she did, and there's no undoing it."

"I never spoke of it to anyone else," said Rhinehart. "It wasn't my place, or my business."

"I appreciate that," said Pettle. He recalled how Sallie had told him of Rhinehart's clumsy efforts to seduce her, if repeatedly trying to feel her up in the storeroom could be counted as any form of enticement. Pettle loathed this man, and all he represented.

"And I always did like Donna Lee," Rhinehart added.

Pettle's hand tightened on the coffee cup.

"I was out there, when they found her," said Pettle. "I looked upon her face. They called me, and told me that a girl had died badly, but there was only so much they could tell me over the phone.

They said I didn't have to come if I didn't want to, and no one would think less of me for it, but they were trying to identify her, and thought I might be able to help. It's strange, but as I was driving along Govan Road, and the police cars came in sight, I was sure it was Donna Lee. I knew it, even before they pointed out her remains. I think it was God readying me for what was to come, but it wasn't enough. Nothing could ready a man for that. I made them show me what had been done to her. They wanted to keep her covered up, but I needed to know. It was important that I bear witness."

"Jesus," said Rhinehart, then, "Sorry."

But Pettle gave no indication of noticing the casual blasphemy. He was staring into his coffee cup, at the surface of the liquid, still and dark, resembling the Karagol itself, as though the lake were less a single body of water than an entity capable of infusing all manner of fluids with its essence.

"I watched that girl grow up," said Pettle. "I cared about her, just as I cared for her mother. In another life, maybe I'd have gone and lived with them both, and taken Donna Lee as my own daughter. If I'd possessed the courage to do that, none of this would have happened."

Rhinehart shifted in his seat. He wanted Reverend Pettle gone. He didn't wish to listen as he poured out his guilt and regret, because he'd heard so many variations on the theme in the past. It came with the territory. The difference here lay

420

only in the ending of the tale, and a body mutilated with sticks. Yet he remained curious to understand the reason for the reverend's presence in his bar.

"My wife knows," said Pettle. "About Sallie and me."

"Women have a way of sensing indiscretion," said Rhinehart. "In my experience, men are more lacking in perception."

"My life has become a misery in the wake of it," said Pettle. "Delores says she'll stay with me for the sake of our mission here, because it's God's will that we should build a great church in Burdon County, and by raising it I may make reparation for my sins. But we sleep in separate beds, and she won't let me touch her. Says she doesn't know if she'll ever permit me such intimacies again."

Rhinehart, as he feared, had become Pettle's confessor, just as he had for countless men and women before, even though he could offer no absolution, and often failed even to rouse himself sufficiently to care.

"Who else knows about you and Sallie?" said Rhinehart.

"I don't know what others Sallie might have told. I was angry that she'd shared a confidence with you. She said it was an accident."

"It was," said Rhinehart. "It slipped out one night when she'd had too much to drink."

"She was beset by that weakness," said Pettle. "It was one of many."

Here's sanctimony, thought Rhinehart.

"Just as you were afflicted by your own," he said.

"I know it. I've knelt before God in shame."

"I'm sure that helped. Bet He forgave you, too."

"What about Leonard Cresil?" said Pettle, ignoring the sarcasm.

"What about him?"

"Does he drink here?"

"I'm happy to say that he does not."

"But you know of him?"

"I'd have to be blind not to, him and Shire both."

"Are you in contact with either of them?"

"Why are you asking?"

"I'd be obliged if you'd answer the question."

"I prefer not to keep the company of such individuals," said Rhinehart primly, and Pettle marveled at the bar owner's mendacity, especially as he had failed to ask the reason for questioning him about Cresil. Pettle was now convinced that Rhinehart was in touch with Cresil, and it was he who had first shared with Cresil his knowledge of Pettle's affair with Sallie Kernigan.

"As for your wife," said Rhinehart, "my opinion is that she'll say nothing about the affair outside the safety of her own home. She'll see no reason to risk further humiliation. So it's just us, then, barring evidence to the contrary, and I have no interest in undermining your position in this community. We have to find ways to work together, all of us, if this town is to prosper."

This much Rhinehart meant sincerely. If Pettle

had come here seeking assurances that Rhinehart would remain quiet about his indiscretion, then he would give him what he wanted, but only because it would put the churchman in his debt. Rhinehart had plans to extend his bar once Kovas commenced building. He even had a local contractor lined up to do the work, and had paid a deposit—more of a bribe, really—to ensure that he wouldn't be forgotten when the time came. In time, he might even open another premises, something more upscale. He was weary of selling pretzels, greasy sausages, and Bud Light. There was money in it, admittedly, but not enough for his liking.

Yet that kind of expansion inevitably involved paperwork and permits. It would also draw objections, particularly from the religious types in the county. An ally would be helpful in countering them, and should Reverend Pettle prove reluctant to oblige, a reminder of his own intimate experience of human frailty might cause him to reconsider.

"You know what the really sad part is?" said Pettle. "Because my wife wouldn't have relations with me, it drove me back to Sallie, and she welcomed me again to her bed."

This Rhinehart hadn't known. Jesus, the reverend was playing with hellfire, and no mistake.

"Man is not meant to be alone," said Rhinehart, in the absence of anything better to offer. He'd read that somewhere, or heard it at a wedding.

"But you're alone," said Pettle.

"Marriage doesn't appeal to me. But I do like

women—more than they like me, which is a heavy load to bear."

"Is that why you insisted on bothering Sallie with your attentions?"

"Hey!" Rhinehart waved a finger in Pettle's face. "I won't take that shit, not from you, not after what you just told me."

Pettle nodded glumly. "I'm sorry," he said.

"Yeah, well."

An awkward interval ensued until Rhinehart broke it with a question.

"Are you going to tell the police about your involvement with Sallie?"

"It wasn't my intention," said Pettle.

"There's a chance they won't find out about it, but in a town this size, who can say? It might be better to make a clean breast of it, before they come calling. You know Griffin has a detective working the case, some ex-cop from New York? He was in here last night. I didn't warm to him."

"His name is Parker."

"Yeah, Parker, that's it."

Rhinehart recalled the man in the bar, and his brief confrontation with Rich Emory. This Parker, he reflected, wasn't afraid of causing trouble.

"What about you?" said Pettle.

"What about me?"

"Do you have anything to hide?"

"What's that supposed to mean?"

"Everyone has something to hide. We are all sinners, and sin requires concealment."

"My sins aren't the kind that concern the police," said Rhinehart. "The IRS, maybe, but not the police."

He went to fetch more coffee. He was feeling anxious. Pettle was still circling, but to what end? And that wasn't all: there was something the preacher had said earlier, something that bothered Rhinehart as soon as he heard it, but which had since slipped from his memory. He wanted to retrieve it, though. It was important.

Rhinehart came back with the pot and refilled both cups, even though Pettle had drunk only a mouthful or two. He didn't bother returning the pot to the machine, but sat it on a coaster instead.

"What are you trying to say, Reverend? I'm getting tired of listening to you beating about the bush."

Pettle removed his spectacles, wiped them with a cloth that he took from his pocket, and restored them to the bridge of his nose. When he regarded Rhinehart again, it was with a new clarity that had nothing to do with the cleaning of the lenses.

"I was at Sallie's on Thursday," he said. "I was sitting at the kitchen table when Donna Lee came home from school. Donna Lee was used to me calling around occasionally, and I'd like to believe she didn't think ill of it. She was upset, but wouldn't tell her mother what happened. They'd been fighting a lot lately. I suspect it was mostly Donna Lee's teenage hormones, although Sallie also had a short fuse. If someone tried to pour oil on troubled waters, Sallie would set fire to it."

There it was again. Rhinehart had it now, but said nothing.

"So I went in and talked to Donna Lee. I always had a way with her. I never judged her, never spoke harshly to her, always encouraged her in her studies and her music. I could have been a good father to her."

"So you said before."

"Because it's important. Donna Lee was vulnerable because of her background, but also on account of how she looked. She was beautiful, inside and out. She needed to be cared for, and her mother couldn't do it, not the way she should have. She tried, but her vices undid her, and caused her attention to wander. There were men who might have tried to take advantage of Donna Lee under those circumstances. Men like you, Denny."

"Get out of here," said Rhinehart softly.

Pettle didn't move. "She told me what you did," he said. "How you offered her a ride home, how you laid hold of her breast, how you pulled at her hair as she ran, pulled it so hard that she thought her scalp would come away in your hand. She didn't want to go to the police, because she said it would just be her word against yours and she didn't want to cause trouble. She didn't want me to tell her mother, either, because she knew you and Sallie were tight, even though Sallie had warned her to be wary around you."

"That's all lies."

"I don't think so. Donna Lee didn't tell lies. She'd prefer to say nothing at all than offer an untruth."

"She was no angel," said Rhinehart. "She was whoring around. Her momma said so, but wouldn't tell me who the guy was. Said she had to be careful, but I had my suspicions."

"I don't want to hear you spout such poison about a dead child."

"You ought to listen. Maybe that man was the one who killed her."

"Or maybe you killed her, Denny, because she didn't like your hands on her."

"I didn't kill her."

"That should be for the police to decide."

Pettle stood, and Rhinehart stood also.

"You go spreading slander and I'll ruin you," said Rhinehart. "Once the whole town finds out about you and Sallie, you'll be finished here. Your bitch wife won't have any reason to stay with you, and you'll be a congregation of one. And don't think the finger of suspicion won't point at you when it comes to Donna Lee. You were fucking her mother, and they'll wonder if you didn't have an eye for the daughter as well."

"You're a vile man," said Pettle.

"That may be true, but I'm no creeping Jesus, not like you. It might even be that you're worse than a charlatan, and you got more than fucking on your conscience."

"You're insane."

" 'Had,' Reverend. 'Had.' "

"What?" Pettle was confused by the sudden turn.

"When you were speaking about Sallie just now, you said she *had* a short fuse, and she *had* a weakness for liquor. Not has: *had,* like you know she's already dead. But last I heard, Sallie was missing, and the police were still hoping to trace her. Why would you do that, Reverend? Why would you speak about Sallie as though she's in the ground? Those are hard questions, and I wouldn't like to be the one required to answer them.

"So you go talk to the police, and you tell them what you think I might have done. And when they ask me about it, I'll share with them what Sallie told me, and what you said here today, and we'll see which one of us still has a future in Cargill by the end of it. Now take your stink of hypocrisy from my bar."

Pettle didn't reply. He turned his face from Rhinehart and got unsteadily to his feet, using the chair for support until he was confident in his ability to remain upright unaided. He walked to the back door, unbolted it, and closed it again behind him as he stepped into the parking lot, all without acknowledging his tormentor.

Rhinehart resumed his seat. His heart was beating rapidly and his palms were sweating. He felt as though he were about to have a seizure. It would be bad for him if Pettle went to the police. Word would get around that he was alleged to have sexually assaulted Donna Lee Kernigan

428

in the days before her death. Even if it was only hearsay, and could never progress further because the girl could offer no testimony, it might harm his business, although perhaps only for a while. Even if Pettle were believed, the regulars would accept it if Rhinehart claimed the allegation contained more exaggeration than truth, and it had all been a misunderstanding between him and Donna Lee. They'd believe him because they wanted to: not believing him might require them to drink elsewhere, and the options in town were limited. In addition, Rhinehart was certain that he could account for his movements during the time Donna Lee had been missing, because he'd spent most of it at the bar. He went home only to rest, and then for just a few hours, because he'd never been a good sleeper. In the end, the police wanted to find the killer of those girls, and any other crimes, actual or alleged, would pale into insignificance beside the fact of the murders. He'd get through this, whatever happened.

He brought the coffeepot back to the hot plate and turned the plate off. He'd boil the pot up again later. No sense in letting even such modest fare go to waste. He went to his office and stared at the piles of invoices and receipts. Earlier he'd been dreading the paperwork, but now it would serve as a distraction. He sat at his desk and put on his glasses.

A noise came from the doorway. He looked up.

And Reverend Nathan Pettle started shooting.

CHAPTER
LXIX

Pruitt Dix's last known address was an apartment just south of 630 in downtown Little Rock. Neither Knight nor Griffin had any great desire to visit the city at the best of times, even before the Bloods and Crips started using it as a shooting gallery, but someone had to go up there to question Dix, and certainly not alone. Griffin didn't want both Knight and himself to be out of the county simultaneously at such an early stage of the investigation. On the other hand, Dix had a bad reputation, one that his address did nothing to counter, since the only people who lived in that district were either too poor to be able to live anywhere else or too criminal to care.

Griffin made a call to the Little Rock PD to call in a favor, resulting in a detective named Tommy Robinett agreeing to meet Knight at Franke's Cafeteria on North Rodney Parham, and keep him company while he went calling on Dix. After Knight headed off, Griffin tried to touch base with the rest of his officers. Giddons and Petrie, the two most reliable part-timers—now essentially full-timers because of the killings—were continuing the door-to-door interviews. Colson's cell phone was out of range, and she wasn't answering her radio; Griffin guessed that she was probably dealing with someone out in the boondocks. Naylor did respond from his car, though. He sounded out of breath.

"You climbing a hill, son?" asked Griffin.

"Silverbell Lane," said Naylor. Silverbell Lane snaked up into the Ouachita, and the rains had made some of the private roads that led to its houses virtually unnavigable for now. If Naylor had wanted to talk to anyone up there, he'd have been forced to make his way partly on foot.

"If you fall," said Griffin, "you're paying your own laundry bill, so best stay vertical."

"I just spoke to Bill Tindle," said Naylor.

"I know Bill." Tindle had been a trainer of racehorses before old age rendered him unfit for duty. He lived near the top of Silverbell Lane with his daughter Min, a spinster who had a depth of feeling for Kel Knight, and wouldn't have allowed his marital status to get in the way should he have been of a mind to reciprocate. Kel Knight avoided Silverbell Lane like the plague itself.

"Well, he says Min was driving him into town last week, along Bloodroot, and he saw a girl matching Donna Lee Kernigan's description picking up her schoolbooks from the ground. Her hair was all messed up, he said, and she looked like she might have been crying. A truck had just pulled away from where she was. Mr. Tindle told Min to stop and make sure the girl was okay, but she took a cut into the woods before they could speak with her. He thought he knew the truck, though."

"Tilon Ward?"

"No, Denny Rhinehart. Mr. Tindle said he recognized it because Denny has all those German stickers on his rear fender."

Denny Rhinehart was third-generation German-American, but persisted in collecting flag decals relating to his ancestral homeland, although he eschewed swastikas and twin lightning bolts on grounds of taste. Griffin had never had any trouble with Rhinehart beyond the occasional disturbance in his parking lot on weekends. Nevertheless, he knew Tilon Ward was a regular at the Rhine Heart, along with assorted men and women whom Griffin strongly suspected of being minor dealers, and only the lack of probable cause had so far prevented him from attempting to prove these suspicions right. It meant that Denny Rhinehart was willing to turn a blind eye to illegality, if not actively engage in it.

"You talk to Min about this?" said Griffin.

"Mr. Tindle let me use his phone to call her at work. She says he's remembering right, and it was definitely last Thursday, although she wouldn't swear that Denny's truck was actually pulling away when they saw it, and she didn't get a good look at the girl. Mr. Tindle is sure it was Donna Lee, though, on account of how tall she was. I took down everything he told me, read it back to him, then had him sign it. You know, just in case."

Just in case Tindle's condition suddenly deteriorated, leaving no proof of what he'd seen or said. Naylor was smart. It was only a matter of time before he moved over to the state police.

"You did good," said Griffin. "Better than good."

He told Naylor to return to town, replaced the handset, and walked to the nearest window. He could see the Rhine Heart from where he stood. The parking lot was empty, but he knew that Denny usually parked his truck around back. He'd probably be in his office by now.

If Bill Tindle wasn't mistaken, he'd witnessed the fallout from an altercation between Denny Rhinehart and Donna Lee Kernigan. It might have been something as simple as the girl crossing the road at the wrong time, but Griffin had heard from a cop in the Little Rock Vice Squad—a brother of Tommy Robinett, the detective who'd agreed to assist Kel Knight with the Dix inquiry—that Rhinehart had been questioned by police after being spotted emerging from an apartment block in Geyer Springs, a building suspected of housing a brothel on its top floor. Rhinehart had claimed to be visiting a friend, but declined to name the acquaintance in question, and the police had no reason to detain him. When the brothel was raided the following night, it was found to contain only black women, most of them in their late teens and early twenties. Rhinehart might just have been experimenting, or was guilty of being in the wrong place for entirely legal reasons; but he might also have enjoyed a predilection for young girls of color, and Sallie Kernigan had formerly worked at the Rhine Heart, and still frequented it as a customer. On the other hand, Mina Dobbs claimed to have witnessed Donna Lee Kernigan climbing

433

into a newish red truck, while Rhinehart drove an old blue Jeep Comanche that wouldn't have been worth the effort required to set it on fire.

And there remained the fact that the only print retrieved from Donna Lee's remains had come not from Denny Rhinehart but from Hollis Ward. Rhinehart would have known Hollis from around town, but they weren't close, or even on good terms; one of the reasons that Tilon Ward had always liked the Rhine Heart was because his father didn't frequent the place, so he wasn't likely to bump into his papa while he was drinking. Then Hollis Ward had gone missing for years, only to return to leave his mark on a murdered girl. . . .

So Evan Griffin now had a man long believed to be dead as the main suspect in the Kernigan killing and, by default, the murder of Patricia Hartley as well. Meanwhile, that same man's son might well have been the last person to see Donna Lee alive, but he was currently nowhere to be found, and was apparently keeping company with a known felon linked to Randall Butcher: strip club owner, would-be property tycoon, and an individual reckoned to be a dealer in narcotics. Finally, one of the friendly local bar owners, previously best known for serving warm beer and cold food, and possibly for frequenting a brothel specializing in younger black women, had seemingly been glimpsed driving away from a distressed Donna Lee Kernigan days before her murder.

Griffin tried calling Parker. The detective had a

New York cell phone, which would have crucified him with charges, so the Cargill PD had ponied up for a local phone on condition that Parker didn't go crossing state lines, or even range much farther than the adjacent counties. Parker picked up on the third ring.

"Where are you?" said Griffin.

"Driving to a meeting with Nealus Cade. He appeared anxious to talk, and I thought it couldn't hurt."

Griffin briefly brought Parker up to speed on developments.

"They're sure it's Hollis Ward's print?" said Parker.

"Yes. Why?"

Parker explained to Griffin about the statement from Ward that was missing from the file on Estella Jackson's murder.

"Did Jurel have anything to say about it?" said Griffin.

"Only that anyone could have removed that document from the file, which is probably true. The sheriff's office doesn't keep much under lock and key, and we're already familiar with how it handles evidence."

"Nothing goes on there that Jurel doesn't know about. If he didn't purge that file, he knows who did."

"I don't think I can go back and ask him again. Our working relationship shows few signs of improvement. He did say something interesting, though. He thinks we're looking for two killers: one for Jackson, and the other for Donna Lee Kernigan, and therefore also Patricia Hartley."

"Did he give a reason?"

"The damage to Estella Jackson was far greater than that inflicted on Donna Lee and Patricia. Also, in Jackson's case some of it was meted out while she was still alive. The conduct of the Hartley investigation means we don't have much more than Cade's word for most details, but we've both seen the instant photographs taken by the forensic analyst. Those branches were inserted very deliberately, and very deeply, into Patricia Hartley—even the fall down the slope didn't succeed in dislodging them entirely—but the other injuries occurred when the body hit the rocks, not from the actions of her killer. With Donna Lee, you got to see the body exactly as the killer intended. Again, he didn't go tearing at her face or groin, despite the stab wounds: what mattered was the placement of the branches. So, bearing all that in mind, I'm disposed to agree with Cade."

"Two killers," said Griffin. "And I already thought events couldn't get any more complicated."

Parker added to Griffin's woes by telling him of his conversations with Ferdy Bowers and Loyd Holt, and the apparent removal of Wadena Ott from the county, almost certainly at the instigation of Jurel Cade.

"If that's what passes for cooperation around here," said Parker, "I'd hate to encounter obstruction."

"Damn Jurel and his ways," said Griffin, "but you wouldn't have got much out of Wadena anyway."

"I'd bought her a bottle of cherry brandy."

"Then I retract my last statement."

"What are you going to do next?" said Parker.

"I'm going to wait for the autopsy results to come back, just in case they throw up any more surprises, before I go sounding the alarm. I've already pulled up the most recent photos of Hollis Ward in the hope that we can start circulating them once we receive the full report from the ME. But most everyone in the county of a reasonable age knows what Hollis looks like, so it's not as though they're going to require pictures to jog their memories. We still need to talk to Tilon Ward, but we may have to find Pruitt Dix first, and if we can't, we'll rattle Randall Butcher's cage."

"And Rhinehart?"

"I'll be speaking with Denny soon enough. Right now, though, Jurel Cade doesn't know about Hollis Ward's fingerprint, and the longer that state of affairs persists, the better."

"Why?"

"Tilon Ward. If Jurel finds out about the fingerprint, he'll use the excuse of the father to go after the son, and this will stop being about dead girls and become more about narcotics and settling scores. Tilon Ward is connected to Randall Butcher. We know that because Pruitt Dix is the one who took Tilon out of town, and Dix comes running when Randall Butcher whistles. The Cades would enjoy nothing better than to see Butcher put out of commission, because he's unwanted competition in the county, and Ferdy Bowers would be collateral damage. That's a lot of pieces wiped off the board with one move."

Once again, Parker resisted the urge to question Griffin about his own links to Tilon Ward. He had a feeling the inquiry wouldn't be welcomed. If the mood struck, he thought he might try Colson or Naylor, who might be more amenable to sharing such information.

"What about you?" said Griffin. "What are you planning to do after your sit-down with Nealus Cade?"

"I want to talk to Eddy Rauls. Even if Jurel Cade is right about two killers, there has to be a link back to Estella Jackson. I don't believe that whoever murdered Patricia Hartley and Donna Lee Kernigan decided to desecrate their bodies with branches just because of some half-remembered detail from an older murder. It means something, and Rauls may have some inkling of what it could be. Also, I want to find out what he remembers about Hollis Ward's statement, and why it might have been important enough for someone to make it go missing."

"Call Colson," said Griffin. "Her father and Rauls have been friends for a long time. It might help to make the old fart more amenable to conversation. He took being forced out of his job pretty hard."

"I'll do that. Once I've spoken with him, I'll get back to you. I made a list of names from the case files, and thought we should look at talking again to some of the people on it, but it may be that whatever Rauls has to say will enable us to narrow the focus, especially if he can point us toward anyone familiar with Hollis Ward."

"Okay. Man, Hollis Ward."

"Does it surprise you?"

Griffin ruminated on this. "I believe Hollis had it in him to kill someone. He had a streak of cruelty to him a mile wide, and no love for any living creature. But I'd convinced myself he was dead, and I dislike having my illusions shattered."

"One fingerprint," said Parker.

"A *perfect* fingerprint. I think it would be hard to leave unintentionally. I've messed up my share of fingerprints, and I've lost count of the number I've taken. If it is Hollis, he wanted that print to be found. He wanted us to know it was his handiwork."

"Did Ward have a grudge against the Cades?"

"Hollis worked for Pappy for a time, until he didn't. He was a fixer, of a kind."

"What kind exactly?"

"The kind that dealt with problems requiring a firm hand."

"What changed between them?"

"That's a question for the Cades to answer."

One fingerprint, thought Parker.

"It's a shame there was no autopsy on Patricia Hartley," he said.

"Because it might have revealed a similar print on her body?"

"Yes."

"If the evidence hadn't been destroyed, I could have prevailed upon Tucker McKenzie to go back to the negatives and try to enlarge them."

"Don't worry about it. If you get Hollis Ward for Donna Lee, you'll also have him for the Hartley killing. Speaking of which, did Billie have any luck tracing the Hartley family down in Lucedale?"

"Nope," said Griffin. "She managed to talk to someone else in their building, though, who said the Hartleys moved out yesterday, leaving no forwarding address."

"Just like Wadena Ott," said Parker. "As you said, damn Jurel and his ways. Look, I have to go. I'm at the Dairy Bell now."

"Be careful of the peach pie," Griffin advised. "It may look light, but the memory of it lingers in the digestion."

"Thanks for the advice. I'll avoid it."

"Don't be too hasty. If you see fit to pick one up on your way out, I'll reimburse you out of petty cash."

"I thought you said it lingers."

"It does," said Griffin, "but it lingers good."

CHAPTER
LXX

Leonard Cresil returned to the motel and knocked on the door of Charles Shire's room.

"It's me, Mr. Shire."

"Come in. It's unlocked."

Shire was sitting at the room's single table. His laptop was open and connected to the Internet. Cresil did not use the Internet, and distrusted cell phones—all phones, if he was being honest. He had never yet encountered a situation that could not be best handled in person. Those who were forced to contend with Cresil's physical presence in their lives might have differed, but he bothered little with their opinion.

Shire paid Cresil well for his work, and didn't ask too many questions about how the ends were achieved. Unlike Cresil, Shire was married and had a family. He spoke to his wife twice daily on the road, once in the morning before his children left for school, and once in the evening before they went to bed. Cresil had occasionally been privy to these conversations and was struck by the absence of warmth in the exchanges. Shire might as easily have been checking on a set of underperforming minor investments, or the progress of some repairs on his car. He was a man almost entirely without amiability, or anything approaching character or charisma, yet he was extraordinarily good at brokering agreements and gaining the confidence of politicians and businessmen. Perhaps those with whom he had dealings believed that no man so dull could ever prove untrustworthy, because duplicity required imagination. In this much they might have been correct: Charles Shire was corrupt down to the marrow of his bones, but his corruption was undisguised, and balanced by an innate understanding of the corruption of others, whether actual or potential, which made him an adept negotiator. His was also corruption for its own sake: Shire did not live an ostentatious existence, drive a particularly expensive car, or overly resent staying in motels as unremarkable as the Lakeside Inn. Neither did he indulge in narcotics, drink to excess, or cheat on his wife. It was simply in his nature to manipulate and undermine—whether people, systems, or institutions both private and public—for the ultimate benefit of his employer, Kovas being only the most recent in a long line. Once the agreements were signed, Shire would remain in place for a few months to ensure that his efforts were bearing fruit, before accepting a generous payoff and moving on to pollute pastures new.

Cresil would not be going with him, though. His experiences with Kovas in Arkansas, and especially the maneuverings in Burdon County, had caused him to conclude that, at some point in the future, Charles Shire would end up in prison—sentenced, because of the depths of his delinquency, to the kind of period of incarceration typically associated with mass murderers. Cresil did not intend to go down with him. He would arrange what needed to be arranged in Burdon County, his fee would be paid into an offshore account, and he would stay low for the rest of his life. And if, by some misfortune, his actions came back to haunt him in the guise of state or federal investigators, Cresil would feed Shire to them like chum to sharks.

"How did it go with Butcher and Bowers?" said Shire.

"As well as could be expected, given the parties involved."

Shire continued to tap at the keyboard. He was analyzing figures, and making adjustments where required. His fingernails were trimmed so short that swathes of the nail beds lay exposed. Cresil couldn't fathom how Shire accomplished this, short of prying the nail itself from the bed before he began to cut. The man's obsession with his own hygiene knew no bounds.

"Butcher and Bowers," said Shire, "are both unreliable, but each in their own individual way: Bowers because he sets his sights too low, and Butcher because he sets his too high."

"Funny that they're both going to end up disenchanted," said Cresil. "You'd have thought they could have settled somewhere in the middle, and avoided a shitload of trouble."

"In which case they'd be like the vast mass of humanity, and each aspires to more."

"If you say so."

From the bathroom came the sound of a tap running. Cresil hadn't known anyone else was in the room with them. He glanced over to see the door open and a woman emerge.

"Hello, Mr. Cresil," said Delphia Cade. "I hope you've been having a productive morning."

CHAPTER
LXXI

The Dairy Bell was peaceful, with only a sprinkling of customers, none of whom was under sixty or displayed more than a passing interest in Parker's arrival. Nealus Cade was seated at a booth away from the window, his presence partially concealed by a pillar. He had also parked his red coupe behind a big rig making a delivery to a warehouse in the adjoining lot; Parker wouldn't have spotted it had he not been watching out, so he doubted a more casual eye would pick up on it. He took a seat across from Nealus. When the server arrived Parker ordered coffee and a peach pie to go. Nealus already had a hot tea before him.

"You must really like peach pie," said Nealus.

"Not so much, but I was asked to buy one for a friend."

"If the rest of my family is to be believed, it's a surprise that you have a friend for whom to buy it."

"Are you trying to prove the exception to the Cade family rule?"

"I don't know you, but I believe in giving people a chance. I got that from my mother."

"And from your father?"

"I got little from my father, other than a name."

The coffee and pie arrived, the latter wrapped in plastic. It was heavy, with the kind of crust that could withstand an earthquake. Parker set it aside and waited for Nealus to get to the point. If he wanted to unburden himself of his daddy issues, Parker would have to charge him by the hour, or at least ask him to pay for the pie. But when Nealus did speak again, it was with the bluntness of the very young and the very rude.

"Did you give up being a detective because of what happened to your wife and daughter?" said Nealus.

"I haven't 'given up' being a detective. That's why I'm sitting here."

"I think you know what I mean."

"I know what you mean. I just don't consider it any of your business."

"No, I don't suppose it is. Consider it unsaid."

"Mr. Cade, I'm very busy, so—"

"Do you know a man named Leonard Cresil?"

Parker tried the coffee, but it was lukewarm so he set it aside. He had a vision of his life, the days marked by countless unfinished cups of bad beverages.

"I know of him," he said, "but we haven't been formally introduced."

"He's not a very nice human being."

"I can believe it. Do you have personal experience of this?"

"I only know what I overhear."

"And what have you overheard?"

A mist had descended over the land. Nealus Cade watched a state police cruiser drift through it, like a big fish hunting amid turbid waters.

"My family doesn't communicate very well," he said, "or not with one another. My father likes to believe that he's still in charge, but he seldom leaves the house anymore, not since he got sick. Of course, he won't admit that he's seriously ill. It would be a sign of vulnerability, but I think he's also afraid that to acknowledge his infirmity would be to allow it dominion over him, and hasten his end.

"It's hard to maintain control when you're largely trapped inside your own four walls, so he has to work through my brother and sister. Jurel is his voice and strong hand in Burdon County, and Delphia performs the same functions in Little Rock. Jurel listens to him, Delphia less so. Jurel wishes he didn't have to cooperate with you and Chief Griffin, but he understands why it's necessary. Delphia contends that it would be better if you weren't involved."

"And how does Leonard Cresil enter into this sibling difference of opinion?"

"Delphia has asked Cresil to find a way to harm you."

In the kitchen of the diner, two male voices were discussing the fortunes of the Razorbacks. Everyone in Arkansas had an opinion on the Razorbacks. It was the Razorbacks or nothing.

"Are you sure?"

"I heard her speaking to him on her cell phone. I didn't catch everything she said, but she doesn't want Cresil to do it himself. She wants him to get

447

Randall Butcher to take care of you instead. You can be hurt up to a point, but she'd prefer to avoid a killing. Did you do something to offend her? Because her grievance sounded as much personal as professional."

"I may have declined to be employed by her, or sleep with her—or perhaps to be employed to sleep with her. The terms of recruitment weren't completely unambiguous."

"That would suffice to aggrieve her," said Nealus. "If it helps, my sister is more particular about her bedmates than rumor might suggest."

"Should I be flattered?"

"It's probably too late for that, if she's involving Cresil and Butcher. Do you know who Randall Butcher is?"

Griffin had given Parker a brief account of Butcher in the course of their earlier conversation, which meant he didn't know a lot about him, but enough.

"I've heard the name."

"My father thinks that Butcher and a local businessman named Ferdy Bowers are working against our family interests, and may even jeopardize the Kovas negotiations, if inadvertently."

"How?"

"Butcher is a criminal, and therefore unpredictable. He's also an exploiter of women. He wants his share of the Kovas wealth, but my father believes that no good can come of him being involved, and Delphia agrees. Leonard Cresil works for Charles Shire, who is set to make a great deal of money in bonuses and kickbacks when Kovas finally arrives in Burdon County, on top of whatever he's already earned in bribes. My father has been cultivating Shire, and Shire has been cultivating my father in turn, but Shire is also engaged in discussions with Butcher, and to a lesser extent Ferdy Bowers. Shire likes to keep his options open, but in the end, he'll almost certainly be forced to cut Butcher and Bowers loose. My father will insist upon it, but the severance will also make sense for Kovas. The company has a reputation to protect, which is why it's letting Shire and Cresil do the grunt work before it formally sets foot in the county.

"If Cresil and my sister can convince Butcher to make a move against you, it's a win-win situation. If Butcher succeeds, the murder investigation will lose momentum, and Griffin may be more amenable to waiting until after the Kovas paperwork is signed before continuing with his inquiries. If Butcher fails, any blame for the attempt will fall on him, giving the police an excuse to move in and close down his operation. And when they do, it will be my brother at the head of the arresting team."

"You got all this from one partly overheard conversation? I'm impressed."

"I didn't have to hear it all. I know how my sister thinks, and my brother, too. It wasn't hard to join the dots."

"I appreciate the warning. Now I have another question for you. What do you know about Hollis Ward?"

Nealus Cade barely reacted to the name, but it was a reaction nevertheless.

"Why are you asking about him?"

"It was my question. You can have your turn later."

"He and my father grew up together, and were partners for a while. Hollis helped him with some property and business deals in the county, back when my father was still laying the groundwork for luring companies like Kovas."

"Your father doesn't strike me as the kind of man who requires a lot of help making deals, or not from someone like Hollis Ward."

"Hollis knew who was hurting for money," said Nealus. "He was aware of who might be vulnerable to blackmail, or simple threats. and whose claims to land might be open to challenge. He was particularly knowledgeable about potential cases of heirs' property. Do you know what that is, Mr. Parker?"

"No, I do not."

"It's a form of property ownership based on inheritance, but not backed up by a will, and is common in black communities."

Black, Parker noted, not *colored.* Here was no Ferdy Bowers.

"It dates back to a time," said Nealus, "when legal advice was not available to black people,

450

and has persisted to the present day because the courts are regarded, not without cause, as being ill-disposed toward the interests of poor minorities. If they don't have clear title, these people are ineligible for federal loans and disaster relief, and are unable to use their land for collateral with lending institutions. And if they can't prove ownership, their property can be taken from them and auctioned without their consent. More than a third of the land owned by blacks in the South is heirs' property, representing a potential windfall for those who are sufficiently unscrupulous. My father more than qualified in that regard, and in Hollis Ward he found the perfect agent.

"Through Hollis, my father could exert a great deal of influence without getting his hands too dirty—not that dirty hands ever concerned him greatly, but this was his county, and his people, and he wanted an element of deniability when things got rough or unpleasant. He didn't want the community turning against him, and Hollis was comfortable with playing the bad guy, because that's what he was. But then Hollis disappeared, and nobody's heard from him in years."

That, thought Parker, had just changed, but he decided not to mention it to Nealus. The print found on Donna Lee Kernigan's body would become public knowledge soon enough.

"Do you think Hollis Ward is still alive?"

"He could be. He was a strange man. My father was as close to Hollis as anyone, but I don't believe

451

he ever really knew him. They didn't socialize together, or even seem particularly friendly toward each other. My father used Hollis, and Hollis used him."

"And what did Hollis gain from this arrangement?"

Nealus Cade took a few seconds to decide on an answer. "Power," he said, finally, "or a semblance of it. Money, too, but mostly power."

"What kind of power?"

"The power to alter the trajectory of lives, even to ruin them. Sometimes, I think he'd have worked for free for my father, just because his role elevated him and gave him an authority he would otherwise have lacked. Then he and my father fell out. Hollis's conviction made it inevitable."

"The child pornography?"

"Yes. My father had to end their association. He was left with no choice."

"And how did Hollis take that?"

"It probably didn't come as a huge surprise to him, but he was still angry about it. He came to the house a month or two after he got out of jail. He wanted money from my father. There was a huge argument. Jurel arrived and threatened to put Hollis back behind bars if he ever showed his face on Cade property again. Hollis stopped coming around, and eventually he stopped being seen anywhere."

"That was convenient for your family, given the knowledge Hollis possessed about your father's affairs."

"It certainly was," said Nealus. He smirked. "My father has that kind of luck."

"Was Hollis the only person to help your father out in this way?"

"He was the main one. There were others, but not as important, except perhaps for Reverend Pettle."

"Why Pettle?"

"He has influence with the black community."

"Did Pettle know Hollis Ward?" said Parker.

"Of course. I can remember him sitting down with Hollis and my father at the house. Pettle only ever drank soda. My father and Hollis would mock him about it. Of course, Pettle had just a small congregation in those days, but people listened to him and his wife. It's surprising, really. I could never figure out if Pettle was a weak man pretending to be strong, or a strong one pretending to be weak.

Parker picked up his pie. It was time to go.

"I'm curious, Mr. Cade," he said. "Why are you telling me all this?"

That smirk flashed again. "Why do you think?"

"Don't take this personally, but I suspect you suffer from a great deal of resentment."

"It's all about power, Mr. Parker. I learned that from Hollis Ward. There's no point in having power, even the little I possess, without using it. My knowledge of my family's past dealings in the area of heirs' property has enabled me, belatedly, to put pressure on my father to ensure that there is no repeat of such behavior. Now, in return for one conversation, and the price of a pie and some beverages, I've managed to make life difficult for my sister while doing some good along the way— although the attraction was more the former than the latter, if I'm being honest."

"Yes," said Parker, "if you are. Goodbye, Mr. Cade. Thanksgiving with your family must be a sight to see."

"Good luck avoiding that beating," said Nealus, as he called for the check. "And I hope your friend enjoys the pie."

4

Yonder come little David
With his rock and sling
I don't wanna meet him,
He's a dangerous man.
                —"Sit Down Servant" (Traditional)

CHAPTER
LXXII

Franke's was the oldest restaurant chain in Arkansas, dating back to 1919. The original Franke's location on West Capitol had closed in the sixties, but the other outlets continued to thrive, mainly because the menu hadn't changed much over the years. As long as it continued to serve meat loaf on Mondays, catfish on Fridays, and some variation on fried chicken virtually every day of the week, with Karo nut pie to finish, Franke's wouldn't be hurting for customers anytime soon.

Kel Knight found Tommy Robinett sitting alone at a table, making serious inroads into an egg custard pie. The two men had met a couple of times in the past. Robinett was a distinctive-looking man, thanks to a scar that ran from his hairline to the base of his right cheek, a relic of a botched surveillance operation on a Little Rock Crips leader named Winston Holmes back in the early part of the decade. By then Holmes was already a millionaire, thanks to his undeniable business acumen when it came to selling narcotics, and wasn't about to allow the police to prevent him from becoming a multimillionaire. Holmes promised $20,000 to whoever made an example of a narc, and two brothers, the Embrys, took him up on the offer. Had they decided just to shoot him, Robinett would almost certainly have ended up dead. Instead, the Embrys elected to use blades, which meant they had to work up close. Robinett killed one of them and wounded the other, but not before acquiring the scar that was now his distinguishing feature.

"I eat only one of these a month," he said, as Knight pulled up a chair opposite.

"Did I say anything?"

"You have an accusatory demeanor, but I can never tell if it's general or specific."

"I like to think it's capable of being both, but either will serve."

They shook hands.

"How've you been, Kel?"

"Good, until someone started killing young women in our county."

"Rumor is there's pressure growing to involve the state police," said Robinett, "some of it coming from the governor himself, but this Kovas deal has to go through first. After the tornadoes, the state needs all the investment it can get. We're millions of dollars in the hole for the damage."

"I know that. Doesn't help us right now."

"Where does Pruitt Dix fit in?"

"Evan didn't tell you?"

"He said only that you wanted access to Pruitt. He didn't say why."

That was Evan not wanting to spread the word about Tilon Ward, Knight knew, unless he proved untraceable by more discreet means.

"The last person known to have seen Donna Lee

Kernigan alive may currently be keeping company with Dix," said Knight. "For obvious reasons, we'd like to talk to him."

"Does this person have a name?"

"All people have a name. That's why they're called people."

"You just be like that, then," said Robinett, but he wasn't holding any grudges, because he offered Knight the last piece of the egg custard pie.

"I will be like that." Knight ate the pie with a coffee spoon. It was good: not too sweet, and better than his wife's version. Even after all these years, she retained a heavy hand with the sugar. "Is Dix still running errands for Randall Butcher?"

"Yep."

"Is the Little Rock PD interested in Butcher?"

"Might be."

"Any particular branch of the Little Rock PD?"

"Perhaps, and it might not be alone. How about you tell me the name of the man you're looking for?"

"You know Jurel Cade?"

"Some."

"You like him?"

"Not greatly," said Robinett. "If that's what's worrying you, you're expending needless energy. Whatever is said here won't go any further unless it has to."

"A man named Tilon Ward was with Donna Lee shortly before she died, or so we believe. We think Ward has also been cooking meth in the Ouachita for distribution across the southwest, and maybe even farther afield."

"Tilon Ward, who is an associate of Pruitt Dix."

"Who works for Randall Butcher."

"Who may be a person of interest to the Little Rock Narcotics Unit—among other parties, in answer to your earlier question."

"Is he under active investigation?" said Knight.

"Very active. Old Randall is slippery, though, and has friends in the legislature. One thing about Randall: his checks always clear."

Robinett wiped his mouth with a napkin.

"Time to go," he said. "By the way, if you do lay hands on Tilon Ward, we'd appreciate a heads-up, and the chance to talk with him."

"I'm sure that won't be a problem."

They walked to the exit and into the parking lot.

"You know," said Robinett, "Pruitt Dix is kind of an asshole."

"I won't contest it. I've met him once or twice, and it's a wonder the air doesn't emerge black from being inside him."

"What about Tilon Ward?" said Robinett. "Is he an asshole too?"

"He's a suspected criminal."

"That apart."

"That apart," said Knight, reluctantly, "he's sort of an okay guy."

"Do you think he might have killed the Kernigan girl?"

"No," said Knight, and it gave him some small

pleasure to see Robinett's mouth gape as he added, "we think Hollis Ward did."

Parker sat in his car and watched Nealus Cade drive away. He had encountered some poisonous clans in his time, but the Cades must have had Eden's own serpent somewhere in their lineage. He took in the parking lot and the diner. He observed the customers entering and leaving, and tried to find some bond with them, but failed. He was not of this place, but perhaps he was no longer of any place, because his absence of feeling for these people extended to most of humanity.

He gripped the steering wheel with both hands and thought about his next step. He could go to Evan Griffin and tell him about the supposed threat, but he didn't think there was much Griffin could do short of giving him an escort, or wrapping him in cotton wool and hiding him in a closet. Griffin could always have tried warning off Leonard Cresil, or even Delphia Cade, but they'd have looked at him as though he were speaking in tongues.

Parker took out his New York cell phone, but for various reasons, including the cost, put it away again before pressing a button. Instead he went back into the diner, asked them to make change, and used their pay phone to call New York.

"Hello?" said the voice on the other end of the line.

"It's Parker."

461

A brief silence, followed by: "It's been a while. How are you doing?"

"I'm in southern Arkansas."

"Not so good, then."

"I may have a problem."

"What kind?"

"Some people have it in mind to hurt me, or worse. When it comes, I won't know the faces."

"Last time we met, you wanted to die."

"Maybe I still do, but not here, and not yet."

"So you'd like us to watch your back?"

"I can cover your expenses, but it may take me a while. I'm still waiting for the insurance money to come through."

"We're not accepting your money. Tell us where you are."

Parker felt his eyes grow hot. This voice. These men. Such memories. He gave the name of the Lakeside Inn, and said he'd book a room for them.

"We'll check flights. With luck, we'll be there late tonight."

"Thank you."

"Sure. Be seeing you."

Parker hung up the phone. He walked back to his car, got in, and closed the door. He recalled the cemetery, and the uniforms. He recalled two groups of mourners, and words exchanged with the parents of his dead wife that could never be taken back. He recalled rain falling, and handshakes— endless handshakes—and a numbness behind which lurked all his pain.

And he recalled, beneath a tree, the forms of two men watching the interment from afar, and he felt their grief for his loss. Although they would not, could not, stand alongside police and federal agents, marshals and prosecutors, still they wanted him to know that they were with him, and of him, and would be there for him later and always, just as they were there for him now.

"When it comes time, you only have to ask. You call our names, you hear? You call our names."

Parker put his head in his hands and wept.

Pruitt Dix's apartment building wasn't anything to write home about, not unless the folks at home were really interested in poor workmanship and social decline. It stood at a nexus of fortified grocery and liquor stores; of restaurants selling food that managed to be both cheap and overpriced; of dwellings that seemed destined to remain forever for sale until they fell into decay; and of patches of waste ground that were awaiting development in the same way the dead await the promise of resurrection. A handful of older teenagers regarded Knight and Robinett curiously as they pulled up to the curb, before raising a chorus of warning that brought men and women to windows and front steps.

Robinett rang the bell to Dix's apartment, but got no reply. He tried all the other bells until a man in a blue short-sleeved shirt appeared in the hallway to see what the commotion was about. He saw Knight's uniform and Robinett's shield, and opened the door.

"We're looking for Pruitt Dix," said Robinett.

"Top floor," said the man, "but I don't think he's home."

He stepped back to admit them, and they took the stairs to the fourth floor. Of the apartments on that level, only the door to Dix's was made of reinforced steel. They tried knocking, but received no answer.

"Better call the super," said Robinett.

The man who had admitted them turned out to be the super. His name was Madrigal, and if he wasn't familiar with Pruitt Dix's reputation, he gave a good impression of someone who was. His features twitched with apprehension, and his mouth was a woebegone slash of regret at ever having admitted the two men ino the building, or even leaving the safety of his apartment to answer the bell. A couple of residents drifted into the hallway to take in the show.

"I don't believe Mr. Dix would like us to be trespassing on his property," said Madrigal.

"We're not trespassing," said Robinett. He removed an official document from his pocket and handed it to Madrigal.

"You know what this is?"

Madrigal read the document.

"It's a search warrant."

"That's right."

"So open the door."

Madrigal opened the door. Inside, the apartment

was tidy and unadorned with personal effects, apart from a couple of shelves of books, CDs, cassettes, and vinyl, a high-end stereo system, and a good TV. The only incongruous item was a small bar fridge against the living room wall. As far as Robinett knew, Pruitt Dix wasn't a drinker.

"You got a screwdriver?" said Robinett.

"On my knife," said Knight.

He handed it to Robinett, who used it to unscrew the back of the bar fridge, revealing the bags of crystal meth concealed inside.

"Well, now," said Robinett. He didn't touch the drugs, but instead began to scribble down a name and number from a sticker affixed to the back of the fridge, left there by an appliance repair service. Knight guessed what he was doing. If the service turned out also to have worked on jobs for Randall Butcher, investigators might be able to establish a link between Dix and Butcher: one more small detail that could be added to building the case. He and Knight continued their search, but came up with nothing else.

"I'm going to call a patrol car," said Robinett, "and get them to keep an eye on this place. We'll also log that meth as evidence. If Dix comes back in the interim, they'll hold him so you can ask about Tilon Ward, but my feeling is that he won't be returning anytime soon."

"Because by now he already knows we're here."

"That's right. He probably got a call as soon as we started knocking on his door."

"Is this the moment to ask how you came by that warrant?" said Knight.

"Therein," said Robinett, "hangs a tale . . ."

The call had come through to Pruitt Dix's cell phone as he entered Little Rock.

"Pruitt, man, they in your place."

Dix parked two blocks away from his apartment, the hood raised on his jacket, and walked to a corner from which he could watch the police emerging from his building. He recognized both men and found them equally troubling, if for different reasons. Robinett had always maintained a hard-on for Randall Butcher, and could only be hoping to get to Butcher through Dix. Knight's presence, meanwhile, meant that Burdon County law enforcement was interested in Dix. He wondered if Tilon Ward's mother had failed to keep her mouth shut about her son's recent visitor.

Dix could have called a lawyer. He didn't know if the cops had a warrant. If they didn't, it was an illegal search, but he had dealt with Robinett in the past and was under no illusions about the detective's intelligence. If paperwork was required to nail someone, it would be found, even after the fact.

Dix left the keys to his car at his local convenience store, and told the owner that someone would drop by to pick them up within the hour. His Chevelle was too damn conspicuous, and Robinett and Knight could soon have every

466

prowl car in the state looking out for it. He caught a cab to a bar in Boyle Park and called Randall Butcher along the way. It might, he thought, be a good idea if Butcher made himself hard to find for a few days. Butcher, when he came on the line and learned of the situation, agreed.

At the bar, Dix ordered a soda, and waited for one of Butcher's people to arrive with another vehicle. Whoever was killing those girls in Burdon County was causing a profusion of trouble for everyone, and the sooner he was stopped, the better. If Dix found him before the cops did, he'd save the state the cost of a trial.

The soda was flat, and the ice tasted gritty. Dix told the bartender to turn down the music because it was hurting his ears. The bartender didn't argue. He didn't know Dix personally, but he'd crossed paths with enough men like him to listen when they spoke, and do whatever it was they asked of him, legality and common sense permitting. He returned to reading his paper and wondering at the life choices that had brought him to this pass.

CHAPTER
LXXIII

Griffin parked in front of the Rhine Heart. He tried the main door, found it closed, and went to the back entrance. This, too, was locked, although Denny Rhinehart's Jeep Comanche was parked in its usual spot, and someone had left a delivery of hot dog rolls on the step. Griffin knocked, but no one answered. He gave it a few minutes, just in case Rhinehart was in the can, and knocked again, before giving up. Rhinehart could have gone on an errand, in which case Griffin would take a drive around town in the hope of spotting him. Rhinehart would return soon enough to welcome his paying customers. Griffin would speak with him then.

Parker dropped the peach pie off with Bille Brinton before calling Colson and arranging to meet her at a gas station near South Spring Road, which was the nearest landmark she could offer to the home of the former Burdon County chief deputy Eddy Rauls. The gas station was long boarded up, its pumps rusted and locked. At some point in the past it had accommodated an ice cream parlor or soda shop, because Parker could see faded illustrations of sundaes and shakes on the side wall. Behind the gas station stood the screen of an old drive-in movie theater, grass growing through the gaps in the pavement and pools of standing water waiting for the arrival of insects to give them life. As if Parker wasn't feeling depressed enough, a dead possum lay on the patch of grass by the entrance to the theater.

He decided to wait for Colson in the car.

His phone rang while he was still trying to forget the possum. It was Evan Griffin calling to ask if Nealus Cade had come up with anything useful.

"He told me that his sister wants me hurt, but not killed," said Parker.

"That's charitable of her. Did he give any reason why?"

Parker decided to leave out the part about turning down Delphia Cade's advances, professional or otherwise.

"She hopes it might temporarily derail the investigation."

"Did she cook this up herself? It's crude."

"Leonard Cresil may have guided her on the specifics, even if Nealus is convinced that the derailment was her idea."

Griffin absorbed this information.

"Will Nealus swear to it?"

"Nope, and to be honest, I'm not sure how far I'd trust anything that boy said. If you approach Cresil or Delphia about it, they'll obviously deny it, and try to find another way to cause us difficulties."

"Leaves you hanging, though, doesn't it?"

"That depends. I have some friends who might be willing to watch my back."

"Friends from here?"

"Friends from elsewhere."

"How friendly are they?"

"Not very friendly at all."

"I'd feel better if you had one of my people with you."

"They're stretched as things stand. Also, your people have their own lives when they're off the clock."

"And your friends don't?"

"They take a more holistic view of existence."

"I don't even know what that means."

"It means they live to cause trouble."

"Well," said Griffin, "they're coming to the right place."

The conversation ended, but Parker could still see the possum in his rearview mirror.

Colson pulled up moments later. She had spent much of the morning at the county courthouse, testifying in a number of minor cases and acting as the department's representative at various arraignments and sentencing hearings, before continuing with the canvass of those who might have known Donna Lee and her mother. Later, back at the station, she'd assisted Billie Brinton in coming up with a list of persons who might have known all three of the dead girls. The only solid link shared by Estella Jackson, Patricia Hartley, and Donna Lee Kernigan was that they had all attended the same school, which was Hindman, for the duration of their studies. Then Evan Griffin had shared the news of the discovery of Hollis Ward's fingerprint on Donna Lee's body, which seemed to render futile any further efforts to look for a culprit at the school.

Colson joined Parker, who was squatting close to a patch of grass, poking at a dead possum with a gloved hand. The possum looked as though some other animal had gnawed on it, and its body was pitted with wounds. Parker asked if Colson wanted to take a closer look at the possum, and wasn't surprised when she declined.

"Why would I want to look at a dead possum anyway?" she asked.

"You picked the venue," said Parker.

"Because it was a landmark you could easily find, not because of a possum. Oh, and also because it used to be owned by Hollis Ward. He closed it after his conviction on the child pornography charges, since no one would buy it from him as a going concern. I think Pappy Cade might have taken the land off his hands out of sympathy, but never did anything with it. Kovas might change that."

"What about the movie theater?"

"That went out of business before the gas station, but it was another Ward family enterprise."

"Hollis Ward doesn't seem to have enjoyed a surfeit of good fortune."

"The child porn didn't help, but it's also what comes of getting into bed with the Cades. They use people, then throw away the husks."

There was no mistaking Colson's bitterness.

471

"You make it sound personal," said Parker.

"The Cades cheated my uncle out of most of his land. They offered him a line of credit through their tame bank, and waited until he was overextended before calling in the debt. It was legal, but it wasn't moral. If you want to know how the Cades operate, that about sums it up. A lot of people around here have similar stories, and not all of them are prepared to forgive or forget."

Parker looked back at the gas station. Its doors and windows had been covered up with steel plates, either bolted to the walls or secured with heavy-duty locks.

"Do you have any airtight containers in your car?" he asked.

"I have some evidence bags, and a cooler box," said Colson. "I also have a feeling I'm going to regret admitting that to you."

The replacement vehicle, a Toyota 4Runner with tinted windows, arrived as Pruitt Dix was finishing up in the men's room. He left a couple of bucks on the bar to cover the lousy soda, and stepped outside. The driver's side window rolled down, revealing Randall Butcher seated behind the wheel.

"Get in," he said.

Dix took the passenger seat. Butcher pulled away and headed for the interstate.

"How much trouble are we in?" he asked Dix.

"Depends what they found at my place, but I could be in a lot. As for you, I can't say for sure."

"What were you holding?"

"About a key and a half, and I had a buyer lined up."

Dix didn't usually get involved directly in sales and distribution, but these were desperate times. Dix had taken Butcher's last two keys the previous night, and had already offloaded a quarter of the meth before dawn.

Butcher's cell phone rang. He picked up and kept driving, listening closely all the time, saying little in response. At the conclusion of the call, he said only "I understand," and killed the connection. Dix waited.

"There's a sealed grand jury indictment in my name," said Butcher. "Conspiracy, bribery, and five counts of wire fraud."

"A federal indictment?"

Butcher nodded. That explained why they'd heard nothing about it until now. If it had been purely a state matter, the drums would have been pounding long ago. Also, if a grand jury had been convened, it meant federal prosecutors had confidence in their case. Whatever problems Dix might have, Butcher had bigger ones. Depending on the legality of the search, Dix could be looking at felony possession, which carried a sentence of six years or less. Butcher, on the other hand, could be facing a sentence of twenty years on the wire fraud alone—and that was per count. It made the issue of the meth cook even more urgent, because Butcher now needed funds for a better lawyer than he already had.

"I'll supervise the damn cook myself," said Butcher. "In the meantime, start making calls. Tell the buyers I want their money lined up and ready to be counted."

"And Tilon Ward?"

"Tilon stays aboveground. He cooks, we move him, he cooks again."

Dix was sorry to hear this. Tilon Ward had always bugged him.

"If you're sure."

Butcher patted him on the arm.

"We'll work him to the bone, then you can get rid of him. But," he added, "if you see the police coming, you shoot Tilon in the head. We don't need him talking on top of all this other shit."

Which cheered Dix up some.

CHAPTER
LXXIV

Eddy Rauls lived in a neat house in a neat yard surrounded by trees that were also neat, as woodland went. Parker pulled up behind Colson and took in the view. Two other vehicles stood in the yard: a Ford truck that bore mud splatter from the recent rains but was otherwise in good condition, given that it was at least a decade old, and beside it an Acura Integra bearing a disability sticker.

A small brown mongrel dog appeared from the house, leaped the three steps to the yard in a single bound, and nuzzled up to Colson as soon as she emerged from her car. A big man holding a cup of coffee followed the dog outside, although he stopped short of also jumping into the yard and nuzzling Colson. His shoulders and chest were massive, and tapered to a waist that wasn't much wider than Parker's. He wore loose-fitting cargo pants, and a baggy bowling shirt over a white T. His silver hair was cut in a flat top, while matching curly strands peeked out curiously over the neck of his undershirt. As Colson walked over to meet him, he put the coffee cup down on the rail of his porch, and enveloped her in a hug.

"It's been too long, girl," he said.

"It's been two weeks, Uncle Ed," Colson replied.

"Still too long."

He released her, and shook hands with Parker. His palm had a sandpaper grip.

"Mr. Parker," he said. "You're quite the talk around town."

"Should I be pleased?"

"Well, someone once dumped the carcass of a cat over by the Dunk-N-Go, and there was a week's worth of conversation in that, so we may be setting a low bar. How are you finding our little county?"

"Vexing."

"Hard to contest. Come inside. I just made a fresh pot."

The dog, Milo, skipped at their heels and tried to bite the ends of Parker's trousers. Parker didn't mind. He liked dogs. Susan had been allergic, but Jennifer had wanted a dog really badly, and they'd been asking around for advice about breeds that didn't shed.

He pushed aside the memory.

The interior of Eddy Rauls's home was as tidy as the exterior. Even the newspaper was aligned perfectly with the edges of the kitchen table, and the jars and cans in the cabinets were stacked with the labels facing out. The floor was clear of obstacles, and every surface shone.

Rauls noticed Parker taking it all in.

"My wife is going blind," he said.

"I'm sorry to hear that."

"I was always an orderly person. I learned it in the army. Now it serves a practical purpose. Helen needs to know where things are, particularly when I'm not around. She's sleeping right now."

The kitchen table already had cups and spoons laid out, along with milk and sugar. Rauls poured the coffee and offered them vanilla pound cake that he'd baked himself. The coffee was a lot better than the cup Parker had taken with Nealus Cade, and the cake was light. Eddy Rauls was a man of contradictions. Parker wondered if he still had the blackjack and ball-peen hammer used to maintain order back in the day. He was obviously keeping in shape, and only the color of his hair gave away his years. His face remained relatively unlined, and his eyes were clear. Parker wouldn't have crossed him for all the tea in China.

"How far have you got on the killings?" Rauls asked, once they were all settled.

Parker let Colson answer.

"We pulled a print from Donna Lee Kernigan's body," she said.

"You get a hit?"

"Hollis Ward."

Rauls shook his head. "Hollis Ward is dead."

"Officially, Hollis is missing," said Colson.

"That doesn't matter a damn. He's dead, and we all know it."

"How?" said Parker.

"Hollis wasn't the kind to pack his bags and run, didn't matter how much people might have taken against him. It wasn't as though he was particularly sociable to begin with, and he could handle himself."

"If he's dead," said Parker, "how did he die?"

"I'd say someone killed him. Hollis wouldn't have taken his own life, if only out of spite. It's possible he might have met with some kind of accident out in the woods, I suppose, but my guess is he was murdered, and his body dumped somewhere it wouldn't be found."

"Any thoughts on who might have done it?"

Rauls looked at Colson.

"It's nothing I haven't heard before," she said.

"I think his son did it," said Rauls.

"Tilon?"

"Unless he has another."

"Why?"

"Because of what Hollis did to him."

"You think Hollis abused Tilon?"

"I have no proof, but I wouldn't have put it past him. Hollis Ward was a debased son of a bitch."

"I read your case files on Estella Jackson," said Parker. "I could tell you liked her father for the killing, but he had an alibi."

"Yeah, I liked Aaron Jackson for it at first. Subsequently, I had a change of heart."

"Why?"

"I began wondering about Hollis. That's also in my notes."

"Not any longer. They're gone."

Rauls reacted as though a stick had been poked in his face.

"They cleaned the records," he said.

"Who?"

"The Cades."

478

"Why?"

"Because they're rewriting their history in preparation for the addition of a glorious new chapter."

"Do you remember what was in the Ward material?"

"Sure. He had two alibis for the night Estella Jackson disappeared—one from his wife, and the second from Pappy Cade—and another from Cade covering the hours during which she probably died. The Cade alibis were never officially recorded."

"Why?" said Parker.

"Because Pappy didn't want his name associated with Hollis any more than it already had been, not after the child porn business, but he owed Hollis, and said he wasn't about to stand by and see him railroaded for a crime he didn't commit. Pappy advised that he was prepared to give a sworn statement, if it came down to it, but it never did."

"You believed him?"

"There's believing, and there's lacking a solid reason *not* to believe. Pappy and Hollis were thick as thieves, and I use the term advisedly, but it's one thing to pick a man's pocket, and another to torture a girl to death. When it came to Harmony Ward, I had more doubts. She's a sad, bitter woman, but she loved Hollis. She'd do whatever it took to protect him. She told us she received two calls from Hollis during the killing window. Phone company records confirmed that the calls came from the Cade property."

"Which doesn't necessarily mean that Hollis Ward made them," said Parker.

"No, but combined with Pappy's alibis and an absence of evidence, it left us with little to pursue."

"Were you still with the sheriff's office when Hollis Ward disappeared?"

"I was, but I already had one foot out the door, thanks to Pappy's efforts. I hung on for another year because of my pension, then embraced the inevitable."

"Did Harmony Ward have any opinion about what might have happened to her husband?"

"None, but my impression was that she genuinely didn't know where he was."

"You don't think she had anything to do with it?"

"His death, you mean?"

"His presumed death," Parker corrected.

"Whatever way you look at it, the answer is no. It's my conviction that she really did love him."

"What if it came down to a choice between her husband and her son?" Parker asked.

"I've considered that question over the years," said Rauls. "If Hollis was abusing Tilon, Harmony either knew and turned a blind eye, or she didn't know, which I find hard to accept. So if she knew and did nothing, then she chose Hollis over Tilon. That's what makes me think it was Tilon that killed him."

"If he did, and was avenging childhood abuse, he waited a long time before acting."

"There's no statute of limitation on rage."

"No, I don't suppose there is."

"But what if you're wrong?" said Colson. "What if Hollis Ward isn't dead?"

Rauls appeared to physically struggle with this challenge to his assumptions, twisting in his chair.

"Then I'd have to accept that he's returned, and has started again, but I don't know where he could have been hiding during that time, or where he might be holed up now."

"That's a lot of forest you have out there," said Parker.

"Yeah, but hunters and hikers use it, and it's harvested. There's also the Forest Service."

"Although the majority is pine," Colson pointed out, "and clear-cutting has been banned since '93. It would be easier to vanish into it than some might think, if you picked the right areas and knew how to avoid the rangers."

Rauls scratched his chin. "It's just about credible, I admit, but it still doesn't sit easily with my conception of Hollis Ward."

"What about his son?" said Parker.

"What about him?"

"According to Chief Griffin, he may be involved in meth production in the Ouachita, but nobody seems to know exactly where."

"Those boys use mobile labs. They hide them in RVs and campers."

"If you can hide a meth lab out there," said Parker, "you can hide a man."

Rauls conceded the point.

"If Hollis is alive, could Tilon be helping him?" said Colson. "What if you're wrong about Tilon killing Hollis, and they're now working together?"

"Killing women?" said Rauls. "Why would Tilon do that?"

"Because Hollis is his father," she said. "Some fathers do terrible things to their sons, but their sons never stop loving them, and sometimes even want to become like them."

"I don't know what kind of magazines you're reading, girl," said Rauls, "but I think you ought to stop."

Colson slapped his arm.

"Tilon Ward may have been one of the last people to see Donna Lee Kernigan alive," said Parker.

"Seriously?" said Rauls.

"She was sleeping with someone, but keeping it secret," said Colson. "It could have been Tilon."

"If that's true," said Rauls, "and Hollis is alive, then he killed his son's girlfriend."

"Or Tilon fed her to him," said Parker.

"I'm still not of the opinion that Tilon has such capacities," said Rauls.

"A few minutes ago, you had him pegged for the murder of his father," said Parker.

"That was different," said Rauls.

"Different how?"

"Hollis was asking for it."

Which answered that question. They batted ideas back and forth. Rauls poured more coffee, and told them about the discovery of Estella Jackson's body and the investigation that followed. He didn't have much more to add to what was in the files, although the tale of Pappy Cade's intervention on Hollis Ward's behalf bothered Parker. Then again, it probably shouldn't have: Ward had been doing Pappy's dirty work for a long time, and might have called in a favor with the alibi in return for keeping quiet about his activities on behalf of the Cade family. But lying for a man accused of the brutal murder of a woman was a service beyond the usual, and there was also Nealus Cade's account of the falling-out between his father and Hollis Ward after Ward's release from prison. Why would Pappy Cade have been willing to stand up for a man that his son had threatened to jail?

"I'm still troubled by the removal from the Jackson file of your notes on Hollis Ward," said Parker. "There must have been more to it than the Cades' reluctance to be associated with an old murder, however peripherally."

Rauls thought for a time.

"I can't recall everything that was in it," he said, "and I lost a lot of my old papers in a house fire about a year ago. It was lucky we didn't all go up in flames."

He resumed thinking. Parker and Colson waited.

"I do recall that while Pappy had offered to corroborate Hollis's alibi, he said he could provide other witnesses too, which was why I was prepared to cross Hollis's name off my list faster than I might otherwise have done."

"Do you remember who those witnesses were?"

"Delphia was one. It might even have been Jurel as well, although I'm struggling to recall, but certainly Delphia."

"Did you interview them?"

"Only Delphia, and that was an informal conversation. I didn't keep notes."

"Why?"

"It wasn't worth the ink. She confirmed what her father said."

"Which was?"

"That Hollis Ward had been staying at the Cades' guesthouse at the time the medical examiner determined Estella Jackson was killed."

"Did she say why he was there?"

"She claimed that Hollis sometimes stayed over at the property, if I remember right. He and Pappy both liked drinking into the night, even after Pappy officially cut Hollis loose."

"That makes for a lot of potential alibis," said Parker.

"And it's possible," said Rauls, "that none of them was completely true."

"Leaving Hollis Ward as the killer of Estella Jackson."

"It's not beyond the bounds of likelihood. Aaron Jackson, the girl's father, was a known associate of Ward's. He helped Hollis when there was work to be done among the coloreds, so Hollis knew the family, and knew those roads. Hollis also liked very young girls, as that child porn conviction demonstrated, although Estella was closer to a woman when she died. But thinking it and proving it are different animals. It's just a feeling, that's all, and unless the justice system has transformed itself in my absence, the courts don't convict on the basis of whatever may come between me and sleep."

"I have one last question," said Parker. "Could the Cades have killed Hollis Ward?"

"A few minutes ago," said Rauls, "you had Hollis pegged for the murder of Donna Lee Kernigan."

"I'm happy to assess alternatives," said Parker.

"Why do you think the Cades might have been involved in Hollis Ward's death," said Colson, "assuming he is dead, which is a stretch, seeing as how he's leaving his fingerprints around?"

"Aside from the fact that they're involved with everything in this county?" said Parker.

"Aside from that."

"I understand why Mr. Rauls here was prepared to accept the alibis the Cades offered for Ward, if only to a degree, but that doesn't mean Pappy and the rest of them weren't lying. What if Hollis knew enough about the Cades' activities in Burdon County to blackmail Pappy into speaking up on his behalf? Once Pappy had acceded, he was in danger, because that's how blackmail works. All things considered, it would have been easier for the Cades if Hollis were to have disappeared permanently in the aftermath. It would silence him, and help prevent the alibi from coming back to haunt Pappy."

"It still leaves us with Hollis Ward's fingerprint on Donna Lee Kernigan's corpse," said Colson, "and her getting into Tilon's truck just before she vanished."

Rauls poured himself another cup of coffee. Parker didn't know where the man was putting it all.

"What you have here," said Rauls, "is what's called a mystery."

CHAPTER
LXXV

Dr. Ruth Temple went through the Kernigan autopsy results with Griffin over the phone shortly after 4:30 p.m. She didn't have a lot to add to what he already knew, apart from confirming that the branches had been placed in Donna Lee Kernigan's body after death. While force had been applied in order to lodge them in place, resulting in considerable internal damage, they were not the kind of injuries associated with a frenzied attack, but suggested instead a degree of deliberation.

Griffin asked if she could pull up the autopsy results from the murder of Estella Jackson.

"I'm already familiar with their contents," she said, "and I know what you're going to ask me."

"They hiring psychics up there at the crime lab now?"

"I don't think the executive director would approve—although if I were actually a psychic, I'd be able to say for sure. No, I believe you're going to ask me if the injuries to Jackson were similar to Kernigan's, in which case I'd say they weren't. Those branches were jammed repeatedly into Estella Jackson's mouth and vagina, which was done while she was still alive—and that's leaving aside the multiple stab wounds. I can go into more detail if you like, but it won't make you feel any more positive about humanity, or help you much either way."

"I'll pass, then."

"Wise move. Suffice to say that most of Estella Jackson's teeth were knocked out, her spine was partially severed below the skull, and her uterus was pierced several times. That kind of damage bespeaks rage, which isn't to say that the same individual couldn't be responsible for both killings, but that would involve psychological profiling, which is beyond my remit." She paused. "It's a shame we weren't able to look at Patricia Hartley's body."

"Yeah, a damn shame, and a double damn shame that she was cremated, so we can't even seek an exhumation."

"Speaking of which," said Temple, "it might be politic for me to contact the Burdon County Sheriff's Office after I'm done talking with you."

"I understand. I appreciate your tact."

"It's my pleasure. I'll send on hard copies of the report by morning."

Griffin hung up. It wouldn't be long before he heard from Jurel Cade about Hollis Ward, and when he did he'd be forced to share with Cade the likelihood that Hollis's son, Tilon, was the last known person to have seen Donna Lee Kernigan alive. That would give Cade an excuse to start tearing up the place looking for both Hollis and Tilon. Once, Hollis Ward had been tight with the Cades, but then Hollis went missing, and Tilon drifted into criminality. Now nothing would give Jurel Cade more pleasure than to see Tilon Ward incarcerated, and maybe Tilon's old man, too.

There was an aspect of the relationship between the Cades and the Wards that was beyond Griffin's comprehension, and his inability to pinpoint it bothered him. It was possible to construct a narrative that ran from the bond between Hollis Ward and Pappy Cade; continued through the carving up of the county, and Hollis's fall from grace and subsequent disappearance; and ended with Jurel Cade's natural antipathy as a lawman toward someone reckoned to be involved in the production and supply of methamphetamine, namely Tilon Ward. But this narrative wasn't sufficient to explain the rancor that seemed to underpin the current state of affairs between the Cades and what was left of the Ward family— unless, of course, Tilon Ward was convinced that the Cades had something to do with his father's disappearance, but that would explain only his animosity toward the Cades, not vice versa. Now, it appeared, Hollis Ward was back from wherever he'd been—the Ouachita, or the grave—and had started, or resumed, killing young black women.

Kel Knight appeared in the doorway of Griffin's office. He looked exhausted.

"That's not the face of a man bearing good news," said Griffin.

"Pruitt Dix is in the wind," said Knight, as he flopped into a chair, "and when Robinett and I paid a courtesy call on Randall Butcher at his club, we found it in the hands of one of the assistant managers, who pleaded ignorance of his boss's whereabouts."

"Any reason why Butcher might not want to be found?"

"Unofficially, there's a federal indictment imminent. Robinett told me so, but only because by 'imminent' I mean within the next twenty-four hours, although it could be less now that Butcher is running."

"Man, they kept that quiet," said Griffin. Usually a dog couldn't bark in Little Rock without the fact being remarked upon.

"Because they were afraid Butcher might hear about it," said Knight. "And if Butcher is conclusively dealing meth, then Tilon Ward may also be involved."

"Which would explain why Dix didn't want us talking to Tilon."

"Wasn't Sallie Kernigan a dancer at one of Butcher's clubs when she was younger?" said Knight.

"I knew she did some club work. I didn't know it was for Butcher."

"I remember hearing something about it. Denny Rhinehart might have mentioned it. Can't think who else would have."

"Yeah, about Denny," said Griffin. "I know you're tired, but I'd be grateful if you could take a run over to the Rhine Heart and ask him why he might have been arguing with Donna Lee. I dropped by earlier, but the bar was all locked up.

I'd go back myself, but I think I'm going to be hearing from Jurel Cade soon, and I'd prefer to be sitting in my own chair when that happens."

Knight pushed himself to his feet.

"Where's Parker?" he said.

"With Colson, talking to Eddy Rauls."

"He find out anything from examining those records at the sheriff's office?" said Knight.

"Only that Jurel doesn't like him any more now than he did yesterday, but my hope is that Parker might have spotted something that Jurel overlooked—and even Rauls, too. Fresh eyes. Why, you missing him?"

"I'd like to be given the opportunity to miss him."

"You and Jurel ought to get together, now that you've found something to agree on. Me, I'm starting to like our Mr. Parker."

"He's ours now? I worry about you, Chief."

"We need him," said Griffin, waving Knight on his way. "Plus he works cheap, and has his own gun."

CHAPTER
LXXVI

Leonard Cresil spent most of the afternoon and early evening driving Charles Shire to and from a series of meetings, at which Shire was required to offer assurances that the investigation underway in Burdon County would not impact negatively on the Kovas contracts, or endanger any investments and payments—official or undocumented, legal or illicit—already made. Occasionally, Cresil would be asked to interject to offer a word of support, but for the most part his presence alone was enough to reassure those who knew of his particular reputation. While they traveled between venues, Shire would carefully disinfect his hands with sanitizer. When traveling together on commissions like this, they ate only in chain restaurants, usually McDonald's, because Shire said that the company's hygiene standards were higher than the norm. The food played hell with Cresil's guts.

"I think Delphia Cade likes you," said Shire, as they returned to the motel. They had not spoken of Delphia's presence in Shire's room. Cresil knew that it was not for him to decide when, or if, to raise the subject.

"If you want me to sleep with her, it'll cost you extra," said Cresil.

Shire permitted himself what might have been mistaken, in the wrong light, for a smile.

"There are some things even I wouldn't ask of a man."

Cresil doubted that, but let it pass.

"Did you permit her to use your toilet?" he said. Cresil had become adroit at removing motel toilet seats in order to replace them with Shire's own. It was, in its way, one of the more reasonable of the man's phobias.

"No, only the sink. She said she wanted to wash her hands."

"Of what, blood?"

"She's too clever for that."

Again, Cresil elected not to offer an opinion. He also wouldn't have put it past Delphia Cade to piss on a man's toilet seat out of spite. Instead, he said, "I'm now ambivalent about the wisdom of going after Parker."

Cresil had decided to be straight with Shire about the involvement of the former NYPD detective, and the moves being planned against him. He didn't want to be left hanging in the wind if they didn't work out. As it turned out, Delphia Cade had already made plain to Shire her thoughts on the subject of Parker.

"We're not going after him," said Shire. "Butcher and Dix are."

"Nevertheless."

"It's what Delphia wants. Apparently she has taken against Mr. Parker. He has proven resistant to her charms, possibly due to his state of grief."

On this, Cresil empathized with Parker. As

493

far as he could tell, Delphia Cade's charms were negligible.

"And that doesn't dispose her to be more understanding?" he said.

"No, it does not."

They reached the outskirts of Cargill, passing on the left the body of water that gave the town its name, or some semblance of it. An early moon lay perfectly reflected on its surface, undistorted by the slightest of ripples, even though a wind was troubling the trees. Cresil had a vision of himself dipping a hand into the lake, and watching blackness drip like oil from his fingers.

"You know," said Cresil, "I think there's something wrong with this county."

"That's unfortunate, given the significant investment our employers are about to make in it."

"I wonder if it's to do with that lake. The water's not right. It may have poisoned the land, and the people along with it."

Shire took in the sight of the Karagol as they passed.

"It's just dark. Some might consider it beautiful."

"They'd be wrong."

"Once we're done here, you won't ever have to return."

"Music to my ears."

"Have you considered that the fault might lie not in the county, but in yourself?"

"What do you mean?" said Cresil.

"You've lived too long with corruption and

violence. They have infected you, and now you carry them with you everywhere, like a disease."

Cresil wouldn't have taken this from anyone else, but Shire was a singular man. His distance from ordinary human emotion meant that even the subject of Cresil's potential moral delinquency was something to be considered only in the abstract, as though it did not directly concern either of them.

"And you?" said Cresil. "Are you somehow immune?"

"No, I am corrupt, but the corruption is entirely my own. I believe I may have been born peccant."

Cresil was minded to agree. He pitied Shire's wife and children, and their ongoing exposure to this man—although the former at least had some choice in the matter.

They swept through the town and pulled into the parking lot of the motel.

"Will we be leaving tomorrow?" said Cresil.

"I have to report back on what's been happening here. I'd prefer if you'd remain a few more days, just to monitor developments. Your proximity will also serve to reassure the Cades."

"All of them, or just Delphia?"

"Delphia is the only one that matters. She's going to become a very wealthy woman in the near future, and she'll be adrift once the divorce goes through. You're a single man. Her issues with her father make her an unsuitable mate for someone her own age. She requires an older, steadier hand. Perhaps you should reconsider your attitude toward her. I believe you might find some of her appetites amenable to your own."

Cresil was under no illusions about Shire's knowledge of his appetites. They had worked together too long for that.

"Wouldn't that entail staying here?" said Cresil.

"Probably."

"Then I'll pass. This is the worst place I've ever been. I told you: I'm going to retire to Florida, and open a bar."

"You're not going to retire, Mr. Cresil."

"No?"

"Men like us don't retire. We just die."

"If you make it to Boca Raton, you can look me up and I'll disprove your thesis. I may even pour you a free soda."

Shire opened his door to get out. More cars were now parked in the lot than before. Shire didn't look pleased to see them. More cars meant more people, and people were potential contaminants.

"If *you* make it to Boca Raton," he said, "I'll pay for your bar myself. Have a good evening."

Cresil sat in the car and waited until Shire was safely in his room. He'd meant what he said. Burdon County was oppressing him. The sky was too low and the air tasted sour. Whatever was debased in his own nature found no echo here, but rather shied away from a deeper, darker aspect in the land. Kovas might build in Cargill, but Cresil was of the view that it wouldn't thrive, and neither would its employees. Cresil was sure that if he were to check back in five or ten years, he would discover a litany of broken marriages, alcoholism, abuse, and general domestic unhappiness. Not that he had any intention of doing so: he would be in Florida, listening to tourists complain about the humidity, and recalling his time in Cargill only when the smell from the drains got to be too much.

He turned off the engine, and checked that he had his wallet and room key.

When he got out of the car, Charlie Parker was standing before him.

CHAPTER
LXXVII

Jurel Cade put the phone down. In front of him was a sheet of notepaper with only a few scribbled words on it, because he had stopped writing shortly after Dr. Ruth Temple mentioned the name Hollis Ward.

"Are you sure it's Ward's fingerprint on the body?" he asked Temple.

"There's no doubt."

"Have you spoken to Evan Griffin about this?"

"I talked to him before I called you."

Cade noticed that she didn't specify how long she had waited before contacting him, but her tone caused him to believe that she'd taken her sweet time about it. He had only met Temple on a couple of occasions, and got the impression she didn't like him. Under ordinary circumstances, Cade tended to reciprocate dislike with dislike, but it paid to keep on the right side of the folks in the state crime lab, so he was forced to be polite to her.

"I'm grateful for the courtesy."

"It's my job," said Temple, and this time there was no mistaking the edge.

"Have I done something to offend you?"

"I think it would have helped the progress of the investigation had this lab been given the opportunity to examine Patricia Hartley's body before it was consigned to the flames."

"That was the county coroner's call to make."

"Was it? You enjoy the rest of your day."

Then the bitch had the temerity to hang up on him. Cade filed away that final slight for future reference. Down the line, he'd give Temple cause to regret it. Kovas's investment in the state would buy the Cades a lot of influence and goodwill. Jurel thought he might use some of it to ensure Temple's career path became one of briars and tangles.

He considered contacting Griffin, but decided he'd learn more from a one-on-one conversation, or gain more personal satisfaction from shouting in Griffin's face. He informed Sandi, the dispatcher, that he was heading for Cargill. He got in his car and began driving, only to pull over by the side of the road when he was barely outside town, because there were times when a man could think and drive, and times when he had to choose one or the other.

Hollis Ward. Jesus. As far as anyone knew, Hollis Ward was dead. Pappy wouldn't be pleased to hear that this assumption now appeared to be erroneous, because a deceased Hollis Ward had been best for all concerned, Hollis himself possibly excepted. But that fingerprint on Donna Lee Kernigan's body explained a lot, because if Hollis had returned with a grudge against the Cades, then potentially undermining the Kovas agreement was a good way to go about indulging it. Pappy had overextended himself in every way to make Kovas happen— financially, politically, even physically, because his efforts had taken a toll on his health. Not only the future prosperity of the county but also the Cades' long-term wealth and influence were dependent upon the agreement going through. If it didn't, they'd be left with a lot of worthless land in Burdon County, a long line of disappointed investors, both actual and potential, and a family name that wouldn't be worth the breath required to say it aloud.

But Jurel didn't want to speak with his father about Hollis Ward, not before he'd had a chance to sit down with Griffin, and certainly not until he'd discussed everything with Delphia. His sister always said they should have killed Hollis themselves for what he'd done. When Hollis vanished, Jurel even suspected that Delphia might have been responsible: not directly, of course—Delphia was a Cade, and Pappy had instilled in his children the importance of subcontracting illegal acts, and using layers of middlemen—but it wouldn't have been beyond her abilities to sow the seed of Hollis's destruction in the mind of another. She had denied this allegation when Jurel put to her, but he hadn't wholly believed her. Now, it seemed, she'd been telling the truth after all.

Maybe she was right, though, and they should have killed Hollis Ward when they had the chance. But if that was true, they should have killed someone else as well.

They should have killed Pappy.

The lights were out at the Rhine Heart when Kel Knight arrived, and the doors remained locked.

Two cars were parked out front, and he recognized the drivers: a couple of Denny Rhinehart's regulars, wondering why the bar wasn't open.

"Have you seen Denny around?" Knight asked one of them, a guy named Leon Hornbeck who used to work as a metal fabricator but now stacked shelves part-time at the IGA. Leon's brother, Milton, was a familiar face in local law enforcement circles, being always on his way to jail, from jail, or actually in jail. Without jail, Milton Hornbeck's life would have been utterly without meaning or purpose.

"His truck's here," said Hornbeck. "I tried knocking, but I don't think there's anyone inside. I'm going to give him a few minutes more, then head over to Boyd's. I got a thirst."

Leon Hornbeck always had a thirst. He'd once had a good job, a pleasant wife, and two kids that he saw each evening after work. Now he had a crappy job, no wife, two kids he saw a couple of weekends a month, and that thirst. Even if Kovas settled on Cargill for its facility, Knight thought it would come too late for Leon. He was lost. Eventually he'd wrap his car around a tree while driving drunk, or set himself on fire by falling asleep with a cigarette in his hand.

Knight walked over to check out the interior of the bar. The shutters on the windows were closed, but through a busted slat he saw a single coffee mug sitting on one of the tables inside, and thought he could faintly hear music playing. He didn't want to go breaking down any doors, not if Denny Rhinehart had been delayed somewhere. Then again, Rhinehart was, in Knight's opinion, a slothful individual, and if he ever went anywhere, he did so behind the wheel of his truck. Also, he wasn't in the habit of locking the back door when he happened to be inside, except at the end of the night when counting the takings.

Knight decided to give Rhinehart another half hour. After that, he had a crowbar in the trunk of his car, and the bar owner could bill the town for the damage.

"If Denny shows up anytime soon," he told Hornbeck, "tell him to give me a call."

Hornbeck looked at his watch.

"Okay," he said, "but he better not be long. I got—"

"A thirst," Knight finished for him. "I know."

This town, Knight thought. *This dying town.*

CHAPTER
LXXVIII

Until earlier that day, Leonard Cresil had paid attention only in the abstract to the fact of Charlie Parker's existence. As far as he was aware, the Cargill PD had engaged some passing deadbeat ex-detective, a guy who couldn't make his nut in the NYPD, to help them with their case in return for beer money. As a former detective himself— although one who had managed to monetize his experience in a significant way—Cresil was aware of plenty of ex-cops who had gone down the private investigator route, or hired themselves out as security. Some of them were good, but a lot weren't, and even the ones that were up to snuff still didn't meet Cresil's idiosyncratic standards.

And, yes, Parker's story, once revealed, was different from most: a cop father with blood on his hands, who had taken his own life rather than face a prosecution for killing two young people, the reasons behind the shootings still unexplained; a career in the NYPD that seemed set to make up for his old man's sins, even as the son began to inspire unease in those who served with him because of the odor of bad luck about him; the slaying of his wife and daughter, which appeared to confirm all those doubts; a resignation from the force that was neither entirely unexpected nor especially unwelcome; suspicion of involvement in the death of a pimp named Johnny Friday, the investigation into which remained open but was likely to slide for lack of proof and a general reluctance to pursue a man who had suffered so much already; and finally, rumors that he was hunting the one responsible for murdering his family, aided by information that might, just might, be coming from a rabbi within the Federal Bureau of Investigation.

Charles Shire's money had bought a lot of information on Charlie Parker.

Yet Cresil's instinct had still been to dismiss Parker as an irritant, one that would, despite Cresil's own reservations, be dealt with by whatever hillbillies Randall Butcher might round up to deliver a beating—though Butcher would undoubtedly be less willing to oblige were he to learn that he was effectively doing Delphia Cade's dirty work, and that whatever resulted from the attack would doom him in the long run.

But now, faced with Parker in the flesh, Cresil realized that he had been wrong to underestimate him. Parker might have been young—early thirties, according to the intelligence Cresil had received—but he carried himself like someone much older, although that was almost certainly a consequence of all he had endured. He radiated watchfulness without fear, and a self-aware intelligence. Cresil probably had about five inches and thirty pounds on him, but decided he wouldn't want to face Parker in a fair fight. Parker might go down, but he wouldn't stay there, and whatever demons impelled him would keep him coming until his opponent made an error, permitting the delivery of the killer blow.

And if Parker lost, he wouldn't care, because a part of him wanted to die. All this Cresil recognized in an instant, and understood that he was suddenly afraid of this man.

Cresil leaned against the driver's door. He slid his left hand into a pocket of his pants, pushing his jacket back to reveal, almost casually, a gun in its shoulder holster.

"Can I help you with something?" he said.

"Your name is Leonard Cresil," said Parker. "The only reason you're not behind bars is because police forces in three states were too embarrassed by your conduct to risk a court case, and instead quietly showed you the door. You're a rapist, and an abuser of women. You may have murdered a union organizer named Marvin Wright in Pensacola, Florida, and you left a federal witness, Enrique Figueiras, in a vegetative state after cracking his skull with a Louisville Slugger in Macon, Georgia, but they're only the most recent of your victims. You work for the wealthy and powerful, and prefer your employers to possess even fewer moral scruples than you, which is a select group. Because of your actions, I believe you're living on borrowed time. If you die in your bed, you'll do so in a pool of your own blood."

Cresil made an odd biting gesture, an animal response to provocation that was both instinctive

505

and quickly smothered, as though the feral core of his being had briefly been exposed to light.

"And you're Charlie Parker," he said, "a failed son, a failed husband, a failed father, and a failed cop. You killed an unarmed man in a bus station restroom because you can't control your rage, and now you're wandering aimlessly in the hope that, somehow, it will bring you closer to the man you're looking for, and ultimately result in the termination of your own existence.

"And wherever he is, the one who left you this way is laughing at you, because he took everything you loved and there wasn't a damn thing you could do about it. You couldn't protect your wife and daughter, and you didn't even have the decency to die with them. If you're lucky, their killer will come for you and put you out of your misery. But it may be that he'll just leave you to suffer, and you'll float from town to town while all that anger and grief eats away at you like a cancer."

If Cresil was hoping for a reaction, he was destined to be disappointed. Parker showed no anger or hurt, and Cresil knew that he had said nothing to this man with which he had not tormented himself a thousand times over in the months since the loss of his family. It left Cresil feeling strangely angry with himself, as though even his own moral turpitude was unworthy of the words he had spoken.

"So now we know each other," said Parker. "I hope it's you that takes a run at me. I might be willing to put you out of your own pain."

"Perhaps I was mistaken," said Cresil. "I mistook you for one who had mastered his pride, but I was in error. You're still young, which might explain it some, but you won't live long enough to make an old corpse. I have a quarter of a century on you, all hard miles, and I've watched the dirt cover better men than you who thought they had the measure of me. When you die, I'll read about it in the newspaper and struggle to remember what you looked like."

"We'll see," said Parker. "In the meantime, you tell the Cades I said hello."

He nodded to Cresil and walked away. Cresil stared at his back and envisioned putting a hole in it. At the very least, he wanted this man to suffer the planned beating, but he mastered this urge. He'd call Delphia Cade and advise her to call the dogs off Parker. If she decided to proceed, let it be on her own head, because he knew now that it wouldn't go well. In a few months, or even a year—assuming the man who had killed the detective's wife and child didn't decide to reunite the family—Cresil would come looking for Charlie Parker, and he'd deal with him in his own way: quietly, from behind, with the minimum of fuss.

And then he would never think of him again.

CHAPTER
LXXIX

Kel Knight didn't have any luck finding Denny Rhinehart around town. He even swung by Rhinehart's home, just in case he'd been forced to leave his vehicle at the bar for mechanical reasons, or due to some personal indisposition, but there didn't appear to be anybody there. He called Ivy Muntz, Rhinehart's cook, to find out if she'd heard from him. She hadn't, because this was one of her evenings off, but she did have a spare set of keys for the Rhine Heart, and agreed to meet Knight at the bar so he could go inside and take a look around.

By the time Knight returned to the Rhine Heart, Leon Hornbeck had left the vicinity in an effort to slake his unquenchable thirst elsewhere, and had presumably taken any other prospective customers with him. As Knight waited for Muntz to arrive, he saw Parker's rental pass, the man himself behind the wheel. Parker noticed the prowl car, spotted Knight, and made a U-turn to pull into the lot.

"Everything okay?" Parker asked.

Knight bristled. He couldn't help it. Here was this interloper, this suspected killer, acting as though he owned the damn town. The visceral nature of his own animosity struck Knight with such force that he tasted copper in his mouth.

Yet even as he stood before Parker, Knight was

nagged by an ambivalence that might not have been unfamiliar to Leonard Cresil, albeit one with markedly different origins. Knight thought he might have some inkling of how Parker's fellow officers felt about him up in New York City, and how one who should have been part of a brotherhood in blue—Knight still didn't hold with female cops, Colson excepted, and then only because he knew her people—could have found himself so isolated. Yet Parker hadn't come to Cargill in order to interfere with the workings of the community, or personally offend the morals and sensibilities of Kel Knight, but because something in the staging of one killing, and the unofficial details of another, had reminded him, however mistakenly, of what had been inflicted on those he loved. Knight had to remind himself that Parker was doing them a favor by remaining in town. He had set his own inconvenience against the needs of others, and the scales had tipped in favor of the latter, but that didn't mean Knight had to be ecstatic about it.

"The place is still locked up, and Rhinehart's usually pouring drinks by now," he said.

"Do you have a reason to be worried?" said Parker.

"This is a town of routines. Any break in them is odd." Knight relented somewhat. "Did the chief tell you about Rhinehart and Donna Lee?"

"Only that she was seen looking distressed, and Rhinehart might have been responsible."

"That's still all we have, but it would be good to hear his side of the story. His cook is coming over with a set of keys so I can take a look around."

"If you need company—"

"No, I can manage. What about you?"

"I thought I might have a talk with Nathan Pettle."

"Why Pettle?"

"He knew Hollis Ward, and is—or was—on good terms with Pappy Cade."

"Did Eddy Rauls tell you that?"

"No, Nealus Cade."

"That family is a nest of vipers."

"You may be doing a disservice to vipers."

Knight was about to smile, but caught himself just in time.

"I hear Delphia Cade wants you off the case."

"Or off the face of the earth. I believe she'd settle for the first, but prefer the second." Parker glanced back toward the motel, which was visible from where they were standing. "I just had a conversation with Leonard Cresil."

"Sometimes, things learn to walk that should only have crawled," said Knight. "Cresil was a dirty cop, and he's even dirtier now. You ought to keep away from him."

"I'm not sure that's my decision to make. According to Nealus Cade, his sister may have left it to Cresil to deal with me."

Kel Knight thought that life seemed intent on testing him. Just as he was starting to get a handle on how he felt about Parker, a further embroilment was added to the mix.

"The chief won't stand for it," Knight said. "Neither will I. It's no secret I have reservations about your involvement in our affairs, but that doesn't mean Cresil and the Cades get to ride roughshod over the law."

"No reflection on the law in this county," said Parker, "but I think that's exactly what Cresil and the Cades get to do. And if anything did happen to me, you'd have a better chance of connecting it to Mother Teresa than to them."

"I don't want to see you end up in the hospital," said Knight. "We'd have to cover your expenses."

"And come visit," said Parker. "With grapes."

Knight's expression suggested that, in the event of such a mishap, Parker would be waiting a long time for the pleasure of his company.

"You'd better head out to Pettle's place before the light fades much more," Knight said. "Given recent events, people will start to become jumpy once night falls."

"On my way," said Parker.

He left the lot just as Ivy Muntz pulled in. Perhaps, Knight considered, Parker wasn't the worst guy to have around while all this was going on, not with men like Leonard Cresil circling.

Then he recalled the scars on Parker's hand, and his heart hardened once more.

CHAPTER
LXXX

Billie Brinton rarely heard Evan Griffin raise his voice. He wasn't disposed to shouting. In fact, the softer he spoke, the more reason the object of his attention might have to feel concerned, and therefore to pay attention. But the chief's voice was certainly raised right now, and Jurel Cade was hollering right back at him. Mostly they were shouting at each other about Hollis and Tilon Ward, but it also sounded as though Chief Griffin had endured his fill of Cade's obstructionism, and wasn't going to stand for it any longer. Eventually Cade stormed out of the chief's office, and as he departed he used a word to describe Griffin that Billie could later only bring herself to refer to as "C U Next Thursday."

Griffin himself arrived at her desk a few moments later. His face was red.

"Where's Kel?" said Griffin.

"I assume he's still down at the Rhine Heart."

"And Parker?"

"I don't know. He hasn't been in touch."

"Colson? Naylor?"

"I can find out."

"Am I running this goddamned department alone?"

Billie peered at him over the top of her spectacles.

"You got me," she said.

For a moment she thought the top of Evan Griffin's head might be about to pop off, until some of the tension and anger seemed to drain from him as though a valve had been turned at the base of his skull.

"That's something, at least," he said. "Please find out where they are, and ask them to come back here as soon as possible."

"Can I tell them why?"

"Inform them that Jurel Cade just declared war."

"On us?"

"On everyone."

Ivy Muntz unlocked the rear door of the Rhine Heart, and Kel Knight called out Denny's name. He received no reply, but could hear the radio playing from somewhere in back.

"Should I come with you?" said Muntz.

"No, you stay here. Anyone else arrives, you make sure they remain outside."

The hairs on Knight's neck were standing on end, and he had a cramp in his stomach. A man just grew to know when something wasn't right. He unclipped his holster, but didn't draw his weapon. He went behind the bar and entered the private precincts of the Rhine Heart, containing the storage areas, the kitchen, and Denny Rhinehart's small, windowless office. That was where he found Rhinehart lying on his back with a new hole in his face, another in his belly, and the room stinking of blood and death. Knight checked for a pulse, but only so he could later confirm that he'd done everything right. Rhinehart's skin was cold and rigor mortis had already set in.

Knight had never liked Denny Rhinehart because he'd never trusted him, and Knight could never like someone who couldn't be trusted. But now, looking down on Rhinehart's remains, he lowered his head briefly to pray for the man's soul before stepping outside to call Evan Griffin.

Reverend Nathan Pettle lived in a two-story dwelling painted yellow and green, with a small Stars and Stripes fluttering from a flagpole above the front door. A white Country Squire station wagon bearing the ichthys symbol alongside a Clinton/Gore bumper sticker was parked in the drive.

Parker pulled up alongside the station wagon, stepped into the yard, and rang the doorbell. After a short wait, the door was opened by a tall gray-haired man wearing a clean but untucked white shirt and a pair of bargain-store jeans. His face bore the dazed look of someone who had just been woken from sleep, and his feet were bare.

"Reverend Pettle?" said Parker.

"Yes, can I help you?"

Parker identified himself and displayed the temporary ID issued by the Cargill PD. Pettle took it in his hand and examined it closely, squinting.

"I don't have my glasses," he said.

"They're hanging from your shirt."

Pettle dabbed at his chest, found the glasses, and put them on.

"You're the policeman from New York."

"Ex," said Parker, "although I suppose that piece of paper makes me current again."

Pettle handed it back to him.

"What can I do for you?"

"I'd like to talk to you about the Cade family, and Hollis Ward."

Parker saw Pettle's face relax slightly, almost in relief, before it settled into a confused scowl.

"Why Hollis Ward?" he said.

"Perhaps we could discuss it inside."

"This really isn't a good time."

"Reverend, I know you helped identify Donna Lee Kernigan's body. You saw what was done to her. We're trying to stop that from happening to any other young women."

Pettle looked at his watch.

"I'm expecting my wife home shortly."

"Is that a problem?"

"We're obligated to have an important family discussion."

"I'm sure you can delay it."

Parker's tone brooked no further argument, so Pettle conceded defeat.

"I guess you'd better come in, then," he said.

He stepped aside to admit Parker, still holding the door.

"After you," said Parker, and waited for Pettle to lead the way.

Because Kel Knight wasn't the only one that could sense when something was wrong.

Evan Griffin was staring at the body of Denny Rhinehart. Griffin had no personal experience of investigating professional hits, but this didn't strike him as a murder of that stripe. From the mess on the carpet, and the blood on the papers, he got the impression that Rhinehart might have rolled around some as he died, which meant he'd probably also been making a degree of noise, because Griffin didn't believe that men wounded in the belly elected to suffer quietly. For that reason, no professional would opt to kill a man by shooting him in the stomach, which meant that a second shot had been required to finish Rhinehart off. There weren't many good ways to die, and this wasn't one of them either. Griffin also spotted what looked like a bullet hole in the carpet close by Rhinehart's body. He deduced that the killer had fired at least one other shot, which missed its target, before the fatal bullet struck Rhinehart's head, lending further support to Griffin's theory that this was the work of an amateur.

Like Knight, Griffin never had much regard for Rhinehart, but he hadn't deserved such an end. No one could merit that kind of violence, not even the man currently responsible for the deaths of two— or possibly three—young women in the county. Griffin wanted that individual tried in a court of law, judged by a jury of his peers, and, if found guilty, given the needle. Should Bill Tindle truly have witnessed the aftermath of some altercation between Rhinehart and Donna Lee Kernigan, one that subsequently led to Donna Lee's death at Rhinehart's hand, then the latter's murder had deprived the state of its right to justice. Griffin wasn't jumping to any conclusions, but Cargill was a small town. Despite recent evidence to the contrary, homicide was an aberration here, and Denny Rhinehart, as Sallie Kernigan's former employer, had enjoyed a relationship with the Kernigan family.

"Does he have a safe?" he asked Knight.

"Nope. According to Ivy, Rhinehart kept a cash box in the bottom drawer of the file cabinet. He didn't like holding large sums on the premises, but it wasn't as though the bar was doing so well that this was often an issue, so he'd sometimes let a couple of days go by before he made a run to the bank. The cash box is still in the cabinet, and it hasn't been touched. The cabinet was unlocked, and from what I can tell, the place hasn't been tossed."

Papers covered the floor, but the majority were stained with the emissions of Rhinehart's dying, which most likely meant that he'd knocked the documents from the desk as he fell. His chair was still upright, but was pushed back against the wall. The drawers in the desk were all closed. Griffin opened them with a gloved hand, revealing only assorted items of stationery, a couple of bags of candy, and a selection of pornographic magazines. He flicked through the titles, noting that they catered exclusively to the barely legal market: the models were probably all over eighteen, but had been chosen because they looked much younger. Many were black. He put the magazines back where he'd found them.

"It's time to hand the whole mess over to the state police," he told Knight. "This is getting out of hand."

"Won't make Jurel Cade like us any more than he already does." Knight had been about to call in the discovery of Rhinehart's body when Billie came on the radio to tell him that Griffin wanted to see him, because Jurel Cade was on the warpath.

"Can't increase his dislike for us either," said Griffin. "Besides, he has his own agenda. He now knows about Hollis Ward's fingerprint on the body, and that Tilon Ward was seen with Donna Lee shortly before she died. He tried to tear me a new one for letting Tilon—and I quote—'slip through our fingers.' He said he'd find Tilon and the old man himself."

"Does he believe they're in it together?"

"It's never plain what Jurel believes about any given situation," said Griffin. "If he has resolute principles, I've yet to determine what they might be."

He heard footsteps approaching from the bar. Seconds later, Tucker McKenzie, the forensic analyst, appeared at the door, already suited and booted, with Colson beside him. It was the first time Colson had seen the body. She winced, but didn't otherwise react. Griffin didn't feel he had a lot about which to congratulate himself, especially lately, but hiring Colson had been one of his better decisions.

"Any word from Parker?" he asked her.

"None."

"I spoke with him just before Ivy got here," said Knight. "He said he was on his way to talk to Reverend Pettle."

"I'll give him a call," said Griffin, "just in case Billie became distracted before she could get to him."

McKenzie coughed pointedly. He'd just finished assisting at the scene of a house fire over in Polk County when he got the call from Griffin. It hadn't taken him long to get to Cargill, and he still had smudges of soot on his face.

"When you've finished tramping all over the scene," he said, "could you see your way clear to stepping outside so I can get started?"

They did as McKenzie asked. He paused by Griffin.

"You do know I don't get paid per body, right?" said McKenzie.

He looked tired. There was only so much death upon which a man could gaze in any given day.

"I'm aware of that."

"So I don't need any more of your business. Just saying."

He proceeded into the office and went to work.

• • •

Reverend Nathan Pettle invited Parker to take a seat at the table. The house was very quiet. Parker couldn't even hear a clock ticking. There was no hint of disorder, but neither was there any sense of homeliness. It held the ambience of a location in which an occupant had recently died, someone taken before their time: a young person, perhaps, except no mention had been made to Parker of any such bereavement in the Pettle family. A set of double doors, currently open, separated the kitchen from the living room. Parker could see framed photographs on the table beneath the front window, but they were the only indication that living, breathing human beings might actually spend time together within these walls. The contents of the kitchen cabinets were hidden from view, and all of the surfaces were bare.

"I hope you'll forgive me if I don't offer you anything to drink," said Pettle. "As I told you, I'm expecting my wife home any minute. My daughter is staying with friends. She does that sometimes."

Parker kept his expression neutral. He had no wish to signal any awareness of the oddness of Pettle's behavior.

"That's fine," said Parker. "I've had my fill of coffee for today."

His eye was drawn to an image of Christ hanging on the wall. It was the only religious signifier that Parker had noticed so far.

"That was a gift from a friend," said Pettle. "I

didn't think it was appropriate for our church. Some of the congregants remain doctrinal in their attitude to iconography, so I decided to hang it here instead. I consider it as much a piece of art as a religious symbol. Are you a Christian?"

"I was raised Catholic."

A flicker of disappointment signaled Pettle's opinion of Parker's faith, but he quickly rallied.

"Do you still believe?" he said.

"I don't know."

"Because of what happened to your family?"

So Pettle had known about him before he arrived at his door. Parker wasn't surprised. Like many people around town, the preacher had probably been waiting to put a face to the name.

"For lots of reasons," said Parker.

"I didn't mean to pry. Questions of belief come with the territory." He joined Parker before the image. "What do you see when you look at it?"

"I see Christ," said Parker.

"And nothing else?"

"Isn't that enough?"

"Most white people, when they visit, feel obliged to point out the color of His skin. They say it's a black Jesus, and always in the same tone, the one that tells me they wouldn't have nothing like it on their walls at home. For them, the Savior is always Caucasian." He stepped away from Parker and seated himself at the head of the table, the window at his back. "Is that what you are, Mr. Parker: a white protector, come to save the children of the black man, to restore order where he could not?"

Parker sat at the other end of the table, between Pettle and the door.

"I'm not sure what you mean, Reverend."

"I mean that Evan Griffin is relying on you to solve these crimes, and stop the slaughter of our young women, so money can begin to flow into this benighted county."

"I don't think Chief Griffin sees their color—" said Parker.

Pettle interrupted him. "Don't be a fool," he said.

"You didn't let me finish. I was going to say that I don't think he sees their color before any other aspect. To him, they're primarily women who shouldn't be dead."

"And what about you?"

"I see their color. I'm not blind."

"And you believe that it doesn't make a difference to your attitude?"

"Do you judge every man by your worst experiences of mankind, Reverend?"

"You haven't answered the question."

"I didn't come to this town with the intention of solving its racial or social problems. I came because I was looking for whoever took my wife and child from me. To be honest, Reverend, I don't care a great deal about any of you, black or white, dead or alive."

"That's very honest, yet here you are. Why is that?"

"Because I was asked to help."

For a man who hadn't been keen on admitting a stranger to his home, Parker thought Nathan Pettle was proving surprisingly amenable to discourse. Now that Parker had crossed the threshold, it was as though Pettle was grateful for the distraction he provided. On the other hand, Parker had been around many disturbed people in his time, and Pettle struck him as laboring under considerable psychological and emotional pressure. It was visible in his eyes and gestures, and his sweat contributed to a malodor that permeated the room.

"You could have declined," said Pettle. "Might it be that you care more than you want to admit?"

"I don't have to care. In fact, it's easier if I don't. I just have to make the killings stop. It'll satisfy *my* sense of order. Then I can leave."

"And where will you go?"

"Someplace else. Wherever it may be, it can't be any worse than here. Tell me about Hollis Ward."

"What do you want to know?"

"You were familiar with him."

"I was, but we were not close."

"You were familiar enough with Ward to join him in Pappy Cade's home."

"You're well informed. Who told you that? It wasn't Pappy."

"Why wouldn't Pappy Cade have shared that with me?"

"What manner of man would admit to keeping company with a corrupter of children?"

"Is that what Hollis Ward is?"

"Was. Hollis Ward is dead."

"I've been hearing that frequently today."

"Because it's true. There may not be a grave that anyone can point to, but Hollis Ward's soul is gone from this earth."

"His soul may be, but the rest of him is still here. He left a fingerprint on Donna Lee Kernigan's body."

Pettle's shock was unfeigned.

"That's not possible."

"Why?"

"I told you: he's dead."

"You sound very certain."

"Is that an accusation?"

"Not at all," said Parker. "The evidence suggests that Hollis Ward is alive. Eddy Rauls, the former chief investigator for this county, suspected him of involvement in the death of Estella Jackson. Now two more young women have died in a similar fashion, and Ward has left his mark on at least one of them. I'm interested in exploring the general reluctance to accept that Hollis Ward might have returned, because you're not alone in it."

Pettle checked his watch, then licked a forefinger and used it to wipe a mark from the dial.

"I wanted him to be gone for good."

"Because of the child pornography found in his possession?"

"Yes."

"Is that all?"

"Isn't it enough?"

"Not for the level of animosity he's generated."

"He was a brutish man."

"And?"

"There's no smoke without fire. If he had those pictures, he possessed contemptible desires, and perhaps the willingness to act on them. Actually, there was no 'perhaps' about it. After those pictures were found in his house, I heard a rumor that he'd been caught interfering with a white boy over in Fordyce—his perversions knew no impediment of sex or race—but someone called in a favor, and it was hushed up."

"That someone being Pappy Cade?"

"I assume so."

"Did the discovery of the pornography come as a surprise to you, Reverend?"

Pettle grimaced.

"I might have had my suspicions."

"Why?"

"Things Ward said, and the way he looked at children."

"Any child in particular?"

"No."

Parker detected the lie, but didn't immediately pursue it. It was enough for him to know it was there.

"Which brings us back to you, Hollis Ward, and Pappy Cade—because, as you yourself noted, what kind of man keeps company with a deviant?"

"You haven't been in this county for very long, Mr. Parker, but even you must have concluded by now that nothing gets done without the approval of

525

the Cades. I was trying to build a congregation and help my people. We were worshipping in living rooms and backyards. I wanted a proper house of prayer, which meant I had to deal with Pappy Cade, because he'd already begun buying up properties in the area, and those he didn't own directly, he held the paper on. Hollis Ward was his eyes and ears—and sometimes his fist—in this county. In answer to your question, only a desperate man keeps company with a deviant."

"And did you get what you wanted?"

"I did."

"At what cost?"

"A troubled conscience."

"Because the end didn't entirely justify the means?"

"If you want to put it that way."

The light outside was growing dim, but a trace of sunlight remained. Parker could hear a bird fluttering and crying in Pettle's yard, although the creature itself was not visible. Only its shadow danced across the lawn as it circled, like a dead leaf caught by the wind.

"Which child did Ward look at, Reverend?"

"I don't understand."

"Did he err in a particular respect? Did he make an approach to one of your own children?"

"No! How dare you imply such a thing?"

"I'm not blaming anyone for it except Ward himself. Who was it, then?"

Pettle grew very still, and the silence that

followed went on for so long that Parker began to wonder if the preacher would ever speak again. It was possible that he had overstepped the mark, but even if he had, there were other questions that needed to be asked and answered before Reverend Nathan Pettle was left alone once more.

"Donna Lee Kernigan," said Pettle at last.

"How do you know?"

"I saw him do it. I was over by the school, and Hollis Ward was parked nearby, smoking a cigarette, his hand hanging from the open window. He was watching the boys and girls go by, and then Donna Lee came out. She was only eleven years old. I saw his eyes follow her, and I could tell what was in his heart."

"And why was Donna Lee more important to you than the other children?"

"I didn't say she was. It would have been as bad had he looked at any of them."

"And did he?"

"He might have done."

"Yet it's Donna Lee you recall."

"I knew the family."

"Donna Lee and her mother?"

"That's right."

Parker waited. There was more here.

"Sallie Kernigan was troubled," Pettle continued, after a pause.

"In what way?"

"She drank too much, ran with bad types. I tried to help her."

"How?"

"I ministered to her."

"So she was a member of your congregation?"

"Yes—or no, not as such."

"Which is it, Reverend?"

Parker spoke softly. He thought he understood now where this was going.

"She wasn't, but I hoped she might join us."

"And did she?"

"No."

"Were you very close to Sallie?"

Pettle nodded dumbly.

"You cared about her?"

A pause, and a closing of the eyes.

"Yes."

"More than you should have?"

"Yes."

"And her daughter? Did you feel protective of Donna Lee?"

"Very much so."

"So when you saw Hollis Ward looking at her, you acted."

"Yes. I spoke to him. I told him his behavior was unacceptable."

"How did he react?"

"He laughed in my face."

"What did you do then?"

"I wanted to hit him. I might even have been tempted to kill him. I prayed later for God to forgive me and help me to restrain such impulses."

"And once you finished praying?"

"I went to Pappy Cade. I told him I couldn't guarantee my support in the future unless he did something about Ward."

"Specifically, that he should be warned away from Donna Lee Kernigan?"

"Yes."

"And did that happen?"

"I believe Pappy spoke to him, or it might have been Jurel. Whatever was said, and by whom, Ward didn't hang around the school after that, and he stayed well away from Sallie and Donna Lee."

"Did Ward ever raise the subject with you again?"

"No, but . . ."

"Go on."

"Pappy Cade knew about Ward and his predilections, but still he kept him close, and not only because of his usefulness. Whatever Pappy had on Hollis Ward, I believe Ward had more on Pappy."

"Do you think they shared similar tastes when it came to children?"

"Pappy Cade wasn't interested in anything except money and power, and he was prepared to do whatever it took to accumulate both. If that necessitated fraud, threats, beatings, even burning properties to the ground in order to force out the owners, then Hollis Ward took care of it on his behalf. Pappy had to keep Ward sweet. He didn't want Ward making trouble, or turning on him in a court of law. But eventually . . ."

529

"Ward would have become a liability."

"Yes."

That, thought Parker, tied in with the possibility of blackmail raised by Pappy's willingness to provide Hollis Ward with an alibi for the Estella Jackson killing.

"Is that why you believed Ward was dead, because you thought Pappy Cade had killed him?" said Parker. "He was no longer of use to Pappy, and what he knew of the Cades' activities was potentially damaging enough to justify his murder?"

"I had no proof, but that was my intuition."

"Mistaken, according to the latest developments."

"I still find it hard to accept that Ward might be alive. Where could he have been hiding for all this time?"

"I don't know this territory well enough to speculate," said Parker.

He felt his phone buzzing in his pocket. He'd silenced it before he rang the doorbell. He checked the display and saw Griffin's name. He'd also missed an earlier call from the station house.

"Time for me to go," he said.

"I hope I've helped."

"You've clarified some issues," said Parker. "I do have one more question for you, though."

Parker returned the phone to his jacket pocket.

"Yes?" said Pettle.

"I'm wondering where the blood on your watch face came from."

But Pettle did not answer, or not in so many words.

His right hand emerged from under the kitchen table, and it was holding a gun.

CHAPTER
LXXXI

Horrace Sneed was a small man: small in stature, small in mind, but grand in ambition. Like a great many unintelligent people, he lacked the wherewithal to perceive his own frailties, and had somehow convinced himself that only a combination of misfortune and the machinations of others had deprived him of his rightful position further up the food chain. Faced with this existential injustice, Sneed had decided that his only recourse was to be duplicitous in all matters. Rarely in the conduct of his affairs did he encounter a back he did not wish to stab or a wagon he did not want to de-wheel. He was, by nature and inclination, profoundly deceitful.

Sneed earned a modest income at Warnell's hardware store—the largest provider of home-improvement products in Burdon County—which he supplemented with various forms of criminal activity, including, but not limited to, theft, embezzlement, and the sale of narcotics. Unfortunately for Sneed, he belonged to the class of malefactor that possessed all the instincts for wrongdoing without the acumen to carry it off successfully. This had brought him to the attention of Jurel Cade, which was not the kind of scrutiny that Horrace Sneed relished. In return for not being consigned to the state's prison system, where he would undoubtedly have floundered,

Sneed had agreed to act as an informant for Cade.

Thanks to his innate dishonesty, Sneed turned out to be a virtuoso snitch—so good, in fact, that he had convinced himself his guile was sufficient to cozen even Cade himself. For this reason, Sneed had decided not to share with Cade the details of his professional relationship with Tilon Ward, because his part in the distribution of Ward's product enabled him to enjoy some of the finer things in life, such as a big-screen TV, Minute Man hamburgers, and hookers who could speak English. He had also become a minor cog in the meth-manufacturing machine by occasionally altering orders and invoices in order to redirect supplies of muriatic acid and other chemicals.

Sneed still lived in the house in which he had been born. It was left to him after his father died, his mother having predeceased her husband by many years—almost certainly to her relief, since Sneed's old man had given even habitual domestic abusers a bad name. The house was too big for one person, but selling it wouldn't have significantly improved Sneed's prospects as its location and condition meant that he wouldn't have been able to afford anywhere better with the proceeds. But Sneed kept the interior reasonably clean and made sure the yard was clear of trash. It wasn't as though he entertained many visitors—any visitors at all, to be honest; it was purely a matter of personal pride. He didn't want to be like his father, who had lived and died in squalor.

On this particular evening, Sneed opened the front door of his home to be greeted by his cat, Poindexter; the smell of the stew he had cooked the previous night, which he planned to reheat as soon as he'd fed the animal; and the sight of Jurel Cade sitting in Sneed's favorite armchair, a black wooden baton in his right hand, its leather thong looped around his wrist.

"Hello, Horrace," he said. "Better close that door. Don't want your cat getting out."

Sneed closed the door, although Poindexter wasn't the straying type. He put his car keys on the hall table.

"Am I in trouble?" said Sneed.

"Yes, you are. Get in here and sit down."

Cade used the baton to point at the couch. Sneed sat.

"What can I do to get out of trouble?" he said.

"You can tell me where to find Tilon Ward."

Lying was so ingrained in Sneed that he did it without thinking. He was predisposed to telling an untruth even when honesty couldn't hurt him.

"I guess Tilon's over in Cargill, where he always is."

"That," said Cade, "is the wrong answer."

He twirled the baton and got down to business.

CHAPTER
LXXXII

Pettle's hand was shaking, which meant the gun it held was also shaking. This didn't make Parker feel any better about looking down the barrel. The hammer wasn't cocked, which was something, although it didn't qualify as reassurance. The weapon dangled lengths of the duct tape used by Pettle to secure it to the underside of the table. Parker had already been moving his hand toward his own weapon when Pettle beat him to the draw. He'd underestimated the preacher: another error to add to a growing catalog, although one that might now have reached the final sum of its increase.

"You don't need that," said Parker. "However difficult your position may seem, holding a gun on me is unlikely to improve it."

"You have no idea what I need or don't need," said Pettle. "Right now, I'm not happy that only one of your hands is visible. I'd really like to see the right as well as the left."

Parker placed both palms flat on the kitchen table.

"Why were you concealing a gun, Reverend?"

"I told you: my wife and I are overdue for a conversation."

"What kind of conversation requires a firearm?"

"My wife won't listen to me. I try to tell her I'm sorry, but she walks away. I require her undivided attention in order to explain certain facts to her. It's very important."

"Why is that?"

"So she'll understand."

"Understand what?"

"Why I did what I did."

"Is this about Sallie Kernigan?"

"Yes."

"Does your wife know about your relationship with Sallie?"

"She does. That knowledge lies at the heart of our current difficulties. She won't forgive me, and I require her forgiveness."

Parker tried to keep his breathing even. He didn't want to die here, in a too quiet house, at the hands of a disturbed preacher. But if he didn't want to be shot, he had to keep Pettle talking. He needed to persuade him to put the gun down. Strange, he thought: there was a time, not long before, when he had wished only to die. Now, faced with the reality of his dispatch, he was reluctant to embrace its immediate likelihood. He still wanted it, but— in the manner of St. Augustine—not yet.

"Why are you smiling?" Pettle asked.

"I hadn't realized I was."

"Aren't you frightened?"

"Some, but not as much as you might think."

"Why?"

"Because fundamentally I believe that you're a good man. I wish you weren't pointing a gun at me, but I'm not going to give you cause to use it.

I want to help you. Situations like this never have only one possible outcome. It can appear that way, but it's not the case."

"But you don't know what I've done."

"Then tell me, Reverend. Tell me about the blood."

Pettle's left hand stroked his shirt, as though to wipe away whatever residue remained of his sin.

"He wouldn't leave Donna Lee alone," said Pettle. "He was just like Hollis Ward. Neither of them could keep their hands off young girls."

"Who wouldn't leave her alone?"

"Denny Rhinehart."

"Did Rhinehart kill Donna Lee?"

"I don't know. He said he didn't, but I wasn't sure whether to believe him or not. Then he said he'd tell the police about Sallie and me. He never did like me, and the feeling was mutual. But I would never have ruined him, not the way he was threatening to ruin me."

The phone buzzed again in Parker's pocket, the vibration audible in the quiet of the room.

"Do you hear that?" said Parker.

"What about it?"

"I think that's Chief Griffin. He's been trying to call me ever since I got here. I told Kel Knight I was coming to talk to you. If I don't answer, Griffin will send someone to find out what's the matter. Once that happens, everything will start to go downhill very fast."

"You want me to let you answer it?" said Pettle. "Do you think I'm an idiot?"

"I don't think you're an idiot, Reverend. You've had a hard time lately, and you're doing what you feel is necessary to bring it to a conclusion. Sometimes, when we're under pressure, we act out of character. I'd very much like you to let me answer this call and confirm to Chief Griffin that I'm okay. After that, we can keep talking, and I'll do my best to find a way to help you resolve your difficulties. I have nothing against you, beyond the fact that you're holding a gun on me, but it's likely that I won't be safe until we find a solution to your problem. With that in mind, it's in my best interests to assist you. Can I reach for my phone?"

Pettle's inner debate played out on his face. It went on for so long that Parker didn't think he'd permit the call to be answered, but Pettle surprised him.

"Go ahead," he said, "but slowly."

Gingerly, Parker extracted the phone and flipped it open. It was, as he'd anticipated, Griffin on the line.

"Where are you?" said Griffin.

"I spoke to Knight."

This was met with a confused silence.

"What's that supposed to mean?"

"Just what I said. This isn't a good time."

"It isn't a good time for anyone, least of all Denny Rhinehart. Somebody shot him to death."

This put a different complexion on affairs. Parker was watching Pettle's face, and wondering if some alteration in the reverend's features might reveal his intentions just before he pulled the trigger. It could be the difference between living and dying.

"I may have an answer to that," said Parker.

"Are you in trouble?"

"Very much so, but I'm hoping for a positive outcome."

"We're on our way."

Griffin hung up.

"They're coming, aren't they?" said Pettle.

"They'll give us the time we need, and they won't enter your home unless they have to."

"Did they find Rhinehart?"

"Yes."

"I didn't mean to kill him. I didn't confront him with that intention."

"I believe you."

He didn't, or no more than he believed Pettle had just wanted to talk to his wife with a gun in his hand.

"What happens now?" said Pettle.

"What would you like to see happen?"

"I'd like to rewind time. I'd like to undo all of my mistakes."

"In the absence of that."

Pettle stared at a place beyond Parker, beyond this world.

"I believe Pappy Cade fed children to Hollis Ward before betraying him," said Pettle. "In return, Hollis Ward has come back from hell to destroy the Cades. Now I think I'd like to die."

Reverend Nathan Pettle put the barrel of the gun beneath his chin and pulled the trigger.

CHAPTER
LXXXIII

Technically, Jurel Cade "escorted" Horrace Sneed into the Burdon County Sheriff's Office, although it would be more accurate to say that he virtually carried him inside. Sneed's face had suffered severe bruising, and he walked as though some of his ribs might be busted. The sheriff, Harold Swanigan, roused himself sufficiently to peer out through the blinds of his office window. Cade looked back at him, daring him to intervene, but Swanigan merely adjusted the blinds so that he could see nothing at all before going back to whatever it was he'd been doing, which was likely to have involved pondering his future once the Cades decided he was surplus to requirements. The Cades had masterminded his election and ensured that his two terms were free of strife and excessive labor, just so long as Swanigan minded his own business and permitted Jurel to operate without impediment. But with Kovas about to move into the county, and Pappy of the opinion that his son was now ready to become sheriff, Swanigan was more of a lame duck than ever. He wouldn't be sorry to step down. Even for a man with so little pride, he had suffered an abundance of humiliation.

Lyall Mathis, the office's longest-serving deputy, arrived to help Cade with Sneed.

"Put him in a cell," said Cade, allowing Mathis

to take on the full weight of the prisoner, "and summon Doc Gould to tend to him. No other visitors, and no phone calls. We'll let him leave come morning."

"What did he do?"

"He obstructed an investigation, but I'm not going to hold it against him."

"What if he asks for a lawyer?"

Cade turned to the injured man.

"You're not going to be asking for a lawyer, are you, Horrace?"

Sneed shook his head.

"See?" said Cade. "When you're finished with him, get back up here. We have a lot to do."

Mathis led Sneed to a holding cell and laid him flat on the bunk. It was rare for Jurel Cade to leave marks. Usually he didn't even have to raise a hand to encourage cooperation. Either Horrace Sneed had seriously irritated him, or Cade had been seeking an excuse to vent some rage and Sneed had provided it. Once he had Sneed settled, Mathis called Doc Gould, who knew better than to ask too many questions, and informed him that a prisoner required medical attention. Mathis then rejoined Cade, whose office was bigger than the sheriff's, and saw more frequent use. Cade had a map of the Ouachita spread out on his desk.

"There," he said, pointing a finger at an unmarked section.

"What am I looking at?" said Mathis.

"The old Buttrell property."

"Where Estella Jackson's body was found?"

"That's right, and now owned by a company based up in Little Rock. According to our friend Horrace, it's one of a number of shell corporations set up by Randall Butcher, although his name doesn't figure on any of the paperwork. That farm is also where Tilon Ward is currently holed up, cooking meth for Butcher."

Cade told Mathis about the discovery of Hollis Ward's fingerprint on Donna Lee Kernigan's body, and Tilon Ward's connection to her.

"Does Griffin think Tilon was fucking the Kernigan girl?" said Mathis.

"Evan Griffin wouldn't lower himself to using such language, but that's about the size of it. And when Tilon was done with her, he either gave her to his father or they killed her together, just as they did with Patricia Hartley. If Hollis Ward is still alive, his son has got to be protecting him. Whatever the truth might be, we'll discover it at that farm, and destroying Butcher's operation will solve a lot of this county's problems along the way."

"Are we working with the Cargill PD or the state police?"

"I think we'll handle this one ourselves," said Cade.

Mathis looked doubtful. The Burdon County Sheriff's Office didn't have the manpower to mount an operation such as this unassisted.

Cade scribbled some names on a sheet of paper and handed it to Mathis.

"Way ahead of you," he said. "You call each

of these people—just you, nobody else—and tell them I want them here at five o'clock tomorrow morning, locked and loaded. They'll be deputized before we head out. You don't share with them anything of what I've told you. You don't speak of it to anyone, not even your wife."

Cade then rattled off the names of three more deputies, who weren't rostered for the next day, and instructed Mathis to let them know that they were to report for duty by 4:30 a.m.

Mathis departed, leaving Jurel Cade to make some calls. Between them, Evan Griffin and Horrace Sneed had handed him Tilon Ward and Randall Butcher on a plate. If he could take down Tilon and his crew, Butcher would fall, because one of them would inevitably rat him out, assuming Butcher wasn't dumb enough to be supervising the Ouachita cook himself. If Cade could apprehend Hollis Ward as well, thus solving the mystery of the killings, the Kovas deal would go through without a hitch and the rule of the Cade family would be confirmed in Burdon County, providing a stepping stone to greater influence in the state of Arkansas and beyond.

Within minutes, Cade had apprised both his father and sister of developments, but Pappy barely reacted to the mention of Hollis Ward's name.

"It makes sense" was all he said. "Hollis did know how to bear a grudge."

Finally, Jurel Cade made one more call, this time to Charles Shire.

"If we handle this right," he told Shire, "it'll show Kovas that we're serious about dealing with our share of the meth problem, but it will also mean no more Randall Butcher, and no more dead girls."

"I'd like Leonard to go out there with you," said Shire.

Cade didn't want Cresil anywhere near this. Being in the enforcer's presence for too long always made him feel as though his skin might erupt in boils.

"Why is that?"

"We've been hearing rumors out of Little Rock," said Shire. "It appears that Randall Butcher has vanished, just as he was hours away from being indicted on federal charges. He's gone into hiding, and now it seems you might have found out where he is." Shire paused for Cade to absorb this information, then resumed: "It would be better if Butcher didn't return to Little Rock to face those charges. Who knows what lies he might tell to save himself?"

Jurel Cade didn't want to hear this. It was one thing to see Butcher ruined, but another to let Leonard Cresil put a bullet in his head. Cade had done many bad things in his time. He had manipulated and broken the law, sometimes in what he perceived to be the larger interests of justice, and occasionally out of expediency, or to benefit his family or its confederates, but he had yet to collude in a killing.

"That's not how we operate here," he said.

"It is now."

CHAPTER
LXXXIV

It was called a delayed discharge. Parker didn't know how old Pettle's gun was, or the condition of the ammunition. Given his success in using it to kill Denny Rhinehart, the cartridge might just have been a dud. Whatever the reason, when Pettle pulled the trigger, the primer in the cartridge went off, but the bullet didn't immediately fire. Parker didn't bother reaching for his own weapon as soon as Pettle turned his gun on himself, because there was no percentage in threatening to shoot a man already intent on suicide. The priority was to disarm him.

But Pettle wasn't used to handling a gun, particularly not one that had malfunctioned. He removed the barrel from beneath his chin just as the pressure from the propellant built up sufficiently to fire the bullet. It entered Pettle's lower jaw from the right, and exited through his left cheek, taking bone, teeth, and most of Pettle's tongue and palate with it. By the time Evan Griffin arrived with the cavalry, Parker was holding a towel to the injury with one hand and trying to dial 911 with the other. He let Lorrie Colson, who had emergency medical training, take over, and sat back against the kitchen cabinets. His ears were ringing from the shot, and he was shaking from the rush of adrenaline. Griffin handed him a bottle of water before walking with him to the front yard. The neighbors had already gathered, and Kel Knight and Naylor were keeping them back.

"Why did he kill Rhinehart?" said Griffin.

"I'm still not sure," said Parker. "I think Rhinehart was threatening to ruin him by informing you—and, by extension, the rest of the town—about his affair with Sallie Kernigan, potentially bringing him into the frame for Donna Lee's murder. But Rhinehart was also bothering Donna Lee, and Pettle felt very protective toward her."

"Anything more than that?"

Parker shrugged. "Who can tell?"

"Could Pettle have murdered Donna Lee?"

"I don't think he did."

"What about Rhinehart?"

"Pettle didn't say that he held Rhinehart responsible for Donna Lee's death. Mainly, he just didn't like him."

"There are a lot of people I don't like," said Griffin, "but I've left their skulls intact."

The ambulance arrived, and they stepped back to let the crew enter the house.

"I think Pettle was going to kill his wife," said Parker. "After that, he'd have killed himself."

"He may wish he'd succeeded with that last part. His face is a mess."

"I should never have let it get that far."

"Do you feel sorry for him?" said Griffin.

"Just enough. Don't you?"

"The prosecutor will probably push for second-

546

degree murder, so he'll be spared the needle. I was going to call in the state police to help us with the Rhinehart case, and to hell with the consequences. Not much cause to do that now."

Parker sipped the water slowly. His belly felt ready to rebel, and his hands were shaking. Had he eaten more during the day, he would probably have puked on the lawn.

"Pettle told me that Pappy Cade might have colluded with Hollis Ward in the abuse of children," he said.

"Did he offer any proof, or names of victims?"

"No."

"Then where does that leave us?"

"As we were. Still, it's interesting to know."

"I have another question," said Griffin.

"Shoot."

"Why is there a dead possum in the department's freezer?"

But before Parker could answer, a car turned into the street and pulled up behind the crowd of onlookers. Delores Pettle emerged from behind the wheel, one hand raised to her mouth. Griffin prepared to meet her.

"I don't even know," he told Parker sadly, "where to begin."

CHAPTER
LXXXV

It was not that Delphia Cade was devoid of faith in her brother Jurel, but rather that she lacked sufficient trust in him to rely on his word or authority alone in any given set of circumstances. Nevertheless, the news that Randall Butcher's future was likely to include extensive involvement with prosecutors and defense lawyers, followed by a long period of federal incarceration, was a source of no small pleasure and relief to her. If Jurel could be the one to lay hands on Butcher, so much the better, but even should he fail to do so, Butcher's ambitions would no longer be a problem for the Cade family.

On the other hand, having spoken briefly with Leonard Cresil, Butcher's flight from justice meant that it would now be impossible to call off the men he had dispatched to deal with Charlie Parker. This fact did not unduly trouble Delphia. Parker was an outsider, a jinx, and, in all likelihood, a killer. There was also the matter of her personal pride: he had rejected her offer of an olive branch, and Delphia was not about to let that slight pass unpunished.

Now, in her apartment in the Hillcrest area of Little Rock, she sipped vodka with just a splash of tonic and leafed through the clippings file on Parker assembled by her assistant. The reports on the deaths of his wife and child were admirably, if frustratingly, discreet, but Jurel and Cresil combined had provided her with a more detailed description of the end suffered by Parker's family. It had been almost artistic: cruel, yes, but also strangely beautiful. Delphia thought she would be most interested to meet the man responsible for killing them.

If nothing else, he had an admirable level of ambition.

Parker returned to the Lakeside Inn shortly after 8 p.m. He showered and changed his clothes before driving out to Evan Griffin's home for a late supper. He had been reluctant to accept the chief's invitation, but Griffin had insisted. His wife, he said, felt they were being inhospitable to a stranger; and after the day Parker had endured, a home-cooked meal would do him more good than eating at Boyd's or alone in his room.

The table was set for three when he arrived, and Ava Griffin came out of the kitchen to greet him. She was a tall, slim woman, with a touch of austereness to her looks, although it disappeared as soon as she smiled. Her hair was very dark and her skin very pale. Parker guessed that she was at least fifteen years younger than her husband.

Griffin offered him an O'Doul's, apologizing for not having anything stronger to hand.

"I've lost my taste for any beer," said Parker. "Water or soda is fine."

Griffin went outside to bring in some more wood for the fire, although the night was not cold, leaving Parker alone in the kitchen with Ava and the dog, Carter.

"I'm glad to meet you at last," said Ava. "Evan's told me a lot about you." She put a hand on Parker's arm. "And I am sorry for all you've been through, and all you're still going through."

He thanked her. He'd grown used to acknowledging by rote people's sympathies, but the way in which she spoke to him, and the touch of her hand, caused him to respond with more sincerity than usual. Griffin returned with the firewood, and soon they were all seated at the table, sharing beef short rib. For a time they spoke of general subjects, including how Griffin and his wife had met. Griffin had been married once before, but his first wife, Embeth, had drowned in Lake Ouachita in the fourth year of their marriage. He'd considered leaving the state in the aftermath, he admitted, but everything he knew was here, and so he stayed. After a couple of years he met Ava through a mutual friend, and they hit it off. Parker saw a look pass between them and recognized the depth of their feelings for each other.

Ava rose to clear the plates and get some ice cream for dessert. Both Parker and her husband offered to help, but she shooed them away.

"I don't require either of you to be under my feet," she said. "Evan can do the dishes later."

Griffin and Parker went out to the back porch

to get some air. Parker made sure Ava was out of earshot before speaking again.

"Why didn't you tell me about your first wife before now?" he said.

"I never saw a justification for it," Griffin replied. "And what would I have said: that I'd lost someone too, that I knew how you felt? It wouldn't have been true. We may both have suffered bereavement, but our experience of it is not the same."

"I'm surprised nobody else chose to share it with me discreetly."

"You're a stranger, and even my own officers would have left it for me to tell you. They wouldn't have considered it their part to do so."

"That's admirable," said Parker. "I notice you wear a cross."

It was silver, and very plain. Griffin touched a hand to it.

"I still have my faith. You?"

"I don't know."

"I had to reach an accommodation with it," said Griffin. "With God, too. I decided it wasn't part of His plan for my wife to drown. Anyone that said otherwise was deluded."

"What, then?"

"Who can say? Maybe God is old, and His attention wanders; or He has so much to take care of, what with famine, floods, and war, and people trying to kill one another on a minute-to-minute basis, that small occurrences, like a woman struggling in a lake, sometimes slip through His fingers."

"I've yet to reach that stage of reasoning," said Parker.

"I can believe it. And, you know, I may be wrong about everything. Ultimately, this is a being that allowed His own son to be nailed to a tree. Callousness may be endemic to Him. If that's the case, I choose not to consider myself made in His image, and I reject His disorder. For the most part, though, I think He spends His days just fighting off despair, like the rest of us."

Griffin reached into his shirt pocket and handed Parker a folded sheet of paper. Parker opened it to reveal the mug shot of a man with features that were almost familiar.

"That's Hollis Ward," said Griffin.

Hollis Ward resembled his son gone to seed, the face bloated, the skin marked by broken veins and patches of redness that could have been the result of dermatitis or eczema. His eyes were too small for his head, and darkly belligerent. Even had Parker not been aware of Ward's history, he would have identified this man as one mired in degradation.

"When are you going to put this out?" he said.

"We had planned to do it this afternoon, but events conspired to delay any approaches to the media."

"Rhinehart's death?"

"And a call from Jurel Cade, backed up by one

552

from Pappy. We've been asked to hold off on alerting the public to the possibility of Hollis's involvement."

"Why?"

"Jurel claims to have a lead, although he declined to elaborate, he and I having parted on bad terms earlier today. He said he didn't want to alert Hollis Ward to the fact that we're searching for him, which makes some sense. Even had I disagreed, Pappy has made it clear that his newspapers won't cooperate with us unless Jurel gives them the go-ahead."

"What will happen when Jurel becomes sheriff?" asked Parker. "Because I assume that's part of the family plan."

"Jurel will take over from Swanigan after next year's election, barring a calamity," said Griffin. "When that happens, I'll consider early retirement. But Pappy's aspirations for Jurel go further than his becoming county sheriff. He'd like to see Jurel up in Little Rock, with a ringside seat in the General Assembly. In that case, I won't just retire, I'll leave the state. And if Jurel makes it as far as Washington, I'll emigrate."

Ava came out with the ice cream, and a bowl of strawberries to add some nutrition.

"Why does Jurel hate the Wards so much?" asked Parker, as they ate.

"People here have extensive, if selective, memories," said Griffin. "I know families that have been feuding for so long that the original offense has been forgotten, and now all that remains is the feud itself. With Jurel, it seems to me it's Hollis he despises, and Tilon suffers the blowback because he's Hollis's son. We all suspected Tilon of being involved in the meth trade, but no one could ever nail him. Kovas won't want narcotics being an issue for contractors or its own staff, so it's in the interest of the Cades to put an end to whatever is coming out of the Ouachita. But Jurel also has a sense of right and wrong, however warped I may sometimes consider it to be. He doesn't like meth being produced in Burdon County. He considers it a personal affront."

"And how do you feel about it?"

"I don't want meth being cooked or dealt in the county either, but my people were right when they said that I'd always liked Tilon Ward. They just didn't elaborate on why. Embeth drowned because of a cramp. Dumbest damn thing. She was swimming with friends, and stayed out in the water when they returned to the jetty. Boats were going by, and music was playing on the bank, people shouting and laughing, so when Embeth got into difficulties, no one could hear her cries. Tilon was the only one who saw she was in trouble, and he swam out to help her. By then she'd already gone under, but he dived down to get her, brought her back up, and swam with her to shore. There was a nurse in Embeth's group who tried to resuscitate her, but it was too late. So yes, I admit to a greater tolerance than is wise for Tilon Ward's flaws, suspected or proven, and it would have pained me to see him go to jail before now, because I'd always hoped he'd see sense and find a new path to follow. But if he had anything to do with Donna Lee's death, I'll hold him down myself while they put the needle in his vein."

Which brought an end to that particular conversation. They watched clouds scud across the moon, and listened to the cries of night birds, before Ava sent Griffin inside to do the dishes, leaving her and Parker to finish their coffee together on the porch.

"I'm going to have a baby," said Ava.

"I'm pleased for you both."

"Thank you. Evan wasn't sure that we should tell you."

"I've decided," said Parker, "that secrecy may be ingrained in this county."

"I won't argue the point, but in our case Evan was worried that the news might compound your own sense of loss. I think he's spent lot of time since your arrival contemplating what happened to your wife and daughter, and more so after he learned he was going to have a child of his own. It'll sound strange, but it's almost as though he feels the need to do something about what befell you, even though there's nothing that can be done, is there?"

"Not too much," said Parker, which wasn't the same thing, and she noticed the distinction.

"I don't know you very well," she said, "so I'm reluctant to speak out of turn."

"Please, don't be."

"You're a victim as well. What your wife and little girl endured was horrific, but it's over now. Your torment goes on."

She wasn't looking at him, and it was instead as though she were carefully choosing her words from an array that only she could see, plucking each one from the darkness.

"I sensed it when they died," said Parker. "I felt them being torn from me."

The ground shifted under Ava's feet, and the landscape tilted. She had buried her mother a year before. That death had come far too soon—a heart attack when her mother was barely into her sixties—but it was not like this. The magnitude of the visitor's suffering was incomprehensible to her.

"My God," she whispered.

"I should have been with them," he said. "Had I been there, I might have prevented what happened, even if only by the fact of my presence. But do you know where I was?"

She did not respond. There was no need.

"I was in a bar, feeling sorry for myself. The last word I spoke to my wife was an obscenity."

Ava recalled the arguments she sometimes had with her husband, and the occasions on which one or the other left the house on a harsh word. It would happen again, she knew, because they were people, not saints. But she prayed now, as she always did, even after the worst of their quarrels, that the day would end with Evan sleeping safely by her side.

Soon, God willing, she would be praying for Him to watch over another. Her left hand touched her belly, where the child waited.

How can this man carry on? What is it that keeps him from embracing oblivion?

And the answer came to her: wrath.

"I still find myself talking of them in the present tense," he said, "but not as often as before. I'm losing them, and I don't want to let them go."

His voice caught. He stopped talking.

"Evan always talks about those left behind," said Ava, "the people who have buried loved ones because of drunk drivers, domestic abusers, strangers, whatever. He tries to stay in touch with them, and keep them notified of progress. He doesn't want them to feel they've been forgotten, because he knows that they can't forget, just as you never will."

She reached for him. His body was shaking.

"Whoever killed your family knows that you're in pain," she said. "He knows you're angry and grieving. That knowledge may even give him pleasure. Don't let yourself become his pawn. Don't let him ruin what's good in you. Whatever else you're forced to remember, and whenever you start to doubt yourself, don't ever forget that you came back here when you could have just kept on driving. You came back to help my husband stop another man from killing young women, even though there was no obligation upon you to return, and no one would have judged you harshly if you'd chosen otherwise. There's a light inside you. Don't allow it to be snuffed out."

She went back inside to make some coffee, leaving him alone.

When she returned with her husband, Parker was gone.

CHAPTER
LXXXVI

The three men in the truck—Bobby Needham, Ryan Vinson, and Gary Reeve—were all either current or former employees of Rich Emory, he of the just-about-surviving sawmill and the missing fingertips. They had been present at the Rhine Heart for the exchanges between Parker and Emory, listening from nearby, and had taken the view that the interloper should be brought down a peg or two through the judicious application of steel-toed boots. They had made this opinion known to any number of individuals, both over the course of the night in question and subsequent to it, including within earshot of Denny Rhinehart, whence they found their way to Pruitt Dix, who liked to kept abreast of events in the county. Thus it was that when willing bodies were required to teach Parker a lesson, their names immediately sprang to his mind.

The truck, a Ford SVT Lightning, was brand new, Vinson having come into money following the death of his stepfather, who—unlike every other stepfather of Vinson's acquaintance—hadn't been a complete asshole. A more sensible human being might have put some of that cash away instead of blowing the bulk of it on a truck and the rest on a custom paint job inspired by the cover of Molly Hatchet's *Flirtin' with Disaster* album, but Ryan Vinson was not sensible. He was overweight, single, and dumb as a brush. He was also an optimist at heart, and firmly believed that the impending arrival of Kovas would transform Burdon County into the Southern equivalent of the land of milk and honey promised by God to Abraham.

The men had been following Parker for much of the evening. They had earlier considered gaining access to his room at the motel in order to deal with him there, before deciding that the risks of being overheard while delivering a beating were too great—possibly even greater than being shot by their target, although that was touch and go. When Parker later left the motel, they stayed with him, and were only seconds away from forcing him off the road when it became apparent that he was on his way to Chief Evan Griffin's home—was, in fact, only a hundred feet from Griffin's drive as they closed on him—and if they screwed up, and Parker got away, they'd be in jail before the Ford's odometer had time to clock up another mile.

But Pruitt Dix, who had delivered his instructions to Bobby Needham by phone that morning, had made it clear that Parker was to be put out of commission before another day dawned, or else not only could the three men forget about any form of payment, but they would also incur Dix's personal animosity, which was the only thing worse than his impersonal animosity. It was now getting on for 11 p.m., which meant time was running out, and so it was with a sense of relief that they saw Parker's car emerge from Griffin's drive. With Vinson at the wheel, they came up behind him within minutes, and Reeve racked his shotgun. After some discussion, fueled by most of a bottle of Crown Royal, it had been decided that Reeve should shoot out one of Parker's back tires, because Needham and Vinson had seen it done in a couple of movies and thought it looked cool, after which they'd deliver the beating to end all beatings.

But just as Reeve was rolling down his window prior to taking the shot, Parker accelerated rapidly, and before they could close the gap they were being overtaken by another car, a brand-new SVT Mustang Cobra. It immediately inserted itself into the space between them and Parker, and stayed there until they reached Cargill. Every time they tried to pass it, the Cobra would speed up, or nudge over the white line, until Reeve was seriously thinking about shooting up its tires instead, just to give himself something to do. They couldn't even see the driver, because the interior was dark and the glass faintly tinted, although Needham, who had good eyes, thought he glimpsed two people inside. The end result was that Parker made it back to the motel without incident, the Cobra took the next left and drifted from sight, and the would-be brutalizers were faced with the choice of kicking Parker's door down, which seemed more than unwise; giving up, and taking their chances with Pruitt Dix, which struck them as equally unwise;

or waiting until morning in the hope that a better opportunity might present itself, and Dix would forgive them missing the deadline on the grounds that they'd managed to get the job done eventually. They all agreed that the third option was easily the best, and so Vinson dropped the others back at their homes before returning to his own.

"That fucking Cobra," said Reeve, as he jumped out.

"I know," said Vinson. "If I see it again, I'll leave the imprint of my grille guard on its bodywork."

And, he thought, on the driver, too, given the chance.

Cleon, the desk clerk, waved at Parker as he pulled into the parking lot of the motel, diverting him from the sight of the Ford Lightning reluctantly vanishing into the night, along with the three assholes inside. Parker had never seen a truck decorated like a Molly Hatchet album cover before. He hoped never to see one again, but briefly wondered what kind of person might attempt vehicular assault while driving the most easily identifiable truck in the state of Arkansas.

Parker got out of the car as Cleon approached. He was holding a white business card in his hand.

"Someone came by asking after you," said Cleon. "He left this, and said he'd wait for you at Boyd's."

Cleon gave the card to Parker.

"I've never been handed an FBI agent's card before," said Cleon. "Do you know him?"

"Yes, I know him." Parker looked at his watch. "What time does Boyd's close?"

"Not until after midnight. Was this one of the guests you were expecting?"

"No, I wasn't expecting him at all."

Cleon thought that Parker appeared neither pleased nor displeased by the sight of the card, only curious, which was a relief. He was worried that Parker might be in trouble. Cleon would probably have helped him get away if he was, but only on condition that Parker took him along. Even if they ended up being shot, or driving off the edge of the Grand Canyon like Thelma and Louise, it would still be better than being alive and well but living in Cargill. More than ever, Cleon wanted to escape the town; he just couldn't figure out how. The main obstacle to decamping, he had concluded, was himself.

"Will you still be needing the other room?" said Cleon.

"If that's okay. My friends will be along in their own time. They keep unsocial hours."

"I'll be around whenever they arrive. They'll just have to ring the bell. I've left two complimentary bottles of water in their room, and some fruit."

"Thank you." Parker handed the card back to him. "For your collection."

"I don't have a collection," said Cleon. "I suppose I could always start one." He held the card between his thumb and forefinger, the details facing out. "Or just pretend to be an FBI agent."

"That would be a crime," said Parker, "although I admit it would be entertaining to watch you try."

He looked toward Boyd's, and his expression changed. For a moment, Cleon glimpsed an immensity of pain in his eyes. Had he known this man better, Cleon might have reached out and held him in his arms. And then the shutters came down, and the pain was once again hidden from sight.

"If your friends come, should I tell them where you are?" said Cleon.

"You can tell them, but they won't be joining me. They prefer not to keep the company of federal agents."

"You make them sound like criminals."

"They'll be pleased to hear that."

"Why?"

Parker's smile let in a little light.

"Because that's exactly what they are."

CHAPTER
LXXXVII

An exhausted Tucker McKenzie arrived at the state crime laboratory in Little Rock with material from the scene of the Polk County fire; the accumulated evidence from the killing of Denny Rhinehart in Cargill; and his notes and film from the scene of Reverend Nathan Pettle's botched attempt at self-destruction. McKenzie could have waited until morning before driving up, but given how busy he was currently being kept, he fully expected the new day to bring fresh calamities.

He was also carrying, in a cooler box, the remains of a dead possum.

CHAPTER
LXXXVIII

Only a handful of drinkers remained in Boyd's by the time Parker arrived, but they all watched him cross the bar and slip into a booth—coincidentally, the same booth he'd been occupying when Evan Griffin first came calling. It was now partially filled by a large, overweight man who appeared to have stepped from an old dime novel. He wore a crumpled tan suit, and a yellow silk tie resembling a rag dipped in mustard. Upon closer examination, Parker saw that small dancing skeletons adorned the tie. On the table beside the visitor sat a brown fedora, similar to the one he had been wearing when he and Parker first met over the body of a woman named Jenny Ohrbach. Back then Parker had been a detective third grade, and the man currently sitting opposite him was still just Special Agent Woolrich of the Federal Bureau of Investigation. Now he was Assistant SAC Woolrich of the Bureau's New Orleans field office. He was also the source of all Parker's information on unusual murder scenes and possible serial killings, including the deaths of Estella Jackson and Patricia Hartley, and of the intelligence on Leonard Cresil.

Only days after Parker had buried a wife and child, Woolrich had approached him to offer his sympathies, and assure him that he would do all in his power to aid the investigation into the murders.

And when Parker resigned from the NYPD, Woolrich had again come forward, this time in a less formal capacity, and invited him for a drink, although by then Parker had already forsworn alcohol, and much else.

"I understand your reasons for leaving the force," Woolrich had told Parker as they sat together in Chumley's, the old West Village speakeasy. "It's not for me to tell you that you're doing the right or wrong thing, because it's your decision to make. But if you're serious about looking for whoever did this, perhaps I can be of assistance."

"How?"

"Susan and Jennifer weren't the first. What was done to them was too accomplished for that. There must be false starts, botched efforts—apprentice work. Their killer will have left other bodies: maybe not displayed in the same way, because otherwise the Bureau would be all over it, but he's had practice. I'll send you what I can. Most of it you can probably set aside after a single glance and never look at again, but who knows what you might notice?"

Woolrich had been as good as his word, and now here he was in Cargill, a beer in front of him and a few shards of french fries congealing in a basket. He and Parker exchanged a handshake and made some small talk. Woolrich was divorced, and alienated from his only daughter, Lisa. While in New York, he'd been seeing a nurse named Judy, who lived in Boston. The distance had suited both

567

of them, but Woolrich wasn't sure if it would continue to be the case now that he was based all the way down in New Orleans.

"You want one?" said Woolrich, shaking the near-empty beer bottle.

"No, thank you."

"I forgot, you don't do that anymore. So: Did you kill him?"

"Kill who?"

"Johnny Friday."

Parker extended his hands, holding the wrists close together as though in anticipation of the bite of cuffs.

"I'm not wearing a wire," said Woolrich, "if that's what you're worried about."

"I'm not worried," said Parker. "But if you're looking for a confession, you've traveled a long way for nothing."

"Not so far. I had business in Shreveport before driving on to Little Rock. One of the local boys, Randall Butcher, is in big trouble: bribery, wire fraud, all that good stuff beloved of federal prosecutors."

"I heard."

"Butcher nurses ambitions to expand his business interests into northern Louisiana and east Texas, perhaps even New Orleans and Baton Rouge, so he was on my radar. As it happened, I arrived just in time for him to vanish, but he'll turn up. Anyway, I didn't drive three hours just to talk about Randall Butcher, or Johnny Friday—who won't be missed, so no one is going to be looking too hard for whoever flipped his switch."

Woolrich wet his mouth with the beer.

"Do you have news?" said Parker. "About Susan and Jennifer?"

"I wish I did," said Woolrich, "but no."

"Then why are you here?"

"To ask you the same question."

"Estella Jackson and Patricia Hartley. Their deaths were among the files you sent me."

"Strange that they should have been the ones to catch your attention."

"There were others. This is the fourth town I've visited in ten days, and the eleventh unsolved case I've looked into since the start of the year."

"And?"

"Nothing."

"So what makes this one different? Why stay?"

"Nobody in the other towns suggested that I should." He thought for a moment. "And perhaps because I can."

"Can what?"

"Take your pick: can help, can advise. Or just can. I have nowhere else to go, except back to New York. All these cases have been dead ends so far. By staying here, there's a chance that the whole effort may not prove pointless."

"I'm sorry," said Woolrich, again. "I'm still looking for similarities that might help you. If you want me to stop . . ."

Parker took a deep breath.

"No," he said. "And I apologize."

"For what?"

"For being short with you ever since I arrived here tonight. I'm grateful for what you've done. It's frustration on my part, and not only because the leads you sent me haven't panned out. This whole county is toxic, and it's as though the fumes are blinding me to something about these killings that I should be able to see."

"Tell me," said Woolrich. "I have nothing better to do than listen."

So Parker told him. He went through everything he had seen, heard, and learned so far, right up to the attempted suicide of Reverend Nathan Pettle. He excluded only the tale of the truck that had followed him from Griffin's house, because that would have involved mentioning the car that had intervened in the pursuit—or, more particularly, its occupants.

"You're right," said Woolrich, when Parker had finished. "This is one fucked-up county."

"Confirming the diagnosis doesn't cure the disease."

"It sounds like you have a suspect, so the cure is to catch him."

"Hollis Ward as the chief suspect still doesn't make sense to me. The Cades might have cut him loose after his conviction, but it's a big step from being fired to killing women on their territory, especially after so much time has gone by. And from what I've learned of him, Ward wasn't a man to keep a low profile, yet somehow he's contrived to remain hidden for years."

"But this guy Rauls believes Ward might have murdered Estella Jackson," said Woolrich, "which means there's precedent."

"Yes, but Jurel Cade raised the possibility of two killers, and apparently the medical examiner, Dr. Temple, who conducted the autopsy on Donna Lee Kernigan, isn't dismissing it either."

"You always had a fondness for making situations more complicated than they need to be."

"This one was already complicated when I got here."

"Then look at it again, but from a different perspective," said Woolrich. "Why should these killings have recommenced now, so long after Estella Jackson's murder?"

"Kovas. There can be no other reason."

"You're sure of that?"

"I'm no longer sure about anything, but my gut says it's down to Kovas. Donna Lee Kernigan's body was left within sight of land earmarked for development by the company, and owned by the Cades."

"But Patricia Hartley's body was dumped elsewhere."

"Yet if Griffin is right, her remains were first left on federal land, because the killer hoped that would bring in outside agencies to investigate. Jurel Cade's intervention meant that didn't happen, so the killer had to try again, this time closer to the proposed Kovas site."

"Why not dump Kernigan on the site itself?"

"It's fenced off, and the Cades have already commenced sprucing it up in preparation for the laying of foundations, so the area is exposed. I'm surprised they haven't already strung a ribbon from some trees, and started sharpening a big pair of ceremonial scissors. Gaining access to the site wouldn't have been impossible, or even difficult, but it would have required effort and risk. Leaving Kernigan's body nearby would have been less trouble for almost the same reward."

"So someone wants to see the Kovas deal go up in smoke?" said Woolrich.

"Which will ruin the Cades."

"And the entire county, as well as damaging the state."

"It feels personal," said Parker. "I think the Cades are the target."

"Okay, let's go with it," said Woolrich. "If that's the case, the identities of the victims themselves—their color, sex, age—are of no consequence. He picked them because they were easy, or came his way at the right time. Sometimes the personal is concealed by the impersonal, and vice versa."

For a moment, Parker was distracted. Woolrich's use of those words—*personal* and *impersonal*—brought him back to the hours and days following the murders of Susan and Jennifer. It was the question the police had asked, and that he had asked of himself: Was the choice of victims random or specific? Had their killer waited until Parker was away from the house before striking, or had he hoped to take Parker down as well? How had the killer chosen them? It wasn't a crime of opportunity, but one that had required careful planning so the scene could be properly organized. Their killer had made a form of pietà out of their remains, leaving his daughter's body stretched across her mother's lap. But why target Susan and Jennifer? What if, as Woolrich was suggesting in the case of the Cargill killings, they had been selected only out of expediency? Yet the question remained: How had the killer of his family come to select them?

Sometimes the personal is concealed by the impersonal.

And vice versa.

But now Woolrich was speaking again, calling him back.

"I'm curious," Woolrich was saying. "If a personal vendetta against the Cades is behind what's happening, why not kill one or all of them and be done with it?"

Parker took this in. The question had not previously entered his mind. Why not kill one of the Cades? Why go to the trouble of trying to ruin them in this way?

"He wants the Cade family to witness its own fall," he said at last.

"And also, he isn't roaming," said Woolrich. "He's murdering and dumping in a defined territory, and taking his victims from the same locality."

"Meaning?"

"Meaning it's a good way to get caught. The real human predators keep moving."

"You think he doesn't realize that?" said Parker.

"He may just be stupid, but this doesn't strike me as the work of someone entirely lacking in intelligence."

"Unless it's the point."

"That he wants to be caught?"

"Eventually," said Parker. "Because whatever revelation his capture brings with it will ensure that everything—the Kovas deal, the Cades, all of it—is destroyed."

He was close now, but still the final link dangled frustratingly beyond his grasp.

The bartender announced last call. Woolrich lifted his bottle and weighed it in his hand, as though debating whether he would be happier were it to become full again or remain empty. In the end, he decided on the latter, and dropped some bills on the table.

"I'm done," he said. "What about this Leonard Cresil?"

"I'd hoped that he wasn't going to be a problem in the short term," said Parker, remembering the benighted truck and its occupants. "I may have been mistaken."

"Did you confront him?"

"Yes."

"Of course you did. I'm surprised you didn't slap his face with a glove and challenge him to a duel."

"Absent the glove, that's close to what went down."

"You're not bereft of troubles as it is. Why ask for more?"

"Cresil was about to crowd me. I wanted space to move."

"If you like, we can put a foot on his neck. Cresil's time is coming. He's running out of road, and he knows it."

"No," said Parker, "I have it in hand now."

"If you're certain." Woolrich picked up his hat and jammed it on his head.

"Where are you staying?" said Parker.

"Not here. Too many people in this county are winding up dead. I'll start heading home, and find somewhere to sleep along the way. I like driving at night. It's more conducive to reflection."

Together they walked from the bar.

"I don't want you to get your hopes up," said Woolrich, "but I might, just might, have better news about Susan and Jennifer when next we meet. It's a whisper, but it could grow louder over time."

"Should I come down to New Orleans?"

Parker heard the eagerness in his own voice, or the desperation.

"No, not yet. If it sounds promising, I'll let you know."

The night was mild and quiet, but the town didn't look much better in the dark than it did in daylight, and the air was feculent.

"Why would anybody come here?" said Woolrich.

"I came."

"To hunt, not to settle."

"I'll be moving along when this is over."

"Back to New York?"

"For now."

"And after?"

"Who can say?"

Woolrich placed a hand on the back of Parker's neck. His palm was warm and damp.

"Bird," he said—sadly, fondly. Woolrich was one of the few who still called Parker by that name. Parker had given up asking him not to, just as he had with the others who liked to use it. The sobriquet held no meaning, except to remind him of the seeming impossibility of any escape from all that bound him to this earth. Now, with Woolrich beside him, he felt something of the same sorrow that had overcome him in the parking lot of the Dairy Bell earlier that day. Without Woolrich and a handful of other men he would be entirely alone, and it struck him that all were older than he, as though he were seeking to create out of them some amalgam of a father.

"Why are you helping me?" said Parker.

"Because I can. If you want more than that, you're destined to be disappointed."

"Then 'because I can' will have to do."

"It will, for both of us." Woolrich turned his back on Parker and ambled toward his car. "I'll be seeing you, somewhere down the road."

CHAPTER
LXXXIX

Upon returning home from his unsuccessful mission to put the investigator named Parker out of commission, Ryan Vinson had eaten a bag of Doritos, finished off what remained of the bottle of Crown Royal and, with nothing better to do, opened another. He then rewatched—for the hundredth time, or thereabouts—his worn copy of Chuck Norris's *Delta Force*, and concluded that life, all things considered, was good. He had a truck, a home, a big TV, and friends upon whom he could rely in times of crisis. The only cloud on his horizon bore the shape of Pruitt Dix, but Vinson knew Dix from way back and was confident of his ability to talk him around on the Parker business. If that didn't work, Vinson would resort to pleading. He wasn't proud.

Vinson went to bed shortly after 2 a.m., and set his alarm clock for six hours later.

Because he was, as has already been established, an optimist.

Ryan Vinson, the optimist, woke to the sight of a tall masked man standing over his bed, and another, smaller masked man seated to his left, the latter holding a gun to Vinson's temple. Vinson wouldn't have woken at all, even allowing for the touch of the gun, if the standing man hadn't rapped

577

him hard on the forehead with his knuckles. Vinson could see the gun only by moving his head slightly, which caused the muzzle to be pressed even harder against his skin. No one had ever pointed a gun at Ryan Vinson before, never mind poked him in the head with one. He really didn't like it.

"How you doin'?" said the man who wasn't holding the gun, and was therefore of marginally less immediate concern to Vinson. He sounded black, which didn't make Vinson feel any better. Vinson didn't have any black friends, and he guessed that this man's presence in his life wasn't about to alter that state of affairs substantially.

"Not so good," said Vinson.

"You ought to clean your house more often. I think I got bitten by a flea."

"I'm sorry about that."

"Yeah, well, you should be more aware of your domestic and personal hygiene. Being bitten has put me in a bad mood, and I was already feeling sore. Is this your truck?"

He held up a gloved hand to show Vinson a photograph taken with an instant camera.

"I can't see," said Vinson. "It's too dark."

The man holding the gun turned on the bedside lamp with his free hand so that Vinson could see the picture better. It did indeed show Vinson's beloved truck sitting in his driveway.

"Yeah," said Vinson, "that's my truck."

"No, it's not. Actually, this is your truck."

The black man dropped the first picture. The next

one was also a photo of Vinson's truck, except that it was no longer in his driveway, but was instead positioned worryingly close to the edge of a rocky precipice.

"No, wait a minute," the man continued. "I tell a lie. I think *this* is your truck."

Vinson's truck was no longer on the edge of the precipice. In a demonstration of considerable photographic skill, the photographer had managed to capture the image of the truck in midair, its hood just beginning to tilt downward.

"Okay, this," the man concluded, holding up the fourth and final print, "is *definitely* your truck. Look, you can see the paintwork bubbling."

Vinson's truck, or what was left of it, lay at the bottom of a quarry, which could have been one of any number in the vicinity of the Ouachita. The truck seemed to have only recently started burning, because Vinson could still make out the custom paint job amid the rising flames.

Ryan Vinson began weeping. That truck was the nicest thing he'd ever owned.

"Don't cry," said the man. "The good news is that you could have been in it when it went over, but I tossed a coin and you won. Admittedly, that was before I got bitten by one of your fleas. Now I've a mind to toss the coin again, and keep tossing until it comes up on a side more akin to my frame of mind."

Vinson heard the sound of the pistol cocking beside his left ear. If he lived, he thought, he'd have to change the sheets.

"Who told you to go chasing after the detective from New York?" said the black man.

"Pruitt Dix," said Vinson. This wasn't the time for lying.

"And who is Pruitt Dix?"

"He works for Randall Butcher."

"And Randall Butcher is . . . ?"

"Randall owns some titty bars."

"And did either of these gentlemen tell you why they wanted the detective hurt?"

"I didn't ask."

"Of course not. Why would you?"

"It wasn't personal," said Vinson. "I just do what I'm told."

"I'm sure that would have been comforting to Mr. Parker had you successfully completed your task. Now I'm going to tell you to do something, and for my associate and me, this really is personal. Mr. Parker is a friend of ours, and we like him just the way he is, which means unmarked. You call those two ofay assholes that were driving around with you, and you inform them of what has transpired between us. You let them know that if we have to come calling on them, we'll burn their homes down around their ears, sow their land with salt, and kill all their pets. You understand?"

"Yes. What do I tell Pruitt Dix?"

"Tell him we may be paying him a visit. Same goes for the titty bar guy, because I do hate titty bars."

The hammer clicked as the pistol was decocked.

From the folds of his jacket, the gunman produced a pair of solid handcuffs, with which he secured one of Vinson's hands to the frame of the bed. The bedstead was heavy and made of black iron. It would take Vinson a while to free himself. Otherwise, he'd be forced to yell until someone heard, or else find a way to disassemble the frame.

"We'll be on our way now," said the black man. "Remember what I said about cleaning up occasionally."

They left Vinson on the bed, along with the photographs.

So he had something to remember his truck by.

In the comfort of the Cobra, the driver removed his mask and tossed it out the window. He was, as Vinson had surmised, black. His name was Louis.

"That went well," he said.

Beside him, the gunman disposed of his own mask in the same way. He was of indeterminate race, and his name was Angel.

"You certainly seemed to enjoy destroying the truck," said Angel.

"You know, I kind of did," said Louis. "I think I might like to do it again someday."

Cleon heard the bell ring above the office door. He'd been sleeping soundly on the couch in the back room, but he sprang up at the sound and went to see who had entered. Standing at the reception desk was a tall, elegantly dressed black man, and a smaller and considerably less elegantly dressed second man who might have been white, Latino, some combination of both, or none of the above.

"I believe Mr. Parker made a reservation for us," said the black man. "My name is Louis, and this is Angel."

"Yes, sirs," said Cleon. "Mr. Louis and Mr. Angel. If you'd just like to register . . ."

He took a registration card from a drawer and placed it on the desk. The black man looked at it, then looked at Cleon.

Cleon put the registration card back in the drawer.

"One room, is that correct?" he said.

"One room."

And something in the way he said it made Cleon's gay heart soar. Like most men who are brave, Cleon did not consider himself to be so. There were only two ways to be gay in Cargill, perhaps even in most of the South, except for pockets of tolerance like New Orleans or Miami. The first was to conceal one's nature and reveal it only in secret, if at all. Burdon County had no shortage of closeted gay men, and Cleon had met his share of them. He'd taken beatings from a few as well, sometimes after moments of intimacy when desire, now exhausted, was replaced by self-disgust.

The other path was the one chosen by Cleon. He would not hide—or if he did, he would hide in plain sight. This course also led to its share of beatings, but the pain of them was easier to bear because it was unaccompanied by shame. Now, as he looked at these two men before him, he wanted to ask how they had come to be as they were, because he perceived in them a strength that he erroneously believed to be lacking in himself.

"What's your name?" said the one named Angel, who had not spoken before now.

"Cleon. I'm the night manager. The day manager, too, depending on how short-staffed we are."

"Are you a native?"

"Of Cargill? Yes, sir."

"You like it?"

"No, sir, I don't like it at all."

"Then why are you still here?"

Cleon opened his mouth to tell the stranger about his lack of funds, and his distance learning course in design studies, and how once he had a qualification he'd think about moving, maybe. What emerged, instead, were words he had never previously spoken aloud.

"I guess because I'm scared. Shitty as this town is, I know how it works. I can navigate it without getting hurt too badly."

"Then it'll destroy you," said Angel.

"I have nowhere else to go."

"There's always somewhere else to go."

"Hey, Ann Landers," said Louis, "leave the man in peace."

Cleon handed over the key to the motel's second-best room.

"Will you be staying longer than one night?" he asked.

"We don't know yet," said Louis. "Anything to do around here?"

"Lately," said Cleon, "people are mostly causing trouble, and killing one another."

"Then," said Louis, "we'll fit right in."

5

But as for the cowardly, the faithless, the detestable, as for murderers, the sexually immoral, sorcerers, idolaters, and all liars, their portion will be in the lake that burns with fire and sulfur, which is the second death.

—Revelation 21:8

CHAPTER
XC

They began gathering at the Burdon County Sheriff's Office before there was light in the sky; first the men in uniform, then the rest. These others carried an assortment of weapons: pistols, shotguns, and semi-automatic rifles. Some were dressed in full camouflage clothing, but most wore more casual hunting garb: waterproof trousers and jackets, with old shirts and T-shirts underneath, so they could add or subtract layers as required; and boots that had seen years of wear, and would see more still. Two women, both in their forties, and big and hard-faced as the men, were among the group. Conversation was limited, and no one joked. The darkness was like a mesh before their eyes, and settled like soot upon the skin. Coffee was poured from thermos flasks, and someone passed around biscuits that had been baked in preparation the night before.

Then Jurel Cade appeared among them and laid a map on the hood of one of the cruisers. He spoke to them of Hollis Ward and Hollis's son, Tilon. He talked of dead girls and methamphetamine. He reminded them of what was at stake for the county: a choice between continued poverty and steady decline, of half-lives for them and all who came after; or the prospect of a new start with well-paid jobs, and further employment down the line for their children and grandchildren.

And from the shadows of the sheriff's office, Leonard Cresil watched over all, the hunting bow in its case by his side.

"Each of you will be temporarily deputized," Cade told the group. "If you elect not to participate, we'll be obliged to make you comfortable in one of our cells until we're done. We can't afford to have anyone give this operation away with careless talk."

But nobody demurred. Cade had made his selection well.

He had his posse.

Parker, never a morning person, woke shortly after 7:30 a.m., and could not return to sleep. He got up to shower, and saw that Cleon had slipped a note under his door, informing him that his guests had arrived safely during the night. He decided to give Angel and Louis a few minutes more to rest while he showered. As he emerged, dripping, he heard his local cell phone ringing. He didn't recognize the number, but picked up anyway.

"Is this Mr. Parker?"

"Yes."

"My name is Dr. Ruth Temple. I work at the state crime lab. You sent us a dead possum."

"That's right."

"We don't usually examine possums."

"I was hoping you might make an exception for this one."

"Were you and the possum very close?"

Parker decided that he already liked Dr. Ruth Temple.

"We never really got the chance to become intimate. I'm working with the Cargill PD on the Kernigan and Hartley cases."

"So I understand."

"We're struggling."

"I understand that also."

"Therefore the possum is a long shot."

"I'm still listening," said Temple.

"Someone took a blade to it. There were blood-stains around the remains when I found them, so I'm guessing it might have been done while the animal was still alive. In my experience, the kind of person who would do that to a possum might also be capable of doing the same to a human being."

"What do you want to know?"

"If the blade used on the possum might be similar to the one used on Donna Lee Kernigan or Estella Jackson."

"That's the second time someone from Cargill has mentioned Estella Jackson to me in the past twenty-four hours."

"Evan Griffin told me he'd spoken about Jackson to someone at the crime lab," said Parker. "That was you?"

"It was."

"He also said you were of the opinion that we might be looking at two killers."

"That's not my area of expertise. Chief Griffin and I were speculating, and nothing more."

"For what it's worth, I'm leaning toward the same theory, but I'm still interested in the wounds to the animal."

"I'll take a look at the possum. If anyone asks me why I appear to have lost my mind, I'll refer them to you."

"Do that. In the meantime, I'll try to come up with a name for it."

"You're a strange person, Mr. Parker."

"I'm not the one about to cut up a possum before breakfast," said Parker, "so it's all relative."

While Parker spoke with Dr. Ruth Temple, Cade's posse was finally moving into position.

Everything about the operation had taken longer than anticipated, because Cade didn't want to send a bunch of armed civilians into a potentially dangerous situation without all of them understanding their responsibilities, and ensuring that they were clear on the positions they were to take up. Basically, he instructed, their role was to cut off routes of escape, and their weapons should be regarded primarily as tools of intimidation, not harm. If they saw someone approaching, they were to instruct them to drop any weapons and lie on the ground. They were not to fire unless they believed their lives were under imminent threat, even if that meant allowing suspects to go free. Cade didn't want this turning into some kind of free-fire calamity. He organized them into groups of three, placing one of his men in charge of each, and emphasized the necessity of obeying any orders given by their group leader. Even then, Cade knew he was playing with fire. He had deputized armed men and women, and was introducing them into a confrontation with drug dealers who would themselves be armed. His hope was that the occupants of the farm would mostly be local boys, and reason might prevail once they realized they were surrounded by their own kind, but his experience of life in Burdon County was that reason was often in short supply there.

So, too, on this particular morning, was luck. The dark was reluctant to yield to the day, and the first of the rain began to fall before the convoy had even reached the first meeting point, after which they would proceed on foot for the last half-mile. There was only one road to the farm, and Cade wasn't convinced that they could travel up it in force without alerting the suspects to their approach. He didn't want Butcher's people scattering into the woods, because it would be hard to round them all up again, not to mention risky for his deputies and those with them.

The rain meant that visibility was limited, although it would keep those in the farmhouse from ranging too far, which would make it easier for the posse to close in on them unnoticed. Cade wanted everyone in position before he started negotiating the surrender of the operation's targets.

He had decided against going in hard; his aim was to prevail without bloodshed on either side. He didn't want to have to tell the wife of one of his deputies that she was now a widow, or a mother that she had lost a son or daughter because of his posse, but neither did he want to make a martyr of Randall Butcher or anyone else on the old Buttrell property. Deaths would also bring bad publicity, which he wanted to avoid. Nice clean arrests would be best for everyone. He'd drummed that into the posse, and checked with each of them in turn to make sure that he or she understood.

Only Leonard Cresil had looked away. It was all Cade could do to convince him to leave behind the hunting bow, and its arrows with their broadhead tips. But Cresil still had a gun, and Cade's conversation with Charles Shire, and its likely implications, continued to prey on his mind.

Cade raised his hand as soon as he saw the roof of the farmhouse through the trees. Everyone around him stayed silent, even as the posse split up and moved to encircle the building. Cade duck-walked to the edge of the woods, Deputy Mathis close behind. Cade saw the farmhouse, with two trucks and three cars parked in the yard, and one man, armed with a pump-action shotgun, leaning against the shed in which Estella Jackson had been found, its tin roof providing him with shelter from the rain. He had a two-way radio strapped to his shoulder, and was eating beans from a can. He appeared to be the only lookout.

The door to the farmhouse opened and Randall Butcher emerged. He had a cup in his right hand, and a gun tucked into the waistband of his jeans. He yawned, stretching his arms.

And someone shot him in the chest.

CHAPTER
XCI

Later, once the smoke had cleared, both literally and figuratively, it would be decided that Leonard Cresil fired the first shot in what became known locally as the Battle of Buttrell's Farm. For a number of reasons, it would prove impossible conclusively to establish Cresil's culpability, and therefore a degree of doubt would always remain.

For now, though, all Jurel Cade knew for sure was that a person unknown had just put a hole in Randall Butcher. The lookout with the shotgun, having stood frozen while his boss set about the business of dying, started running for the farmhouse while simultaneously firing random blasts into the forest. Pellets from one of those blasts hit Deputy Erwin Franks in the side of the head, removing most of his right ear and a section of his scalp, and rendering him immediately unconscious. The three deputized civilians assigned to Franks, having concluded, not unreasonably, that their lives were almost certainly under threat, returned fire, and suddenly Cade's operation was spiraling out of control before it had even properly begun. He was already scrambling for the bullhorn to order everyone to stop shooting when four armed men emerged from the trailers parked at either side of the farmhouse. One of those men was Pruitt Dix.

Dix had many unbecoming qualities, but

disloyalty was not among them. He had stood by Randall Butcher's side for nearly twenty years, and what he felt for him was as close to love as he had ever known. The sight of Butcher writhing on the porch, a blood angel forming behind him, caused something to break inside his lieutenant. Dix's only instinct was to try to save Butcher, even as what remained of the logical part of his brain recognized that his employer—his friend—could not and would not survive. But shots were impacting around him. Glass was breaking, and wood splintering. Dix could hear shouting from inside and outside the house, and a voice repeating "Stop firing! Stop firing!" over a bullhorn. But this couldn't have applied to Dix, because he hadn't yet fired a shot. He was about to rectify that situation.

Dix was carrying a Beretta AR90, one of a number of weapons that had fallen foul of the Federal Assault Weapons Ban signed into law in 1994 by President Bill Clinton—for whom Dix had not voted, and whom he regarded as a disgrace to the state that birthed him. This particular AR90, with its wire folding stock, was one of three that Dix had acquired from Mexico, and was fitted with a hundred-round C-Mag drum, the contents of which Dix now commenced emptying into the forest.

Jurel Cade's voice was subsumed in the tumult, but by then he had given up on the bullhorn, and—like everyone else around him—had his face buried in the dirt.

On the porch, Randall Butcher stopped writhing. Because Randall Butcher was dead.

Tilon Ward lifted the hatch in the floor of the RV and dropped to the ground below. He lay unmoving, his ears ringing from the noise of gunfire. He could see Pruitt Dix's muscles jerking as the assault rifle bucked in his hands, and two of Butcher's other subordinates shooting from positions of cover. A third was working his way from the rear of the farmhouse when a bullet took him in the right ankle and he went down. At the same moment, the back door burst open and three figures in blue protective overalls commenced a run for the forest. Running had also been Ward's plan. Initially he was annoyed at these others for doing the same before he could get around to it, thereby attracting unwanted attention, until he realized that their overalls would make them stand out until they could be discarded, and therefore they, along with Pruitt Dix's fusillade, would provide just the distraction he required.

Tilon Ward crawled from under the RV and broke for the trees.

Leonard Cresil had two men on his shoot-to-kill list. The first, and most important, was Randall Butcher. The impending grand jury indictment had served as Butcher's death warrant. He would have every reason to cooperate with the federal authorities as part of a plea bargain, and would be in a position to throw any number of individuals under the bus, including Cresil and his employer, Charles Shire. It was therefore a matter of some urgency that Butcher should not live long enough to be served with the indictment. Cresil had solved that particular problem with one shot.

The second person on Cresil's list was Pruitt Dix. Dix was an integral part of Butcher's enterprise, which meant that it wouldn't be long before he, too, was being questioned. In fact, according to Shire's sources, local law enforcement had raided Dix's apartment in Little Rock the previous day, and a warrant had already been issued for his arrest on narcotics charges. If Butcher couldn't be relied upon to keep his mouth shut, it was unlikely that Dix would be any different.

Of course, Butcher's demise now gave Cresil another good reason to ensure that Pruitt Dix didn't leave the Ouachita alive. Were Dix to survive, and escape the police cordon, he might regard it as his duty to seek a measure of revenge for Butcher's death. Cresil didn't want a lunatic like Dix potentially spoiling his retirement, and was certain that Shire wouldn't care to have him haunting the shadows either.

Cresil was maneuvering himself into position when he was saved the cost of another bullet. Out in the woods, at least one of Cade's people had decided that they were tired of being pinned down by Dix's fusillade. In a brief gap between bursts from the AR90, Cresil heard a single shot with a lot of powder behind it. By the time he had identified the noise, and the direction from which it had come, a .300 Winchester Magnum round, popular with deer hunters because of its accuracy over long distances, had removed part of Pruitt Dix's skull.

Dix emptied his magazine into the air in a final dying spasm, and Cresil immediately heard shouts of surrender from inside and outside the farmhouse. It was over. He wondered how many of Cade's deputies and posse might be injured or deceased. He hoped they'd all had the sense to stay low, and that casualties had been kept to a minimum; Shire might have wished to see Butcher and Dix dead, but not at the cost of endangering the arrival of Kovas Industries. Then again, Shire was skilled at media manipulation, and the image of good, honest men and women risking—or laying down—their lives in order to rid their county of the meth menace, and create a safe and secure environment for families and business, could play well. If Kovas were to let God-fearing people put themselves in danger only to be betrayed at the last by the very company whose investment they were fighting to secure, well, the optics would be poor.

Cresil's attention was drawn to a man scuttling into the forest from behind one of the RVs. Cresil thought it looked like Tilon Ward. Cade had shown the posse a picture of Ward from a DUI bust a few years earlier, along with photos of Ward's father, Hollis. The old man was someone else's problem, but it might be useful to Cresil if he could present

Cade with the son, particularly if Cade was of a mind to kick up a fuss over the killing of Randall Butcher.

Of course, Tilon Ward would have to be dead when Cresil gave him to Cade. If he was involved in the murder of black girls, it was no more than he deserved—and even if he wasn't, he'd been an intimate of Butcher and Dix, and represented a loose thread that should be tied off. Cresil's only regret was that Cade had talked him into leaving his hunting bow back in Hamill, because he had been of a mind to use it. He consoled himself with the knowledge that he'd dispatched other men with it, although the thrill of a bow hunt never faded.

Cresil brushed dark earth from his hands, hitched his pants, and went after Tilon Ward.

CHAPTER
XCII

Parker met Angel and Louis at Denton's, a little diner at the edge of Cargill that opened only from 5 to 10 a.m. Parker had not previously given Denton's his business, big breakfasts being anathema to him, but Angel and Louis were cut from a different cloth. He found them at a center table, their plates a cholesterol nightmare. Even glancing at the contents threatened Parker's circulation.

Parker sat beside Angel and across from Louis. He ordered coffee and toast, which made him feel virtuous by comparison.

"Did you have to hurt anyone?" he said.

"Only some feelings," said Angel. "We did destroy a truck, though."

"Molly Hatchet?"

"Is that what the shit paint job was?"

"I thought it was sort of impressive."

"Impressively fucking dumb."

"The man we spoke with," said Louis, "the one who used to own a truck, said someone called Pruitt Dix hired him to take care of you, and that Dix works for a titty bar owner named Randall Butcher."

"I've never met either of them," said Parker, "but I know who they are."

"If you've never met them, why do they want your bones broken?"

"Probably because Leonard Cresil, the Kovas goon, told Butcher and Dix to get it done."

"Where's Cresil now?"

"The desk clerk told me that he checked out of the motel before sunrise. Cresil's boss is a guy named Charles Shire, who's the fixer for Kovas. Shire's room is also currently vacant. To be honest, I was surprised at Cresil. I thought he'd be smart enough to back off once I'd made it clear that I knew he was holding the leashes. But if he left the details up to Butcher and Dix, then it makes some sense."

"Why?"

"Because, as of yesterday, Butcher and Dix are wanted men. Maybe Cresil couldn't get in touch with them in time to stop them from proceeding with their half-assed plan."

"You almost sound like you're looking for an excuse to forgive him."

"No, just to forget. Going after Cresil makes no sense unless it's absolutely necessary. He's a moral void, and the world will find a way to deal with him in its own time."

"So you're just going to wait and see whether he comes at you again?"

"I have you to watch over me, but my gut feeling is that he won't, or not until the Kovas agreement has been nailed down. It's not worth the trouble to him or to Shire."

Parker checked his phone. The volume on it was screwy, and he sometimes missed calls coming through.

"Expecting to hear from someone?" said Angel.

"Yes, about a dead possum."

Louis took a moment to reflect on this.

"I think," he said, "that you've already been down here too long."

Kevin Naylor was driving to Cargill when the first of the ambulances from the Hamill Medical Center passed him on the road, followed by two state police cruisers and a second ambulance. He didn't have a police radio in his off-duty vehicle, so he used his cell phone to call Billie at the Cargill PD, inform her of what he'd seen, and advise her to find out what was going on. In the meantime, he was going to tag along behind the last ambulance, just in case Chief Griffin wanted a more personal perspective on whatever was happening.

Within minutes, Billie knew as much as the state police dispatcher with whom she'd spoken, which was a report of gunshot fatalities in the Ouachita resulting from a Burdon County Sheriff's Office operation of which, until only a short time before, the staties had been completely unaware. At this point, a less self-possessed individual might have rushed to share this information with her superiors, but Billie knew that Griffin would want to know more, so she took the time to call Cecile Hardgrave, the dispatcher at the sheriff's office. Cecile was in a hell of a state, but she was also a pro and told Billie what she knew as clearly and succinctly as possible before asking her to pray for all concerned. Billie, who was an atheist, lied and said she would, because it wasn't as though she was going to hell for it. Seconds later, she was at Griffin's door.

"Jurel Cade led a posse into the Ouachita this morning to take down a meth cookhouse," she said. "He also hoped to arrest Tilon Ward, possibly Hollis Ward, and anyone else found on the premises. There are at least two dead, and five more injured. Cecile Hardgrave says sheriff's office personnel aren't among the fatalities, so far as she can tell, but they are among the casualties. She doesn't know if they got Tilon Ward or his father. Kevin is on his way out there now. He spotted the ambulances heading west and decided to follow."

Griffin restrained himself from breaking something, but only just. Jurel Cade had screwed them all over, and perhaps endangered the entire investigation in the process. Duplicity was bred in the Cade bone.

"Get in touch with Kel." Knight had spent the night up in Little Rock, waiting for doctors to permit him to speak with Reverend Nathan Pettle, who was recovering from what was likely to be only the first of many surgeries. Pettle wouldn't be able to say a whole lot, but it would be sufficient for their needs if he could nod and shake his head, or even raise and lower a pinkie to indicate yes or no. "Tell him to leave Pettle and get down here. I'm going to send Naylor back to you once I get out there. The reverend will just have to wait."

"What about Parker?"

"What about him?"

"What should I tell him?"

"Tell him to stay around here and do whatever he can to help Naylor." Griffin grabbed his hat and his weatherproof jacket. "And if anyone asks, you know nothing about what's been happening in the Ouachita. Just refer any inquiries to the sheriff's office."

"Does that include Harmony Ward? Because rumors are going to spread fast."

Griffin stopped fighting with his jacket long enough to say: "Have Parker take Harmony into protective custody. I want her brought in here and kept behind bars until you hear from me. If she has a cell phone, relieve her of it. If it rings, note the number."

"And if her son is among the dead?"

Tilon, Tilon. Why did it have to be like this?

"If he is, I'll inform her. No matter what you hear, you keep it to yourself. From now on, you're dumb as the dead."

"I understand."

Griffin gave her right arm a squeeze.

"At least one of us does."

Tilon Ward was still alive, if only for the present.

He looked back to see the bulky form of Leonard Cresil pursuing him through the trees. Tilon knew Cresil by sight and reputation, although he had been spared any personal dealings with the man. He was aware that Randall Butcher had never trusted Cresil or his boss, Charles Shire, but had been forced to work with them in order to profit from Kovas's impending arrival. Equally, Cresil and Shire had probably been wary of Butcher, especially if they had knowledge of his involvement in the supply of illegal narcotics. But how much had they known, and when had they become aware of it? Was Shire the kind of man who would risk contracts worth tens of millions of dollars by allowing a drug dealer to become a fixed part of the arrangement?

Probably not.

Now Randall Butcher was dead, and Pruitt Dix also, while Leonard Cresil was moving deeper and deeper into the Ouachita, tracking their meth cook. The odds on Tilon's survival were shortening by the second until Cresil briefly lost sight of his quarry thanks to a stand of hickory. Tilon went to ground, and was now debating the wisdom of remaining where he was, partly concealed by the rotting trunk of a fallen tree, in the hope that Cresil would pass him by, enabling Tilon to retrace his steps for a while before heading southeast. Tilon didn't have a cell phone, though, which was a problem. While there was no coverage out here in the woods, he might have picked up a bar or two once he got nearer to a road, and made some calls. He had people who would be willing to help him, but as things stood he had no means of contacting them, no car, no weapon, and virtually no hope, not as long as Cresil kept coming.

"I only want to talk to you, Mr. Ward," Cresil called, not for the first time. "I mean you no harm. I just need some information."

Yeah, thought Tilon, *like how much blood my body contains.*

"I can help you get out of here," Cresil continued. "You're a wanted man. The police are convinced you killed those girls."

This was a new tack from Cresil, but it struck home. Tilon squeezed shut his eyes. So someone had seen him with Donna Lee. Someone knew. What Cresil said next confirmed it.

"They have a witness who spotted the Kernigan girl getting into your truck," said Cresil. "You were the last one seen with her, and now the police have drawn a bead on you. They want this over and done with so everyone can get to making good money from Kovas. You think the sheriff's office went to all that trouble just to take down a meth lab? You think all those guns were sent in here only for Butcher and Dix? It's you they want, you and your old man."

His father? What the—

Tilon almost asked the question aloud. His father was dead. Everyone said so.

"You require the services of a good lawyer, Mr. Ward. I've heard tell that riding the needle doesn't hurt, not after the first sting, but I've never believed it myself. I've been a witness at executions, and I've looked in men's eyes as they died. They've been filled with agony, and that's after years of living with the fear of what's to come while the process of taking a life worked its way through appeal after appeal. I used to be of the opinion that the waiting was worse than the end itself, but that was before I glimpsed the end and learned it wasn't true. Dying is worse than any waiting, and dying like that, strapped to a gurney while all those folks will you to suffer, and suffer hard, is as bad as dying gets.

"So you need me, Mr. Ward. We can find you a lawyer and a place to rest up while you consider your options. Depending on what you tell us, and the choices you make, we may even be in a position to help you in other ways. I know about you. I know you tried to save Chief Griffin's wife all those years ago. A man who'd do a good deed like that isn't the kind to murder women. The law isn't always right, and sometimes justice is better served by leaving legality out of matters entirely. Are you listening, Mr. Ward? Because right now, I'm your best hope for living to old age."

Hollis Ward hadn't raised a fool. Tilon was prepared to accept that the police might have entered the Ouachita to arrest him, because if Cresil knew he'd been seen with Donna Lee then that information had probably come from law enforcement. But Cresil had pushed it too far with all that execution shit and offers of help with a lawyer, even with the suggestion of a possible escape route for Tilon. Some men simply didn't know when to shut up.

Which was when Leonard Cresil finally stopped talking, and began screaming.

Naylor followed the ambulances and cruisers up the dirt road to the Buttrell land, past neat rows of nascent pine and signs advising that this was private property. A bearded asshole in a hunting vest, probably a member of Cade's ill-fated posse, tried to step in front of him as the farmhouse came in sight to his left, but Naylor kept on rolling, forcing the asshole to dive for the ditch. In his rearview mirror, he saw the asshole raise his rifle as if to fire before some small semblance of rational thought flared briefly in his brain. It was probably the realization that the Negro behind the wheel just might—for better or worse—be an officer of the law, especially given the blinking blue light on his dashboard, in which case shooting at him was likely to have repercussions.

The asshole lowered his weapon, and Naylor made a mental note to have a quiet word with him before the day was done. He turned toward the farmhouse, where he saw two men lying in its vicinity, one on the porch and another in the dirt close by two RVs, both clearly dead. He took in four more men sitting against a fence with their hands cuffed behind their backs, two of them dressed in blue protective overalls, and three others with blood on their clothing who were being watched carefully by sheriff's deputies and civilians. One of the bloodied men was staring glassy-eyed in Naylor's direction, his face gray and his jeans soaked red. Naylor was fairly certain this man was going to die. To his right an ambulance crew was already running to take care of the wounded. One of the deputies was on his feet, leaning against a tree with his arm in a makeshift sling, but the second was lying on his side, and half his head was raw and bloody.

Naylor was the only black man on the scene, which was not an unfamiliar situation to him, but still made him stand out more than he might have wished. He identified himself as a police officer to the state trooper who was approaching him, a statement confirmed by the trooper's colleague, a sergeant named Ogden who was seeing a woman who lived in Cargill and sometimes drank with her in Boyd's. Zachry, one of the Burdon County deputies, joined them. He smelled as though he might have puked recently.

"What the hell happened?" said Naylor.

"Someone shot Randall Butcher," said Zachry, "then a bunch of people started shooting at us from around the farmhouse, and suddenly everyone was shooting at everyone else. It couldn't have gone on for more than a minute or two, but when the dust cleared we had two men dead and a whole lot more injured."

"But why target this place to begin with?" said Naylor.

"It's a meth lab," said Zachry, "but Jurel said

Hollis and Tilon Ward might be in there too. He thinks they killed those girls."

"And did you find the Wards?"

"No sign. If they were here, they're gone now, but nobody is talking without a lawyer, so we can't say for sure."

Zachry rubbed the butt of his service weapon with the palm of his right hand, as though his skin was itching.

"I didn't even fire a shot," he said. "I was scared shitless."

Naylor took in the injured, the dying, and the dead.

"Then maybe they'll let you keep your job after the investigation," he said.

Zachry followed his gaze. When he'd signed up to be a sheriff's deputy, it wasn't for this.

"You know," he said, "I hope they don't."

About eighteen months previously, the now-deceased Randall Butcher had been taking an evening stroll through the environs of the Buttrell property when he'd stumbled across a black bear and her five-month-old cub. Black bears are typically solitary animals, and prefer to avoid contact with humans, but sometimes a bear's preference didn't enter into it: the black bear population of the state had risen from about fifty in the 1930s to thousands in the present day, and in places like the Ouachita they occasionally bumped up against man. Black bears weren't large by the standards of other American ursids, but a male could still weigh 700 pounds, and even a 300-pound female was enough to put the fear of God into a man if he wasn't anticipating her company.

And if he came between her and her cub—well, that was pretty much a guarantee of pain.

Randall Butcher had backed away, but he could see Momma Bear was contemplating teaching him a lesson, and he didn't begin to feel safe again until he was back in the farmhouse with the door locked behind him, surrounded by a couple of guns and about $100,000 worth of methamphetamine. Subsequently, Butcher invested in bear traps for the property, although in truth he'd been thinking for a while about adding them as a security precaution against snoopers. He acquired a range of devices, including some old Victor, Triumph, and Newhouse wolf and bear traps that dated from less enlightened times, when the main purpose of said instruments was to inflict maximum pain and damage on prey. The traps were in poor condition, and rusted as all hell, but some TLC and lubricant restored them to reasonable working order. Butcher made sure his people knew where they were located, but as far as anyone else was concerned, he figured they could just take their chances.

It had been Leonard Cresil's misfortune to lose his footing close to one of those locations, and therefore land with his right knee on the plate of a vintage Kodiak bear trap designed to disable animals up to ten feet tall and weighing as much as 1,500 pounds. The toothed jaws instantly crushed Cresil's right femur, along with the tibia and fibula in his lower leg. They also tore apart his femoral artery, so that by the time Tilon Ward found him the ground was already soaked with blood and Cresil was dying. Cresil was in so much agony, though, that he probably didn't realize the imminence of his own demise, which might have explained his next words.

"Help me," he said.

Tilon was carrying a thick length of branch that he'd picked up along the way, just in case Cresil, for all his hollering, proved to be less incapacitated than he sounded. Cresil stretched out his left hand, and Tilon instinctively moved to take it, which was when Cresil brought up his right, a gun still gripped firmly in its fingers. But his movements were sluggish, giving Tilon plenty of time to lash out with the branch, catching Cresil hard on the head and causing his body to twist. There was a final spurt of red from the ruined artery, and Cresil gave a whine of pain, which was the last noise he would ever make. Tilon stood over him, watching him bleed out, and was surprised at how little he felt. When Cresil was dead, Tilon searched his pockets and relieved him of his cell phone, his billfold, and his gun before continuing on his way. He walked for about ten minutes until he came to a pool of standing water, in which he disposed of the branch. After another ten minutes, a signal bar appeared on the phone.

Tilon called his cousin Ernest and asked him to come find him.

Parker had a cuffed and unhappy Harmony Ward in the back of his car when he pulled into the parking lot of the Cargill PD. She hadn't been working at the Dunk-N-Go that morning, so he'd been forced to confront her at home. She'd been more sad than angry, and hadn't kicked up too much of a fuss. She was worried about her son, but Parker couldn't tell her much other than that Chief Griffin was on his way to the scene, and as soon as they heard anything, they'd let her know.

Parker led her to a cell and handed her phone over to Billie Brinton. By then Naylor had returned, and informed them that there was no sign of either Hollis or Tilon Ward at the Buttrell place. While none of the men arrested at the scene would either confirm or deny if Tilon had been present, they all claimed never to have seen his father.

"I'm heading out again," Parker told Billie, when Naylor was done.

"May I ask where to?" She heard the aggrieved tone in her own voice, and regulated it for the follow-up. "Just in case the chief wants to know."

"I'm going to visit Pappy Cade."

"Uh-huh? We got a blender in the kitchenette, should you prefer to stick your face into that instead."

"It's tempting," said Parker, "but I'll continue with Plan A."

613

CHAPTER
XCIII

The same dour woman who had haunted the spaces of the Cade residence when Parker last visited now answered the door to him again. He was shown into the same office, where Pappy Cade was once again seated behind the same desk, wearing the same cardigan and what might have been the same shirt and pants. The same clock ticked, and the same sad sour smell of bitter old age filled the air. Nothing, it seemed, changed at the Cade house, or nothing of consequence.

"Take a seat, Mr. Parker," said Pappy. "Your company is most welcome."

"Why is that?"

"Because you represent novelty, which means that you'll suffice as a distraction until you tire of these regions and move on. May I offer you coffee, or hot tea?"

"No, thank you. I hope my visit will be brief."

"I'm surprised to see you here at all, given the morning's events. A lot of action out in the Ouachita, or so I'm led to believe."

"Two dead, and more injured, including a number of sheriff's deputies. I don't think the execution of the raid will reflect well on your son."

Pappy Cade's shoulders jerked in an approximation of contained mirth.

"Then you don't know this county," he said.

"From what I hear, none of those deputies is in any danger of expiring soon, while Jurel and his people, aided by concerned citizens, just took down a meth operation that was contributing to the debilitation of our populace, and might have caused Kovas to reconsider its intentions. I don't see any problems at all with that story. Men have successfully run for office on less."

Perhaps he was right, Parker thought. Jurel Cade might yet emerge smelling of roses.

"They found no sign of Hollis Ward out there," said Parker.

"Didn't they?" Pappy's voice gave nothing away. It was studiedly neutral.

"Most of those with whom I've spoken think he's dead," said Parker. "I'm curious to hear your opinion."

"I'd prefer to see a body before I make pronouncements like that, but if you pressed me, I'd lean toward considering him deceased."

"Why did Hollis Ward hate your family so much?"

"I don't know that he did."

"But you dispensed with his services after he was convicted for possession of child pornography."

"That's true, but I'm not convinced Hollis took it too personally. He knew the lay of the land, and he'd profited from his dealings with us."

"Just as you had from his efforts on your behalf."

"True."

"So despite what some might think, your view is

that Ward—if he's alive—would have no particular reason to derail the Kovas deal?"

"No, I suppose he would not. May I ask where you're going with this, Mr. Parker?"

Parker stared the old man in the face.

"I reckon you know who's been killing those young women," he said. "Perhaps not for sure, but you have your suspicions."

Pappy Cade stared back.

"That's a hell of an accusation to make," he said, but there was no real indignation to the response, and the expression on his face remained unaltered. It displayed only a vague disinterest, as of one regarding a fly that refuses to cease buzzing after a hand has crushed it.

"Yes, it is," said Parker.

"Do you have any evidence to support your theory?"

"Nothing substantial, or not yet, but I will. I believe Hollis Ward is involved, but not in the way everyone seems to fear. There appears to be a lot of hatred in your family for a man who was willing to strong-arm the poor and vulnerable into property arrangements that benefited the Cades. What agreement did you reach with Hollis Ward, Mr. Cade? What did you give him to cause such resentment among your own blood?"

Pappy Cade's expression changed, and for a moment Parker glimpsed the toxic fury that dwelt inside the old man, a rage that would evanesce only with his final breath.

"You don't know anything about this land," Pappy said at last, "and you know nothing about those who live on it."

"People don't differ so much from one another," said Parker. "They love, they lust, they hate. They get angry, they get frightened. They live, they die. The rest is just details."

"Then you haven't seen enough of life."

"Oh, I've seen enough."

Pappy was overcome by a fit of coughing. Parker poured a glass of water from a jug and passed it to him, but Pappy's hands were shaking so badly that Parker had to assist him in raising the glass to his lips. Pappy turned his head away when he had drunk enough, and Parker saw red worms of blood uncoil in the water before dissolving; whatever was ailing him, Parker thought, it was not Parkinson's alone. Pappy did not say thank you. Instead, his face flushed briefly with embarrassment.

"Whatever passed between Hollis Ward and this family is long done with," said Cade, as Parker resumed his seat. "Any lingering resentments that my offspring may feel toward me for slights and hurts inflicted over the years will fall away once their security, and the security of their children, grandchildren, and great-grandchildren, has been guaranteed by the wealth and influence that Kovas will bring. The rest, as you say, is just details."

"If you really believe that," said Parker, "then your children are destined to disappoint you."

Through the window behind Pappy, Parker

watched a car pull up before the house. From it emerged Delphia Cade, as though summoned by Parker to provide proof of his thesis.

"It's a shame," said Pappy.

"What is?"

"That your own child didn't survive long enough to disappoint you. You, unfortunately, lived long enough to disappoint her."

But his words had no power to wound Parker, or none beyond the superficial. Pappy Cade was a hateful old man, and death would take care of him soon enough. Parker heard a key turning in the lock of the front door, followed by the sound of Delphia Cade's heels tapping across the hardwood floor of the hall, and the creak of the office door opening behind him.

"Mr. Parker," said Delphia, as she drifted into sight. "Have you changed your mind about my offer?"

Pappy raised an inquisitorial eyebrow.

"I asked Mr. Parker to consider working for us," she explained. "Or rather, for me. I felt I might have need of a factotum, among other services."

"Whatever you needed, Ms. Cade, I couldn't provide," said Parker.

"Then why are you here?"

"Your father and I were exchanging views on family."

"I didn't think you had a family," said Delphia, "not anymore."

Parker couldn't help but smile. It was the only

appropriate response to such genetic incorrigibility.

"It seems that your father's blood runs in your veins," he said. "That's unfortunate." He returned his attention to Pappy. "If it's any consolation to you as your health deteriorates, I don't imagine your children will permit you to suffer long. One of them will put you out of your misery before the pain becomes too great."

"It's beyond time for you to leave here," said Pappy. "If I were you, I'd fill your tank in town and keep driving until the gas runs out."

"I'll be doing that soon enough," said Parker. "But no more young women are going to be butchered. That's coming to an end."

"You think I wanted those girls to die?" said Pappy.

"No," said Parker. "I'm just not convinced that you, or anyone under your sway, cared enough to stop it from happening."

Parker watched a shadow cross Delphia Cade's face, and the shards of silver in her eyes flashed brightly for an instant. But she was looking only at Pappy, and her hatred for him was manifest. As Parker moved toward the door, Pappy's voice followed him.

"Whatever you do, it won't bring your child back," he shouted, "or your wife neither! Dying will be a mercy for you. Dying—"

But the rest was lost in another fit of coughing, which continued as Parker walked to the front door. He glanced back to see the patriarch hunched over his desk, racked with pain, thick gobbets of blood spattering the leather inlay and the papers spread upon it, and Delphia, contemplating her father's suffering, the water jug held in her right hand as she poured its contents onto the floor.

And through the trees, over water and sky, the dead moved in unison.

CHAPTER
XCIV

Charles Shire took the call from an unfamiliar number as he waited by the gate at Adams Field for his flight to Atlanta. He had been expecting to hear from Cresil, but the voice on the other end of the phone belonged to Jurel Cade.

"Cresil is dead," said Cade, without preamble.

"How?"

"He landed in a bear trap."

"Is that a literal description of his fate?"

"Very much. He probably bled to death within minutes."

Shire felt no particular regret, beyond that which a man might feel at the loss of a useful tool from his kit. In some ways, Cresil's death might even be for the best, because their shared secrets had died with him.

"And the rest?"

"Randall Butcher was shot and killed at the scene, along with Pruitt Dix. They were the only other fatalities. We're dealing with a lot of media. We got the TV, the newspapers—"

"Is the situation under control?"

"I think so. Only bad guys died."

"Are you including Mr. Cresil among their number?"

"Officially, or unofficially?"

"I think that answers my question."

"Cresil fired the first shot. He killed Butcher."

"You're sure?"

"As good as. Nobody else has admitted to firing at Butcher, and I don't doubt they're all telling the truth. We'll know for sure once the ballistic examination of the slug is concluded."

"And how will you paint these events?"

"Cresil was part of a group of deputized citizens that came under fire in the course of the operation. Two deputies were injured, one of them seriously. Shots were exchanged. Cresil's actions may have saved lives."

"That was very heroic of him. Call Tammy Barker. She'll help you with the nuances."

Barker was one of the partners in the Little Rock PR firm engaged by Kovas Industries to smooth ruffled feathers in Arkansas. Even by the standards of her industry, she was breathtakingly mendacious.

"And what about Hollis Ward?" Shire asked.

"I don't think he was ever there. His son, maybe, but not Hollis."

"Where's Tilon now?"

"We're looking for him."

"Do you still consider him your chief suspect?"

"In the absence of a better one."

Shire grimaced. Only his best efforts, combined with certain assurances from Pappy Cade and promises from Little Rock of a further sweetening of the tax arrangements, had kept Kovas from bolting to Texas after the Kernigan killing. Another female corpse would lead to serious financial and reputational damage for all concerned.

"I told you," said Shire. "No more dead girls."

"We're working on it."

Shire heard his flight being called.

"Work harder," he said, and hung up.

Angel and Louis were waiting for Parker as he emerged from the gates of the Cade property. They had offered to accompany him inside, but he didn't regard himself as being at risk from the dying Pappy, or not physically: the potential taint to his soul from exposure to the old man's virulence was another issue.

Parker's phone rang as he pulled up. It was Evan Griffin.

"Where are you?"

"I just finished visiting with Pappy Cade. I think he cut a bad deal with Hollis Ward and it's returned to haunt him and everyone else in this county. I believe Patricia Hartley and Donna Lee Kernigan died because of it, possibly even Estella Jackson, too."

"Did Pappy sign a statement to that effect?"

"Yeah, and he also wrote me into his will before I left. He told me I was the son he never had."

"He already has two sons."

"Like I said."

Parker heard Griffin mutter something. It sounded like a prayer for patience.

"I thought you might be interested to hear that

623

Leonard Cresil is dead," said Griffin, once he'd sent his message to God.

"How?"

"He was part of Jurel Cade's posse. Seems he fell into a bear trap and bled to death."

"Fell, or was pushed?"

"There was no one around to witness his end, so I guess we'll never know for sure. But I saw the body: it looked like Cresil took a blow to the head shortly before he died, one that almost knocked his left eye from its socket."

"I warned him he'd come to a bad end."

"I'm sure that was a solace to him as he walked into God's light."

"Anything else?"

"Tilon Ward was in the vicinity at some point. He left his wallet in one of the RVs, which means he departed in a hurry, most likely when the shooting started. As for Hollis Ward, he was never there."

"Because he's dead," said Parker.

"He left his mark on Donna Lee's body."

"I think someone did, but not him."

"I have to confess that I struggle to follow your line of reasoning. I'm heading back to town, and Kel has returned from Little Rock. If you could see your way clear to joining us at the station, I thought we might have a conference to establish where we're at. You could take it as an opportunity to clarify your thought processes for us."

"Then I'll probably see you there."

"That word *probably* troubles me," said Griffin,

but the only response he received was dead air, because Parker had already killed the call, and was dialing the number for the state crime lab. He got through to the switchboard and asked for Dr. Ruth Temple. He was advised to hold the line, and five minutes went by before Temple eventually picked up.

"We have bodies on the way," she said. "Human bodies."

"I know."

"From Burdon County."

"I know that, too."

"Are you responsible for any of them?"

"No, but the word is that one of them will have a bear trap attached. Just warning you."

"I hope to meet you someday," she said.

"Really?"

"No. I examined your possum."

"And?"

"I can't say with certainty that its injuries resulted from the same blade that was used on Donna Lee Kernigan."

Parker picked up on the inflection in her speech.

"But?"

"The dimensions are similar, and so is the depth of the wounds."

"So it could be the same blade?"

"It could be, yes."

"Thank you."

"You're welcome." She paused. "I hope it helps."

"It hasn't hindered," said Parker. "Right now, I'll settle for that much."

He said goodbye, and walked to the driver's side of the Mustang. Louis let the window down.

"Cresil's dead."

"With Butcher and Dix also gone," said Louis, "looks like your back is safe."

"Do you want to leave?" said Parker.

"Do you want us to leave?"

Parker looked north, toward Cargill. Sometimes, he thought, you operated on evidence, and sometimes on instinct. Mostly, it was a combination of both.

"I may need a lock picked," he said.

Beside Louis, Angel visibly brightened. Angel had no great fondness for anywhere farther south of Manhattan than Tottenville. The fact that he was present at all spoke volumes for his loyalty to Parker.

"More than one?" he asked hopefully.

"You never know," said Parker, turning toward his car. "And if you're very good, I may even let you steal something."

CHAPTER
XCV

The rain had cleared, but thin, persistent clouds hung like gauze over the sky, soaking up all warmth so that only a vestige reached the earth. The sun was a coral orb, bleeding burnt orange and carmine crimson into a lacteal sea. Upright crows stood like thorns upon the topmost branches of the trees, and the air smelled of rot and standing water. Parker felt an ache in his fingers and toes, and a sense of deep, unanchored regret that caused his throat to seize up and his eyes to sting. He knew now that the dead spoke with one voice, and the final agony was the same for all.

A memory came to him of a walk in Prospect Park with Jennifer, only a month before she died. They had found a small form lying curled upon the grass: a squirrel, puncture marks on its neck.

"What happened to it?" said Jennifer.

"I think a dog might have caught it."

"It's so little." Jennifer's voice was full of pity, and wonder, and sadness. Her hand tightened on his. "Do we have to leave it out here all alone?"

"No. We can bury it, if you like."

"Okay."

He lifted the animal in his hands. It was still warm. Its head hung loosely over his palms, and his fingers found the break in its neck. Yet what struck him most forcefully was how heavy it was, how dense with mortality. Life had lent it grace, but death had restored its substantiality. Even after they placed the squirrel in the ground and covered it with dirt, he could feel the memory of its mass, the burden of its absence.

"I'm sorry," he said, and he was speaking not to one dead girl but to four dead children. He thought that were he to pull over and descend into the woods, he would discover them waiting, paused in the act of shadowing: three young black women, and with them a fourth—a white child, wandering. He saw darkness curl into a tunnel of smoke, and a light shining like a vermilion wound at the heart of the world. Moisture touched his cheek. He wiped it away with the back of his hand and his skin came away bloody. He looked in the rearview mirror. A line of red trickled from his scalp and dripped onto his face. He had no recollection of injuring himself. He pushed back his hair to reveal the source, but could not locate it.

There was only blood, except that he could no longer say with any certainty that it was his own.

CHAPTER
XCVI

The two cars pulled up in front of the abandoned gas station, and the stained, pitted screen of the drive-in theater came briefly alive with the shadows of passing clouds, like the remembrance of some old movie retained in the aluminum panels.

"Why this place?" said Angel, as he and Louis joined Parker in the forecourt.

"Because someone took a blade to a possum here," said Parker. He had cleaned the blood from his face with the sleeve of his jacket, and now could no longer detect the stain on the material. It was as though it had never been.

From somewhere in the untidy depths of his clothing, Angel produced a zippered leather pouch, which he opened to reveal an old but well-tended set of picks, torsion wrenches, and skeleton keys. Angel rarely traveled without the tools of his former—and, Parker suspected, periodically current—trade. He walked to the garage building and began testing each padlock with a pick, although without trying to open any of them. To Parker's eye, all the locks looked old and rusted, but he said nothing and left Angel to finish his work.

"The lock on the side door is in use, and so is the one on the main garage entrance on the left," said

Angel, when he was done, "but the side door more than the other. The rest haven't been opened in a long time."

"Can you get me in?"

"Which door would you prefer?"

"Side."

"Done."

It took about ten seconds. The smell hit Parker as soon as Angel opened the door: putrefaction, and something older resembling the mustiness of a tomb. Parker took his gloves from his pocket and pulled them on. He reached inside the entrance and located the light switch. Only one of the fluorescents flickered into life, but it was enough for him to see what lay within: a Toyota Tercel with Arkansas plates, a human shape seated behind the wheel; and a body cocooned in plastic in a corner, its outline distorted by what appeared to be spikes beneath the covering.

Louis unfolded a clean white handkerchief and offered it to Parker. It smelled of expensive male scent—not sufficiently to mask entirely the stench from the garage, but enough to take the edge away.

"Get the cars out of sight," he told Louis.

The road was quiet, and the property didn't appear to be overlooked, but Parker didn't want whoever was responsible for maintaining this place to be alerted to signs of intrusion should they happen to chance by. He held the handkerchief to his nose and stepped into the garage. He went first to the car and opened the passenger door. The body in the driver's seat was heavily swollen, and the bugs had begun to colonize it, but he could still tell that he was looking at a dead black woman, her mouth forming an oval around the branch that had been jammed down her throat. There was dried blood around her nose and chin, but he could see no other signs of injury. The make and license plate number matched that of Sallie Kernigan's vehicle.

Parker did not touch the body, but gently closed the door before moving on to the plastic-wrapped remains. They were much older, and almost skeletonized, but Parker could tell they were male. Sharp sticks had been driven deeply into the legs, arms, and torso, held in place by the plastic even as decomposition had gradually excised the flesh. A larger stake protruded from the damaged jaws, and another appeared to have been inserted deep into the victim's rectum. Two fingers were missing from the right hand, but the damage seemed old. On a shelf nearby, Parker saw a jar of yellowing preservative. Lying at the bottom of the jar were the amputated digits. If Parker was correct, he was looking at what was left of Hollis Ward.

He made a cursory search of the rest of the garage, but found nothing more than old pornographic calendars, rusting equipment, and disintegrating tires. He went back outside, removed the handkerchief from his face, and breathed deeply of the fresh air, although the smell of the woman's rot now clung to him. He took out his cell phone and found the number for Eddy Rauls.

The former chief investigator picked up on the second ring, as though he spent his days sitting by the phone, perhaps waiting for this very call.

"Mr. Rauls? It's Charlie Parker."

"What can I do for you?"

"What do you know about the abandoned gas station at the end of your road?"

"Hollis Ward's old place? I don't pay much attention to it. It's a Cade property now."

"Who looks after it for them?"

"I don't think it's much looked after at all. It's just waiting for the wrecking ball. But the son comes by now and again to check the locks. He told me once that Pappy threw him a few bucks a month to keep an eye on unoccupied premises, and make sure kids couldn't break in and start a fire."

"Which son?"

"The younger one, Nealus. Said it gave him a sense of purpose . . ."

CHAPTER
XCVII

Nealus Cade drew closer to Cargill. He wasn't driving the Nissan or even the beat-up Dodge, but an Acura with a cloned plate, bought for cash from a junkyard in Linden, Texas, and stored in the garage of one of the properties he tended for the family. From the trunk of the car came a faint thudding, as of feet banging against metal. Beside Nealus lay two thick branches. They were very straight, and each had been sharpened at one end. Nealus was learning from his earlier mistakes. The sticks went in easier if they were spiked.

He crested a rise and the Karagol lay before him, the sunlight barely visible on the surface of the water. It remained black, with only the faintest trace of fire reflected upon it, like pitch set to burning. Once the girl was dead, he'd park up nearby and wait until full dark. He'd chosen the spot earlier, marked by two young pines that had been brought down crossways. It wouldn't take much effort to move the topmost, and make them perpendicular.

After that, he would tie the corpse to the trees and wait for them to come for him.

CHAPTER
XCVIII

Parker caught Griffin on his cell phone as he was leaving his house, the chief having headed home to change his clothing after hours spent trudging through the Ouachita.

"We're looking for Nealus Cade," said Parker, and told Griffin of what he had found at the garage.

"Jesus. This may have nothing to do with it, but Kel Knight just got a call from a woman named Nora McCullough. Her daughter Maryanne didn't come home from a half-day at school. Kel told her not to panic, and to check with Maryanne's friends. Now, though—"

"Nealus drives a red Nissan coupe, but he has another vehicle, a Dodge," said Parker. "He told me it was undergoing repairs, but I wouldn't put it past him to have lied."

"We'll find it—and him. Stay at the garage for now until I can get someone up there to relieve you."

Parker didn't want to stay at the garage. He wanted to hunt for Nealus Cade, but he could understand Griffin's reasons for asking him to remain there.

"Okay, I'll do it," he agreed, reluctantly.

Which was when a silver Acura came around the bend, slowed at the forecourt, then continued on its way, but not before Parker caught a clear view of the driver.

"He's here," said Parker. "It's Nealus."

• • •

Nealus Cade put his foot down but didn't panic. In a way, this was the best outcome he could have hoped for. He hadn't wanted his brother to be the one to corner him at the end, just as he hadn't wanted it to be Griffin or his people. Jurel had managed to cover up Nealus's killing of Patricia Hartley and block any attempt Griffin might have made to involve the state police in the Kernigan investigation. But Parker was an outsider and unbeholden to the people of the county or the state. To bury the truth of what Nealus had done, they would have to bury Parker as well, and Parker didn't strike Nealus as the kind of man who'd go down easily.

The final act was never destined to take place at the gas station. Oddly, his father had dictated the setting by insisting on placing a big sign on the main Kovas site, trumpeting the company's arrival and thus advertising his arrogance. Everything would conclude there with a crucified girl, and the land would be poisoned forever as a consequence.

But it had been poisoned all along, as Nealus knew, poisoned ever since some explorer with a smattering of classical education had come upon this place and named it the Karagol, followed by men foolish enough to raise a settlement nearby. Nealus's acts were simply the natural conclusion to a sequence of events that had begun a century and a half earlier. It might even have been said that the land made him do it, because he and his family were a product of it. The land was in their blood, and their blood was bad as a consequence.

Maryanne McCullough had stopped kicking. Perhaps she sensed a change in circumstances with the acceleration of the car, and now had hope. She might even have cause for it. Nealus was no longer sure he'd have time to kill her, or not as he might have wished. He'd try, though, he certainly would. He'd thought about dumping Sallie Kernigan's body at the Kovas plot, but he hadn't enjoyed killing her as much as the others, and her death had not been a matter of choice, but necessity. It had been her bad luck to turn up the narrow road to her home just as Nealus was dragging away the unconscious body of her child.

But the appositeness of this conclusion was appealing to him: a chase, a confrontation, and an arrest on property earmarked for Kovas, with a dead girl at his feet. Besides, he didn't think he'd get another chance. Whatever happened in the minutes to come, no more young women would pass through his hands, which was a source of regret to him. What began as revenge had transmuted into something much greater.

Nealus Cade had become a god of ruination.

Parker was trying to stay on the phone with Evan Griffin, but the signal kept cutting out. Louis was following on behind in the Mustang, Angel having elected to stay at the garage and wait for whomever Griffin might be sending.

"Where's he—?"

Griffin cut out for the third time. By now, Parker was beginning to tire of hitting redial. When Griffin's voice came through for the fourth time, Parker didn't bother with any niceties. He knew now where Nealus Cade was heading.

"The big Kovas site," he said. "Just get to it."

Nealus could now see the Karagol to the west, like a smear of dirt on a painting of the landscape. He turned toward it. As he did so, Parker's car appeared in Nealus's rearview mirror, a second vehicle close behind. Nealus was only a minute ahead of them, but a minute was all he required. He was approaching the main Kovas site on the left, with its bright new sign promising a bright new future to which Nealus, by his actions, would give the lie.

But then a Cargill PD patrol car pulled out from among the trees at the site entrance, and another ascended from behind the brow of a hill a little way farther down the road. Nealus twisted the wheel to the right, sending the Acura over a shallow ditch and through the fence that marked the boundary of the Karagol Holding. The lake was ahead of him as he bounced over the rough ground, coming to a sideways halt by the low brow that surrounded it. As he did so, the trunk popped open, and it was a miracle that the McCullough girl wasn't sent sailing into the air. Instead her body slammed against the upper frame of the trunk, breaking two of her ribs but also preventing her from being thrown from the car. Nealus got out and ran to grab her, but some preservation instinct caused the girl not to try to run, or even fight, but to pull the trunk closed again with her bound hands. Nealus heard it lock, but the keys were still in the ignition, and he didn't have time to get to them, not with the pursuit cars now pouring through the gap he'd left in the fence. He retreated up the bank of the lake, stones slipping beneath his feet as he climbed, until he was standing above them all, watching his destiny unfold. One, two, three, four cars, the first of them now grinding to a stop before him. Evan Griffin emerged from it, already reaching for his gun. Kel Knight came next, then Parker, and finally a black man whom Nealus did not recognize, but who had been with Parker back at the garage.

Nealus was happy now, happier than he had been since his mother died.

Griffin raised the gun and leveled it at him. He didn't look angry, just sad, as though he had expected better of Nealus.

"Have you got a weapon, son?" he asked.

"I have a knife."

"Then throw it aside, and get down on your knees."

"I don't think so, not yet."

"Why is that?"

"Because I want you to listen."

"Okay, I'm listening."

But Nealus was looking beyond Griffin, to where

Parker stood. He also had a gun drawn, as did Kel Knight and the black man. Nealus thought that Knight didn't seem happy at having an unknown black man standing so close to him with a sidearm, but the black man didn't appear bothered one way or the other.

"Do you want to tell them," said Nealus to Parker, "or should I?"

"Hollis Ward," said Parker.

"What about him?"

"I think he abused you, and your father colluded in it, or chose to let it slide."

"And why would my father have done that?"

"Because Ward was useful to him, more useful than you were, and he was the keeper of the family's secrets. So you waited: you waited until you were strong enough to tackle Ward, and then you tortured him to death; you waited until your father was on the verge of concluding the deal that would crown the efforts of a lifetime, and assure the Cade family of a place in Arkansas history, before you started killing vulnerable young women; and you waited for someone like me to come along, someone from outside, before baiting the hook, because you wanted to be captured, but only by the right person."

"That's very good," said Nealus. "You glossed over the nastier details of what Hollis Ward did to me, but that's understandable. Also, our relationship was more complex than you make it sound. I think I had a kind of love for him. He cared for me, or perhaps it was just easier for me to believe that he did. He killed Estella Jackson, you know. I watched him do it. I might even have helped him a little, although it's hard for me to remember all the details. I suppose you could say I learned from the best."

"Why did he kill her?" said Parker.

Nealus tilted his head in surprise, as though the question were so unnecessary as to be hardly worth answering.

"Hollis liked inflicting pain. He said he'd hurt other girls—boys, too, because he wasn't particular—and I can't see why he would have lied. He thought Estella Jackson was uppity, and wanted to teach her a lesson, but I didn't think she was uppity. She was just a regular girl."

"Did you tell Hollis that before he started hurting her?"

Nealus laughed. "No, I didn't want to spoil the fun."

While he was talking, Maryanne McCullough had resumed banging against the roof of the trunk. Kel Knight walked to the front of the car and popped the trunk with the lever. He removed the gag from the girl's mouth and told her to stay where she was for now, because she was safe. He then resumed his position.

"Nealus," said Griffin, "I need you to get rid of the knife."

Nealus reached to the back of his belt and removed the blade from its scabbard. It was about four inches long, and shone dully in the sunlight.

"Would it be better if there was a trial?" he mused. "If I plead guilty, it'll go straight to sentencing, but that might be too quick. If I were to plead not guilty at first, then it would all last so much longer, and I could always change my mind when it became tedious. I'd like to give evidence. Will they let me do that? Can I speak in my own defense? Will I be permitted to explain why I had to do what I did?"

"I'm sure you'll have the very best lawyers," said Griffin. "They'll act as you instruct."

"Well, they sound like the very *worst* lawyers," said Nealus. "I don't suppose it matters, though. I've ruined my father and my family. I've destroyed this land and everyone in it. It'll stay poor until the world turns to ash, and all of you will stay poor with it. Take a look at that sign over there, because it's as close to escaping poverty as any of you will ever get—except Mr. Parker, and he's got bigger fish to fry."

Nealus Cade cast the knife aside. Its purpose was ended.

"I hope you find the one who killed your wife and daughter, Mr. Parker, I really do," he said. "I have nothing against you. You've done me a favor by bearing witness. Your testimony will be the final nail in the coffin of this county."

Evan Griffin knew that he was right. Nealus had damned Burdon for eternity and impoverished thousands both in and beyond it, men and women who had caused him no harm. He had killed at least four people, and was set to kill a fifth when he was stopped. Nealus Cade was a monster, but one not entirely of his own creation. Even now, Griffin felt a semblance of compassion for him, but Griffin's greater sorrow was for those whom he had sworn to serve. He had failed them, failed them all.

Griffin advanced, moving in from the right so the men behind him could keep Nealus in sight. He began to lower his weapon, and reached for his cuffs.

"Get down on your knees," he said.

Nealus began to lower himself to the ground.

And a single shot rang out.

CHAPTER
XCIX

Evan Griffin stood on the raised bank of the Karagol, staring at Nealus Cade's body floating in the blackness of the lake. Griffin had not looked back after hearing the shot. He did not want to know the identity of the man responsible. He had endured enough disappointments, enough sorrows, and would accumulate more in time.

Anyway, he was about to commit a crime of his own.

He descended to the shore, where he began to gather stones. Kel Knight joined him, then Parker, and finally the third man, the one whose name Griffin did not yet know.

Together they weighed down the body of Nealus Cade, and gave it to the Karagol.

CHAPTER
C

Parker drove with Evan Griffin to the house of Pappy Cade, their trousers still damp from the lake, but Parker did not enter, and whatever passed between Griffin and Cade remained private. By then, Nealus Cade's car had already been set alight by the bank of the Karagol, and Kel Knight had visited Eddy Rauls to smooth out any bumps in the narrative that was under construction: a kind of cousin to truth, or what Thoreau once termed a "consistent expediency."

Later, Parker would wonder at the efficiency of it all: an investigation that was smothered at birth; a single witness, Maryanne McCullough, who had not managed to get a good look at the man responsible for abducting her and could recall only snatches of a conversation overheard by the banks of the Karagol, and what she thought might have been a gunshot; a figure reportedly seen fleeing into the Ouachita, and a subsequent pursuit that yielded no results, because those were deep woods in which a man could lose himself, if he chose; the revelation that, theoretically, a great many people had access to the garage in which the bodies of Sallie Kernigan and Hollis Ward were discovered, because there were multiple copies of the keys, including some held as far afield as Little Rock; and the decision by the Cades' tame judge to regard

Parker's entry into that same garage as an illegal search, making the discovery of the bodies inside fruit from a poisoned tree in evidentiary terms.

And hovering in the background, presences from the state legislature and beyond, all with a shared interest in wealth and silence, even as the disappearance of Nealus Cade became its own mystery, one that was linked to the deaths of young women only through whisper and conjecture, until a corpse was found deep in the Ouachita: a male in his late thirties, rotted beyond identification, with a rusted four-inch blade beside him, the same weapon believed to have been used in the killing of Donna Lee Kernigan and her mother, and perhaps others too, although who could say for sure? His body bore the marks of a dissolute life.

A drifter, it was said, a stranger found dead in some gutter by Jurel Cade—or so it was whispered—and rendered fit for the purpose of providing a scapegoat.

Someone not of that place.

Two days after the death of Nealus Cade, Parker checked out of his room at the Lakeside Inn. A new clerk stood behind the desk. He appeared harried, and was unfamiliar with the running of a motel. Cleon was gone. He had gathered his belongings and departed in the company of the men named Angel and Louis, one of whom, Angel, had spoken with him long into the night. Eventually Cleon would find his way to Springfield, Vermont, where he would open a boutique bed-and-breakfast with his partner, Erik, and design costumes for the Springfield Community Players.

Only Evan Griffin was present to see Parker leave. He paid Parker's bill and walked him to his car. They shook hands, and a few words were exchanged.

"Where will you go," said Griffin, "back to New York?"

"In time," said Parker. " First, Mississippi."

"Why there?"

"Someone crucified a woman named Eliza Tarp in Belzoni, and crowned her with thorns."

"You of a mind to discover who that someone might be?"

"I am."

"You be careful about making promises to the dead. They'll hold you to them."

"I expect them to," said Parker.

And then he was gone.

NOW

CHAPTER
CI

Parker heard down the phone line the whispering of years.

"So I thought you should know," said Evan Griffin. "About the body. The Karagol had started to flood, and stank worse than usual. Someone over at the Kovas facility thought dredging might help, which is how the remains were found."

"Have they been identified?"

"From dental records," said Griffin. "It's Nealus Cade. It's a curious thing, but he was in a state of semi-preservation. Something to do with the temperature of the water, they're saying, and maybe the strangeness of the Karagol. Jurel was there when they laid the body down on the shore, once they'd freed it from the mud. He'd spent a long time looking for his brother, but I think he suspected where Nealus was all along. He's the county sheriff now, you know? Good one, too, or so they tell me. He's the last sibling left. Delphia died of cervical cancer a few years ago. And Pappy—well, Delphia took care of Pappy in his final months. I'd like to believe her solicitude might have been a boon to him, but I'm disinclined to lie to myself. The neighbors said they could hear him screaming in the days before he passed away."

Parker didn't care. He had rarely thought about the Cades since leaving Cargill, and only once had the events of that time intruded with force upon his thoughts. A few months earlier, down in Houston, he had caught sight of a man walking with a woman in Tranquility Park, a pair of teenage girls alongside them. Parker thought the man looked like Tilon Ward, who had vanished without trace from Arkansas in the aftermath of the confrontation at the Buttrell property. Ward did not notice him, and Parker made no effort to confirm his identity.

After all, he might have been mistaken.

"What about you?" said Parker.

"I retired a decade ago," said Griffin. "I got three kids now, and we all live in Siloam Springs. Cargill grew too busy for me, once Kovas got situated and started to expand. Too many faces I didn't care to get to know. It's become a wealthy town—or it is for some, but still better than it was for most."

He drew in a long breath, before speaking again.

"I saw that you found the man who killed your family."

"Yes," said Parker.

"Did it bring you peace?"

"Not immediately."

"But now?"

"I have a kind of peace."

"That's more than a lot of people can say."

"I suppose it is."

"You still making promises to the dead?"

"On occasion."

"Old habits. There is one more thing."

"Yes?"

"They dug a bullet out of a sycamore down by the Karagol about five years ago. The tree was being milled over at Rich Emory's when someone found it. The bullet had been there a long time: more than a decade, judging by the growth around it. Rich called me himself, in case I wanted to take a look. The slug was messed up, but I thought it might have been a ten millimeter."

"What did you do with it?"

"Took it away, then lost it. Careless of me."

Griffin said goodbye. Parker collected his car keys, his phone, and his notebook. He thought about the 10 mm Smith & Wesson he no longer possessed, and the Glock pistol that Kel Knight was carrying as his sidearm on the day that Nealus Cade died: a G20, chambered in 10 mm.

And Parker cast Cargill from his mind forever.

ACKNOWLEDGMENTS

It seems odd to compile a list of acknowledgments without adding the titles of a slew of reference works, but *The Dirty South* is different from some of my other books. I began writing this novel just a few days after delivering *A Book of Bones* to my publishers. Since each novel tends to be a reaction to the one that preceded it, and *A Book of Bones* was a mammoth endeavor, requiring enormous amounts of research material, I wanted *The Dirty South* to be less bound to other texts. And so, while I read newspaper articles relevant to the period and the occasional piece on recent Arkansas history, most of this book derives from my imagination, aided by a little time in the Ouachita and the assistance of the kind and knowledgeable former executive director of the Arkansas State Crime Lab, and—as Colonel J.R. Howard—former director of the Arkansas State Police. What he doesn't know about Arkansas law enforcement probably isn't worth knowing, but I suspect there isn't anything he doesn't know. I can think of few more pleasant ways to have spent an afternoon than in J.R.'s company at a Burger King in Searcy. He is an extraordinary man, and his expertise, and generosity of spirit, made *The Dirty South* a better book. Its flaws are entirely mine, not his. Brian Cliff and John Couzens facilitated my introduction to J.R., and I owe them a debt of gratitude.

I am hugely grateful also to Ryan and Rebecca Webb, who took the time to speak with me about growing up in Arkansas, and to share their recollections of the tornadoes that struck the state in the 1990s. The novel may be called *The Dirty South*, but my experiences of Arkansas were entirely positive, and the best of the characters in this book are based on people like J.R. and the Webbs.

Emily Bestler Books/Atria has remained faithful to me down the years, and I'm indebted to my American editor, Emily Bestler, and all who work with her, including Lara Jones, David Brown, Gena Lanzi, and the staff at Emily Bestler Books, Atria, and Simon & Schuster. Similarly, my novels continue to find a home with Hodder & Stoughton, just as they have since 1999. Thanks to my British editor, Sue Fletcher, and all those at Hachette who support, improve, and promote my work: Swati Gamble, Carolyn Mays, Lucy Hale, Auriol Bishop, Alice Morley, Ruth Mundy, Alasdair Oliver, Breda Purdue, Jim Binchy, and the Hachette sales teams around the globe. To my foreign publishers and editors, and all my sub-agents, thanks for bringing my books to far-flung shores; and to booksellers and librarians everywhere, long may you run.

My agent, Darley Anderson, and his crew are as fine a bunch of folk as a man could hope to have guarding his interests. Huge thanks, and much affection, to you all. Ellen Clair Lamb, as well as being friend, fact-checker, and advocate, holds the online fort together, and Cameron Ridyard does a sterling job on making that online presence as beautiful and easily navigable as possible. Jennie Ridyard, meanwhile, was the first to read the manuscript, and contrived to save some of my blushes, as did Cliana O'Neill, supplementing the efforts of various staunch copy editors and proofreaders.

Finally, love to Jennie, Cam, Al, Alannah, and Megan. At the very least, I hope I keep you all amused.

John Connolly, January 2020

Books are produced in the United States using U.S.-based materials

Books are printed using a revolutionary new process called THINKtech™ that lowers energy usage by 70% and increases overall quality

Books are durable and flexible because of Smyth-sewing

Paper is sourced using environmentally responsible foresting methods and the paper is acid-free

Center Point Large Print
600 Brooks Road / PO Box 1
Thorndike, ME 04986-0001 USA

(207) 568-3717

US & Canada:
1 800 929-9108
www.centerpointlargeprint.com

THE

AMERICAN

CENTURY

YALE UNIVERSITY PRESS   NEW HAVEN AND LONDON

THE ☆ ☆ ☆ ☆

AMERICAN

☆ ☆ ☆ ☆

CENTURY

The Rise and Decline of the

United States as a World Power

DONALD W. WHITE

Excerpts from "Colloquy for the States" and "America Was Promises," from *Collected Poems, 1917–1982* by Archibald MacLeish. Copyright © 1985 by The Estate of Archibald MacLeish. Reprinted by permission of Houghton Mifflin Co. All rights reserved.

Excerpts from "Iron Horse," from *Collected Poems, 1947–1980* by Allen Ginsberg. Copyright © 1966 by Allen Ginsberg. Reprinted by permission of HarperCollins Publishers, Inc., and Penguin Books Ltd.

Excerpts from "America," from *Collected Poems, 1947–1980* by Allen Ginsberg. Copyright © 1956, 1959 by Allen Ginsberg. Copyright renewed. Reprinted by permission of HarperCollins Publishers, Inc., and Penguin Books Ltd.

Set in Times Roman and CgTowerCd type by The Composing Room of Michigan, Inc.
Printed in the United States of America by Book Crafters, Inc., Chelsea, Michigan.

Library of Congress Cataloging-in-Publication Data
White, Donald Wallace.
The American century: The rise and decline of the United States as a world power / Donald W. White.
p.   cm.
Includes bibliographical references (p.) and index.
ISBN 0-300-05721-0 (alk. paper)
1. United States—Foreign relations—1945–1989.   2. United States—Politics and government—1945–1989.   I. Title.
E744.W538   1996
327.73—dc20   95-506
                    CIP

A catalogue record for this book is available from the British Library.

The paper in this book meets the guidelines for permanence and durability of the Committee on Production Guidelines for Book Longevity of the Council on Library Resources.

10 9 8 7 6 5 4 3 2 1

To my mother and father,
and to my students

CONTENTS

Preface ix

Prologue 1

Part I   The Origins of a World Role

1   The Frontiers 17

2   A Circuit of the World 28

3   The Elemental Forces 47

4   The Legitimacy of Power 65

Part II   The Growth of a World Role

5   The Pressure from Abroad 89

6   The Formulation from the Past 111

7   The View from the Present 127

8   The Consensus Theories 142

Part III   The Manifestations of a World Role

9   Economic Enterprise 161

10 Foreign Aid 189

11 Cultural Thrust 211

12 Political Structure 243

Part IV   The Crisis of a World Role

13 The Consensus Dilemma 275

14 The Internal Crises 295

15 The Dissenters 309

16 The Activists 320

Part V   The Decline of a World Role

17 Discord at Home and Abroad 339

18 The Military Costs 369

19 Criteria of Declining Power 383

20 The New World 404

Epilogue 427

Notes 439

Bibliography 497

Index 531

PREFACE

The origins of this study lie in the experience and education of a post–World War II youth. When I was a boy, I learned in school from textbooks depicting skyscrapers, wheat fields, mile-long factories, oil derricks, and the other symbols of prosperity, supported by the statistics of industrial production and standard of living. They called America an affluent society and the most powerful of world powers. America had its faults—racial segregation and pockets of poverty—but, the textbooks implied, these failings could be overcome by men and women of good will using the resources at their command. When I traveled by railroad from a suburban home in the northern New Jersey hills to New York City, I passed from streams and fields to factories with smoking stacks, power-generating plants, and great fuel tanks, over multilevel engineering feats combining tunnels and tressels, and beneath the soaring New Jersey Turnpike, until beyond a tunnel, there appeared the skyline of New York City dominated by the spire of the Empire State Building. Crossing the Hudson River by ferry, I saw in the harbor ocean liners and freighters entering or departing with commerce of the world's greatest port. I wondered why.

Why did America—as one book declared at the time—have the greatest national industrial output on earth; the largest merchant marine at sea; the largest number of transport and commercial airplanes in the sky; an agricultural plant capable of contributing to feeding hungry peoples; the greatest national production of steel, petroleum, cotton, and other vital products; vast holdings of monetary gold and silver; the most powerful navy that had ever sailed the five oceans; and the biggest and hardest-hitting air force the world had ever known? I was never satisfied with the lists of these assets that sufficed for the explanations in textbooks. The answers were not that easy. It was not just because of America's talents, and it was not just because other centers of power in a war-weary world had fallen on hard times. The significance of an elusive mixture of elements was uncertain to me.

When I went to college, I began to direct my studies toward understanding how nations had achieved exceptional world positions. But by the time I had written a prospective senior thesis on the theories of history to which were attributed the rise and expansion of nations, I had to adjust my thinking to new realities—to deal with the decline of power.

After another America was taking form in the 1960s and early 1970s—its society divided by protests and its military mired in the jungles of Vietnam—as I entered graduate school, I faced new questions. Why was the nation being torn from within? Why was its prowess in trade lessening? Why was its massive military power ineffectual?

The answers in the textbooks, once unsatisfying, were now worthless. I had mastered statistics and geopolitical theories—the levels of steel production and computer chip output, the rate of capital investment, and the first principles of Mackinder, Spengler, and Toynbee. My readings on the cold war had revealed the lack of a generally recognized context in which to study the logic of American internal dynamics during the post–World War II period. The traditional accounts of the cold war, uncritical of government policy, were oblivious to dangers, and the revisionist interpretations, rooted in economic or Marxist theory, lacked awareness of the benefits of national strength. Neither argument addressed the fundamental issues of rise and decline.

My goal was to understand how this world I knew had come to be, its virtues and faults, because I also wanted to know what had gone wrong. I sought a means of organizing economic, social, cultural, and political attitudes within the context of America's place in the world. To accomplish this study, I read for a period of years all I could of the great bulk of primary source material, traveled across reaches of the country, interviewed those who had lived through events, and immersed myself in the period's popular culture of film, music, television, and radio. For whatever limitations the study has, I alone am responsible.

A work of many years and vast scope would not have been accomplished without the generous help of many people. First, I am indebted to Paul Baker, a professor, colleague, and friend for many years. He was my dissertation adviser, when many of the ideas of this book were taking shape, and I want to express my deepest thanks for all he has done since he allowed me to embark on a study of unusually broad scope. His unselfish and honest guidance then and since, his warmth of encouragement, and patient dedication to fair-minded thought were invaluable. I also want to thank the members of my dissertation committee. I am especially grateful to Irwin Unger for impressing on me the need for clarity of thought and for his constructive suggestions on careful writing. David Reimers challenged me to ask significant questions in examining the validity of my ideas and methods. I also thank Albert Romasco and Vincent Carosso for their help and inspiration. Marilyn Young, the chair of the New York University History Department, read with insight parts of various drafts. I thank too Thomas Bender, Carl Prince, David Hicks, Frederick Schult, and Michael Lutzker.

I am indebted to some leading historians of international affairs. At a critical point Akira Iriye encouraged me to proceed with this larger study after he had read one of my journal articles presenting the arguments of part 1 of this book. John Lewis Gaddis offered an exceptionally insightful evaluation of the opening chapters. From McGeorge Bundy I gained a sense of the political world, apart from the world of ideas and intellect to which scholars retreat. My years of work assisting him in his massive study of the political decision-makers of nuclear weapons taught me a great deal about the constraints under which government officials are compelled to operate. His encouragment of my project, which necessarily departs from certain policies he participated in making as national security adviser to Presidents Kennedy and Johnson, is a measure of his generous and open-minded spirit, and his rigorous evaluations of some early drafts still leave me in awe of one of the most brilliant individuals I have known.

I also wish to note the great assistance rendered by the librarians and archivists of the many institutions I visited in the course of my research. I have spent countless days over many seasons at the New York Public Library on Forty-second Street, where the excitement of doing primary source research, often in dusty, dated periodicals and ancient books, unfortunately now crumbling, first took hold while I was researching my senior college thesis. I have returned again and again to use the library's unique collections up to the final efforts of checking this book's citations. The librarians at the Elmer Holmes Bobst Library of New York University have also extended innumerable courtesies and unflagging aid, particularly in the reference room, the social science division, the microform center, and the Avery Fisher Media Center. To archivists, I am most grateful: at the National Archives and the Library of Congress in Washington, D.C.; at the Franklin D. Roosevelt Library, Hyde Park, N.Y.; at the Harry S. Truman Library, Independence, Mo.; at the Dwight D. Eisenhower Library, Abilene, Kan.; at the Time, Inc., Archives, New York City; at Columbia University Library, New York City; at Yale University Library, New Haven, Conn.; and at Princeton University Library, Princeton, N.J. I especially appreciate the help of Edward Reese at the Military Archives Division of the National Archives, and of David Haight at the Dwight D. Eisenhower Library.

Supporting my research was a generous grant from the National Endowment for the Humanities. The funds helped to provide a block of time so essential to productive scholarship. I am also appreciative for postdoctoral research funds from the History Department at New York University.

Formative chapters of the book originally appeared in several journals, and I wish to thank their editors and editorial readers for their valuable comments, especially Michael Hogan of *Diplomatic History,* Norris Hundley of *Pacific Historical Review,* Jerry Bentley of *Journal of World History,* and Robin Higham of *Journal of the West.* Jack Hopper brought his editing skill and fresh perspective to a draft of the completed book manuscript.

I don't know how to thank properly my students, graduate and undergraduate. Colloquia and seminar classes on foreign policy and culture offered uplifting discussion and beneficial critique of parts of the manuscript. Some outstanding graduate students read extended sections of the book at various stages: David Cowen, Saverio Giovacchini, Peter Braunstein, Renqiu Yu, James Eber, and David Gluck. This book is truly for my students. When I was finishing the manuscript for publication, they successfully nominated me for an Outstanding Teaching Award of the College of Arts and Science at New York University. I have firmly believed that scholarly research and excellent teaching are not at odds but are interdependent, and that teachers may learn from the questions and insights of students as much as students may learn from the knowledge and wisdom of teachers. At least, I recall the influence a few teachers had on me in public school and college: Ruth Ann Wichelman, who in a sixth-grade classroom first opened up to me the wonders of world history and comparative geography through maps and original outlines; James Nicholas and William Gilliam, who in high school expanded this knowledge of America and the world; and in college Alban Hoopes, who revealed in his masterful lectures on diplomatic history both the irony in history and the joy of learning it.

The association with Yale University Press has been long and fruitful. My editor, Charles Grench, has offered enthusiastic support and valued friendly advice at every stage of the publication process. Otto Bohlmann was instrumental in meticulously cutting a manuscript that was considerably longer than the final version. My thanks too to the anonymous outside readers, who made thoughtful suggestions. To those who helped in many ways but whom I neglect to mention, I express my apologies.

My brother, Richard White, a former professor of English, read extended versions of the manuscript, offering suggestions to improve the literary quality. My grandmother, Mrs. Donald Wallace, granted me permission to spend weeks over several summers writing at her cottage at Cranberry Lake, N.J. My mother and my father were most generous and supportive over this enduring effort.